PRAISE FOR *THE BOOKSELLER'S SECRET*

"A delight from start to finish. Michelle Gable skillfully twines the narratives of two effervescent heroines. The result is a literary feast any booklover will savor!"

—**Kate Quinn,** *New York Times* **bestselling author of** *The Diamond Eye*

"A thoroughly entertaining tale. Gable expertly and cleverly delivers wit, humor, and intrigue in full measure on every page."

—**Susan Meissner, bestselling author of** *The Nature of Fragile Things*

"Featuring a colorful, witty, tenacious cast, *The Bookseller's Secret* deftly connects two authors separated by generations while unraveling a mystery that keeps the pages turning."

—**Kristina McMorris,** *New York Times* **bestselling author of** *Sold on a Monday*

"An ingenious story. Filled with crisp dialogue and populated with delightful, intriguing characters, the novel sings with wit and wisdom."

—**Fiona Davis,** *New York Times* **bestselling author of** *The Magnolia Palace*

"Gable's witty narrative effortlessly moves between two time periods and is enriched with cameos by historical figures and authentic, memorable characters. Historical fiction fans will be riveted from the first page."

—*Publishers Weekly* **(starred review)**

"A cunning blend of historical fiction, fetching romance, and literary thriller, Gable's newest novel is sure to reinvigorate interest in [Nancy] Mitford and beguile fans of light-hearted relationship fiction."

—*Booklist* **(starred review)**

"A riveting page-turner that will leave you exclaiming, vive la littérature!"

—*Toronto Star*

Also by Michelle Gable

A Paris Apartment
I'll See You in Paris
The Book of Summer
The Summer I Met Jack
The Bookseller's Secret

THE
LIPSTICK
BUREAU

a novel

MICHELLE GABLE

GRAYDON
HOUSE

GRAYDON
HOUSE®

Recycling programs
for this product may
not exist in your area.

ISBN-13: 978-1-525-80497-7

The Lipstick Bureau

Graydon House
22 Adelaide St. West, 41st Floor
Toronto, Ontario M5H 4E3, Canada
www.GraydonHouseBooks.com
www.BookClubbish.com

Printed in U.S.A.

To Lisa Kanetake,
For the many miles and roads (literal and figurative) we've traveled together. I would not have made it to 2022 without you!

THE
LIPSTICK
BUREAU

NIKI

Niki's stomach flip-flops, and there's a wild fluttering in her chest. *You're fine*, she tells herself. In this buzzing, glittering room of some three hundred, she's unlikely to encounter anyone she knows. Not that she'd recognize them if she did. It's been almost forty-five years.

"Jeez, what a turnout," her daughter, Andrea, says as Niki takes several short inhales, trying to wrangle her breath. "Did you know this many people would show up?"

"I had no idea what to expect," Niki answers, and this much is true. When the invitation arrived three months ago, she'd almost pitched it straight into the trash.

> *You are invited*
> *to a Black-Tie Dinner*
> *Honoring*
> *The Ladies of the O.S.S.*

The ladies of the OSS. A deceptively quaint title, like a neighborhood bridge club, or a collection of wives whose given names are not important.

"You should go," Niki's husband had said when she showed him the thick, ecru cardstock with its ornate engraving. "Relive your war days."

"Manfred," Niki had replied sternly. "Nobody wants to relive those."

Though he'd convinced Niki to accept the invitation, it hadn't been the hardest sell. Manfred was ill—dying, in fact, of late-stage lung cancer—and Niki figured the tick mark beside "yes" was merely a way to delay a no.

The week before the event, Manfred was weaker than ever, and Niki saw her chance to back out. "I'll just skip it," she'd said. "This is for the best. You'd be bored out of your skull, and no one I worked with will even be there!"

"Zuska," Manfred said, using her old pet name. As always, he'd known what his wife was up to. "I want you to go. Take Andrea. She could use a night out. It'd be like a holiday for her."

"I don't know..." Niki demurred. Their daughter did hate to cook, and no doubt longed for a break from her two extremely pert teenagers.

"You can't refuse," Manfred said. "What if this ends up qualifying as my dying wish?" It was a joke, but what could Niki possibly say to that?

Now she regrets having shown Manfred the invitation and is discomfited by the scene. Niki feels naked, exposed, as though she's wearing a transparent blouse instead of a black sparkly top with double shoulder pads.

"Do you think you'll spot anyone you know?" Andrea asks as they wend their way through the tables, scanning for number eighteen. Every Czech native considers eighteen an auspicious number, so maybe this is a positive sign.

"It's unlikely," Niki says. "The dinner is honoring women,

and I mostly worked with men." *Most of whom are now dead*, she does not add.

Soon enough, mother and daughter find their table, and exchange greetings with the two women already seated. Niki squints at their badges and notes they worked in different theaters of operation. Onstage is a podium, behind it a screen emblazoned with *O.S.S.* Beneath the letters is a gold spade encircled in black.

"What a beautiful outfit!" says one of their tablemates in a tight Texas twang.

"Thank you." Niki blushes lightly, smoothing her billowy, bright green chiffon skirt.

"You're the prettiest one in the place," Andrea whispers as they sit.

"What a load of shit," Niki spits back. In this room, it's sequins and diamonds and fur for miles. She pats Andrea's hand. "But thank you for the compliment." And thank God for Manfred, who'd raised their girl to treat her mother so well.

Manfred. Niki feels a quake somewhere deep. She is losing him. She's been losing him for a long time, and maybe *this* is the reason she came tonight. Those three letters on-screen call up—rather, *exhume*—a swarm of emotions, not all of them good. But they also offer a strange kind of hope, a reminder that Niki's survived loss before, and this old body of hers has lived more than one life.

PART ONE

PREPARATIONS

1

NIKI

October 1943
Washington, DC

"You let me do the talking." It was not the first time Niki had said this to William Dewart, and it wouldn't be the last. "You're the one who got us into this mess," she reminded him. "And I'm going to get us out."

"Let's agree that honesty is the best option here," Will said, and Niki passed him a look. The man had his charms, but after a week of training, he'd proved the rumors were true. The Office of Strategic Services was nothing but a hodgepodge of army castoffs and every rich family's one stupid son.

"That," Niki said, "is not going to happen."

Will furrowed the part of his face where his eyebrows had once been. "I still think—" he began but was interrupted by the thwack of a thrown-open door. Will and Niki jumped to their feet and offered salutes.

"Sit," the man grunted—he was some major or another. Niki couldn't keep it all straight. Because she was a woman, everyone was of higher rank than her, which was frustrating but also convenient in terms of figuring out who she was supposed to pay deference to, not that she always followed the rules.

After plunking down into his chair, the major flipped open a folder and scanned the report. Through it all, Will violently jiggled his leg. "You two have gotten yourselves into quite the pickle," the man said. "Care to explain what the fu—" His eyes flicked toward Niki. "Care to explain what in tarnation happened out there?"

The official assignment was to detonate a bomb on the ninth green at Congressional Country Club—the regular stuff—and skedaddle while leaving no evidence of themselves behind. Unfortunately, the bomb had been slow to wake up, and Will went to inspect the thing at the exact moment it decided to ignite.

Upon seeing the blast of flame, Niki screamed and scrambled over to find Will lying in the grass, clutching his oft troubled stomach. "Are you okay?" she'd cried, jostling his shoulders as he swatted her away. When the commanding officer happened upon them several minutes later, Will remained splayed on the green with Niki hovering over him.

"It's really quite straightforward," Niki told the major. "We've already gone over this with the CO." Sure, Niki could talk a good game but, between this incident and failing knife combat class, it was possible she didn't have the makings of a very good spy.

"Straightforward?" the major barked. "The exercise was supposed to involve hand grenades and bunkers, not TNT and fairways. The golfers are not going to be happy."

"Well, that's a shame," Niki said.

"The worst part," he continued, and Niki was oddly pleased

there was something worse than blowing up a golf course. "The worst part is that, in addition to ruining a perfectly good hole, you two dingbats didn't even have the brains to hide. You just stood there, waiting to be captured by the enemy."

"The instructor told us to wait," Will said, his leg still antsy. "We weren't supposed to leave until we confirmed the bomb went off."

"Which does not explain why you were found minutes later still hanging—"

"It's a new technique," Niki blurted. Both men whipped in her direction as an idea formed like a fog in her mind. Niki smiled, though mostly on the inside. One did not survive years in a Nazi-occupied country without the ability to push around the truth. "The idea is to stand there and act shell-shocked, so to speak," she explained. "Innocent. As though you have no idea what's going on. It's quite brilliant when you think about it. If you run, you might get caught, and there will be no denying what you've done."

Niki threw on another smile, hoping the men didn't hear the break in her voice.

"So, you just took it upon yourself to employ a new technique?" the major said, narrowing one eye.

"Yes and no," Niki said, and Will made a loud puffing sound. "Our instructor told us that the ability to think on one's feet is critical, and we should take every opportunity to do so." Niki snuck a glance at Will, who looked awfully pale for a person who'd just burnt half his face. "When we realized someone handed us a bomb instead of grenades," she said, turning back to the major, "and then the bomb acted a little fussy, we decided to change course."

Will threw back his head in silent agony, though notably did not counter Niki's retelling. Was this an American thing, to never go against a lady? That couldn't be right. George contradicted her all the time.

The major exhaled and then released a soft chortle. If he was finding some humor in the situation, maybe they would be okay. This ragtag organization was new to the intelligence game, Niki understood, and they hardly knew what they were doing one minute to the next. The OSS *needed* her; they'd recruited her. Where else would they get a Czechoslovakian national turned American citizen with several degrees and fluency in multiple languages? Niki lowered her shoulders and began to relax.

"Can we return to training now?" she asked. "I suspect you're compelled to write us up or whatnot. Feel free to get to it." She waggled her fingers. "But we'd like to get back out there sooner rather than later, right, Dewart? I've been told that next week we get to practice sabotaging the Richmond ironworks?" If there was one thing Niki had learned in her twenty-five years, it was that the best way to get through something was to rev the engine and plow straight ahead.

"Oh. No. Absolutely not," the man said, laughing again. Niki's skin prickled, like nettles on the skin. "Clandestine work is out for you."

"But that's why I'm here!" she protested. "It's why the OSS picked me."

"I'm sorry, but not every recruit pans out, and it's become patently obvious that we can't drop you behind enemy lines."

"After one minor slipup?" Niki said. "I'm perfectly capable..." She paused, heart pounding triple-time as she watched the major stretch back to open a drawer.

"You are a clever woman," he said. "But you're not dramatic enough."

"Dramatic?" Niki said, her eyes starting to cross.

"She can be a *little* dramatic," Will mumbled.

"Contrary to popular notion," the major said, "in order to sell one's story, a good agent needs to be able to engage in histrionics. A personality like yours would never work. You're too insouciant for a girl. Too devil-may-care."

Will snorted, and Niki shot him a glare. "This was *your* fault," she hissed.

"You'd never keep your cover," the major said. "I imagine you getting made, then attempting to persuade your captor that your blowing up his factory was a good thing."

"Seems like this would be a positive attribute?" Niki said.

The major slapped a piece of paper onto his desk. As he scribbled, Niki drew forward for a better look, but his left hand blocked her view. Will stayed suspiciously quiet, the only sound the occasional stirring of his gut.

Niki cleared her throat. "But, sir," she said. "I can learn to be histrionic if that's what's necessary. Back in my home country, I was a lawyer, and a journalist before. Which is to say, I'm capable of being more than one thing."

The major affixed the mysterious paperwork with a gigantic red stamp.

"Not to mention," Niki added, "you need my skills. How many American citizens have you met who speak eight languages *and* want to help the cause?"

Niki recognized that she sounded pleading, borderline desperate, and that's because she was. Being perfect for a busted-up group of outsiders meant she wasn't qualified for much else, and Niki couldn't lose this opportunity. An intelligence organization that sent people overseas was her best and only chance to find out about her parents and brother. Czechoslovakia was a black box, and not even her husband, who worked for the Office of War Information, could tell Niki what was going on there.

"I presume everyone wants to help the cause," the major said. "Otherwise, they wouldn't sign up."

"Not everyone signs up, and not everyone can go behind enemy lines in multiple countries." Countries like the former Czechoslovakia, if given her druthers.

"Don't worry, Private," the major said. "You'll still contribute to the war effort. The big boss saw *something* in you." He smirked and gave Niki the kind of once-over that made her wish she had mastered close knife combat, after all. "I think there's a better role." He slid the paper across the desk. "Tomorrow at oh-nine-hundred hours, please report to room 112 in the Q Building. Here's the address."

Niki skimmed the form, though it didn't tell her much. She saw her name and something about "Morale Operations."

"So, I'm moving over to this…" She flapped the paper. "Morale Operations? And he gets to stay?" For fear of bruising his ego, Niki wouldn't say it out loud, but six-and-a-half-foot timorous men were not especially undercover, William Dewart in particular. The man moved about the world as though someone once called him a bull in a china shop and he'd actively avoided teacups ever since.

"Just worry about yourself, sweetheart." The major stood, signaling the meeting's end. "When you arrive at the Q Building, give a false name and address to the receptionist."

"Do you know whether Morale Operations is sent overseas?" Niki asked as she begrudgingly lifted onto her feet.

"Depends," the man said. He walked around his desk, brushing his arm against hers as he reached for the door. "Wherever you end up, good luck. You'll do a swell job."

Before stepping out into the hall, Niki glanced back and found Will's eyes, a hint of apology in his gaze. Why was she the one getting booted when it was Will who'd grabbed the bomb? Will who'd nearly blown off his face? Niki had only hung around to make sure he was alive.

As far as Niki was concerned, the world had it all wrong. Men were supposed to be the heroes, the saviors, the rescuers of kittens in trees, but she'd seen scant evidence of this trait. Men seemed to cause the problems, not solve them. And, somehow, they always got in her way.

2

May 1989

A waiter makes his way around the table with a pitcher of water. Nearby, another server is lifting silver lids two at a time to reveal butternut squash and salmon fillets.

"Interesting crowd," Andrea notes, surveying the room. "Lots of jewels."

"It was a notoriously eclectic group," Niki says. "The men were a bunch of misfits but the women were usually high society types." She scans the faces again. Though Niki doesn't know these ladies personally, they are likely some combination of ambassadors' daughters, manufacturing heiresses, and countesses of this or that. Marlene Dietrich was in the OSS, as was Julia Child. Evidently, she couldn't even boil an egg back then.

"Were most of the women translators, too?" Andrea asks.

Niki shakes her head. They weren't all translators and, contrary to what she's let her daughter believe, neither was she.

"Ladies and gentlemen," a voice says over the speaker. "Please welcome your host for the evening, Geoffrey Jones, President of the Veterans of the OSS."

Applause rolls through the room as Geoffrey Jones struts toward the podium, looking like central casting's version of a middle-aged government man—tall, fit, with close-cropped, gray-speckled hair. Attractive but hardly memorable.

"Greetings, everyone," Geoffrey Jones says, and the crowd settles. "What a wonderful night! You are all probably accustomed to attending events that celebrate your *husbands'* achievements, but this evening, we are charged with honoring *you*, the women who worked for the Office of Strategic Services."

"This guy is already on my nerves," Andrea murmurs, and Niki mimes an elbow to her ribs.

"The OSS came in many shapes and sizes," Geoffrey Jones continues, "and the organization has carried several names over the years. When you served, the letters stood for the Office of Strategic Services, but you might've known it as the Oh-So-Social."

Niki joins the tepid laughter, though she was never like the rest of the girls—plucked from the social register and chock-full of poise and savoir faire. Niki was simply a foreigner who wound up in the right place at the right time. Or the wrong place, depending.

"Now, the OSS is known by a different acronym altogether." Geoffrey Jones hits a clicker, and the telltale blue circle fills the screen. There's no mistaking the proud eagle and the yellow words beneath it: CENTRAL INTELLIGENCE AGENCY.

"Are you kidding me?" Andrea pivots toward her mother. "You never told me you worked for the CIA!"

"I didn't," Niki says. "The OSS was its *precursor*." She picks up her roll and, like an anxious squirrel, begins tearing off small pieces and shuttling them into her mouth.

"Same thing," Andrea says. "Seriously, Mom. What the hell?"

The woman across from them gives a shush.

"It's not like that," Niki whispers, and waves her daughter away. "I wasn't a *spy* or anything." Despite her best efforts, she thinks. "I worked in an office. They liked my language skills."

"Classic Nikola Brzozowski dodge," Andrea grumbles.

"From when it was founded in 1942," Geoffrey says, "to when it ceased operations three years later, a total of forty-five hundred women served in the OSS, and their jobs were as varied as the magnificent gowns I see in this room."

Again, the crowd titters and Niki rolls her eyes. The OSS could've dredged up a better emcee. A broad would've been nice.

"You worked in intelligence and counterintelligence," Geoffrey says. "You manned the home office and served as drivers, clerks, decoders, radio operators, and interpreters."

The man prattles on. Should Niki say something to Andrea? She probably should. This presentation might be headed anywhere, to a place where her "just an office gal" shtick would fall apart.

"The OSS was comprised of over a dozen different divisions," Geoffrey says, and an organizational chart appears on-screen. "And I want to recognize each one."

Shit, Niki thinks.

"Whaddya say, ladies? When I call your unit, will you please stand?"

Niki instantly breaks out in a cold sweat. She dabs her forehead with a napkin as Andrea studies her, confused. In truth, Niki is confused, too. Would it be so terrible if Andrea found out she worked for the OSS? Not really, Niki decides. The source of her consternation is not her former employer, or some basic description of her job. Once Geoffrey gets rolling, Andrea will have questions, and Niki might have to unpack everything she thought she'd banished to permanent storage.

"Are we ready?" Geoffrey says. "Let's show the world who we are, and how this group of women contributed to Allied victory."

3

NIKI

October 1943

At three minutes after nine o'clock—Niki was always running behind—she entered the Q Building, a sprawling, unsightly prefabricated structure with a thousand unmarked doors. Niki considered herself decent with maps, but had to double back three times before locating room 112.

Though she was good and late by now, Niki paused in the hallway, listening to the chatter on the other side of the door. None of this was what she'd envisioned when George's colleague had recruited her, but at least she was away from home-made bombs and that oafish William Dewart.

Taking in a gulp of air, Niki threw open the door. She made one faltering step into the room, only to find herself stuck at the end of a very long line.

"What in the world?" Niki said, looking around. The place was mobbed with women of a preposterously specific type, a sea of pearls, sweater sets, and high-coiffed blond victory rolls. "Oh, no thank you," she whispered, and began to back up. Niki wasn't interested in joining a secretarial pool and hoped that leaving now would not qualify as desertion.

As she reached for the door, the girl in front of her whipped around. "Hello!" she said, nearly blinding Niki with her diamond-bright smile. "Glad to have some company. What's your name? I'm Tina. It's so lovely to meet you."

"Niki," she answered, and warily shook Tina's outstretched hand.

"Don't worry," Tina said. "It looks worse than it is. The line moves quickly. Or that's what I've been told."

Niki rose onto her tiptoes and craned over the crowd, but at five foot five, she wasn't tall enough to see past the hairstyles. She thought of what her sister-in-law had told her last Christmas. *Niki, it's time to grow out your hair. No one wears it short anymore. It's all about shoulder-length.* Every once in a while, Moggy knew what she was talking about.

"What are we queuing for, anyway?" Niki asked.

"Didn't anyone tell you?" the girl said. "This is the OSS fingerprinting room. Very top secret!"

Niki made a face, wondering how top secret it could be when a girl two feet away was speaking loudly about everyone who'd attended her recent wedding. They were surrounded by posters instructing them to BUTTON YOUR LIP! but the babble was so high she had to work to hear Tina.

"Do you know what you'll be doing? I'm R&A," Tina said. "Research and Analysis. It doesn't sound very glamorous—positively *everyone* wants to be a spy—but R&A is the heartbeat of the organization." This Tina sounded rather like a parrot and was plainly trying to talk herself into the idea.

"How nice," Niki said.

"It *is* nice," Tina agreed. "R&A produces studies—economic, social, political, military—to keep other divisions apprised of what's happening. Things like assessing civilian requirements in newly liberated areas, or analyzing the supplies necessary to maintain ration levels, and so on. What about you?"

"I was initially slated to be part of SI. Secret Intelligence." Niki flashed a smile. "As you said, everyone wants to be a spy. Alas, we are not all cut out for it. Now I'm supposed to be with…" She checked her paperwork. "Morale Operations. I don't even know what that means," Niki admitted.

"It's a new division," Tina said. "Propaganda, if I'm not mistaken."

Niki frowned as they shuffled forward. She was trying to stay positive about the change of assignment, but while Niki was glad to avoid the "tricks of silent killing" course, this was not what she had in mind.

"Do you know whether many Morale Operations folks go overseas?" Niki said, hoping Tina had more information than the major who'd sent her to this room.

Tina shrugged. "My sense is that we won't really know what we're doing until we're out in the field," she said.

The line moved again. "Why are there so many of us?" Niki asked, dizzy from the size of the crowd combined with the overpowering miasma of Chanel No. 5. "And why does everyone look the same?"

Niki hadn't meant to speak the second question out loud, but Tina was apparently good-natured and responded with a high, tinkling laugh. "Oh, that is very much by design! Miss Griggs seeks a precise kind of girl." Tina scanned Niki once, head to toe, no doubt thinking, *Gosh, how did this scrappy thing fall through the cracks?* "You weren't recruited by Miss Griggs, were you?" she guessed.

"Never even heard of her," Niki said.

Tina smacked a hand to her chest. "Oh, lordy!" she gasped. "Sounds like you have some information to catch up on. Miss Griggs was the first woman hired by the OSS, and she finds all the girls." Tina pulled a face. "Most of them, I suppose. According to her, the best OSS girl is a cross between a Smith graduate, Powers model, and Katie Gibbs secretary. She plucks them right out of the social registry."

Niki rattled her head. Boy, was she swimming in the wrong pond. "Why the social registry?" she asked, possessing only the vaguest notions of what this meant. "What's so special about it?"

"I think the question is why *not* the social registry?" Tina said. She turned around, and they walked forward several feet. "It makes sense if you think about it. Girls of a certain social class know one European language, minimum. We've all been to France on vacation, so are familiar with the terrain."

Niki smirked. She'd also been to France, but in her case, it was to study journalism at the University of Paris.

"Not that we'll all be sent abroad," Tina said, "but you get the point. Also, we're used to large groups, and don't have to worry about money or paying bills." She threw a look over her shoulder. "How'd you get here, anyway, if it wasn't through Miss Griggs?"

"An acquaintance of my husband's," Niki said. "George is with the Office of War Information, but this fellow works for the OSS. I met him at a party."

The fateful meeting happened a few months before, during the trailing days of summer, when Washington was at its stickiest, buggiest worst. On that night, Niki was tired, and headachy, and in no mood to trek to Capitol Hill. But George was days from leaving for Bern, and Niki figured to play the dutiful spouse, even though he only wanted her company because of his mistaken belief that a small, Eastern European wife gave him cachet. George was the third son of a prominent family, and Niki often contemplated whether he'd only married her to stand out in his ritzy circles.

An hour into the party, George was loudly bragging about his wife's mastery of foreign languages when a trim, silver-haired man in a Savile Row suit appeared, slicing clean into their conversation, all knife. "You speak how many languages?" he'd asked.

"Seven," was her reply, and he ogled Niki, waiting for her to elaborate. "English, Czech, German, French, Italian, Slovak, and Russian," she said. The total was eight if she included the mix of German and Czech specific to the area she'd grown up in, but there wasn't much use for that now. Niki hadn't spoken a word of Brünnerisch—or Czech, for that matter—since leaving home two years before.

"Her accents are perfect," George informed the interloper. "When we went to Paris, everyone thought she was French. In Venice, they thought she was Italian! Sometimes, she even manages to pass for American. My old lady's half chameleon, I'll tell ya what."

Smiling with approval, as though Niki had passed some test, the man reached into his coat pocket. "For you," he said, transferring a piece of paper into Niki's hand. It was a job application for the Office of Strategic Services, but George was quick to swipe it from her grasp.

"You must be joking, Bill," he said. "My wife can't work for the government! She was already making noises about joining WAC, which I shut down. The OSS is simply out of the question."

"I'm not joking at all," the man said, his translucent blue eyes taking on a soft, tired look, as though George's protestations were putting him to sleep. "Missus Clingman, we could use someone like you," he said. "As long as you're willing to volunteer for hazardous duty, potentially behind enemy lines."

"Yes, of course!" Niki said. She barely knew what constituted "enemy lines" these days, but anywhere in Europe, Niki was game.

"Donovan, get a hold of yourself. This woman wasn't even born in the States," George said, and the man smiled again. The OSS preferred foreign-born citizens, he explained, because they were more comfortable abroad. "She just escaped Europe," George protested. "You can't send her back."

"It's been two years…" Niki said.

In no mood for someone else's marital spat, the man asked Niki to please think about it and then disappeared.

That night, George lectured her about propriety, and how terrible it would look for him to have a wife who worked for the *government*. Niki pretended to listen but submitted her application once he shipped out. It wasn't that she *wanted* to disobey him, but this was war, and the OSS might be her only chance to find out whether her family was still alive. Plus, Niki wasn't the sort of wife who'd happily knit socks for soldiers while awaiting her husband's return. He should've known this by now.

"I can't believe you were hired at a cocktail party," Tina said after Niki relayed the details of the encounter. "What did your husband think? He must've been so proud."

"He was…apprehensive," Niki admitted.

"Who was this colleague, anyhow?"

"Colleague might be too generous a term. They don't even work in the same unit. Let's see…" Niki twisted her face, thinking back. "A Mr. Donovan? He was very dashing. I think he's fairly high up in the OSS."

Eyes ballooning, Tina clamped down on Niki's arm with one perfectly manicured hand. "Mr. Donovan?" she chirped. "Niki. Bill Donovan *is* the OSS!"

"Oh. Right. George might've said something about that." Living in Washington, it was hard to keep all those agencies and bureaucrats straight.

"You've been holding out on me," Tina said. Tightening her grip, she leaned forward, and Niki felt her warm breath on her cheeks. "You're not from America, are you? You seem American, but there's something about you that's a little…off."

"What a good ear you have," Niki said, smiling as she seethed inside. She must have tripped on something, accidentally pronounced a silent letter, or overly emphasized the first syllable of a word. As George had told Bill Donovan, impersonating other nationalities was one of her greatest skills. Niki thought she'd perfected the American intonation, but so much for that. "I am a citizen," she was sure to clarify. "But I'm from Czechoslovakia originally."

The "where are you from?" question rankled no matter how many times Niki was forced to answer because home as she'd known it was no longer a place. They were born the same year— she in a hospital, Czechoslovakia from the ruins of the Great War—but Niki had already outlived her own country. Czechoslovakia was once the heart of Europe, an island surrounded not by water but by mountains and dense, thick forests, until Germany annexed Austria, and they found themselves encircled by the encroaching tide of the Third Reich.

To mollify Hitler, France and England took it upon themselves to cede the Czech borderlands to Germany, leaving Niki to debate whether she'd misunderstood the definition of "allies." With this opening, Hitler quite predictably gobbled up more, eventually dividing Niki's beautiful home into the Protectorate of Bohemia and Moravia, where her family lived, and the newly declared Slovak State. Through it all, America looked the other way, as she was prone to do.

"Czechoslovakia?" Tina said, and popped a brow.

"Rather, the former Czechoslovakia," Niki clarified. "Moravia is what they're calling it now. I lived in Brnö, the capital."

"How awful," Tina said as tears filled her wide brown eyes. She released Niki's arm, which continued to smart even after she let go. "We have all these big ideas about what it must be like over there, but you've actually lived it. I can't fathom seeing it up close. Sometimes the war, it seems—" she nibbled on her bottom lip "—abstract. No. That's not the right word. Remote. Impossibly far away. In America, we're lucky to have the distance. Every now and again, I can convince myself it's not really happening."

"We *are* lucky to be in the States," Niki agreed, though she figured this remoteness cut both ways. It was easier to feel murderous rage toward Nazis once you'd seen them in action. For American soldiers, the enemy was faceless, and they had to trust what they were told.

"What about your family?" Tina asked. "Are they still there? Did they come to America with you? You married an American, yes?"

"So many questions," Niki said as she felt her composure slip. They were nearing the front, and the line was moving, though not quickly enough. "My husband is an American citizen, yes. Unfortunately, my parents and brother decided to stick it out in Brnö. They own a wool factory, and it was in full production when I left. In *theory*, the Czech government is still in charge. When Hitler's goons moved in, they promised autonomy. But..." Niki trailed off.

"Have you been able to reach them, or have any sort of contact?"

Niki shook her head. "I've sent letters, though I doubt they're getting through," she said as the fingerprinting lady waved Tina toward her table. "And I haven't received anything from them, not that I expected I would."

"You must be so worried," Tina said, peering back. "You're probably hoping the OSS will send you over there. And who knows? Maybe they will." She smiled, turned around, and wiped her hands on a grimy, much-used towel. "That area is under enemy control, and surely they'd want agents to go in who know the culture and speak the language."

"From your lips to God's ears," Niki said, steeling herself against the slow creep of hope. Were they even dispatching agents into Czechoslovakia? Niki hadn't the faintest idea.

"Well, even if they don't send you there," Tina said, "you should be able to find *something* out. Otherwise, what's the point of the OSS?"

Niki chuckled grimly and took the rag. "That's what I'm counting on," she said, pressing her fingers into the black, greasy ink. "I'm anxious to get moving. Wherever they send me, I pray it doesn't take too long."

4

PALOMA

May 1945
Caserta, Italy

Nikola came to Rome soon after the liberation. The same week, if memory serves, back when celebratory carnations and camellias still littered the streets and *"Viva!"*'s were freshly painted onto the buildings. *Viva America! Viva the Allies! Viva Chicago!* Name your place. We believed that Americans were there to save us, and everything would get better soon.

It was late in the day when I first met her. This much I recall. In my line of work, most of us sat along a brick wall, a meter between each girl, everyone watching over the small pile of tins at her feet. For me this is too much like a conveyor belt. I'm too pretty for factory work, so I conducted my business from the Spanish Steps, close to the high-end shops that sell leather and other premium goods to the GIs. I was sitting on these very stairs when Nikola sat down to smoke a cigarette. I glanced up, and we caught eyes. She hesitated for a second, smiled, and marched over to join me. I'd seen her walk by several times, but it was the first we'd spoken.

"Ciao. Sigaretta?" she said.

"I am fresh out," I lied.

"No, no, no!" Nikola laughed. Her teeth were so unusual— very white and overlapping, as if there were too many crowded into her mouth. "I was the one offering a cigarette to *you*," she said, extending the package in my direction.

"Oh! *Me dispiace!*" I was hit hard by my own shock. Years of war and occupation meant I saw everything as a demand, a payment to someone else.

"Mi chiamo Nikola," she said as I pilfered three cigarettes from the box. Her Italian was pitch-perfect, her words sharp and crisp, not unlike the shirt she wore, which was starched to within an inch of its life. Between her clothes and the cropped, wavy hair brushed away from her face, I wondered if she might be im-personating a man. It was not a bad idea in such unreasonable times, but her cheekbones were too high, her features too deli-cate to get away with it.

"Paloma," I said in response, lighting her cigarette first and then mine. This was how our friendship began.

I know what you are thinking. You'd like to understand why a nice girl might befriend someone like me. Your GI handbook warns: *The type of woman who approaches you in the street in Italy and says, "Please give me a cigarette" isn't looking for a smoke.* In this case, she was the person offering the cigarette, but I was a whore, either way.

Nikola held no judgment about my line of work, maybe be-cause she was born in Europe and didn't see much difference between us. Don't be so skeptical! After all, we're unlucky in the same way—both of us women, born in Europe, between the wars. The world has never had a place for us.

Although I must allow, had she come months or even weeks later, I might've been more distrustful of her overtures, possibly rebuffed them altogether. But in those early days, we looked upon every American with a mixture of gratitude and relief, before we realized you had no vested interest in truly saving us. We were an inconvenience, the sideshow distracting you from Germany, the main event. We'd waited for months, almost a year, and then you arrived, and we were waiting still.

What took you so long? When I put this to Nikola, she offered a long-winded response about feuding allies and second fronts. The Americans insisted on entering through France, she explained, whereas the Brits wanted to go through Italy.

To stop her history lesson, I put up a hand. "No," I said. "Do not speak on behalf of Patton or Montgomery. Speak for yourself."

"Oh." She blinked. "Well, our group was training."

"Training?" I yelped. This was a true surprise as Nikola and her compatriots seemed like the least organized group on the continent. One does not live under a fascist regime without developing an appreciation for orderly conduct. "When did this training begin?"

"Late last October?" she said, and I counted backward.

Last October was six weeks, give or take, after the armistice. Six weeks after the Italian Army disbanded, and the king and prime minister announced they'd abandoned all efforts to defend Italy's capital. They declared Rome an "Open City," a plea for all sides to play nice. Germans viewed it as an opportunity to parachute down and commence their raping and looting and killing. They raided the *Ghetto di Roma*, destroying a neighborhood that had been part of our city for four hundred years. Hundreds of residents left when the fascists took over years before, and the Nazis tried to do away with the rest, rounding up over one thousand Jewish men, women, and children in one night.

After this, while Nikola was still in her *training*, the Nazis went about deporting the remaining Jewish residents. Romans objected to the deportations, and most police forces refused to participate, which meant ordinary people had a small window in which to help our friends and neighbors disappear. We found hiding places for some and sympathetic hospitals took in others, diagnosing each person with *Il Morbo di K*. No German soldier dared approach a "patient," lest he suffer facial convulsions, paralysis, disfiguration, and death. K Syndrome was a deadly neurological disease and entirely fictional.

While these efforts helped many, they remained small bandages on a very large flow. We needed the big guns to step in right away, instead of waiting nine months. How many lives were lost in the hesitation, do you think?

Was this careful approach worth it? Could you have not made better use of your manpower and time? When Nikola began this so-called training, thousands had died, whole neighborhoods had vanished, and we were stripped of nearly everything except our wills to live. Only the Germans and convents had food, and we former housewives had one of two ways to survive—become a nun or a whore. About my choice, I feel no shame. Sex is more lucrative than praying, and we must all do things to get by.

5

NIKI

November 1943

Niki must've been the only one from the fingerprinting room assigned to Morale Operations. Among the people in her unit, she could almost pass for a social register type. The OSS personnel office claimed they employed people representing every country as well as occupation, all the way down to pack elephants and carrier pigeons, and this was no exaggeration. During the first week of training, Niki met a Thai missionary, a Shanghai businessman, and a private detective from the Bronx. Many were new citizens, just like her.

Thanks to her prior attempt at joining SI, Niki was able to skip OSS assessment school. Though it was unlikely to be the worst part of training, Niki was glad not to truck out to a 118-acre estate in Fairfax to be psychologically grilled by a gaggle of tweedy psychiatrists. *What do you dislike seeing people do? What experience made you feel like sinking through the floor? What moods and feelings are most disturbing to you, and how often do you have them?* It was the sort of thing a person should only do once.

Instead, Niki was ordered to proceed directly to the Q Building, where she was shuttled into a long, drafty, overlit room filled with abandoned office furniture. After picking from the twenty or so desks, Niki surveyed her surroundings, counting only three other women.

At twenty past the hour, an instructor stepped up to the front of the room. "Welcome, everyone, to Morale Operations," he said, and promptly dove into the materials. "MO is part of the Office of Strategic Services, an undercover organization established by the Joint Chiefs of Staff. This is a *secret* intelligence agency. Do you know what that means?"

Someone sprang up a hand. "That we can't say anything to anyone?" the eager beaver guessed.

"It means you can get shot for merely knowing the information yourself," the man said, seemingly quite proud of the threat.

Niki struggled to tamp down a brewing sense of disgust. Shot for *knowing* something? This was not the America Niki thought she'd committed to.

"Repeat one word you've heard to anyone, and you'll be tried for treason," the man added. "Understand?" Heads nodded as he signaled to his secretary, one of the previously counted three women. "What is Morale Operations, you might be asking yourself?" the man continued. "It's many things, but MO's primary purpose is to lower enemy morale by spreading disinformation." The secretary snaked between the desks, dropping a booklet on each. "Your role is to act as propagandists. *Black* propagandists, which means your work will be subversive, designed to seem as though it's coming from the enemy. This is important because Germans are more apt to believe something if they think it's from inside their own borders."

Thwack. The booklet plonked in front of Niki. MORALE OPERATIONS FIELD MANUAL, it read. She glanced up to smile, but the woman was onto the next propagandist. *Thwack, thwack, thwack.* Niki flipped past the table of contents and to the first page.

> The term MORALE OPERATIONS as considered in this Manual includes all measures of subversion other than physical used to create confusion and division, and to undermine the morale and the political unity of the enemy through any means operating within or purporting to operate within enemy countries and enemy occupied or controlled countries...

"Propaganda campaigns can take a variety of forms," the man said. "Section five of your book outlines several examples, including bribery and blackmail, forgery, rumors, as well as false leaflets, pamphlets, and graphics. You'll receive more details in the coming weeks, but throughout your training and while devising campaigns of your own, it's crucial that you remember several key points.

"One. Disinformation must be easy to comprehend—nothing too highbrow. Two. It must be addressed to the masses, not the intellectuals. Three. It should hit on emotions, not facts or logic."

It sounded so diabolical, not to mention insulting. Pick on the people who wouldn't think too much?

As the instructor droned on about keeping their lips buttoned and taking things seriously, Niki skimmed a few more pages. *It's not all bad*, she told herself. Sometimes lying and subterfuge were necessary, and besides, Niki had practiced plenty of subversion while still in Brnö. For example, she never let on that she understood German, and regularly "forgot" they'd switched to driving on the right side of the road. Her batted-eye "confusion" sent a minimum of twelve Nazis to the hospital.

"You should know that this branch has the worst security record in the organization. Somehow, MO personnel are always the first ones made. When confronted, every person in MO should pretend he is—" The man's eyes flickered toward Niki. "You should all claim to be file clerks when asked. Are there any questions?"

Before Niki had time to think of one, someone else put up a hand.

"Where will we be sent?" the person asked in a Spanish accent.

The instructor checked his notes. "After you wrap up in Washington," he said, "this group will be sent to Algiers."

"Algiers?" the man balked. "I'd hoped to go into *enemy* territory. Haven't we gained control of North Africa?"

"Not so fast," the instructor said. "There is much to do before we can turn you loose. We do indeed have control of North Africa, but Algiers is at present the base of Allied headquarters, and the training grounds for MO. You'll hone your propaganda skills there before shipping out to other areas, depending on need."

Niki groaned, though only on the inside. More training? Weren't they about to wrap up this war? At this rate, armistice might happen before they stepped one boot on the ground.

After two hours and forty-three minutes, the instructor dismissed the group, dispatching them to another room to practice steaming open envelopes. This didn't seem relevant to their job, but Niki was glad to do something with her hands that did not involve explosives. She was happily one foot out the door when the instructor let out a whistle and ordered all gals to stay behind. He had another manual, for the three of them.

"You girls are not officially part of the Women's Army Corps," he said, handing them each a one-hundred-thirty-page booklet, "but you will need to abide by its rules. It's very important that you go through the manual with a fine-tooth comb to understand what's expected of you. This division has a bad reputation, and we don't need you ladies making it worse."

Niki read the first page.

YOU MUST BE FIT.

YOU are a member of the first Women's Army in the history of the United States. You are one of the small percentage of women qualified in mind and body to perform a soldier's noncombat duties.

These duties are many. The demands of war are varied, endless, and merciless. To satisfy these demands, you must be fit.

You have successfully passed a rigorous physical examination. You are organically sound. Now you must build the strength and stamina, the control and coordination, to do a man's work any hour of the day, every day of the month.

YOUR JOB: TO REPLACE MEN.

"Girls, see if you can't set an example?" the man said as he began packing his briefcase.

Niki looked up from the booklet. *What* had she just signed up for?

"Excuse me?" called out a voice from the back of the room. "Am I in the right place? I'm here for MO training. I might be a little late. They sent me from—"

Niki turned and squinted at the doorway. "FUCK!" she said upon spying a patchy, broken line of eyebrow. All heads cranked in her direction, and Niki smiled sheepishly, waving them off.

Fuck, she said, only in her head this time. The blow-in was none other than Captain William Dewart. A late-breaking entry into the liars' club.

6

PALOMA

May 1945

Captain Dewart? *Avoja!* Yes, I know who you mean. Tall, hand-some, dimpled. Very hard to miss.

Was I attracted to him? I did not sleep with him, if that's what you're asking. Attraction doesn't really play into my line of work. I can see how he might strike the right chord for someone into big, burly Americans, but he was never very appealing to me. He was too lumpish, too artless, always standing around look-ing uncomfortable.

It took me forever to determine what was happening between him and Nikola, whether she despised him or was secretly fuck-ing him on the side. Nikola is a tricky one, which is of course the very reason you're talking to me.

7

NIKI

January 1944

The man appeared on Niki's doorstep at dawn. "Here's every-thing you'll need," he said, handing her a small stack of papers.

Along with official orders, and several explanatory memos, the folder included a special green passport that would allow Niki to freely pass between areas under Allied control, as well as receive "all lawful aid and protection as would be extended to citizens or subjects of foreign governments." Niki pulled back the cover and marveled at her first destination.

ALGIERS—IMPORTANT INTERNATIONAL BUSINESS.

"Did you get all of your immunizations?" the man asked, and Niki bobbed her head. "And your flight bag is ready?"

Again, she nodded, and gestured toward the sack into which she'd crammed a year's worth of clothes. Her footlocker of equipment had already been shipped overseas: helmet, sleeping bag, thermos, flashlight, machete, all standard-issue army stuff, though Niki questioned which items she'd really use. The fatigues, maybe, and the poncho.

"Be at the airport half an hour before takeoff," the man said. "Someone will meet you there. Don't lose your papers. Sew them into your corset or something." With that, he whirled around and vanished into the low Washington fog.

As Niki closed the door behind him, a cockroach skittered across her toes. She didn't necessarily mind that the government was billeting her in the basement of a former house of ill repute. If anything, its history gave the place some character, but Niki hoped future accommodations would be cleaner, less teeming with critters.

She could hardly believe it. Tonight, Niki would be flying to Algiers, via a circuitous route that somehow included both Miami and Brazil, a precaution because "Germans will shoot anything crossing the Atlantic." It was a stark reminder that Niki wasn't going home. She was going to war.

Assuming a safe journey, in a few days she'd be in North Africa, the testing grounds for MO, where Niki and her colleagues would get their footing and support the planned infiltration of France. Once that was complete, and the Allies finished taking Southern and Central Italy, Rome was to be her next destination. Naples had fallen in October, and it made sense to move the Mediterranean Theater of Operations out of North Africa and into European cities with ports.

You're one of the only women in MO who'll be stationed in the Mediterranean Theater, the commanding officer had told Niki when she got her final assignment. *Make us proud.*

After tossing her documents onto a nearby table, Niki crouched to inspect her flight bag, barely able to open it because of her suddenly fat and clumsy fingers. She reminded herself that she'd *wanted* this. Czechoslovakia—she refused to call it the Protectorate—had felt more distant, more out of reach by the day. According to the newspapers, Russian guerrillas were at that moment parachuting into the Carpathian Mountains, but Niki wanted to know what was happening in Brno. George had been in Switzerland for months but couldn't tell her a thing, despite being employed by the Office of War Information, which seemed awfully devoid of the information part.

"They don't trust Americans," he'd said. "The government-in-exile goes to the Brits and Soviets for help, and there's not much we can do about it." It was a lost cause, as George had told her all along. "Your family had their chance, darling, but refused to take it."

George was right, and now Niki's parents and brother could be alive, or dead. They might be imprisoned, or confined to a labor camp, and the family's wool factory was either confiscated or briskly churning out Wehrmacht uniforms and underwear. There was no best-case scenario, only different versions of the worst, and not knowing was its own kind of torture.

For the past two years, Niki had lain awake most nights, worried about her family but also consumed by a sense of unfinished business. She could be quick to pull the metaphorical trigger, which was ironic since during training she'd received poor marks when it came to the literal one. Had Niki *really* done all she could, with her family, her former professors, the people in her town? Or had she cut out as soon as she had the opportunity?

Niki fought back against the Germans in her way, with small acts of subversion and attending the occasional protest, but how much of a risk had she really taken, given her family's position? They weren't wealthy, but they owned a business, a business that followed rules, for better or worse.

"They're keeping our government intact," her father insisted when Niki pleaded with him to *do something*, to stand up against the tyrants. "It will not be bad here, like it is in other places."

Niki wanted to believe him, and, for a brief window of time, the economy still hummed along and not many restrictions were put into place. Schools remained open and their family friend and next-door neighbor, Julius Goldberger, was allowed to freely operate his lumber mill despite being Jewish.

Regardless, the inevitability of disaster hung like smog over the city, and Niki remained tense, bracing herself for the treachery to come. Sure enough, within two years of the Germans goose-stepping into Czechoslovakia, the Protectorate's puppet regime banned Jews from most paid occupations as well as schools, movie theaters, and parks. In the fall of 1941, when the government announced a mass deportation to an unknown destination, a wave of suicides broke out across Brnö.

Niki waited for outrage, for the Czech people to react. Because of its sizable Jewish population, Brnö never felt like a divided culture. Jews had seats in parliament and on city councils. They owned businesses, attended university, and more than 30 percent married gentiles. Surely the Brnˇáci, the citizens of Brnö, would not abide the cruelty, Niki believed, even as she witnessed the torching of synagogues and civilians throwing Nazi salutes in Freedom Square. By the end of the year, Niki recognized the harsh truth. The majority now identified more with Hitler than the country they'd pledged their allegiance to after the last war.

Given her parents' inaction, Niki tried to appeal to their more influential friends, but they also claimed impotence. Meanwhile, with each passing week, more restrictions were imposed, and Niki's legal work eventually ground to a halt. She grew increasingly restless, and hopeless, and could no longer stomach staring into the faces of people she knew, who seemed all too willing to turn the other cheek. One morning Niki woke up and at last accepted there was no saving Brnö, and when George asked her to marry him again, she agreed.

For a moment, Niki could envision some kind of future, until her family refused the visas arranged by George's family. She might've seen this coming with her parents, who were as hard and stout in personality as they were in appearance, but that sweet, curly-haired Pasha stayed behind left her in ruins. After a pathetic barrage of pleas and one or two threats, Niki gave up and sailed to America, the most brokenhearted bride to ever exist.

Though this was her own version of turning a cheek, no one could begrudge Niki for leaving when she did. *Kdo utec̆e, vyhraje.* It was an old Czech proverb meaning, "he who runs away, wins." But Niki didn't feel like a victor, and she couldn't help but play out a hundred different scenarios in her mind. Could she have done more if she'd stayed an extra week, a month, a year? Most likely not, and it was futile to pretend things might've gone another way, and Niki hated the part of herself that still believed she could go back and fix everything.

Rising to her feet, Niki brushed her hands on her pants. She gathered her papers from the table (*sew them into her corset*—the nerve!) to double-check she had all that was required. A sneaky outfit like the OSS would definitely leave something out of the packet as a test to see if she noticed.

As Niki reached the end of the stack, she found a flimsy sheet of yellow paper tucked in among all those documents festooned with fancy signatures and important stamps. When she saw it was a telegram from George, Niki's heart jumped. Her husband wasn't the love note type, and they'd had more than one argument about her taking the job. George only accepted the situation upon learning the reasons his wife was picked—her age, college record, languages, and looks. George saw these not as Niki's attributes but as a reflection on him, as though they were true only after she'd become his wife.

Inhaling deeply, Niki tore open the envelope and skimmed the stunningly brief note. Safe travels. I'll see you when you get here.

"You'll see me?" Niki said, wrinkling her brow. Spouses weren't supposed to be assigned to the same theater of operation, and he was in Bern, not Algiers.

Niki tucked the telegram back in with the other papers. There was no use worrying about it now. George was always confounding her, and Niki would learn the answers when she got to Algiers. This was the OSS, and something told her she'd find many more surprises ahead.

8

PALOMA

May 1945

Maybe I cannot blame Niki and her colleagues for taking a holiday in North Africa before coming to us. Who would want to go to Italy then or even now? But the question remains. Might you have arrived more swiftly had you known the extent of our suffering? By the close of the year, our lives were so wretched we stopped worrying about our disappeared Jewish friends. We'd been stripped of so much, including our humanity.

Winter was bleak but spring was worse because of all our prior deprivation, like a building snowball of penury. In that season of alleged renewal, the Germans slashed our meager bread allotment by another one-third and did away with pasta rations altogether. In some respects, it didn't matter. People were still waiting to buy their November rations in March, and the bread, when we had it, was nearly inedible, an ungodly creation of maize flour and elm tree pitch.

We had no way to procure more food. Rail transport had ceased, and private vehicles were long ago confiscated and reissued to the Gestapo. Even if we had the automobiles to drive somewhere, the bridges were heavily guarded and mined. Commodities couldn't come into the city, and we couldn't go out, and thus the only available food was whatever could be acquired on a very long walk. In a city surrounded by decimated farmland and one hundred seventy-five miles from the sea, this "whatever" was never much.

We Romans survived on a two-to-three-day supply of food. "BREAD! BREAD! BREAD!" the people shouted, as did graffiti on the buildings. "DEATH TO THE PEOPLE WHO ARE STARVING US!" The Vatican's soup kitchens fed one hundred thousand per day, but still people were collapsing, dying on the streets.

Oh, you didn't know it was so bad? Perhaps you fell victim to propaganda. Was it the pictures? The photographs of happy, rosy-cheeked Nazis distributing loaves of bread to a clutch of little ones, their skinny arms outstretched? Don't be fooled. Once the cameras were down, the brutes snatched the bread away, leaving dozens of dirty, hollow-eyed children screaming in the piazze.

Food was not the only problem. So many plants had been bombed that electricity was rationed, as well as water. The minute the faucets turned on, women everywhere scrambled to fill bathtubs and basins and any other container they could reasonably carry.

One by one, shops and restaurants closed, and people hid behind locked doors, afraid to venture outside. The Nazis lived fine, sì, certamente, wearing fur coats as they tooled around in our cars, enjoying the opera and theater and all those loaves of bread. With no other choice, I went where the money was, the food.

Through it all, I refused to imagine my son's face or any of the treacherous places he might be. Paolo was drafted into the Italian Army two years ago, the minute he turned eighteen, but what happened after Italy signed the Armistice and the country was split in two is anyone's guess.

Some of the men from our now defunct army went north, to fight for the Repubblica Sociale Italiana, Mussolini and Hitler's new fascist state. Others joined the former partisans in the south, to fight on behalf of the king and the Badoglio government. Confused about the situation, and where loyalties were supposed to lie, hundreds of thousands of men surrendered to the Allies, or were captured by the Germans, or simply tried to go home. I still don't know which hell my son chose.

The king declared Rome an "Open City" to protect its civilians and cultural landmarks. Yet, during those nine months, I came to learn "open" meant vulnerable, unprotected, exposed. *Any day*, we thought. *Any day the Allies will be here and make it okay.* You'd freed Naples, and Rome was surely next. But you did not come, and you did not come, and we had to accept the possibility you wouldn't ever arrive.

"The delay was necessary," Nikola told me once. The Allies had to work out where to start the second front, and at the same time bolster the troops. They needed fresh people and equipment to combat the beleaguered German forces. Fresh troops *were* key to the Allied victory. Still. How nice to wait it out in Algiers, basking in the sunshine and piles of food, all while working alongside that handsome William Dewart.

9

NIKI

May 1944
Algiers

"How would you rate these beauties?" Ezra Feldman said, pinning one of his drawings onto the wall.

Five of them were in their Quonset hut turned office—Niki, Ezra, Will Dewart, the Rumors guy, and Lieutenant Jack Daniels, whose primary skill seemed to be lifting heavy objects.

"Will the Germans like them, do you think?" Romanian-born Ezra was the group's resident cartoonist, and the only one with experience, having come to Algiers from China, and India before. *This doesn't make me more seasoned*, he'd claim. *Unless the seasoning is turmeric, by which I mean bitter.* Artists like him were in high demand, drafted by the planeload. It was the best way to communicate in foreign lands where the government didn't speak the language.

"Will the Germans *like* them? What's not to like?" said Rumors, leering.

"Could be bigger, to really get the point across," Lieutenant Jack Daniels opined.

"I think they're perfect. Very realistic," Niki said, and felt Daniels's eyes slither in her direction. She didn't have to guess what he was thinking. A woman built like an adolescent boy couldn't possibly identify a good set of knockers.

"Thank you, everyone, for the feedback," Ezra said. "I'm quite proud of the work." He plunked down upon an upside-down bucket. "Do you have anything to add, Dewart?" he asked, though only for show. At present, Will was hunched over his desk, an unmistakable blush creeping up his neck and spreading toward his ears.

"I'm sure whatever you came up with will suffice," he said.

Niki snickered. "Honestly, Will. Looking is not against the law," she said. "But you're very sweet with that halo so firmly in place."

Back at the Q Building in Washington, Niki and Will agreed to leave all prior fracases in the past. Niki considered this a great courtesy on her part but, in the months since, Will had grown on her, like an invasive though innocuous mold. Captain Dewart was an interesting specimen. The man was built like a monument to strength and fortitude, an appearance that was at odds with his internal unrest, and the ever-present crease between his (regrowing) brows. Even his smile was guarded, starting with a twitch at the corners before it spread cautiously across his face. Whatever shortcomings he had, Will was a good man, a conscientious man, and always treated everyone, including Niki, with a level of respect that was unusual around these parts. The fact that he wasn't interested in gawking at Ezra's rendition of boobs was another credit in his ledger of nice qualities.

"Here's my outline for the article," Will said, rattling Niki out of her thoughts. He placed a piece of paper on the overturned crate she used as a desk. "It's about how members of the High

Command are profiteering from the war and living ridiculously lavish lifestyles."

Niki nodded, working out how she'd convey his ideas in German for the inaugural issue of *Nachrichten für die Truppe*, their *News for the Troops* magazine. It was their first real effort after five months of practice, and Niki had to get all the quirks of the language and culture correct. If MO did their job, the average soldier would read *Nachrichten* with its hand-drawn nudes, sports scores, and light brushes with the news, and not notice the odd subversive article tucked between all that tail and boobs.

"This is perfect," Niki said about Will's article, though this was merely a guess. It seemed like a strong message, but she didn't feel any more skilled at this propaganda business than when they'd arrived. Most people they came across in Algiers were British or Free French soldiers, and they couldn't wield their lies and rumors on Allies. Washington advised trying with the locals, but the Arabs were unimpressed by their attempts, and never understood their "jokes."

Now playtime was over, and all military efforts were focused on opening the second front, which was a tactical way to say "invading France." Soldiers were at that moment positioned in camps along the south coast of England, waiting for the sign to move, while Eisenhower calculated the whens and hows. MO's job was to prime Germans for their impending encirclement, as well as provide inaccurate maps of where the Allies would land.

Niki could feel it. She could taste it. Once this operation was complete, the second front would open, and the war's tenor would change. They'd send her unit to Rome and Niki one step closer to home. It was about time, after nearly half a year. She was nervous, but more than ready.

As Niki typed the first sentence of her article, one of Allied Forces Headquarters' messengers rapped on the frame of their hut. "Mail call!" he sang.

Ezra was the first to spring up from his bucket. "How many do I have today?" he asked.

Like Niki, Ezra was a freshly minted United States citizen. Unlike Niki, he hadn't needed a marriage to do it. The artist lived in Italy for almost a decade, having first studied architecture before dropping out to draw cartoons for Italian humor magazines. When war was declared, despite the opposition of its citizens, the government banned Jews from employment, and foreigners were told to go home. The fascist police put Ezra's name on a list of people who were in the country illegally, but his passport had been canceled and Ezra therefore couldn't leave.

Whatever Ezra lacked in material wealth he made up for through a rich group of family and friends who'd already immigrated to the States. They worked to get him out of Italy while raising funds for his passage to America, and repeatedly submitting his cartoons to *Town & Country*, *Life*, *Mademoiselle*, and *The New Yorker*, hoping his talent would get him around the fact that more Romanians left America each year than were let in. With an annual quota of under four hundred for a country with over one million Jews, it was no surprise that the waiting list was forty-three years long.

After a brief stint in a Fascist prison, Ezra eventually escaped to Portugal, and then sailed to the United States only to be turned away because he'd doctored his passport with fake stamps. "Americans are so didactic!" he often said, citing this as evidence. Ezra was forced to spend the Fourth of July weekend at Ellis Island, so close to his dream of America, yet so far away.

While family and friends sorted through the paperwork required for American citizenship, Ezra waited it out in the Dominican Republic. Though it was ruled by a maniacal autocrat, the country was willing to accept an unlimited number of Jews, so long as the proper fees were paid, an option available only to a select, privileged few.

From his exile, Ezra published cartoons for Dominican newspapers as well as *The New Yorker,* until he finally made it to America, where he became a citizen. Ezra harbored no ill will for the difficulties he endured, and loved everything about his new home, as smitten with the country's "big, generous heart" as he was with its chewing gum, shampoo, and inspiring "relentless hope of the oppressed."

Almost immediately, the OSS spotted Ezra's work in a magazine and drafted him into their graphics department, before sending him overseas. From Algiers, he continued producing work for the American press. Back home, there was a great hunger for a front row peek of war, though only if the tale was relayed amusingly, and with none of the gory stuff.

My life is a series of fortuitous encounters and lucky breaks, Ezra often declared, which was a hell of a thing for a Jewish refugee to say. Niki got the sense he was beloved not only by his American contacts but a wide range of people, across several continents. Between friends, fans, and editors, Ezra received more mail than the rest of them put together.

"Four letters for Mr. Feldman," the messenger announced. This was a light load for Ezra, and he responded with an expression of extreme displeasure. "And one for Lieutenant Jack Daniels."

"Which of my fillies is it, I wonder?" Daniels claimed to harbor a string of girlfriends, coast-to-coast, but the only letters of his Niki had seen were written by his grandmother, making him an excellent fit for a propaganda machine.

"Sorry, guys," the man said, eyes skipping from Rumors, to Niki, to Will. "That's all for today. Better luck tomorrow."

Rumors's face fell, Niki shrugged, and Will worked on, same as before, his expectations in check. His wife wrote only on the third Thursday of every month, each letter opening with a set of gardening updates—flowering, pruning, new seeds—followed by a recounting of their children's most recent behavior, as reported by a nanny. Niki didn't mean to snoop, but she'd caught a paragraph, here and there, and usually found herself chafed on Will's behalf. At a minimum, Mrs. Dewart could've *pretended* her husband was missed. Otherwise, why bother? Then again, Niki would've done most anything to see her parents' or brother's handwriting, no matter what they wrote.

And who was she to judge? Niki didn't even have a third Thursday to look forward to and she never heard from her family, or even from George. *I'll see you when you get here*, he'd telegrammed before she left Washington. He had come, for one day, to make sure Niki got settled, without staying long enough to eat or meet the rest of the team. She knew the others found it odd, but Niki never questioned how or why he'd come that far. It made a strange kind of sense in the context of knowing and being married to George. He was always finding ways to check on her, to make sure she wasn't saying or doing the wrong thing.

"Be careful," he'd warned on his way out. "I won't be around to rescue you, and your mistakes will be a black mark on *both* our names." With that comment, Niki switched all her paperwork to "Nikola Novotná." It was an upside to being stationed at the AFHQ.

"What's with the long face?" Ezra said, and clapped a hand on Niki's shoulder. "Ole George isn't much of a letter writer, eh?"

Niki shook her head. Until Ezra mentioned it, she hadn't even known she was frowning. "It's not that," she said. "I mean, he's not, but that's fine. I knew what I was getting myself into."

"Novotná and Dewart." Ezra clucked. "Ironic that the two married folks are the only ones who never get mail. Perhaps the trick is staying away from the institution altogether. That's my plan, in any case. Receiving missives from other people's wives is much more fun." He waved one of his fan letters overhead as proof.

"If only we'd known," Niki mumbled, and turned back to her desk.

"Oh, look! I also have a letter from my Uncle Harry in Denver," Ezra said, flipping to the next page. "He's received a telegram from my parents, courtesy of the Red Cross."

Niki stiffened. "Is that right?" she said, and cleared her throat. "How nice that the Red Cross is able to get into Romania. Has it been a while since you've heard from them?"

"An entire year." Ezra scanned the note. "They are doing well, it seems. Trusting a murderous dictator really pays off sometimes. Who would've guessed?"

All things considered, Bucharest was the safest place his family could be in Axis-controlled Europe. Romania's special brand of ruthless despot murdered "only" the Jews residing in territories lost to the Soviets, refusing to deport those inside Romania proper, in direct defiance to Hitler. As long as people kept their heads down, and learned to pay bribes, they might get roughed up, but had a much better chance of surviving.

"From what you've said, they didn't really *trust* Antonescu," Niki pointed out. "They lacked other options. It's hard to make decisions when you're in the thick of something and can't really see a proper way out." She'd said these very things about her own parents, many times, but compared to Ezra's family, they had options for miles. *Zkurvysyn.* Son of a bitch. Why hadn't they left when they could?

"Oh, they had options," Ezra said. "But my mother's a real terrorist, completely selfish and authoritarian. In that way, Antonescu is her style. Everyone's like that in Romania, which is why I've divorced myself from the place."

He chucked the letter into the trash, and Niki looked away. "You're lucky to know they're alive," she said. "Not everyone is so fortunate."

"What a boon!"

"You're awfully sour today, Novotná," Daniels said. "Wake up on the wrong side of the bed or something?"

"I'm not sour. We are simply having a conversation," Niki said, and wiggled in her seat. Maybe she *had* been overly salty toward Ezra. They'd only known each other for a short while, but Niki understood he used dry humor and a crusty nonchalance—with a dash of his self-described "Balkan fatalism"—to deflect prickly topics. Niki was envious that the Red Cross could get information out of Romania and, deep down, Ezra was probably relieved to hear from them. In a country run by a mercurial dictator, the situation could change at any moment. "I'm sorry, Ezra," Niki said, staring at the floor. "I don't mean to get testy."

"Who's testy?" Ezra said. "You're a delight!"

"Hardly. Again, I apologize. I'm just anxious for the second front business to go off. We need to end this war. I'm ready to move on."

"Aren't we all?" Rumors said.

"Not much longer yet," Will piped up. "That's what they say."

Niki bobbed her head. He was right. Not much longer, and about damned time.

10

NIKI

May 1944

Niki and Will sat on the sun-dappled patio of the Red Cross club, enjoying their day-end whiskeys while the Donut Dollies trolled the premises, restocking their clubmobiles with gum, cigarettes, magazines, newspapers, and the supplies necessary to make coffee and doughnuts on the road. It'd be one day, two at the most, before the ladies ventured back out to visit the servicemen in airfields and camps. If a fella at headquarters wanted to get lucky, he didn't have much time, which accounted for the nearly empty club.

"Sorry you drew the short straw," Niki said, guessing Will had been assigned to keep the lady private company. "Especially with the special guest stars around. The downside to being married. One of them, anyhow. They think you can't appreciate a pretty woman with treats."

"Nah," Will said, batting a hand. "I'm not interested in the Donut Dollies. I'd rather be here."

"Aw, that's sweet." Niki offered a commiserative frown, figuring this was some kind of act. Will wasn't the wolfish type, but what man didn't relish a fresh, pretty face? "You can admit it," she said. "This is a tough gig."

"A gig I'll sign up for every time." Will pushed both khaki sleeves up over his elbows, revealing unexpectedly flexed and tanned forearms, and Niki tried not to gape. If some unwitting Donut Dolly caught a gander, she might mistake him for an honest-to-God athlete, and Niki would have to explain that the bump on his nose was because he couldn't catch a baseball and had broken it twice. "This is good stuff," Will said, swirling his drink, letting the amber liquid catch the sunlight.

"Mmm-hmm," Niki answered, half-heartedly. It was decent, though she would've preferred a Plzeňský Prazdroj. Over the past two and a half years, Niki tried every beer she could find, but nothing held up to a good Czech lager. It was another entry on the list of things Niki might not ever see again. "Two weeks," Niki said, and Will glanced up with a squint. *"Nachrichten für die Truppe,"* she clarified.

It'd been two weeks since they'd finished the first edition of *News for the Troops*. Two weeks since they sent their magazine to the American 422nd, the Special Leaflet Squadron, to drop somewhere over Germany. Two weeks since everything seemed so urgent, on the cusp of a major shift, but now it felt as though they were stuck in a holding pattern.

"When do you think it's going to happen?" Niki asked. "The second front? It might be any day, right?"

Will took a tight sip of his whiskey. The man was not a big drinker, and Niki hoped this outfit didn't have a bad influence on him. "You absolutely hate sitting still, don't you?" he said.

"Who can sit still? Or sleep at night? The second front will be the biggest development of the war," Niki said. "I appreciate the logistics involved, but for the love of dumplings, people are dying out there. Even Russia's getting surly, thinking we're making them do all the work. Never thought I'd agree with Stalin, but here we are."

"Relax, my spirited comrade," Will said, and patted her hand. "Everything will happen soon enough."

"But *when?*" Niki pinched her lips together. Those in charge had been telling them any day, for weeks, and she was ready to move. Niki wasn't naïve. She understood that Rome would be no kind of break, and the situation there was far more tenuous than in Algiers. Italy was such a god-awful mess, it was hard to keep track of who controlled what parts, and which areas weren't destroyed.

No matter. Once the team arrived in Rome, Austria would be the only country separating Niki from Czechoslovakia, instead of Austria, and Italy, and the whole of the Tyrrhenian Sea. Also, her family loved Italy. They'd wanted to open a factory in Tuscany, and her little brother, Pasha, attended university in Milan. Not that anyone was holidaying *in Italia* these days, but this still felt like a huge leap forward. Five and a half months in, and Niki was no closer to her family than when she'd left Washington. If anything, they seemed farther away.

"The waiting must be difficult," Will said. "I'm sure you're eager to be near loved ones."

"Loved ones?" Niki jiggled her head. Her coworkers knew the sketch of her life but not the finer details, and she intended to keep it that way. "Who said anything about my family?" Niki wondered how she'd tipped him off.

Will's cheeks pinked. "I'm sorry," he said. "I didn't mean to presume. I just... I assumed you wanted to be near Switzerland because that's where your husband is?"

"Oh. Right. Right! Well. That's part of it," Niki lied. "When sad married folks like us don't get any letters, we need to hold on to something."

Will laughed flatly. "Yes. Mr. Feldman has all the answers, doesn't he?" he said. "I imagine you miss him. Your husband. What with still being in your honeymoon phase."

"It's fine. We're used to being apart," Niki said, slapping away a fly that wasn't there.

Will signaled the waiter for another drink. "You've never told me how you met," he said. "George has this air of mystery about him. Come to think, so do you. I'm curious." Will crossed his arms and leaned forward onto his elbows. "Tell me, Private Novotná, how did George Clingman sweep you off of your feet?"

"Huh. What a question," Niki said, trying to recall if she'd told anyone this story before. Should she give it to him straight, or did it need to be couched in propaganda? "There wasn't much *sweeping* involved," she admitted. "We met back in '38 when George came to Brnö to divest his family's Czech business interests. Clever devils. Got out right in time."

Niki smiled, landing for a moment on what had been a sweet part of their relationship. Theirs was a whirlwind romance, but she assumed it'd be fleeting, a fairy tale briefly lived, until George popped the question three months after they met. They hadn't known each other long, and with all the uncertainty in Czechoslovakia, Niki declined. He kept asking over the years, and she turned him down, until she couldn't find a reason to say no.

"I was the attorney representing the buyer of several of his family's assets," Niki went on. "So, we had many opportunities to meet before he formally asked me out. We hit it off and went out together whenever he was in town. Things developed from there."

"Hold on a minute," Will said, eyes widening. "You're a lawyer? What? How come I didn't know this?"

"Gosh, Dewart, don't look so flabbergasted. I was also a journalist between university and law school," she said. "I have three degrees, all told."

"THREE?" Will yelped, startling the waiter as he set down

the glass. "This gets worse and worse. For my self-esteem. I'm not sure I know *anyone* with three degrees."

Niki waited for the "much less a woman" part, though it never came. She should've known by now that Will would never say such a thing.

"I'm not so special," Niki said. "Czechs are better educated than Americans, on the whole, particularly the women. This is one benefit to a new country. You can start with a fresh set of mores and rules."

Without male-dominated religious customs or centuries of "tradition" to overcome, women's rights were compulsory from day one, and all the girls Niki knew growing up pursued higher education. By the time she met George, Niki had graduated from the University of Paris, as well as Masaryk, the country's premier law school, though Niki was hardly one of a kind. Over one-third of Czechoslovakia's university students were women. Thinking on this, she felt a punch of sorrow, something like defeat. What would happen to all those clever Czech girls now?

"Jeez," Will said, "maybe America should start over, too."

"It's not the worst idea, but don't let anyone hear you say that, or they'll think you're a communist," Niki teased. "In any case, George proposed eventually, and I moved to the States in late '41. We married a few months later."

Niki ended the story here, at what felt like the end of their relationship, or their romance, at least. The minute Niki stepped onto American soil, George and his family took over her life. Perhaps she should've seen it coming. During negotiations for their Czech facilities, the Clingmans often spoke over her, and always deferred to her male colleagues, which Niki chalked up to cultural differences. But the slights continued in her new home, and George did little to stand up for his wife. *They're right, darling, you shouldn't go to the golf club alone. There are standards, and rules you probably wouldn't understand. You can be a little...capricious.*

As her attraction to George waned, Niki began to second-guess her decision, and with this, her motives. George was admirable, and patriotic, and they shared many happy times, but a multiyear courtship took on a different tone when bookended by Hitler's invasion and the shuttering of all Czech social and cultural organizations. Now everything was muddled, and it was impossible for Niki to parse gratitude from genuine affection, however much of it was left.

"I still can't believe you were an attorney," Will said, shaking his head, and beginning to take on the slightest hint of George. "Scratch that. I *do* believe it," he added, and right on time. "You certainly have the brains. And you can be slippery when it's called for."

"Hey!"

"Damn. Now I'm kicking myself for not going to law school, ideally in Czechoslovakia."

"Yes, you truly missed out on many beautiful and smart women." Niki jerked her gaze away and glugged her freshly poured drink. She didn't know what he meant by the comment and wouldn't dare ask.

"Explain something to me. You're clearly educated, and brilliant. How'd you get stuck in a hut in North Africa with a bunch of misfits?" he asked.

"Because I'm a misfit, too," Niki said with a wink. "I might not have stomach problems keeping me from the front lines, or Ezra's unique combination of ailments." By Ezra's telling, he was in possession of nearly every attribute disqualifying him from regular service, including his personality (meek), several medical conditions (early-stage heart disease, a mitral systolic murmur, myriad visual defects), and the fact the army diagnosed him with a mild psychoneurosis and borderline schizophrenia. "But I check the boxes for 'female' and 'foreign,'" she continued, "and am therefore more than qualified." Niki polished off her drink.

"I'm not convinced. The OSS is considered a bunch of castoffs," Will said. "And MO is the dregs of that. This isn't the right place for you. You must've been hoping for something different."

Niki snorted. "Well, yeah, weren't we all?"

"I meant something loftier. More highbrow. Like SI, and I got you kicked out."

"It wasn't your fault," Niki said. With each passing day, she believed this a little more. "I didn't have to go back, after the bomb went off."

"Yes. You did. Because that's the kind of person you are," he said.

"I don't know about that," Niki answered as she bit back tears. *Prone to going back* was not how anyone at home would describe her.

"Admit it. This wasn't what you wanted," Will insisted.

Niki hesitated, pressing her lips together. "I don't know," she said at last. "Who's to say I wanted the right thing?" Suddenly, her mouth began to wobble, curling into a watery smile. "Things look different now that I'm here. Maybe, when this is all finished, I'll decide Morale Operations was exactly where I was meant to be all along."

11

May 1989

He's really going to do this, isn't he? Geoffrey Jones is going to make them stand up and be counted.

"Let's begin with the most storied group," he says. "SI. The Secret Intelligence unit."

With Geoffrey's encouragement, a sizable portion of the guests stands. The women are all beaming, which they would, because they worked for SI. Niki begins to actively perspire and the jet beads on her dress make the fabric fall heavy, and cling to her skin.

"X-2," Geoffrey says. "Counterintelligence." A half-dozen women rise. Niki claps lightly, along with everyone else.

R&A. Research and Analysis.

FNB. Foreign Nationalities.

CD. Censorship and Documents.

Niki knows they're getting close. Should she stand? She can't not stand. The letters won't mean anything to Andrea. She'll probably get lost in a haze of acronyms, as Niki did more than once.

SO. Special Operations.

Here, Geoffrey Jones seems to pause, as if he's tuned into Niki's internal monologue and wishes to make the moment as dramatic as possible. What will Andrea think? Manfred was agog the first time Niki told him about it. *You lied for a living? You, the most straightforward person I know?*

"It's not like that," Niki shot back, but maybe it was. Their work had purpose, and it produced results, but at what cost? Is lying ever justified? All these years later, Niki still doesn't have an answer, which is why she shut the door on the question long ago.

Geoffrey Jones opens his mouth. "Next up," he says. Niki uncrosses her legs and places both feet on the ground. "MO. Morale Operations." Gritting her teeth, Niki closes her eyes, and pushes herself up from the chair.

Only a dozen or so are standing, none that Niki recognizes, though she never met other MO women after she left training. The ones around her might've worked in the Pacific Theater or, more likely, back in Washington.

"MU," Geoffrey Jones says, moving on. "The Maritime Unit." There are no takers here.

Niki plonks back down. Pulse throbbing, she smiles at Andrea, who lifts one sly brow. "Morale Operations," her daughter says, nodding thoughtfully as she checks the program for a definition. *The OSS Morale Operations (MO) branch produced and disseminated "black" propaganda to destabilize enemy governments and encourage resistance movements.* "Wow, Mom, you're full of surprises," Andrea says, glancing up.

"Oh, sweetheart," Niki says, and blows out a long stream of air. "You don't know the half of it."

12

NIKI

June 1944

After all those months—*years*—of planning, Rome had been liberated. The following day, Niki and the others gathered around the radio. They listened through hours of clanging, tinny music for the next piece of news, jumping with each hiccup in the broadcast.

D-Day was supposed to happen that morning. If all went according to plan, thirty minutes prior to the naval onslaught, the first plane would've flown over Normandy, dropping not bombs but several million pieces of propaganda *they'd* produced, everything from pamphlets hinting at Hitler's poor health to their fake communist newspaper, *Das Neue Deutschland—The New Germany*—which told of a vast partisan underground and heralded the virtues of peace. But weather conditions were murky, and hours later, they still didn't know whether Eisenhower went through with it.

But at long last, the music stopped, and a man's voice crackled over the airwaves. The room sucked in its breath, and Niki and Will grabbed each other's hands.

"Under the command of General Eisenhower, Allied naval forces, supported by strong air forces, began landing Allied armies this morning on the northern coast of France. This ends the reading of communication number one from Supreme Headquarters, Allied Expeditionary Force."

"We did it!" Jack Daniels whooped. "We goddamned did it!"

"Those poor suckers on the coast," Ezra lamented. "Alas, thanks to us, they'll have plenty to read."

Nine million pieces were dropped, all in, and Niki was proud. Their little team had contributed to the opening of the second front.

"When do you think they'll give us new orders?" Niki said now, from atop an overturned crate in the packing room. "Today or tomorrow is my theory." Whatever the case, she hoped it was soon. Seventy-two hours after D-Day, they still hadn't received their change in orders. Now that the Nazis were encircled, getting to Rome felt more urgent than ever, as though they were all sprinting toward the finish line.

"Today or tomorrow?" Jack Daniels scoffed. "That's awfully optimistic." He lobbed a stack of propaganda into a nearby box. Though D-Day had passed, planes kept flying over France, and MO continued trying to attack the enemy's spirit.

"I prefer to think of it as *realistic*," Niki said. "With the second front, everything's changed." This was true, which made it all the more frustrating that they remained in Algiers. "We've invaded France, and recaptured Rome. Our time here is up."

"Oh la la!" Ezra said, and swooped a hand overhead. "Conquering France and taking Rome. So grandiose. Imperialistic! You make it sound as though we had something to do with it."

"We were instrumental," Niki sniffed. "The top brass is happy with our efforts. Colonel Mann used the word *pleased*. We know they've been skeptical about MO, but I think they're coming around."

Ezra laughed. "Maybe one day, *Puis,or*," he said, and rumpled her hair. "Maybe one day. As of now, they still consider MO pointless and stupid, and frankly, they aren't wrong."

"Didn't you say it's *all* pointless?" Niki asked.

Ezra shook his head. "SO and SI have something to show for their work," he said. "A bridge that's blown up, or an intelligence report. What do we have? Nothing. Meanwhile, half the colonels think my sole purpose in life is to draw dirty pictures for them to put up in their villas."

Admittedly, the situation wasn't ideal, but Donovan believed in psychological warfare, even if no one else did. He was the top dog and they had to send the group *somewhere*, especially with the rest of Algiers already on its way out. At that very moment, trunks and crates were stacked in front of Mongol, the white, boxy villa from which the OSS conducted its Mediterranean operations, ready for AFHQ's move to a castle in Caserta, Italy. The enlisted men's Red Cross club was closed, and their Rumors guy had been shipped somewhere else.

"Why am I the only one who wants to leave?" Niki said. "Isn't anyone else tired of this damned place?"

"Algiers is a stupid city," Ezra said, wielding his favorite affront. "But you must understand the military never does anything expeditiously. This is a war of pants, pants destroyed by sitting on hard chairs and waiting."

It was another Ezra aphorism, and Niki was starting to see his point.

"I don't know," Will said, and pitched something into a box. "Part of me wonders whether they'll send us anywhere near Rome. Or, if they do, should we even be excited about it? Italy feels like an insult."

"Of course we're going to Rome!" Niki could feel her voice

escalate, alongside her blood pressure. She was told Italy. She'd been *counting* on it. "Why are you contradicting me? Do you know something we don't?"

"Not at all," Will said. "It's just... You've heard how the higher-ups talk. Italy isn't strategic for us, as a nation."

"Is that what it's all about, then?" Niki said, her words officially entering the territory of shrill. "What's strategic for us?"

"Uh, that *is* why we're doing all this," Jack Daniels said.

"You people are so cynical," Niki grouched. "It's not all about our economic or political interests. Think about the poor Italians! They need the Allies to step in and clean everything up. They'll be so relieved to see us after having endured both Mussolini *and* Hitler."

Will sighed deeply. "I'm not trying to start anything," he said. "It'd feel like a massive demotion. That's all. As if they're getting us out of the way."

"Oh, for the love of Wenceslas," Niki griped.

"Why are you pestering Dewart?" Ezra asked. "What does your husband have to say about it?"

Niki looked at him sideways, pulling her chin into her neck. "George? Why would he know anything?"

"Uh, isn't he in Bern?" Jack Daniels said. "All European intelligence goes through them."

"Yes, but he's with OWI, not the OSS," Niki said.

"Oh...really...the OWI." Daniels cackled.

"'The OWI,'" Will said, using air quotes.

"Aw, Niki." Ezra tsked, and Niki's heart began to race. "You don't have to pretend with us. There's nobody from OWI working in Bern."

"Yes, there is!" Niki said. Her eyes flew toward Will, then back to Ezra. "His name is George Clingman."

"That, my friend," Jack Daniels said, "is what you'd call a cover."

"Why would someone need a cover in Switzerland?" Niki

snapped. Sweat collected at her hairline. Damn, it was hot in that hut. She went to open the door. "It's a neutral country."

"So neutral they'll throw you in jail for picking a side," Ezra said. "The tyrants."

"But...but..." Niki stuttered. Her brain felt like it was going to spin out of her skull. For a second, she was embarrassed on George's behalf. Everyone at OSS had something wrong with them, and Niki wondered what fatal flaw they saw in him. "I thought spouses aren't allowed to work in the same division or theater of operation?"

"This is the government. They make exceptions," Ezra said as a hundred questions flashed through Niki's mind.

Was Ezra right? If so, why had George lied? If he did work for the OSS, why hadn't he stopped her from getting hired? This did explain being at the same party as Wild Bill Donovan.

"He's the attaché for Allen Dulles," Ezra added. "Dulles is the very hub of European intelligence. How is it possible you hadn't known this?"

Niki swallowed, and more questions piled up. What information was George keeping? To what extent had he lied? Did he know more about her family and Czechoslovakia than he was letting on?

"Do you..." Niki's throat had gone completely dry. "If Bern is the center of intelligence, do you think they're privy to what's happening in *all* of Europe? Like, in areas beyond the Mediterranean theater?"

"You can bet on it," Ezra said.

"Wow," said Daniels. "I can't believe *we're* telling *you* where your husband works. I figured he was the reason you had this job."

Normally Niki would've responded with a testy retort, but in her stupefaction, she let the comment hang. Correcting his never-ending stream of dim-witted observations didn't seem important right now.

"That's funny," Will said, out of nowhere. "I assumed the opposite—that he had his job because of her." He turned toward Niki, and they locked eyes. "No offense to your husband," he said, "but you seem like the brains of the operation."

Niki spit out a laugh and felt the prick of something in her left eye. As she wiped it aside, they heard the pound of boots along the dirt road, and a voice calling out to the people in their hut.

"Dewart! Feldman! Novotná!" Gathering in the open doorway, the group peered out to see one of the villa's messengers beating a path in their direction. "Daniels! Colonel Mann wants to speak to you," the messenger said, wheezing as he jogged up the hill.

"Ah! We've uncovered a person in worse shape than I," Ezra said.

"I hope your bags are packed. The four of you are on the next flight to Rome!"

13

PALOMA

May 1945

The end of German occupation rolled in like thunder, with gun-fire echoing across Rome for days. During those final hours, we climbed atop buildings to watch Allied dive-bombers fall from the sky and smoke billow over the rooftops. A river of men flowed north, out of Rome along Via dell'Impero.

It was rather German, the orderliness of this retreat. The soldiers even waited in line to cross Ponte Milvio. Which is not to say they were polite. As they left, they sabotaged our telephone exchange and water supply, and shot at or burned anything they could, though we didn't mind much. We were victorious, and everything would change, finally! How silly we were to believe this. It might've been a new day, but it was still the same war.

PART TWO

MO: ROME

14

NIKI

June 1944
Rome

"Welcome to Rome," the MO chief said as they entered their new base of operations—a large, mostly empty flat in the heart of the city. Their billets were nearby, in a cluster of villas formerly owned by Mussolini devotees who were now on the run. There wasn't electricity or running water, and locals had looted anything that could be picked up, but the team would have big, fancy beds and roofs over their heads, which was more than most people in Rome.

"We'll be sharing the office with a few other divisions," the chief continued. His name was Eugene Warner, and he had a ruddy complexion and wispy red hair. Before the OSS, he'd been a reporter with the Associated Press, which Will hypothesized made him good at propaganda. Niki thought he was probably incompetent, if they'd sent him to look after them.

"Which other divisions?" Jack Daniels asked as he assessed a pair of side-by-side offices.

"Some people from SI," Warner said, "when they're not in the field. Kunkel is here, too. He's R&A chief. Other than that, I don't really know. It's hard to keep it all straight."

"No kidding," Niki groused. The OSS was complicated, and everyone acted so damned secretive, even when conversing with fellow agents, even when conversing with one's spouse.

"Most of our work will be conducted in this space," Warner said, gesturing toward what was once somebody's high-ceilinged, cavernous living area. "We'll procure a few more desks. Hopefully. Over by Daniels, you see two private offices. The third door leads to our printing operation, which is run by Egidio Clemente. We're lucky to have access to it. It'll make our job a lot easier."

"I'll take the office on the left," Jack Daniels announced.

"That one is mine," Warner said. "Dewart and Novotná will share the one on the right. The rest of you will work out of the main room."

"Are you serious?" Daniels said, his nostrils flared. "The girl—a *private*—gets an office, and I don't? How is that fair?"

"They're the ones most in need of a closed door," Warner said, and Niki was relieved he understood the dynamic.

Of their group, Niki and Will were the thinkers, the plotters, the dreamers of mayhem and mischief. Ezra's cartoons added flourish, but he didn't need or even want privacy for that, preferring that everyone have a front-row seat to his brilliance, and Niki didn't blame him for feeling that way. It was best for the new Rumors guy to be out in the open, listening for gossip from the other divisions, and Lieutenant Jack Daniels needed to be readily accessible to carry out other people's commands.

"Outrageous!" Daniels said.

As he continued to bellyache, Ezra padded over to the window. Two men walked in, carrying a desk, and a third paraded past, pulling a black Labrador on a leash.

"Hi, Harvey," Warner said with a wave, and introduced him as Harvey Kunkel, head of R&A Rome. Kunkel brusquely greeted them and then disappeared, without slowing his step.

As Warner scanned his collection of propagandists, his mouth swiftly turned south. He must've realized what he had, which wasn't very much. "Well. I'll let you all get settled," he said. "Let's reconvene in the printing room in fifteen minutes to discuss capitalizing on Project Breakers. It's a great place for meetings, by the way, if you don't want to be overheard. The machine is earsplitting."

With that, Warner rotated on his heel, and the group broke up. Before following Will into their new office, Niki stopped beside Ezra, who remained staring gloomily out the window, toward the alley behind the flat. "Are you all right?" she asked, squeezing his arm.

Ezra shrugged so listlessly her hand didn't even move. "It's strange being back," he said.

Though Niki wasn't fully apprised of the details of whatever horrors he'd witnessed and endured, she knew that Ezra was living in Rome when people "of the Hebrew Race" were no longer permitted to hold jobs, and his Romanian passport was canceled, rendering him stateless. He spent years living like a hunted man, never staying in one place for long. Despite the nightmare of these "cruel and stupid times," Ezra considered Italy home more than he did Romania, which he viewed as a primitive civilization, a country with a fictitious history made up by politicians and kings, a place where he was constantly scolded and corrected, and even dogs looked at him disdainfully because he was a Jew.

"My beautiful Rome," Ezra said, resting his wide forehead against the windowpane.

"It must be hard to return," Niki said, and rubbed his arm.

"Why must everything be so awful? My dearest Italy has turned into my hellish Romanian homeland," Ezra said. "Utter depravity. Dictators that use anti-Semitism as a convenient political tool. Turncoats everywhere you look. I feel betrayed."

Niki sighed. "It isn't the Rome so many have come to love," she said, despite being glad to have finally arrived. "On the upside, the lack of Nazis does give the place a certain je ne sais quoi."

Ezra laughed flatly. "That is a definite advantage," he said. "And the absence of fascism does make for great art."

Knowing he hated conversations that lasted longer than three minutes, Niki squeezed his arm one last time and retreated to her office.

"Well, we made it," she declared, her gaze landing on Will, who was making careful piles with the two dozen paper clips he'd been allotted. "I wasn't sure we would," she said. They'd traveled over in a rickety twin-engine C-47 flown by a wounded military pilot, and Niki's insides were still sloshing around.

"That was rough," Will agreed. He turned to straighten ten sheets of blank paper. Niki sat down.

"Hey, I've been meaning to thank you," she said, spreading her hands atop her new desk. "For what you said to Daniels, back in Algiers. About how I'm the 'brains of the operation,' the operation being my marriage. Anyway, you didn't have to do that, but it was very kind."

"Uh. Thanks? I mean, you're welcome. I mean..." Will stammered. "I wasn't being nice. The degrees and the languages and..."

Niki smiled sadly. His constant befuddlement was almost winsome, and it might've even softened her heart, if she'd let it. But there was no reason to pity the heir to a publishing fortune, not one with those dimples and a debutante wife.

"Speaking of Daniels," Niki said, opening and closing a column of empty drawers. "Do we think that's his real name? Or did he pick an alias before he got to Algiers?"

Head tilted, Will gave this careful consideration. "You know, I had the same thought. Then I realized..." He chewed on this. "I realized he's not very interesting, and I really don't care."

Niki coughed out a laugh. "I fully concur. That said, we should probably come up with our own aliases. We were supposed to by now."

"What do you have in mind?"

"Let's think about this," Niki said, and popped to her feet. "During training, they suggested variations of our real names." The idea was to make it easier to remember, as well as reconcile any awkward run-ins with people from their old lives. Overall, there were no hard-and-fast rules, which was always music to Niki's ears. "What if we swapped names and then changed them around?" she said.

Will's expression bunched up for several seconds before loosening again. Slowly, he nodded. "A trade. I like it, since we're a team. I could be Nick in place of Niki and change my last name. What do you think about... Demart? Nick Demart?"

"Perfect! And Wilhelmina for me."

"Wilhelmina Zovotna?" Will suggested.

"That's not a name! Let's use George's. He'd love that." Niki walked over to Will's desk, arm extended. "Greetings. The name's Wilhelmina Flingman."

"Nick Demart."

"I'm ever so pleased to meet you, Nick." She threw on a grin. "Sorry, Captain Demart. Whaddya say we join forces to make Nazis feel bad about themselves? It's about time to end this war, don't you think?"

15

PALOMA

May 1945

Not long after the Stars and Stripes was raised over Piazza Venezia, things began to turn.

GIs were suddenly everywhere, sleeping in dry fountains, in their trucks, and on the Spanish Steps. Military vehicles clogged the streets—jeeps, and 4x4s, and sleek black limousines, whenever somebody important was in town. The sidewalks teemed with fliers in leather jackets and doughboys spitting peanut shells.

Your men infiltrated the parks, spreading out, taking up maximum space as they gorged themselves on better food than could be found at the Excelsior Hotel. Meat. So much meat. And white bread! We Romans watched, gaping, as if viewing a play or a film.

In Rome, soldiers became tourists. Every day, the GIs queued outside the American Express office for maps and to feverishly consult the *Soldier's Guide to Rome*. Although recommended points of interest included the Baths of Caracalla, the Catacombs, and "the grottoes where Germans shot three hundred thirty-five Italian hostages," the Colosseum was always their first stop. They even hung an enormous banner at one end of the arena, as if preparing to host a sporting event. *Follow the Blue to Speedy Two. Rome, Berlin, and Tokyo Too.* Those Americans were intent on putting their stamp on everything.

"Gee, I hadn't known our bombers did that much damage!" they'd proclaim, with no irony whatsoever as they bobbled around, dancing and whooping to jazz music blaring from transistor radios. Because you do not allow them cameras, the soldiers made their memories stick by carving their names into the ancient stones. *I love Jane! Kilroy was here!* They were a nuisance, outright pests, but they had money, and thus presented an opportunity, a chance to eat.

I know what you are thinking. Better GIs than the Nazis. *Noi dovremmo essere i buoni!* You were the "good guys," but also our newest threat. The words *liberation* and *occupation* had become synonymous, and by the end of that summer, any woman seen with an American GI was dubbed a traitor and at great risk of getting pulled into an alley where a gang of Italian boys would hack off her hair.

When I spoke with the other girls, such as my dear friend Generosa, I pretended to be unbothered by the escalating tensions. *Non importa, non importa,* I'd say, my favorite line. The GIs would feed us, and we would go to bed, and that was the agreement. We survived the Nazis, and we could survive this bunch. *There is nothing else,* cara mia, I would tell them, *except to make love and survive.*

Though I put on a happy face, I understood I'd find trouble with your soldiers, eventually. It was inevitable—one American or another would lead me down some twisted path. On this prediction, I was for the most part right, my only mistake that I assumed the American in question would be a man.

16

NIKI

July 1944

After crossing Via Veneto, Niki, Will, and Ezra walked through a gap in a cracked, vine-covered wall to enter the Borghese Gardens. On brilliant days like these, with the sun sizzling overhead but protected by the soaring oaks and pines, Niki could almost forget the war, and all the bumps they'd hit over the past two weeks.

"Stop stewing," Will said, and placed one of his big, meaty paws on her shoulder. "That's why we left the office. To get away from work."

"Who says I'm stewing?" Niki shot back as Ezra stomped along beside her, angrily smoking a cigarette. It was Friday, which he considered unlucky, and it could really put him in a mood.

"Forgive me," Will said. "Perhaps you're merely deep in thought. Possibly praying to one of your saints?"

Niki passed him a look. Will was being playful, but she did not appreciate the joke, and was deeply regretful of having accidentally called out, "Holy blessed Gunther of Bohemia!" earlier that day. Gunther was the Czech patron saint of personal relationships and, more importantly, warring countries. Like most Czechs, Niki wasn't particularly religious, so invoking the saints was more along the lines of a superstition.

"I already told you. There's *not* a saint for every occasion," Niki said. "If only that there were." As they passed a group of Italian women, something caused Niki to falter in her stride. She peered back. "Huh. They've stopped applauding," she said. "It's only been two weeks."

"I noticed that, too," Ezra said, and held open a black wrought iron gate, the secret entrance to La Casina del Lago.

"Applauding what?" Will asked.

"Romans have been clapping for you," Niki explained, "and anyone else they think is a GI. I can't believe you didn't notice. Americans are so oblivious."

Niki swept past Will, down the graveled path, and toward the patio, where wicker chairs and tables were set up and opera blared from speakers hidden behind huge terra-cotta pots. Once seated, a waiter placed before each of them a serving of apricot ice. The next table over, a GI and a nurse giggled and held hands, and nearly everyone wore a smile. With the cheer, sunshine, and brightly colored umbrellas, the scene might've been halfway to pleasant, relaxing, even, if a million things weren't whizzing through Niki's head.

They were having a hell of a time getting their first campaign off the ground—literally. Despite the cooperation in Algiers, the air force was now refusing to drop their newspapers and leaflets, citing lack of planes, which was both a load of shit and a very large problem. Without air support, MO had no way to get propaganda into enemy territory, and Niki was beginning to entertain Will's notion that they'd been sidelined. To his credit, he hadn't said, "I told you so," not even once. It was a remarkable achievement, for a man.

"What do you think changed?" Niki asked. Will blinked in confusion, not having access to her train of thought. "Why won't they give us help?" she said. "The air force. The AFHQ. Somebody. We've put together a fantastic campaign and can't even get the materials out. I know they have plenty of planes, and are dropping plenty of bombs."

They'd named their first effort *Wie Lange Noch?* or *How Much Longer?* It was a series of leaflets designed to compel German soldiers to contemplate their strife, their very existence, and ultimately give up the fight. How much longer...

Shall our soldiers be forced to fight side by side with the dregs of Europe?
Will they deny that the East Front is a common grave!
Are we to be left behind while the party bosses flee the bombs?

On Will's suggestion, they used wording that would allow people to absolve themselves of responsibility. All those poor innocent Germans hoodwinked by Hitler's promises, what an evil little man! *Don't worry, kind sir, it wasn't your fault. You were absolutely bamboozled.* It was a smart move. Most people would rather cop to being tricked than admit they'd backed the wrong and extremely vile horse, or that they'd been wrong and extremely vile themselves.

To accompany the text, Ezra created a cast of cartoonish Führers. In some, Hitler had a skeleton for a shadow; in others, he resembled a scratchy-furred, two-faced wolf. They'd printed flyers by the thousands, with the plan to drop them in the German-occupied areas of Italy. Alas, it was hard to drop anything without a plane, and now the materials were piling up in the office, cluttering the hallways and blocking doors. "How much longer," indeed.

"We probably shouldn't be talking about our campaigns in a restaurant," Will said. "Rest assured, I am also irritated that Washington and AFHQ seem to have forgotten about us. Alas, all we can do is be patient and trust it will come together. Things usually work out in the end."

As he reached across the table to pat Niki's hand, she yanked her arm away. "Do they just *work out?*" she said. "That has not been my experience, and most of Europe would agree. What a thing to say. For you, baked pigeons must fly into your mouth!"

"Is that another of your Czech sayings?" Will said, and Ezra sniggered.

"The point is, we have to do something," Niki said. "We can't just sit back and hope for the best. Propaganda—"

"Niki! Shhh."

"*The information* must be fresh, and ours is nearing its prime," Niki hissed. As she stretched forward, the nurse at the next table over released a hardy guffaw. "If our work doesn't go out soon, we'll have wasted the past two weeks. I fail to understand why we had a Special Leaflet Squadron during training, and now we're left without a way to perform our job. Never mind *Wie Lange Noch?* What are we supposed to do about Project Breakers?"

"The unanswerable question," Ezra said as Niki and Will shrugged and flubbered their lips.

Exhaling, Niki sank into her seat. Weeks before, intelligence agents had gotten wind of Project Breakers, an ongoing plot by members of the German military to assassinate Hitler, and MO was meant to plant seeds of unrest primarily through articles in *Das Neue Deutschland.* That Hitler's inner circle wanted him dead was juicy enough, infinitely more so if the attempt was made. Predicting the putsch would also grant an air of legitimacy to their fake underground newspaper, but if *DND* never left the printing room, this was all very much beside the point.

"Warner hinted we might get air support at the end of August," Will said, his voice lowered to a hush. "So that's something?"

"Oh, you mean six weeks from now? Breakers is supposed to happen in July!" Niki unleashed a stream of expletives in Czech, English, and three other languages besides. "We're meant to help end this war, but our own damned bosses are standing in the way. It's madness!" She paused and gnawed on her bottom lip. "Maybe we should go around Warner?"

Will coughed. "Niki. We can't go around Warner. That's not how the military works."

"I don't really care about rank, or who does or does not have a golden oak leaf on his shoulder."

"Hear, hear," Ezra said, and raised his glass. The man despised the military's hierarchies and hid under a desk whenever somebody he was supposed to salute came through the office.

"There must be something we can do," Niki said, her mind ticking through a series of improbable options. Reaching out to George was one not-very-palatable choice, but Niki wasn't supposed to know he was in the OSS, and if he could get her air support, she didn't love the idea of owing him yet another favor.

Plus, what if she needed *more* help down the road? So far, living in Italy hadn't proven an advantage in terms of getting information from home. All Niki knew was what she read in the papers. The British were reporting increased partisan activity in the mountains—a positive sign that people were fighting back— but Russia had begun to stake out areas of influence as a base for their communist state. Through it all, George repeated his same old lines—the government-in-exile didn't trust Americans, so no one really knew what the Czechs were up to.

"You could always just strap on a backpack and carry it across enemy lines yourself?" Ezra said.

"Believe me. I would if I could, but the top brass made it very clear I'm not an SI type." Niki swiped the smoldering cigarette from between his fingers and took a serious inhale. "That's it. I'm not doing a drop more work until Warner solves the distribution problem. As of this moment, I'm officially on strike."

Will groaned as Ezra hooted and threw back his head. *"Mi piace!"* he said. "Two weeks of work and you're on strike? *Congratulazioni!* You are a bona fide Italian!"

17

NIKI

July 1944

Niki huffed up Via dei Serpenti, lighting cigarette after cigarette as she dodged an interminable swarm of GIs bumping around like ants. What *were* they doing, anyhow? They couldn't all be on R & R. Surely one was available to fly a damned plane, drop some leaflets.

Four days after going on "strike," Niki had broken. Never the type to sit around and wait for things to improve, she rang George and asked, ever so meekly, if he knew anyone in Bern who might assist their office in getting air support. *Please, George.* It was critical to their work.

"I'm with the OWI," he answered. "Why are you asking me?"

Niki mumbled her apologies but didn't blow his cover. It felt like a card she might need to play later.

George had lied, and Niki struck out, and this afternoon they'd learned that Kunkel and R&A were getting a new secretary. A whole extra body when MO didn't have ample supplies, or even a radio. *"Basta!"* Niki barked, and hooked right onto Via Nazionale.

By the time she entered Piazza di Spagna, Niki was winded and needed a rest, probably on account of smoking all those cigarettes. She plonked down on the Fontana della Barcaccia—the dried-out Fountain of the Ugly Boat—and examined the crumpled pack in her hand. Was this how she was going to spend her time in Rome? Smoking every last cigarette until she, and all of Europe, ran out? Niki had to figure out a way to make this all work. The only question was how. Maybe Kunkel's new secretary would have some ideas.

Sighing, Niki gazed out across the piazza, her attentions landing on a tall, busty woman who was twisting her cascade of coarse red hair into a knot. Suddenly, the stranger glanced up. The women traded smiles, and Niki felt her heart skip.

Ezra often complained that one of the many reasons he no longer felt at home in Italy was that he was always around other Americans. "I used to be one of them," he said, about the Italians, "but now they see my uniform, and count me as a sucker, another tourist who belongs to a strange superior class and is easy to dupe."

Maybe what Ezra needed, what they both needed, was a friend, a non-colleague, a local who could give them a true break from work. Come to think, it would be nice to have another gal around, an occasional companion so Niki didn't have to spend *every* weekend waiting in a fascist's villa for the lights to come on.

A girlfriend. Why hadn't she thought of it before? Energized by the possibility, Niki tromped over to introduce herself. *"Ciao. Sigaretta?"* she said.

Her would-be friend was visibly puzzled by the interaction,

and reached into her dress. It took Niki a beat to realize the woman was trying to pay. "No, no, no," Niki said, waving her hand. "I'm offering the cigarettes to *you*. Would you like one?" She extended the package in her direction, and the woman's face sprang with surprise.

"*Grazie,*" she said, and helped herself to three. She introduced herself as Paloma.

"I'm Nikola," Niki answered, and immediately wondered whether she should've used Wilhelmina instead. Well, it was too late for any covers, and Niki wasn't in the mood to follow the rules. "I'm very pleased to meet you," she added.

"*Allo stresso modo.* You are new to Rome, yes?" Paloma said, and struck a match. "I have seen you before, but only very recently."

"You've seen me?" Niki said, studying her new friend with some curiosity. She didn't imagine herself the type to stand out in a crowded piazza. "Well. What do you know? Yes. We've been here two and a half weeks."

"Did you come with the Allies?" Paloma asked. "You are from...?" She squinted. "England? Canada? Your Italian is perfect."

"Thank you," Niki said. "I'm American, but originally from Czechoslovakia."

Nodding, Paloma sucked on her cigarette. "Where do you live in America?" she asked. "I want to go to Florida."

Niki chuckled faintly. Florida was always the first place Italians asked about. Maybe it had something to do with the climate. "I've never even been to Florida," she said. "Other than a brief layover on my way to Alg—on my way overseas. I live in..."

Niki stopped to think this through. Where *did* she live? There was George's place in Rittenhouse Square in Philadelphia, and the apartment he kept in Foggy Bottom in DC, but after two years in America, neither was home. "Washington?" Niki decided, after some time. Technically her passport said Philadelphia, but DC felt like the most accurate response.

"Ah. *Va bene, va bene.* By the White House."

"Sort of," Niki said, and lit another cigarette as a thinly mustachioed GI sauntered up, his hat clutched against his chest.

"Good afternoon, ladies," he said, and Niki threw him a glare. What was it about men that they couldn't give you ten minutes of peace? "Or would you call it evening?"

"Shoo!" Paloma said. "Away with you." She waggled her hand. "We are not on the clock."

The man slumped off, dejected, and Niki's brows began to slowly rise. Ah. So Paloma was a prostitute. This both did and did not make sense. She emitted an undeniable sultriness, but her clothes and personality were more along the lines of a middle-class housewife. Then again, she'd likely been a housewife first.

"If I'm bothering you," Niki said, "or impeding your, um, business, please tell me to leave. I don't want to get in the way."

"Not at all. I—" Paloma began, then abruptly stopped. Her face came back to life as she took in something or some*one* over Niki's left shoulder. *"Ahò!"* Flicking her cigarette aside, Paloma popped up. *"Ciao!"* she said. "What is your name? Would you like to come sit with us? We have plenty of space. Don't you two know each other? I feel I have seen you together before."

Niki turned, and her body swiftly deflated. Will Dewart's timing was impeccable. At least he wasn't in danger of losing his eyebrows this time.

"If every GI looked like you," Paloma said, "I wouldn't mind Americans so much."

Niki jumped to her feet. "Paloma, this is my colleague, Captain William Dewart," she said, planting herself between them. Why she did this, or who she was trying to protect, Niki couldn't guess. "Will, this is my new friend, Paloma. Paloma, Will. I hope you haven't come to track me down, Dewart. I told Warner I was taking the rest of the day off."

"I'm aware," he said, wielding his crooked, slow smile. "Unfortunately, I *was* told to find you. The new secretary has arrived."

"That was fast. Jeez. Can't let R&A suffer a moment longer than necessary." Niki peered into her package, but the cigarettes were now gone. "What does Warner want with me? It's not even our division."

"It's not Warner who requested your presence," Will said as an impish look consumed his face. "It was the new employee. She asked for you by name. Evidently, she's an old, dear friend. Like family, almost."

Niki crumpled up the packet and chucked it into the street. "You're not making any sense," she said.

"I think it will make some sense, once you see this new employee for yourself."

18

PALOMA

May 1945

I met Captain William Dewart on the same day I met Nikola, while we were smoking our cigarettes.

At first, I thought he was there to seek personal gratification, and I was pleased by the prospect. This is not to say the captain is my sort of man, despite his charming dimples and intriguing, unusual eyes—brown encircled in yellow encircled in green. He is handsome but unreasonably tall. Also, he has the most terrible posture, and the type of nervous smile that can make a person feel scratchy and uncomfortable. Nonetheless, I sensed he was a better breed than I was accustomed to. This didn't mean I wanted to sleep with him, necessarily, but it wouldn't have been the worst thing to ever happen.

Alas, Captain William Dewart did not come for commerce,

but to deliver to Nikola some news. They were to have *una nuova collega*, and Nikola was plainly displeased. Perhaps she wanted the attention for herself, which I understood. It was better to be the only woman around.

"Who on earth would be asking for me *by name?*" Nikola demanded. As the captain simpered, pleased with his game, she gave him a light shove. "Go on. Tell me. Why are you dragging this out?"

Finally, he revealed her name.

"MOGGY?" Nikola said, stumbling backward, as if tripping away from herself. "They've hired Moggy Clingman? My sister-in-law? *Che cazzo di inferno,*" she cursed, and I cackled, wondering how well the captain understood Italian and whether he knew she'd just shouted for all to hear, *what the flaming dick!*

"Oh, sweet Ludmila!" Nikola said, and shook her fists at the sky. After passing a sharp glower to the captain, she informed me that Ludmila was the patron saint of people with in-law troubles.

The captain seemed at once contrite. "I'm sorry," he said. "I wasn't trying to razz you. I didn't expect you to be this upset. Is she really so terrible?"

"I don't know. Is a full-body rash terrible? A lingering cough?" Nikola slung her brown leather shoulder bag against the steps. A pencil, a coin purse, and a small bottle of perfume rolled out.

"You're going to have to give me more," Will said. "What, specifically, is so awful?"

Nikola thought about this. After several seconds, she relaxed her face and dropped her hands. "You're right," she said. "I'm not being fair. We haven't even spent that much time together— only during the holidays and a few weeks every summer. She's been living in Switzerland the entire time I've been married to George."

"*Switzerland?*" I blurted. Before that moment, it hadn't occurred to me there were people moving about Europe, traveling freely, choosing new places to reside in which they might have a nice view of the Alps. "Now that is…fascinating," I said.

"It's something, all right," Nikola said. "Moggy's spent the past few years following Carl Jung. Last I heard, she was enrolled at some institute associated with the University of Basel, where he's Chair of Medical Psychology. Before you commend her academic inclinations…" She held up a finger like a mom would to a naughty child. "Moggy has no intention of getting a degree, despite attending medical school no less than five times."

William Dewart scrunched his face. "Does she keep failing out?"

"Moggy is actually very smart," Nikola said. "Alas, her educational pursuits are not about degrees but a quest to be the 'best version of herself,' which primarily involves waxing on about the latest frocks whilst engaging in endless rounds of psychoanalysis. Evaluating her shadow side. Her animus. Honestly, she never shuts up about it. *I must tell you, Niki,*" she said, deepening her voice, *"until you make the unconscious conscious, it will direct your life, and you will think it's fate."*

"That does sound tiresome," I commented, still mystified by the notion people lived like this.

"Moggy's a sweet girl," she continued. "Well-meaning, but she takes everything so damned seriously. Her personality can be exhausting, but honestly, my issue is not with Moggy. The fact that she's arrived in Rome means only one thing." Nikola looked first at me and then to the captain. "R&A is getting a secretary, and I'm getting a babysitter." She marched over and began collecting her things from the steps.

"Is it possible you're overreacting?" William Dewart asked.

Nikola shook her head. "This has my husband's fingerprints all over it," she said. "They could've sent her to any office, in any theater, but she came *here.*" Nikola cursed again. "Despite everything, my husband still sees me as a bumbling foreigner who can't be trusted. This is what I get for calling him about the planes," she muttered.

"Aw, Nik," William said with a deep and endearing frown. "I'm sorry. I didn't mean to be so teasing about it. I thought it was funny, or that you might be glad to have another woman in the office."

"Don't apologize. It's fine." Nikola used both hands to push her hair back from her face. "Good Lord. What a day." She flashed me a thin smile. "Nice to meet you, Paloma," she said. "I hope we can chat again soon."

"Ciao," I said, truly doubting we ever would. Nikola was a busy and important woman. Why would she have time for someone like me?

19

NIKI

July 1944

You can do this, Niki counseled herself as she walked toward the office. *Moggy means well. She probably has no idea what George is up to.*

"Moggy!" Niki sang as she swept into the room. Grinning maniacally, she threw open her arms. "I can't believe it's you," she said, and smothered her sister-in-law with a quick, sloppy hug. "Wow. Take a gander at that 'do! No one would know you've been traveling."

As was customary, Moggy wore her hair in a complicated style, with the upper part braided and pinned atop her head, the bottom wound into a chignon. The full effect was admirable, especially in this heat.

"Thank you," Moggy said, and gingerly touched the braid. "I do try. That was some welcoming committee, Niki. I waited on that tarmac for darn near forever." She pointed toward her mud-caked shoes, a pair of Red Cross Mary Janes. Niki would've expected something a little higher fashion and was momentarily impressed. "I had no idea who to ask for help! Who's the enemy? Who's a friend? Italy is very confusing. I thought—"

She froze, mouth ajar, and Niki braced herself as Moggy put her nose into her elbow and sneezed. Though multiple doctors had diagnosed her with allergies, Moggy was convinced this affliction was a physical manifestation of some internal quandary, an indication her ego was unbalanced. *Ignore the sneezes*, George and his parents advised. *Just pretend they don't happen.*

"Golly, Mogs, I'm sorry," Niki said. "I was *just* told of your arrival." She cranked her smile up a notch. "But you made it, safe and sound! That's what counts."

"Perhaps." Moggy crossed her arms, lips pursed as she cast about the space. "This is where you work? How dreary."

"Expected more charm, did ya?" Niki said. This was in fact the best their office had ever looked, mostly because they'd moved all propaganda into the printing office to keep it away from curious eyes. "You should've seen it a week ago. Piles of paper *everywhere*. I'm dying to know, what inspired you to make the leap to our rickety, hodgepodge outpost? I assume your brother was involved?" Niki hoped her voice sounded light, inquisitive, but as though she didn't have much riding on the answer.

"It *was* his brainchild," Moggy said as her gaze skittered away. "He thought it was for my own good, and the rest of the family agreed. Don't understand why everyone can't just mind their own business."

"I know the feeling," Niki said, surprised the Clingmans would consider the OSS a suitable choice for their unmarried daughter, given how female service members were perceived overall. The rumors were outrageous, and even the *New York Times* printed an article claiming the WAC gave a year's worth of condoms to every girl they shipped overseas.

"I apologize for being so ill-tempered about it," Moggy said. "But my family could really benefit from some intense analysis. I suspect this whole thing is about them more than it is about me."

"I'll toast to that." Niki took Moggy's hand. "Let me show you the place. Where should we start? Well, that office over there, with the two desks, is mine. I share it with Captain Dewart. Not sure where he's run off to, but you'll meet him soon enough." She whirled around, spinning Moggy with her. "Our cartoonist, Ezra, sits here. Let's see…what else?"

"What do you need an artist for?" Moggy asked as Niki dragged her through the rest of the main room.

"Oh, you know… Illustrations to be placed inside informational packets for the troops," Niki said, snatching the idea from thin air. They were instructed to be circumspect with other OSS employees, to avoid revealing the details of their black propaganda, unless it was unavoidable. Niki thought it was a pointless practice, albeit very "of the government," but now she was grateful for the rule. Moggy would be appalled by the idea of tweaking the truth for a living. Talk about a shadow side. "Anyway!" Niki sang. "Moving on!"

She next led Moggy to an organizational chart pinned to the wall. Wild Bill Donovan sat at the top, and below him were the strategic units—MO, Special Ops, Maritime—on one side, and intelligence services—SI, X-2, Censorship & Documents, R&A—on the other. While this was supposed to explain OSS, the sum total was a mess. Lines traveled every which way, with new ones added and old ones crossed out. Names were scribbled over, and entire positions erased. Niki located Moggy's boss— Harvey Kunkel, CO, R&A—but it was impossible to make out who he reported to, or who reported to him. For the first time, Niki wondered if this was by design.

"This probably needs to be updated," Niki said. "I wouldn't bother memorizing it. Who else is here?" She peered around a file cabinet and into the deepest recesses of the office. "Gosh. It seems everyone's out. Even your boss. The OSS really is a good group, despite what you've heard."

"What I've *heard*?" Moggy said, and wrinkled her nose. "George said the Office of Strategic Services is extremely selective and well regarded."

Niki chortled. "He would say that."

"Why? He works for the Office of War Information," Moggy said, and Niki smiled, pleased George's lies weren't only for her.

"The OSS is a real...riot of personalities," Niki said. "Wild Bill was given no time to put the organization together, so he staffed it with his friends. Doesn't say much for the company he keeps, I'm afraid. But he's sent the smartest woman I know to Rome." Niki smiled again. Moggy was not the *smartest*, but she was unusually bright, and the poor girl probably didn't receive many compliments. She was definitely not the type Miss Griggs would've snatched off the social register.

"That is very sweet," Moggy said with a faint blush, "but I'm apparently not smart enough. I don't understand why we're here. Why *any* of us are in Rome. Wasn't the city just liberated? I thought the Italians were on our side now."

"Depends on which Italian you ask," Niki said. "Or which part of the country you're in. The Allies are running the government here in Rome, but northern Italy is still under German control. As far as what we're doing, the answer is a whole bunch of things. You'll be working for Harvey Kunkel. Filing and cataloging reports, most likely, as well as picking up after his Lab, Pierre. He can fill you in on the rest."

"A dog?" Moggy said, and sneezed again. "This all sounds very complex. I just hope I'm up to the task. I studied, and read all the materials, but everything's hazy. Jobs are described in the vaguest terms, and I don't even speak Italian!"

"Neither does Kunkel. Everything will be fine, Mogs." Niki squeezed her hand. If she was going to have a babysitter, she might as well cozy up, and get on her best side. "R&A is the heartbeat of the organization," she added, echoing Tina's words from the fingerprinting room. "That's all I know, but *you'll* work out the minutiae in no time. You're perfectly capable, and well trained, no doubt. I'm certain you'll be a smash."

"Well trained?" Moggy's expression soured. "Niki, I wasn't trained at all. They hired me as a civilian."

"You have got to be kidding me," Niki groused, thinking of the weeks in Washington, and the six months in Algiers. No training? Some gals had all the luck.

"You don't need to act so outraged," Moggy snipped. "I met the WAC qualifications. It's all right here." She jostled around in her purse and extracted a well-worn piece of paper. Clearing her throat, she straightened it and began to read. "Number one. She must be between twenty-one and forty-five years of age. Check. At least fifty-eight inches in height." Moggy glanced up. "For the record, I'm sixty-nine inches tall."

"Sure, sure. A real long drink of water."

Moggy continued. "Weight of at least one hundred pounds," she said. "I'm one-sixty, though I promised Mother I'd work on this. I also have the required twenty-twenty vision and the strength, stamina, and stability to get the job done." Moggy crammed the list back into her purse. "Do you see what I mean?"

"Oh. Yes. You're very qualified." Niki never read beyond the first few pages of the WAC handbook and was suddenly curious whether she would've passed muster.

"I've also been going through the exercises on a daily basis," Moggy said. "The ones from the 'LEARN TO CONTROL YOUR BODY' booklet. I wasn't able to perform the group activities, unless you think folks around here are up for a game of Steal the Bacon or Catch the Caboose?"

"Er, probably not…"

"I'm trying to train myself to the best of my ability, but…" Moggy let out an exasperated puff. "I feel a bit thrown to the wolves, and so far, it all seems very slapdash. Every man for himself. The situation at the airport…"

"Par for the course, I'm afraid. Being thin on support is the theme around here," Niki said. "Listen, Mogs, I wouldn't worry about the lack of preparation. I'm sure R&A was just expediting the process." Niki was speaking to herself as much as she was to Moggy. "You were already in Europe. Why send you all the way back to America to teach you things you can figure out on your own?"

Maybe Moggy's lack of training was a benefit, a great stroke of luck. She'd be too busy trying to understand R&A that she wouldn't have time to bother with the particulars of other OSS divisions, and Niki could dance around the true purpose of MO, for a while, at least. Just as Niki was about to settle on this conclusion, her thoughts were cut off by the pop of the side door, and Ezra and Will stomping through.

"The very woman we were looking for," Ezra said. "You're wanted at a meeting in the printing office." He stopped and scanned Moggy head to toe. "Is this our new R&A friend? I like your hair."

"Thank you. It's a false braid," Moggy said, tenderly fingering its smooth lines.

"Boys, this is my sister-in-law, Moggy Clingman," Niki said. "Moggy, meet Ezra Feldman. He's the cartoonist I was telling you about. Behind him is my officemate, Captain Will Dewart."

"I go by Margaret now," Moggy said. After greeting each man, she let out another sneeze. "Don't worry. I'm not sick. It's my ego. It acts up when I'm nervous. Although you're both lovely, so I don't know why that'd be the case now!"

Niki smirked, having *some* idea. With his height, jawline, and gently tousled hair, Will was exactly the type to elicit a sneezing fit. He wasn't Niki's taste—she preferred darker, more serious men—but she recognized his generic appeal. Wait until

Moggy learned he was also the scion of a publishing empire. They'd need to stock up on tissues.

"What a relief! It's the much-anticipated sister-in-law," Ezra said. "For a second there, I was worried. Thought Private Novotná was consorting with the enemy."

Niki laughed to herself. Moggy did have a sturdy German look about her, come to think.

"Novotná?" Moggy said, turning toward Niki. "You're using your maiden name?"

"Think of it as a cover," Niki said, and batted a hand. "Not that we need one in this office. Ha! Imagine! I'm only using it because it gives me an international flair. Helps while working abroad, especially because I'm often mistaken for a born-and-bred American."

"Yes. You are," Moggy said. "I've never been able to fathom it."

"But look at us now," Niki said. "It's almost as though I knew you'd come along. We couldn't have *two* people running around this office using the same last name!" She turned toward Ezra and Will. "Moggy here—"

"Margaret."

"Sorry, Mogs, can't do it," Niki said, shaking her head. "I'd wanted to introduce her to everyone, but it seems everyone is out, including her boss. Should we take her to an early supper? The café across the street just reopened."

"No time for eating," Ezra said, his voice unusually gruff. "We need you. Right now."

"It's about Project *Breakers*," Will said, and the words hit Niki hard, stealing her breath. Was it possible? Had Hitler been killed?

"Moggy," Niki said, her voice rickety like an old creaky staircase. "Can you occupy yourself for a few minutes while I step out?" Without waiting for an answer, Niki clambered after Ezra and Will, slipping through the side door as she wondered whether this was the moment in which everything changed—for her, for them, for every person involved in this war.

WESTERN UNION

19 July 1944
WILLIAM DONOVAN=
OFFICE OF STRATEGIC SERVICES WASHDC=
BREAKERS. To Carib and Jackpot.
There is a possibility that a dramatic event may take place
up north, if Breakers courier is to be trusted. We expect a
complete account this evening. However, it is not only possible but probable that any news will be suppressed by violence if necessary.

20 July 1944
WILLIAM DONOVAN=
OFFICE OF STRATEGIC SERVICES WASHDC=
BREAKERS. Apparently Breakers are breaking. In all prob-
ability the movement is the one explained in my #4110 and
earlier Breakers communications. It was planned that certain men in the inner circles would be at the meeting when
the bomb went off because the only chance for planting the
bomb was in conjunction with a conference attended by many
of the chief military leaders.

20

NIKI

July 1944

Niki wiped the sweat from her upper lip and scooted away from the printing press, which was throwing off all kinds of heat. As promised, it was good for drowning out conversations, less so for thinking straight. The putsch happened. There'd been an attempt on Hitler's life.

During a lunchtime meeting between the Führer and twenty officers at "Wolf's Lair," Hitler's chief of staff, Claus von Stauffenberg, placed a briefcase bomb at Hitler's feet, then took a prearranged call. The bomb detonated about ten minutes after he left the room, killing three people and injuring everyone else. Colonel Heinz Brandt's body was found with one leg missing, and the theory was that he'd likely used a foot to push the briefcase away from his boss. Though the incident generated much mayhem, the coup had failed. Hitler was still alive.

"Crap," Will said, aggressively chewing his bottom lip and looking more like a teenage boy than a man eight years Niki's senior. "Crap, crap, crap." Ezra had slumped off somewhere, feeling defeated that Stauffenberg hadn't closed the deal. He viewed everything about this war as half measures and "too little, too late," and for him this was only more proof that chasing victory was a fool's game.

"Remember," Niki said to Will, "where there's discord in the Nazi party, that's good news for us. Of course, if the brass had given us air support, we'd be in a better position because *DND* would have gone out." Niki had written several editorials for their fake underground newspaper, planting the idea that the German General Staff would attempt to get rid of Hitler now that they were on the losing side, but the papers never left Rome. Now they'd have to work twice as hard to stoke the chaos and prove *DND* was a legitimate source of news.

"You're telling me it's *fine* that Hitler is still alive?" Will said, one brow spiked.

"Not fine, but survival was always a possibility," Niki said. "A likelihood, even. And Hitler wasn't unharmed."

"I'd prefer he suffer beyond a perforated eardrum and burnt trousers," Will said. "Plus, it's going to play into the narrative that he's protected by divine providence."

"It's a setback, to be sure, but nothing we can't overcome," Niki said as she watched the papers whip through the feeders. Warner had told them to keep producing materials in anticipation of future air support, but these would be outdated by next week. "The Germans are alarmed," she continued. "I hear the phrase *civil war* is being used. There is additional damage, beyond a busted eardrum. I just hope Washington doesn't blame us for not doing more to feed the panic."

"A memo might be in order," Will said, and scribbled something on a discarded *How Much Longer?* leaflet. The office was always scrounging for scrap paper, and now they had a whole room full of it. "We could remind the brass of the missed opportunity, with a stern warning that we can't let it happen again. It'd have to be worded very delicately to avoid pointing fingers."

"Or damaging any egos. Men and their feelings," Niki scoffed. People like Wild Bill should try being a woman for a day, to toughen them up. "The memo is a good idea, but we need a specific event to capitalize on that will force them to give us the support without further delay." She paused as an idea coalesced in her mind. "What about August third? It's the anniversary of the SA."

"The storm troopers?" Will screwed up his face. "That's a date people already know about."

"We're not going to get lucky with another assassination attempt," Niki said. "Not anytime soon. But maybe we can use all those parades and rallies to lure Hitler out of hiding."

The bastard hadn't appeared in public in months, and Allied military leaders feared he'd gone into hiding and would disappear forever now that the walls were closing in. They wanted Hitler to face what he'd done, and publicly answer for his crimes.

"If we can disseminate propaganda before the anniversary," Niki went on, "promising he'll speak at festivities, he'll either make good on our promise, which should assuage Washington's concerns about him vanishing underground, or we can say the plot worked and he's dead." As she spoke, a thrill rose in Niki's chest with each word, each twist of an idea.

"I like where you're going with this," Will said, tapping his pencil on the printing machine. "But if this coup was theoretically successful, who's in charge now?"

"Göring and Himmler are grappling for power."

"They'll issue a denial…"

"All the better. While the top Nazis are denying it happened, the sycophants will line up to publicly profess their loyalties to Hitler. In *DND*, we can publish the names of those who are 'suspiciously silent.'"

"And those on the list will be immediately killed."

"Don't worry, we'll be careful who we choose," Niki said, and Will's stomach promptly rumbled. "The German people won't know what to believe, and the leaders will be even more wary of each other. Chaos and confusion are the names of the game."

Will sighed. "I'll write the memo," he said, "but this is still Washington. The most likely scenario is that they'll say, 'Good idea, but you're not getting planes until the end of August.' Then we'll be stuck with a plan we can't execute, and they'll wonder why we never followed through."

"You're right," Niki said, noodling on this. "In case we're denied again, we need a backup means of getting the information across enemy lines. We can't let another opportunity go to waste."

"What about the resistance groups?"

Niki shook her head. Partisans near the Swiss border had aided with dropping some information here and there, but it was not a viable long-term solution. Their network in Italy and Switzerland was not big or wide enough, and partisans were on the whole not a terribly organized or reliable bunch.

"You know how I feel about partisans," Niki said. "We barely vet them, and most are loose cannons. We need something new, completely novel."

"But not so novel that Washington will say no."

"Washington?" Niki snorted. "Oh, I'm not waiting for buy-in from them. Whatever we drum up will have to be carried out expeditiously, and bureaucrats will only hold us up."

"Niki..."

"It'll be their fault for denying our request. Believe me, I'd use planes without their approval, if I could get my hands on some," she said.

"Maybe you should go back on strike?"

"Oh. Come on." Niki swatted him with the back of her hand. "I'll *inform* them of our plans, naturally."

"Of course."

"But I'm not asking permission," she said. "We still have to do our job, come hell or high water. The same way we're asked to re-bend paper clips into shape, and use pencils until they're worn to the nub, we'll figure out how to make this work. Trust me, Dewart, this is the right course."

"I don't know how you always sound so confident," Will said.

Niki blinked at him, confused for a second. "Oh, William," she said, and laughed dryly. "You say that as though it's a choice."

21

PALOMA

May 1945

Nikola might've told you I helped devise the plot. As long as it doesn't land me in trouble, I will confirm it is true.

I'd been counting my lire, calculating how few GIs I could bed to keep crumbs in my belly. It was a fragile balance, and I often came up short. On this day, I'd just decided to take the night off when Nikola stamped through the piazza in her terrible baggy pants.

"Ciao!" I called out, waggling a hand overhead. Nikola didn't hear me, and so I put my fingers to my lips and whistled, tangling up her quick, assured pace.

"Oh, Paloma! Hello!" she said with a little wave.

"Come over," I said. *"Venga a farsi una chiacchierata!"*

"A chat?" she said, and inched closer. Her eyes skimmed the plaza.

"Una sigaretta?"

"I could use a smoke," she said. "Are you sure I'm not...interrupting?"

"Va bene, va bene. You are fine," I said. *"Come stai?"*

"It's been quite the day," Nikola said, and dropped down beside me. She held out her package of cigarettes, and I took several, figuring to smoke one or two and sell the rest.

"What is it about your day?" I asked. I pulled a matchbook from my dress and lit a cigarette for each of us. "Do you find trouble at your job? Is it the sister-in-law? Did she come?"

Nikola gave a throaty laugh. "You know, she did, but I'd momentarily forgotten. Blocked it out, more likely. Considering how mad she was that I didn't meet her at the airport, she's going to lose her wig when she discovers I left the office. Hopefully there's someone around to escort her to the billets." She stopped to take a drag.

"She must not be too awful, if you forgot," I pointed out.

"True. Though my brain's been tied up with other things," she said. "I've got a hell of a puzzle to work out, and I have to solve it soon."

"Hmm," I answered, and took a drag myself. The cigarette was heaven, like drinking gold, and far more satisfying than whatever I might've done with a GI. "Not all puzzles are solved," I said. "Sometimes things do not work out."

"That's true, but I won't let it happen in this case," she said. "It's too important, and I can't afford to fail. My country can't afford it, either."

"Santo Cielo! Your *country?* I did not realize I had met someone so renowned," I said, delighted by the thought. All the Americans I'd seen and met looked like *ragazzini*, and I was beginning to think none of the *pezzi grossi*—the big boys, the top brass—had come to Rome. "If you are speaking like this, you must have a lot of responsibility," I remarked, and it dawned on me that my new friend might be able to find out about my son.

"I wouldn't go that far," Nikola said, and my hopes flagged. "I'm probably the only person who thinks my role is important. The situation at work...it almost seems like there's no winning, as though we're being set up to fail."

"And if you fail, what then?"

"Everything will be blamed on me since I'm the only woman," she said. "Well, Moggy's there now, too, but she doesn't really count." Although it had some life in it yet, Nikola stubbed out her cigarette and lit another.

As we smoked in silence, I stared out across the piazza, watching all the hatless women in their wooden-soled sandals, swinging mostly empty string bags. This time of year, the market stalls should've been overflowing with brightly colored produce— peppers, eggplant, apricots, blueberries, and figs—but lack of both public and private transportation had reduced the bounty to a few green pears, some tomatoes, and a bushel of onions, when we were lucky. Women still crowded around the empty stalls, out of habit, and hope, and to gossip about the rumor that the GIs ate four times per day.

"Sometimes I ask myself whether it's all worth it," Nikola said, dragging me back into the conversation. "What am I accomplishing in Europe? Maybe I should go back to Washington or ask if I can join the Red Cross and deliver doughnuts to troops."

Beignets? They were just handing them out? I tried not to keel over in shock.

"*Boh.* Every person's work feels pointless, at some juncture," I said. "But if your job is so taxing, so very much not fun, you could make a change." I wiggled my eyebrows. "You could always come work with me."

I expected Nikola to be offended by my joke. Perhaps she'd even plant a light slap onto my face. Instead, and to my vast shock, she flung back her head and released an enormous guffaw. I was pleased she had not taken me seriously. Nikola wasn't the type to flourish in my line of work. She had an unconventional beauty, but that wiry physique and short, messy hair would almost certainly get in her way.

"That is quite the offer," Nikola said, dabbing her eyes. "I'll pass for now but will keep it mind."

"It pays nicely," I added, "for women's work." I made a face. "Unfortunately, it does involve fucking a lot of Americans."

"*Basta!*" Nikola howled as I flicked my cigarette onto the street. "You poor thing."

"It is quite laborious, especially with all that talking afterward. For hours! Your soldiers have much to say about themselves, and their wartime bravery."

"Hours?" Nikola tossed me a look. "How could they possibly go on that long? Do any of them even speak Italian? I hope they're not spilling military secrets. A person needs to be careful around here."

As a Roman, the comment prickled me, but I understood what she meant. Our allegiances had changed and were changing still. We might all wake up tomorrow and be communists. Perhaps we would give fascism another try. "Do not worry," I assured her nevertheless. "They say nothing of importance. It's all big sweeping tales of valor and narrowly escaped shells. By their telling, American GIs are so fearsome the enemy surrenders at the very sight."

"This kind of talk, I can imagine," Nikola said.

"If I believed everything I heard, the Allies would have captured half the German population by now. Not to mention, loads of Italians…" I frowned. "More war prisoners than soldiers, from the sound of it."

"The POW population *is* quite high," Nikola said, and my heart picked up a few extra beats.

"Is it?" I warbled, and she informed me the latest reports had some two hundred thousand held in northwest Europe. Apparently, there was a large surge of defections after Rome fell, and anyone who wanted out finally knew where to find some Allies to surrender to.

Two hundred thousand. I turned the number over in my head, but it was too big, too cumbersome to bridle. How many were Italians, and how likely was Paolo to be among this group? I wasn't worried about my husband. One of his girlfriends could take care of that. "Have you *seen* the list?" I spit out. "The names? The Roman defections?"

"No, sorry, I haven't seen any names." Nikola studied me. "Are you wondering about someone in particular?"

"No," I chirped, and she stood and brushed off the back of her pants. "That is a lot of men," I noted. "If there are two hundred thousand, or even half that, what do you do with them all? Where are they? Sitting around, locked up, waiting for this war to end? Are they being treated...fairly?"

"These are the Allies we're talking about," Nikola said, and this was meant to assure me, I think. "They're likely engaged in some light manual labor, but they're being properly looked after. Decent accommodations, plenty of food."

"Interessante." If what Nikola said was true, now I wished that my Paolo was in an Allied POW camp. Decent accommodations and food were more than he could get in any other scenario. "Two hundred thousand to house and feed," I marveled. "That is like a whole second army. The Allies should utilize them for something, no? More than 'light labor'? They can send them to clean up Rome."

"Send them to Rome?" Nikola said, her expression one of bewilderment. Maybe she had not noticed the side streets, where overflowing urinals poured across the cobblestones, or the ever-growing piles of excrement on the Church of Santa Maria Maggiore steps. "Rome," she said again, and I could almost see the ideas snapping in her brain. "Oh my God. Paloma," she said, and seized my arm. I thought for a moment that I had done something wrong.

"Mi dispiace," I said. "I was only curious what you did with them. This is a good question, no?"

"It is a *great* question." She beamed, displaying her funny, crowded smile to maximum effect. "A helluva question, in fact. I don't want to jump the gun, but you might've just solved all my problems in life."

SECRET

Office Memorandum | **UNITED STATES GOVERNMENT**
TO: Director of OSS
DATE: 22 July 1944
FROM: Pvt. Nikola Novotna (MO, Rome)
THROUGH: Swiss Desk, Bern
SUBJECT: OPERATION SAUERKRAUT

PERSONNEL REQUIRED

Cpt. William Dewart
Pvt. Nikola Novotna
Ezra Feldman
Lt. Jack Daniels
Edward Zinder
Egidio Clemente
12 German Prisoners of War

SITUATION

On 21 July, we received news that "Project Breakers" had been implemented, leading to a failed attempt on Hitler's life. We have been ordered to "take advantage" of the ongoing situation. Alas, as ordinary methods of dissemination are not available to us, we must consider other, somewhat unconventional methods for urgently spreading black information.

There is a terrific opportunity to create further disharmony ahead of the 3 August SA anniversary celebration. Unless you are able to provide immediate air support, we have determined that the best and indeed only course of action is to use German POWs (carefully vetted, proven anti-Nazis) to carry our propaganda into enemy territory.

OBJECTIVES

1. To expose the troops to a barrage of propaganda that would capitalize on the confusion resulting from the attempt on Hitler's life.

2. To lure Hitler out of hiding by publishing in our underground newspaper, Das Neue Deutschland, that he'll be giving a speech on 3 August.

3. To plant leaflets, stickers, false orders, and proclamations in bivouac areas and on trees, buildings, trucks, and other places accessible by German frontline troops.

4. To assess and observe the reaction of German soldiers to the MO printed material.

5. To evaluate and exploit a new technique for infiltration of MO propaganda behind enemy lines given the lack of support offered to MO Rome.

REQUIREMENTS

1. Helmets and uniforms.

2. Proper identification papers and passes.

3. Weapons and ammunition.

4. 5000 Italian lira each.

5. First aid packets.

6. Italian cigarettes for bartering.

7. 3000+ pieces of MO material.

22

May 1989

Geoffrey Jones hits his clicker. "You ladies performed tremendous work in Washington and abroad," he says. "One-third of you served overseas."

Niki picks at her lightly dressed salad. She feels calmer now, her pulse less charged. As her eyes sweep the room, she ponders where each woman might've been stationed, and her potential job. What happened to their talent, all the training invested in them? Most got married, no doubt, and became mothers. Niki knows several wrote books, a notion that makes her feel sick. She can't imagine reliving the highs and the lows, the good decisions and the terrible. She can't imagine putting it all onto paper for strangers to read.

"From Japan to the Philippines, from Algiers to Rome," Geoffrey says, and Niki startles at the mention of her home base. Immediately she pictures Will and hears his voice. *How nice! Someone remembers we exist!*

Niki shivers. Shifting, she rubs her arms.

"The work you did was tremendous." *You already said that, Jones.* "But in most instances, it's difficult to quantify the results, or point to anything tangible."

When Geoffrey advances the slide, Niki lets out a gasp. It's her work. *Their* propaganda.

"Unless, of course, we're talking about Morale Operations," Geoffrey says as a grin leaks across his face. "For MO, we have some proof."

"You say that now," Niki whispers, and Andrea looks over with her forehead raised.

"The men and women of MO created black propaganda. Subversive propaganda. Propaganda that impersonated the enemy. In this case, the Germans."

On the screen is a drawing of a man and woman having sex. Somebody—Geoffrey? His secretary?—has placed black bars over the woman's breasts. What a shame. Ezra was so proud of this depiction.

Wie lange noch?
Wie lange sollen diese Ausländer noch unsere Fauen schänden?

"This is part of MO Rome's *How Much Longer?* campaign," Geoffrey says. "And what this racy picture asks is, *How much longer will these foreigners disgrace our women?*"

"Mom!" Andrea hisses. "That was you, wasn't it? That's what you did?"

Niki nods as Geoffrey moves on. "Here's the front page of a fake underground communist newspaper," he says. "*Das Neue Deutschland, The New Germany,* was the name of a supposed 'peace party,' and this was their primary mode of communication. MO used this form of media to print stories that would rattle soldier morale. But effective propaganda is multifaceted, and the regular publication of *DND* planted false stories *and* gave the impression that a large, well-organized underground movement existed." *Click*. "That was also the point of these stickers, which were scattered by the millions behind enemy lines."

Niki can't read the screen but remembers them all.

Die for Hitler?

Peace on Earth not peace under the Earth

Later is too late

Hitler's death—Germany's life

✞ = you?

You are fighting for the party, not for Germany!

End the war!

With the next click, the audience erupts in amusement. It's a picture of a piece of toilet paper. As with the stickers, Niki knows the words, and the translation, by heart.

COMRADES! STOP THIS SHIT!

We do not fight for Germany but only for Hitler and Himmler. The NSDAP led us into this damned war but now the bigwigs are only trying to save their own skin. They let us die in the mud; they want us to hold out until the last bullet. However, we need the last bullets to free Germany from this SS shit. Enough! Peace!

On the flip side—the *wiping* side—is a caricature of Hitler. Despite Ezra's fame as a cartoonist, Niki thinks this is some of his best work.

"These pieces were created by…" As Geoffrey checks his notes, Niki fantasizes about shouting, *Rome, damn it! Project Sauerkraut!* "They are all products of Rome," he says, "but you'll note the quality varies widely. If you weren't in MO, you might not appreciate that everything had to be printed on the same machine but appear as though it came from a variety of sources. For example, this from some communist's basement printing machine. That's why so much of it was crude in appearance."

It wasn't all "crude," Niki thinks. *We had to seem professional, too. Items printed in a basement, yes, but also by the meticulous Nazi machine.*

Geoffrey Jones carries on, ticking through more propaganda, such as fake issues of *Time* and *Life* that documented the luxuries of American internment, as well as surrender cards entitling holders to a long-term holiday at the nearest POW camp.

"I'm sure no ladies were involved in the creation of the more ribald materials," Geoffrey says, followed by the thinnest smattering of laughs. *I made those*, Niki wants to say. *That was me.*

Quite out of nowhere, Niki longs for recognition—not for herself, but for all of them. Their work was important, and so were the people who carried it out, but hardly anyone's left to remember. This feels like a great injustice, yet Niki is part of the problem, is she not? After all, she's the one who's worked so hard to move on, to keep those years buried in the past.

PART THREE

OPERATION SAUERKRAUT

23

July 1944

Niki exited the building to find Will where she'd left him, idling with his headlights off in a cargo truck they'd requisitioned for the trip. Even in the dark, she could make out the white star painted onto the truck's exterior, and Will's square, oversize head inside.

"Permission granted," Niki said, popping open the driver's-side door. "Good thing you stayed in the car. I knew it'd go down easier coming from me."

Nothing ever went down easy with the chief, who could get apoplectic over a five-minute delay or a very decent glass of Chianti. With men like him, the key was to tread lightly, to announce a plan, but not request permission to carry it out. Will didn't have the guile to pull off such crafty nuance.

"I can't believe he agreed," Will said. "I am pleasantly surprised."

"Well." Niki considered this. "He didn't *agree* per se," she said, and Will groaned. "But he didn't forbid it."

"Warner just gave up, is what you're telling me."

"I prefer *relented*. Now, scooch over." Niki gave him a nudge. "Your motor handling skills are far too Sunday drive to make the one hundred fifty miles before dawn."

Will sighed as he slid across the seat. After closing the door, Niki studied the cab's interior—its levers and switches and assorted doodads—trying to work out what was what. She hadn't driven a deuce and a half since training, but how hard could it be?

"Did Warner take issue with your being in charge of the operation?" Will asked as Niki flipped a lock to turn on the lights.

"He did not," Niki said. She stepped on the clutch. "Even lowly lady privates have their uses. Hard to believe, I know. Anyway, the man couldn't reasonably object. I *am* the only person in the office who speaks German."

"What about Wild Bill?" Will asked. "I would've thought Warner might want him to weigh in?"

"He didn't mention it. Personally, I don't give a fig about Wild Bill because he doesn't care about us," Niki said, pushing the shift into first gear. "Washington leaves us alone to an alarming degree. We could have ten dead bodies in the printing room, and no one would notice."

As they eased away from the building at approximately three inches per hour, Niki cranked the lever into second, and immediately into third. They lurched forward, the sudden movement combined with the spring beneath their seat causing Will to bottom out and then hit his head on the roof. He cursed, and Niki cranked the wheel hard left, shifted again, and they drove off into the night.

"Are you sure you don't want me to drive?"

"Quite sure. Why does this beast take forever to rev between gears?" Niki said.

"It's not meant to go fast. I don't know if it's your driving, or this entire scheme," Will said, bracing himself against the dash, "but I think I'm going to vomit."

"We're just getting started, my friend," Niki said, even though her insides were in turmoil, too. Deep down, she hadn't expected Warner to agree, and she'd only concocted the plan as a bluff to force Washington's hand. Their memo outlined two paths for getting the materials into enemy territory—POWs or planes—and Niki figured they'd pick the route used before. Alas, she didn't see any planes around, so POWs it was.

They drove several kilometers in silence, Will with a hand cupped on each knee and hunched to avoid again hitting his head on the roof. Niki glanced over once, twice, three times, but he kept his gaze trained on the dark road ahead. Despite the air whooshing through the open windows, not one strand on his head swayed.

"You might as well relax a little," Niki said finally. "We've got hours to go. Plus several detours, I'd expect. There can't be more than four or five bridges left in this part of the country."

"Sorry. I'm a nervous passenger," he said. "And I don't like driving in the dark."

"How fortunate, then, that I'm the one who's doing it," Niki said. "Hey, why don't you light us each a cigarette?"

"Sure thing," Will said, reaching into his coat pocket. He wasn't a smoker himself yet always seemed to have smokes at the ready.

Niki lit up and puffed hungrily for several minutes as Will faintly jiggled one leg. "William," she said, and tossed her partially smoked cigarette out the window. "You're gonna have to speak unless you want me to fall asleep and drive us both off the road. What an embarrassing way to die. In a traffic accident? During a war? Your role right now is to keep me company."

"Okay. What should we discuss?"

"I find the best way to start a conversation is to ask an open-ended question," Niki said. "The more personal, the better. People love to talk about themselves."

"All right..." Will weighed this with great earnest, and Niki couldn't believe she was teaching a publishing scion how to socialize. "I am curious about our newest employee," he said at last. "Moggy, or Margaret, or whatever she's calling herself. You mentioned there's more to the story than what's being presented to us?"

"Yes," Niki said. "A lot more." She'd rung George to ask what the hell was going on, and he swore Moggy wasn't there to babysit. The family just wanted to keep her occupied, give her something important to do, and thought she'd be more comfortable with someone she knew. Though it sounded reasonable enough, Niki didn't buy it. "I don't think Moggy even realizes she's a pawn in her family's game," she went on. "Part of me feels sorry for the girl. She's awkward and unsure of herself and, according to her family, past her prime. They don't view her as having any social prospects whatsoever."

"That's harsh."

"No kidding. From what George says, she's always struggled to fit in."

"Sounds like your exact opposite," Will noted as they whipped around a corner. "NIKI! THE ROAD!"

"You're such a delicate flower," Niki said, through her pounding heart. This cargo truck was far more cumbersome than the jeep they ordinarily used, and for the first time she worried about keeping it on the road. "How am I Moggy's opposite? By the way, I could use another smoke."

"You seem to fit in anywhere," Will said, and produced a cigarette from his jacket. "I first noticed it when we were in Algiers—your ability to switch from Italian to French to German at the drop of the hat, replete with the accompanying mannerisms. Around Italians you are boisterous and loud. Clipped for the Krauts. Then you take on an almost languid bent when you're speaking French."

"Sensual, I think you mean," Niki said, and Will's ears turned red. She leaned toward him, eyes on the road, and let him light her cigarette. "Well, thanks, I guess. When your country is no longer a country, you must learn to change colors. I *am* an American citizen, you know."

"And that's another thing," Will said. "Sometimes you seem fully American, like someone I might've grown up with."

"Ha! Be sure to tell my husband. He still sees me as the Eastern European he sometimes lives with."

"Oh, Niki—"

"No!" she said. "It's fine. I find it all quite funny." This was both true and it wasn't, depending on her mood.

"You don't talk about him much," Will noted. "Your husband."

"There's not much to say. His name is George, and he works for Dulles. Of course, you all had to tell me that second part. For the record, you never talk about your wife, either. All I know is that she was a debutante of the year or some such, and writes you exactly once per month."

"What more do you want to know?" he asked.

Niki made a face. "Nothing, thanks," she said, stymied by her reaction. "Why are we discussing spouses who are presently in other countries? I vote to move on."

Will bobbed his head, and they drove in silence, along the coast, the briny air wafting through the windows.

"Do you think Moggy understands the true purpose of Morale Operations?" he asked, after some time. "From her brother? The fewer people who do, the—"

"The better. Yes, I know. I don't think she's caught on, but Moggy Clingman *is* the most inquisitive person in the northern hemisphere," Niki said. "To wit, tonight she had a million questions about where we were going even though she should've been busy unpacking all her crap. I wish you could've seen it. Maybe *you'd* be able to do the math on how one person can own that many pieces of luggage."

Yesterday, Niki returned from the office to find a mountain of suitcases and assorted valises piled in the courtyard between the villas. The scene was borderline gluttonous. God only knew how many soldiers had to be sidelined as eleven monogrammed trunks made their way across Europe.

"What excuse did you give her about tonight?" Will asked.

"I told her we're working on a project for AFHQ, assessing Italy's industrial capacity." Niki smiled. "Thought of it off the top of my head."

"You're frighteningly good at lying," Will noted.

"Hey! It's not lying. If we're going to get thousands of pounds of propaganda into occupied territory, we'll need decent industrial capacity."

"Except the printing won't be done in northern Italy. This whole adventure... I'm not entirely sold on it."

"Listen," Niki began. Up ahead there was a river, and only one way to cross it with the bridge gone. "Hold on," she said.

Gritting her teeth, Niki pressed on the brakes and toyed with some lever—the hand air valve?—that'd allow her to successfully maneuver the two and a half tons behind her down an embankment. The path was well worn, and the river barely a trickle this time of year, and so Niki was able to successfully navigate the hill, and the water, and the glass and pottery shards lining the soil, all that evidence of destruction from somewhere upstream.

"I understand your qualms," Niki continued when they safely reached the other side. "But what choice do we have? On the plus side, no one is expecting much from us. They'll probably give us medals if we manage to avoid getting ourselves or anyone else killed."

"That is rather dispiriting."

"Welcome to the Club of the Constantly Underestimated,"

Niki said, gunning it as they crested the ridge, grateful that deuce and a halfs were impossible to stall out. Up ahead were two large spotlights, the first sign of life in hours. It had to be the POW camp. The Americans were the only ones with reliable power. "I think I see it!" Niki said. She pressed down and shifted into increasingly higher gears, her right bicep already throbbing from so much yanking and pushing.

When they reached the end of the road, Niki slammed on the brakes. The truck skidded several yards before coming to a halt in a swirling cloud of dirt. They were here. The Fifth Army POW cages.

"A dramatic entrance," Will said once they'd confirmed neither was hurt. "I'd expect nothing less."

"Remember the guy from SI?" Niki said. Gripping the steering wheel with both hands, she stretched forward to get a better look at the tall wooden gates. "He thought I wasn't dramatic enough."

"He didn't know what he was talking about."

As an armed guard marched toward the truck, Niki felt a lump in her throat. "I guess we're really doing this?" She turned toward Will to find his lips were clamped together, as if swallowing a smile. "What?" she said. "What is it?"

"I'm sorry." Will covered his mouth. "I don't mean to laugh. But your hair...it looks like you've been through a twister."

"So many jokes from you," Niki said, half laughing, half scowling as she patted down the disturbance of curls. "All right, Casanova, if you're finished with the flirting, let's go inside and meet the prisoners. Might as well put the poor saps to work."

24

NIKI

July 1944

A torch-wielding man led them down a pathway flanked by barbed wire. Even in the dark, Niki could see the small beads of worry percolating on Will's brow. "Let me do the talking," she whispered.

"Where have I heard that before?" Will said. "And obviously you're going to do the talking. I don't know any German."

"That's not what I meant, but glad we're on the same page."

Up ahead, the camp commandant waited in front of a squat gray building with a corrugated tin roof. He greeted Will and Niki curtly and motioned for them to follow him inside.

"Così chic!" Niki said, inspecting the room, although there wasn't much to see. Only a table, a few chairs, some with restraints strapped onto them, and a flickering bulb dangling overhead.

"Tell me, what is it that you need, Captain Dewart?" the commandant asked. Though his words were sharp, his eyes were sloppy and bored, giving Niki the impression he didn't approve of what they were doing but didn't care enough to object. "You are going to take some of my men?"

"If all goes well," Niki said. She flipped open her notepad and sat down. "We want a very specific type of prisoner, and ask that you bring through as many as you can who fit the criteria. Any branch of the Wehrmacht is acceptable."

The man eyed Will skeptically, as if to ask, *Why are you letting her be in charge?*

"Most important is that they voluntarily surrendered to the Allies," Niki said, "and, at some juncture, publicly expressed anti-Nazi views or engaged in anti-Nazi behavior." She checked her notes again. "If they exhibit an eagerness to immigrate to the United States, all the better."

Will and the commandant traded looks.

"I'm not promising anything," Niki clarified, tapping her pen on the desk to emphasize the point. "I just think the idea of United States citizenship would compel them to do a better job."

After exchanging final details, the commandant went to wrangle the first group of interviewees. Will lowered down beside Niki and resumed with his dancing leg.

"They're the prisoners, not you," Niki said, and placed a hand on his knee.

"But it does feel as though I'm not in charge of my own destiny," Will said. "How did I let you talk me into this? *Nazis?* We're going to sit here talking to a bunch of Nazis?"

Niki removed her hand and ran it over her hair, which remained wild and twisting at all angles. "Anti-Nazis," she said. "We asked him to bring us only the men who hate the Nazis so much they surrendered to *us.*"

"Remind me how double agents work?"

"We're looking for people who can prove they were anti-

Nazi *before* the war," Niki said. "People who never changed their views and defected as soon they could. It's all very specific, which makes success more likely." Niki hoped her voice sounded more confident than she felt. Of the many thousands of men at this cage, would they find more than one or two who fit the criteria? Even if the commandant did manage to wrangle up a decent group, how accurately could she and Will screen for true anti-Nazis versus those who were only pretending to be?

Ten minutes later, the commandant knocked, threw open the door, and pushed the first prisoner inside. Niki listened as the boss's footsteps retreated.

"Hallo," Niki said. "Your name?"

"Stefan Meyer," he answered, and Niki took a beat to examine him. His face was pale, a little drawn, and his clothes were slightly soiled. Otherwise, he appeared in decent health.

"I'm Private Wilhelmina Flingman," Niki said, and invited him to sit. "This is Captain Nick Demart. Thank you for meeting us. Tell me, where were you born?"

So began the list of questions she'd ask Stefan Meyer and the dozens to come. Before long, Niki settled into a routine, ticking off each item, one by one. The origins of the men varied. *Austria. Cologne. Bitburg. Germany.* As did their occupations. *Plumber. Auto mechanic. Steelworker. Electrical engineer.* And their religions. *Protestant. Catholic. Atheist.* Through it all, Niki kept meticulous notes, flagging the best candidates, pausing on occasion to translate something for Will, or get his opinion.

"What actions have you taken toward the Nazi regime, and have these actions drawn unwanted attention to yourself?"

Punished for not joining the Hitler Youth.

Jailed for eighteen months in 1935 after drunkenly speaking out about the Nazis.

Missing three fingers from when he was first caught trying to defect.

"Please describe the circumstances surrounding your desertion."

Drafted at eighteen. Deserted two weeks later, when he heard Rome fell.

While digging trenches at the front, found out his father was taken to a concentration camp.

Learned his entire family had been killed. No longer feared retaliation against family members.

Three months after being drafted, was ordered to execute fifteen partisans but let them go. Fled to Rome and immediately turned himself in.

Never wanted to serve. Attempted to desert three times, starting one month after conscription. Fled to Rome to surrender to the Americans once they finally captured the city.

The commandant brought forth a healthy supply of men, though most had at least one characteristic eliminating him from consideration. *Bit of an eager beaver. Tries to create the impression he wants revenge. Mood changed when it was mentioned some members of our team are Jewish. Thinks it's all for kicks.* The next step, after cutting the group of fifty in half, was to administer a psychological analysis using tactics from the OSS Assessment School.

When Niki handed Will the whittled down list, it was probably near dawn, but in this windowless room, they had no gauge of time other than their weary eyes and pounding heads.

"Twelve adequate men," Niki said as Will scanned the names. She wished they'd drummed up more, but true anti-Nazis were few and far between, despite the masses they had to choose from. "What do you think?"

"Seems fine," Will said, then balked when he reached the end of the list. "This guy?" He looked up. "Really?"

"Really," Niki said, having anticipated Will might throw up a protest to this particular choice. Max Borgwardt had stumbled in second to last, claiming to be eighteen though his face showed not even a trace of stubble. Throughout the interrogation, he stuttered fiercely, and his eyes were wide and wet, as though he'd been plucked from some horror mere hours before.

"How long have you been at the cages?" she couldn't help but ask.

"I don't know..." He rubbed his forehead. "Three months? Four, maybe?"

Max Borgwardt's family opposed the Nazi regime from the start and spent the war hiding with three other families, two of them Jewish, before the group escaped to central Italy. They mistakenly assumed the armistice would make them safe but arrived to discover the brutes were still very much in charge. Within days, Max and his brother were discovered and swiftly assigned to the Panzer Corps. Max defected when he learned the village his family was living in had been burned to the ground. He didn't know what happened to his brother.

"Borgwardt is trustworthy," Niki told Will, even as some part of her understood his reservations. She believed his allegiance to the Allies, but Max did not seem like he possessed the mettle to successfully cross into enemy territory whilst carrying many pounds of subversive material. "I see something in him," Niki added, though did not say this "something" was mostly hints of her little brother, Pasha.

In the end, they brought the commandant a list of twelve men of German descent between the self-reported ages of eighteen and thirty-three. While Niki and Will stood in the doorway, he prepared the paperwork necessary to strike the POWs from army records and transfer them into Will's care.

"As far as the army is concerned," the commandant said, "these men were never captured. You're in charge of them now. When they have completed the work, return them to any POW cage. Tell the commanding officer that they surrendered to you in Rome, and he'll open a new file, as though they're being interned for the first time."

After the commandant handed Will what he called a "receipt," he outfitted the POWs in American fatigue coveralls and brought them out to the truck. As Will ordered them into the back, Niki stood in a swirl of early morning mist, watching everything unfold. With the adrenaline rushing through her veins, Niki no longer felt tired.

"Last chance to change our minds," Will called out.

Niki laughed with some effort. "Why would we do that?" she said.

Will walked toward her, his boots crunching on the ground. "You realize we're about to drive one hundred fifty miles back to Rome, through a desolate countryside, with a truck full of Nazis?"

"They're not Nazis," Niki said, though their political affiliations were far from the chief risk. If these men wanted to escape, or worse, they easily could.

"Fingers crossed," Will said. He turned on a heel and marched back toward his side of the truck.

"They all seemed very eager to do this!" Niki shouted.

"Yes, you were very convincing! Probably the only woman they've seen in months."

"Hey!" Niki flung open her door. "Don't reduce it to that," she said, lunging up into her seat. "That's not fair."

"What's not fair about it?" he said. "Of course they'd tell you what you wanted to hear. Trust me, when it comes to beautiful women, it's an involuntary reaction."

"Don't be so cynical."

"Says the girl who makes a living in propaganda." With a shake of his head, Will slammed the door. "Well. Off we go."

25

NIKI

July 1944

Niki was thirty seconds through her bedroom door when she heard a light rapping. After being out all night interviewing POWs, her brain was buzzing, her limbs were weak, and she was dying to get out of these boots. No one could possibly need her right now.

As Niki gingerly slid off her shoes, the person knocked again. She kicked her boots aside and crept toward the bed, wincing with each step.

"Niki?" the voice called. "Are you in there?"

Moggy. Niki contemplated the bed and then the door and sighed, accepting her fate. The fastest way to dispense with Moggy was to give her attention. Like watering a dry and strange plant.

"Coming," Niki said, her voice dragging along with her feet.

She pulled open the door. "Hello. Oh! Look at you. Neat out-fit." Moggy was sporting a salmon-colored two-piece getup for which Niki couldn't fathom any practical purpose. Then again, she did have to give Moggy credit for wearing what she liked, even when it wasn't suited to her tall and boxy frame. "What a great color," Niki added. "You're bringing a whole lot of brightness to this dungeony old villa. It's such a refreshing change of pace."

"Thank you. Ordinarily I'd be a little more covered up, but I was just finishing my morning exercise routine." Moggy pulled a handkerchief from her bra and gently dabbed her cheeks. "I'm a little glisteny!"

"You have a morning routine?" Niki was astonished.

"It's the one from the WAC manual," she said. "We spoke about this the other day?" When Niki returned a blank expression, Moggy proceeded to demonstrate a series of arm flings, trunk twists, bent-over airplanes, and jumping jacks.

"Ah. Right. Well, you truly have made the most of the morning," Niki said, and stifled a yawn. "I don't mean to chase you away, Mogs, but I was, uh, in the middle of something." She glanced back, toward the bed.

"I was hoping, since it's Friday, we might go out and explore Rome?" Moggy said. "I would love to check out the tourist sites and maybe a café or two? I've marked a few places I'd like to visit in the guidebook..."

"Moggy, you *cannot* pay any heed to that piece of rubbish. The book's only purpose is to prevent GIs from entering unsavory neighborhoods and contracting a VD. We can explore Rome some other time. I really need to get back to—"

As Niki went to close the door, Moggy jutted out an arm. "Wait!" she said. "I'm sorry. It's just... I don't mean to complain, but it's so quiet here, compared to Switzerland. I'm trying to accept the circumstances and view it as sort of a meditation retreat, but I'm just so lonely."

"Moggy. You've been here two and a half days."

"I know." Moggy swept past Niki and fully entered the room. "But I miss the sense of community I had at the Institute with my fellow Jungians," she said. "We're all living together in these villas. Why can't it be more like that?"

"Welcome to war," Niki said as she actively fought the urge to collapse into a heap on the floor.

"We could still—" Moggy's eyes darted toward the perfectly made bed and back again. She appraised Niki's crumpled clothes and hair and sneezed three times. "What in the world...? Are you just getting home?" she said. "Where did you sleep last night?"

"I was out in the countryside, remember? Assessing industrial capacity?"

"You were doing a study ALL NIGHT?" Moggy's eyes grew. "With Captain Dewart? Oh, Niki, do you really think that's a good idea?" She sneezed again. "George would be so concerned."

"George would be fine. We weren't out *all* night, just until very, very late. Your light was still on when we got back." Niki's pulse fluttered as she spoke. She hated to lie but couldn't risk a follow-up barrage of questions, or Moggy reporting anything to George. Moggy had a way of making things sound worse than they were, and giving her the specifics felt like walking into a trap or, worse, a land mine. "In fact, I called 'good night' to you, through your door," Niki added, doubling down.

"Huh." Moggy twisted her lips, no doubt weighing the likelihood of this. "Well. I'm sorry I didn't hear you."

"You were probably asleep. Listen." Niki placed a hand on Moggy's shoulder. "The adjustment to a new post can be difficult. During my first week in Rome, I woke up every morning and had to ask myself, 'Where am I? Is this Algiers or...?' It can be quite jarring."

"But—" Moggy shook her head, as if endeavoring to rearrange what Niki said into something that made sense.

"You really need to get more rest," Niki said, and released her arm. "As do I." She yawned widely, for effect. "In fact, I think I'm ready for a nap."

Moggy frowned deeply and dropped her head. For a second, Niki's chest tightened. George once called his sister the consummate outsider, and Niki didn't want to be responsible for shutting another door. "Let's plan something for another time?" Niki said.

"That would be fantastic. Maybe when you wake up?"

"Slow down. I have a lot going on..."

"I know you're tired, and I'm trying not to be histrionic, but so far this is all such a disaster! I thought it would be different. Tolerable, at least. It's not just the city." She snuffled. "Or the office. I thought... I know this sounds silly, but I imagined *we* might become friends, you and me. With three boys in the family, I've always wanted a sister." She looked up, tears glistening in her chocolate-brown eyes. "Now that I'm saying it out loud, I realize how foolish that sounds."

"Aw, Mogs," Niki said, swamped by another surge of warm feelings. *Moggy doesn't want your pity*, she reminded herself, lest she end up dragged to the Catacombs or Palatine Hill. *Moggy is an extension of George.* "There will be plenty of opportunities ahead to get to know each other better, for you to get to know the entire motley bunch! Come to think, you and Ezra would get along famously, and he *adores* all those Roman tourist traps. His favorite pastime is smoking at the Colosseum and watching American GIs dance to jazz music. They are apparently quite bad at it."

"I don't smoke. And I don't know about being alone with a man I don't know." Moggy chewed on this. "But he *is* a snazzy dresser," she allowed. "The only one who seems to wear a uniform, which says a lot about his character."

"Mmm," Niki said, aware that Ezra wore the uniform because he was a sharp dresser, and because it signaled to any lingering Nazis that he was American.

"When does it get better, Niki?" Moggy said. "You seem to fit in fine. How long will it take for me to make friends? When will I be less lonely?"

"Oh, gosh, it's hard to say." Niki paused, casting about for an answer when, truth was, she'd never thought about her loneliness in this or any other context. Niki was the sort of person who came into and out of places, without really sticking for long. Even as a child, when Pasha trailed her everywhere, Niki preferred to be by herself. Moggy would probably find this sad—and, fair enough—but it was also a way to survive.

"I promise it won't always be this way," Niki said, and Moggy's face lifted, a glimmer of hope. "We all feel isolated sometimes. It's just temporary." Was this true? Niki had no idea.

"That does make me feel a little better, though I'm sorry you've been lonely, too," Moggy said. Suddenly, her expression changed and her lips began to twitch. The corners of her mouth pulled back slowly, dribbling a smile across her face. "Don't worry, Niki," Moggy said. "If you're feeling lonesome and adrift, it won't be for long. A little birdie tells me that a certain husband—and brother—is coming to Rome next week for R & R."

"Husband." With a whoosh, Niki's insides plummeted. "George is coming *here*? To Rome? Why? Are you sure?"

Moggy slapped a hand over her mouth. "You didn't know?" she cried. "Oh, God. I messed up, didn't I? He probably wanted to surprise you." She threw back her head and wailed. "I ruin everything!"

"Moggy, are you *sure* that George is coming here?"

"Positive. He's going to be so mad at me. Niki." Moggy clutched her hands and held them against her heart. "I know it's a lot to ask, but can you pretend we never had this conversation? *Please*. I don't want George to be upset with me."

Niki laughed grimly. Imagining George wouldn't come to Rome wasn't a favor. It was her greatest fantasy. Maybe, if she pretended long enough, Niki could will it into reality. "Moggy, please put your mind at ease," she said. "Forgetting about seeing George is one promise I can definitely keep."

26

NIKI

July 1944

Niki squinted through the mud-splattered windshield to make out the figure standing on the road. She thought it was Will, but as she got closer, Niki did a double take. With the summer sun glinting on his sandy-blond hair, the man *resembled* Dewart, but his face was too relaxed, and he didn't carry himself as though slowly filling with live bees.

As Niki jerked to the side, Will shielded himself from the rocks and gravel flying into his face. "Hey there," she said, then coughed on account of the mess she'd kicked up. Sometimes Niki neglected to consider the repercussions of driving aggressively in a car without windows or doors. "Fancy meeting you here." She wiped a speck of dirt from her eyes. "Whaddya doing? Taking a stroll? You look like a GI on holiday!" Not for the first time, Niki thought that this large bear of a man might be halfway intimidating if not for his complete lack of bluster.

"Niki!" Will threw his hands into the air. "I was waiting for you. Where have you been? You were scheduled to be here twenty minutes ago."

"Sorry. Moggy cornered me again," Niki said. "She's determined to be bosom pals and slowly chip away at my every thought and secret. Maybe we should send *her* across enemy lines. She'd really gum up all that swift Nazi movement."

Since the confrontation in her bedroom four days before, Moggy had been full of queries, forever materializing at Niki's side, seemingly out of nowhere. *Where are you going? What are you doing? Why did I find all these cartoons of Hitler?* Also, she was really sticking to the "we never had this conversation" pact, and Niki had no idea when or if to expect George. Maybe all that praying to Zdislava Berka, patron saint of difficult marriages, would pay off.

"Why are you on the road?" Niki asked Will. "The entire reason you came out ahead of me was to make sure everything was in order. Where's your jeep?"

"Ezra dropped me off," he said. "*Hours* ago. You were so late, I started to get concerned."

"Aw, that's sweet."

"I mean, you're usually late, but with your driving skills, I wanted to make sure you weren't overturned in a ditch."

Niki rolled her eyes. "Maybe not so sweet after all. Hop in," she said as he heaved himself into the car. "I'll drive you the rest of the way."

As they motored down the lane, over the red dirt road and beneath a canopy of umbrella pines, Niki and Will reviewed the progress they'd made since conscripting their men several days before. While they taught the POWs how to drive German and American cars, read maps, and detonate bombs, their fellow OSS agents trolled the Italian front for anything—belts, helmets, weapons, boots—to help Lieutenant Jack Daniels assemble proper Wehrmacht uniforms. Will created German dog tags using a hammer and anvil, and Niki found the appropriate detritus to sprinkle into uniform pockets. Even lint and tobacco shavings needed an authentically German flair. Back at the office, the R&A team dreamed up backgrounds and cover stories for the men, drafting an unwitting Moggy into the subterfuge.

"Why is your division asking mine to write biographies of people who don't exist?" Moggy wanted to know.

"We're all part of OSS, and we help each other, even when we don't fully understand why. Think of what you're doing as compiling personality profiles," Niki said. "Crafting personas can go a long way to understanding the enemy. You should appreciate this. It's very Jungian." She didn't know whether this was true, but it seemed accurate enough.

While forgers created credentials to match the new identities, replete with stamps to demonstrate Nazi Party dues were paid, Niki penned articles for *Das Neue Deutschland*, including a list of supposedly bombed German thoroughfares. Ezra designed a series of blistering cartoons to imply that dirty, hairy foreigners were bedding all the good German wives, and Will made pamphlets with tips on how to fake an illness or desert to Switzerland. When all was said and done, they'd produced three thousand pieces of propaganda in less than a week, all of it currently packed into the back of Niki's jeep.

"The time has come," Niki said as they approached a four-story palazzo on the outskirts of Rome. Before it was a safe house, it was home to a now dispossessed duke. "We've taught the prisoners everything we know and must send them out into the world, to see if they can walk on their own." She pulled up beside the villa's back entrance and cut the engine. "I'm a little teary at the thought."

"I'm only crying over all of the ways this could go wrong."

"Oh, Will." Niki chortled. "Sorry, *Nick*. You are my sweet bundle of sunshine."

When she jumped out of the car, Niki patted her pocket, and the outline of the pistol she hoped to never use. *It's all going to be fine*, Niki assured herself as she approached the house. *You've thought this through, and you're thoroughly prepared. There's nothing left but the doing.* Inhaling, Niki threw open the door and stepped inside.

"Hello!" Niki hollered. "Demart and Flingman are here!" She stumbled and stopped short, gawping, unable to believe her eyes. The house looked worse than it had immediately after it'd been looted, with heaps of clothes, balled-up trash, and smashed Victorian bibelots scattered across the floors. A thick cloud of tobacco smoke hung in the air, but did little to conceal the pungent scent of male body odor. "Holy Wenceslas," Niki said, and kicked aside a shoe. "What a bunch of slobs. Hello!" she called out again. "It's Captain Demart and Private Flingman. Please join us for a conference in the kitchen."

One by one, the POWs straggled into the kitchen, and collected around an upturned table missing three of its legs. "Well, gentlemen," *Wilhelmina* said, once the men were fully assembled. Though her voice was quivery at first, she soon managed to steady it. "The time has come to put your hard work to use."

Niki assessed the room, letting her gaze linger on each face. To their credit, the men were universally solemn, aside from Max, who wielded his customary impish grin. All at once, regret washed through her. He had no business being in this group. What had she been thinking? It was as though Niki were sending her own Pasha off to war.

"Are you okay?" Will whispered, and she nudged him away.

"The operation begins tonight," Niki said, whisking her fingers against the pistol. "A truck will arrive at nineteen hundred hours, and take you to an infiltration point at a forward base near Florence. When you arrive, you'll meet one of our colleagues, who will provide you with credentials as well as weapons, cigarettes, money, and fifteen pounds of material.

"Once it's time to move, you'll be divided into your established teams. Group one will strike out at midnight. Groups two and three will go at dawn. Upon leaving the base, you'll be met by an officer who will lead you across no-man's-land to a point on the Arno River. From there, you're on your own. First, you'll traverse the river and then penetrate the main line of resistance, moving as far into enemy territory as you can manage."

While she spoke, Niki's heart thrummed as if *she* were about to cross. These men were doing the hard part, and all she had to do was wait. Of course, Niki had never been any good at that.

"Once you've breached enemy lines," Niki continued, "you'll distribute the materials in whatever manner you deem appropriate. You might leave the pamphlets in buildings or in trucks, nail them onto trees, or scatter them on the streets. Your only directive is to distribute all of it, every piece, while avoiding detection. Ideally, you'll hang around to see if the enemy reads any of it.

"When it's time to return, you'll reenter through the Allied lines in the Prato area. With your weapons unloaded, hold your hands high and demand, 'Take me to the CIC!' Once you're taken into custody, ask for Captain Rossetti, and he'll arrange your passage back. If reentry is impossible, lie low in the hills or in Bologna and wait for the Allies to overrun your position. It will happen soon enough, and you can surrender at that point."

Niki surveyed the men. They were all nodding in agreement, and she detected nary a whiff of hesitation. At least *somebody* was sure about this.

"If you're challenged in any way," Niki said, "use the de-escalation tactics you were taught during training. According to those in the field, bartering with Italian cigarettes is the most effective. Any questions?"

No one spoke. No one even moved. After wishing the men

good luck, Niki and Will bade them farewell and stepped back out into the hot and dusty Italian afternoon.

"Well, that's that," Niki said. "I hope we didn't forget anything."

"It'll be fine," Will said as they approached the jeep. "I recognize that earlier I alluded to 'crying,' but I have more faith than I let on."

Niki chuckled. "So do I," she said.

"I know, and it's one of my favorite things about you," Will said. They exchanged closemouthed smiles and lunged up into their seats, neither mentioning how visibly the other was shaking.

27

PALOMA

May 1945

When did I see Nikola again? It was maybe one week after the last time. That afternoon, she didn't properly greet me. Instead, she walked over and dropped onto the bottom step. After removing one cigarette, she lobbed the packet in my direction.

"You don't look like a girl who's solved all her problems," I said as she blew out a long stream of smoke. She rotated toward me, her face thoroughly baffled. "The last time we spoke?" I reminded her. "I'd given you an idea—for what, you did not reveal. You thanked me *copiosamente*, and said I'd solved all your problems."

Nikola tittered. "Right. I'd forgotten." She shook her head. "You were immensely helpful. *Grazie*. As far as whether my problems are solved, it remains to be seen. We're waiting for news. It's excruciating."

"Yes," I said tightly. "I know a few things about waiting. Maybe, for you, it will not be so bad. You have food and can spend time with your coworker." I lifted my eyebrows.

"Which coworker? Do you mean Will?"

"Yes, of course I mean the captain. Who else would it be? You two are fucking, are you not?"

"Paloma!" Nikola shrieked, and gave me a playful swat to the knee. "What a thing to say."

"Do you not find him handsome?"

"Oh, sure. He's all right," Nikola said, and her eyes dashed away. "A little tall and beaky for my taste. Anyway, he's married, and so am I."

To this, I shrugged. "What is marriage? A triviality, during a war. Unless one is very much in love. Maybe this is the case for you." I peered at Nikola and found her expression flat. "You seem too young to be tired of it," I said. Maybe her husband had too many girlfriends, like my own. Not every woman can get used to it. "How long have you been married?" I asked.

"Two and a half years," Nikola said as she stared down at the cobblestones, a cigarette smoldering between her fingers.

"*Santo Cielo!*" I cried. "Only two years?" It was worse than I thought. "The man must be a gem. Where is he right now?"

"Not too far away, actually," Nikola said. "Which means, in theory, he might show up anytime. Rumor has it he's about to do exactly that." She examined the cigarette, now burnt all the way down.

"A surprise visit? This sounds very romantic," I said, and felt the pull of yearning, not for my husband—heaven forbid—but because it'd been such a long time since a surprise from a man was associated with anything good.

Nikola flicked her cigarette into the street. "George wouldn't know romance if I gave him a script," she said. "Honestly, I'm trying to pretend he's not coming. Like if I don't think about it, maybe it won't happen. Silly, I realize." She dropped her head.

"He's a fine man. Honorable. Intelligent. But he's not always pleasant to be around. The problem is probably me. I'm not built to stay in one place, and I don't think I'm cut out for marriage. I never should've signed up for the gig in the first place."

I looked at her sideways. A gig? I'd never heard marriage described in such a way.

Nikola kicked out her feet and leaned back onto her elbows. "Sometimes I wonder..." She grimaced, as if gulping down something unpleasant. "What would've happened if I'd chosen a different path? Not that I had a surfeit of options."

I debated what to tell my new friend. If she wasn't meant for marriage, she never should've said "I do." As a devout Catholic, I'm very much against the idea of divorce. Yes, even someone *like me* can hold this opinion. The sex has nothing to do with it. Most Roman wives believe that once we bear children, we've fulfilled our marital obligations, and are free to have fun. What I've done hardly qualifies as such, but you understand.

"You might be young, but it is too late for other paths," I said. "You can't get a divorce."

"Divorce?" Nikola pulled her chin back, as though I'd said a word she hadn't yet learned. "Who said anything about divorce? Although now that you mention it..."

"I know it is very popular with you Americans," I said, "but surely you can find some other way to enjoy your marriage? Another benefit? Children, for example. Sperm production is often the most useful characteristic of a man."

Nikola lit another cigarette. "Children are not on the docket," she said. "Don't get me wrong. They're lovely. Precious, innocent souls, and that's half the problem. We live in a terrible world, Paloma." As she spoke, she held on to my face with those eerie blue eyes. "It's filled with awful people doing awful things. Why would I subject a child to the treachery? That anyone ever ends up happy is a damned miracle."

"No one is promised happy," I pointed out, and she sniggered.

"Oh, Paloma. I do so appreciate having a friend who's not prone to pep talks. I never worry about any wretched positive attitude when you're around. What about you?" she asked. "Any kids in the future, once this is all over?"

"I have a son. Paolo. He's nineteen years old."

"Nineteen!" Nikola blurted. "How old were you when you had him? Seven?"

I slapped the air, pretending to be embarrassed even though revealing his age is a most cherished pastime. Sometimes I round up for fun. The only fortune I inherited was my mother's skin, and I've spent a lifetime taking care of it.

"I *was* young," I said, beaming. "But not that young. Seventeen, to be exact."

Nikola went to say something and then froze. She placed a hand to her heart as the details wound through her brain. "Oh. Paloma. Your son. Where is he? Do you know? Is that why you were asking about Italian prisoners?"

"Maybe." I gave a little shrug. "He *was* with the Italian Army, but where he is now…" I let my words fall off. "I have no idea."

"That's terrible. I understand how hard not knowing can be, with my—" She shook her head and then draped an arm across me, almost like a hug. "Anyway, I'm sorry. I wish there was something I could do."

Before we go further, I must ask, where is Paolo now? This is the only reason I'm entertaining this interview. Now that I think about it, I'm almost certain he fought alongside the partisans, or else turned himself in to the Allies. He would not have chosen to back Hitler and Mussolini's fascist state. Paolo is too nice of a boy.

What do you mean, you can't tell me anything, "at this juncture"? All right. I will say a bit more, but I will not tell you everything, until you do the same for me.

28

NIKI

August 1944

Niki climbed up on the villa's roof. With the power almost perpetually out, Rome was dark most nights and ghostly quiet aside from the occasional hoot of an owl or the metallic rattle whenever a shopkeeper pulled down his door. Ordinarily Niki came here for solitude, and to work things out in her head, but now it seemed like *too* good of a place to think. What she really needed was for her brain to stop.

The POWs had been gone a week and were expected to cross back at any time. Niki and Will had been alternating shifts in the safe house so someone would be there to debrief the men when they returned, *if they returned*. The wait was almost unbearable, each day bringing them nearer to some great or horrible result, each day increasing the number of times Moggy asked why Niki sometimes disappeared for eight to ten hours at a time.

"She's going to figure out things aren't what they seem," Ezra warned. "Your sister-in-law may be naïve, but she's not dumb. You should just come clean."

Alas, Moggy was (mostly) his problem now. Upon Niki's counsel, she'd drafted the cartoonist into a unlikely friendship, and now spent large swaths of time pummeling him with all the usual Moggy things. Where did he get his uniforms tailored? Why did they need a cartoonist on staff? What do you mean some people can't read? I thought everyone went to school!

"Thank you *so* much for encouraging me to befriend Ezra!" Moggy had said earlier that night. "He was a little intimidating at first—calling everything stupid or pointless—but he tells the *most* interesting stories. And I'm thrilled to have another early riser in the office."

Early mornings weren't a preference for Ezra but an old habit that refused to die. When he last lived in Rome, roundups occurred between six and seven o'clock, and so Ezra woke at five thirty to ride his bike around the city to impersonate an ordinary citizen getting on with his day.

Niki's mind slid back to Pasha. Was he doing what Ezra once had and trying to carry on like a regular Czech? Where was he at that exact moment? Working in the family's factory? Serving the Wehrmacht? Was he even alive? Pasha was a man now, with dark, cropped hair the last time she'd seen him, but Niki couldn't stop picturing the curls that bounced as he chased her to school.

"Stop following me!" she'd squawk as her girlfriends giggled. "You'll go to school soon enough."

"He's so cute," her best friend, Jitka, would say. "Like a little pup." She'd then flip around, pinch her fingers together, and make kissing sounds. *"Here, boy!"*

Damned Pasha. For all the big sister shadowing he'd done in the course of his life, Niki couldn't believe *war* was when he decided to hang back. Deep down, she'd known her stern, stone-faced parents were unlikely to budge, but Niki thought if she convinced Pasha to go to America, they would also relent. He was always the favorite child, and in his refusal to follow Niki, he'd shown why.

"I can't leave," he'd said, without a second of vacillation. "This is our home. And our parents need me."

"Don't you care what's happening to our country? To our own neighbors?" Niki had pleaded.

Maddeningly, Pasha shrugged. "It's not my business," he said. "Everything will be fine."

Now Pasha felt further away than ever, and she was too afraid to press George. Niki couldn't risk reminding him that he had a wife he'd intended to visit. Perhaps with Moggy on the ground, he wouldn't feel the need to check on Niki himself. Again, Paloma's words rang in her head. *You seem too young to be tired of it... I know divorce is very popular with you Americans...* Was it? Niki wished she knew. But no, she couldn't do that to George. It'd be a slap in the face.

Alas, it was not the time to ruminate on the state of her marriage. Niki had more important concerns. She was slated to meet Will at the safe house soon, which meant they were one step closer to the conclusion—good or bad—of their first major mission. Pushing this traffic jam of thoughts aside, Niki stood and tossed her cigarette off the roof, into the blackness. There was no point in stewing. It was time to get on the road.

29

NIKI

August 1944

Niki stepped past the OSS guard and walked into the safe house, her feet echoing on the dusty wood floors. "Nick?" she called out. *"Captain Demart?"* The only light was from the full moon through the open windows, and she couldn't see a thing. "Hello?"

Niki took another step and then tripped, managing to stop herself before becoming a splat on the floor. *"Che cazzo!"* she cursed, looking back to see a lump of something on the ground. "Will! I mean Nick? Is that you?" With memories of Congressional Country Club flashing in her head, Niki scuttled to his side, dropped to her knees, and jammed three fingers against his neck. "Are you all right?" she said, feeling for a pulse, her own quickening as if to make up for any shortfall in his.

"Stop it!" Will said, and batted her away. "I'm fine."

"Jesus, you scared me." Niki sat back on her heels. Across the room, the last embers of a fire burned. "Next time tell me if you're going to start a fire," she grumbled. They had a limited amount of the duke's old Latin manuscripts to burn.

"Leave me alone," Will gargled.

"Are you okay? Is it your stomach, or...?" Will burped, fogging the room with Chianti vapor. "Oh. I see. We're crocked." Niki should've been irritated, but all she could think was, *good for him*. "So, what happened?" She lowered onto the floor beside him and tried brushing a sweat-soaked lock from his forehead, but the cowlick made it spring right back. "I've never seen you like this."

"I've never been like this. I was so worked up about what will happen with Sauerkraut, Ezra couldn't stand me anymore," Will said. "He gave me a bottle of red wine to take with me while I waited and said a glass would help. It did, and so I had four more."

"Classic mistake." Niki rolled her trousers up over her calves. "God, it's stuffy in here."

"How are people drunks?" he said. "This is miserable."

"Most people aren't really in it for the booze."

Will draped an arm over his eyes. "Then what's the point?"

Niki laughed as she picked up the bottle and peered inside. "You sound like Ezra," she said. "I suppose it's different for everyone. Many people want to feel something different. Others don't want to feel anything at all." She threw back the last dregs of the wine and smacked her lips. "This is pretty good," she said.

"Is that your trick?" Will said.

Niki glanced over. On account of the dark, she could see only his profile, mostly that strong and distinct chin. "My trick for what?" she asked.

"Your...disaffection. Sometimes I question whether you feel anything at all."

"Wow," Niki said, and felt a kick to her heart. "That's a hell of a thing to say."

"Sorry. That's not what I meant. Well. Maybe it is." His body seemed to slump further into the floor. "You're never truly bothered by anything."

"I'm bothered frequently. How many times did I yell at you during training?" Niki said. "You must have a very short memory."

"I've seen you upset, but it's always a flame that burns out quickly, and then you move on like it never happened. Your feelings...it's like they're fleeting." He sighed. "Which is off-putting but convenient, I guess. You must be the easiest person in the world to live with."

"Ha! That's the dumbest thing you've uttered in my presence," Niki said. "Too stupid to dignify with a response." If Will only knew that the one person who *did* live with Niki likely held a different opinion altogether.

"You never seem to worry for more than a minute or two," he went on. "Then it's back to business as usual. How are you always so positive things will work out?"

"Just goes to show you don't understand me at all." Niki attempted another swig of the wine, but the bottle was dry. "Mostly I figure things *won't* work out, so I usually have a backup plan, and try to stay one step ahead."

"All right, then," Will said. "What if our men are caught, or blow their covers? What's your backup plan then?"

"Desertion," Niki said. Will responded with a short laugh, but she was only halfway joking.

When it came to capitalizing on failed assassinations of maniacal despots and planned storm trooper celebrations, they had only one shot. The risk of failure was high, and the consequences immeasurable. What if the men were caught because they missed some trifle? Teddy, their forger, did good work, but Nazis changed their credentials and insignia constantly, and being one minute out of date could end lives. Not to mention, they produced everything—from identification papers to Nazi stamps to their fake communist rag—on the same printer. Nazi Party cards had to look official and *DND* as though it'd been produced in some dank basement on a hand-cranked machine. Authenticity was just one thing that could easily go sideways.

"Great, you'll desert me," Will said. "And I'll be left to take the fall."

"Oh, please. Even if I did desert, I'm the one they'd blame," Niki said. "I came up with the idea, and convinced Warner, and interviewed the POWs."

"But shit flows uphill, which means I'll be the one covered in it."

Fiddling with the cuff of her trousers, Niki weighed what she wanted to say, other than that Will had no clue. If they bungled this operation, it'd prove to George, and everyone else, that a woman had no business doing anything important. Niki would be sidelined for real, along with probably every other woman in Morale Operations.

"First of all, we're a team, and I'd never let you take the blame on your own," she said. "Second, has it ever occurred to you that if we fail, they'll chalk it up to a woman being involved?"

"What?" Will turned toward her, the dried gel making his hair crunch against the floor. "That's not true!"

Niki frowned, strangely disappointed Will couldn't grasp this. Maybe it wasn't fair, but she'd expected more from him. "The only reason they let me have this much influence is because I'm pushy and speak German."

"That's not true," Will said again. "Warner and the others believe in you."

"Then why is my husband in goddamned Bern, keeping an eagle eye on my activities? Why did he send his sister to baby-sit me?"

"Moggy doesn't have the wiles to spy on you," he said. "And

if George *did* dispatch her to look after you, I'm sure it's only because he's worried, and he cares. You're his wife. He wants you to be safe."

Niki snorted. "I assure you that's not the case."

"Well, if he did send his sister, that is absurd," Will said. "You might be the most capable person I've ever met. Why would you need a supervisor? Moggy told me you didn't even let her hold the bouquet when you signed your marriage license."

"Moggy loves to tell that story," Niki said, though she didn't necessarily believe it spoke to her so-called capability. Deep down, Niki probably just wanted to get the whole thing over with.

"If we were married," Will said, "I'd want *you* to be keeping tabs on me. You have three damn degrees and managed to get yourself out of a war-torn country. What has he done?"

"Oh, a few things," Niki said. For one, George would consider himself instrumental in the getting-her-out-of-Czechoslovakia part, which of course he was. "In any case, I appreciate your faith in me. That is very sweet."

Niki ran the empty wine bottle back and forth along the floor, pondering all the years behind her and those that still lay ahead. War had a way of putting everything else on hold, of focusing a person's attention on only today, which could be good or bad, depending.

"I'm flattered," Will said. Niki looked over and could just make out his eyes glinting in the dark. "This is the most consecutive minutes you've spent discussing your feelings."

"Is that what just happened? My apologies. It wasn't on purpose. Must've been the wind."

"There she goes again," he said, and Niki could practically hear him rolling his eyes. "You're a real expert, you know? Deflecting. Zigging. Zagging. Running constantly onward, no time to think. Always giving people eighty-five, ninety percent, but forever holding on to that last bit."

"You're not exactly an open book," Niki pointed out. "I've said way more about my personal life than you have about yours. I'm not ordinarily the prying type, but now it's your turn. How'd you meet Missus Dewart? Wasn't she a family friend or some such? That's all I've been able to get out of you so far."

"Caroline is the daughter of my father's first business partner."

"How sweet. Combining two powerful families. It was meant to be, I guess."

"Huh," Will said, though it was really more of a grunt. "*Meant to be* is not how I'd categorize it. More like an arranged marriage. It was assumed we'd end up together, just as it was assumed I'd take over the newspaper. Everything was set out for me before I even got there."

"I assume you proposed, voluntarily?"

"Well, yeah, I wasn't *forced* or anything," Will said. "Not directly. On some level, though, I felt I had to. Because I'd screwed up so much by that point, I kind of owed it to my family to step back in line. Prove I was worthy of the name."

Niki laughed, bewildered. "I can't fathom you screwing up, at least not in an upper-crust society way. Explosive devices, on the other hand..."

"Oh, you'd be surprised," he said. "That golf course was not the first thing I blew up. Don't get me wrong. Caroline is kind, and smart, and lovely. Totally devoted to our children."

Excellent at hiring the best nannies, Niki thought to herself.

"She's all the things you'd want out of a wife. There's absolutely nothing wrong with her."

"She does sound *magnificent*," Niki said, wondering not about Caroline but the children. He mentioned them infrequently—then again, so did his wife in her letters, according to him—but Niki could only picture miniaturized versions of Will running around, perhaps a pair of strangely tall eight-year-olds with strong jawlines and deep clefts in their chins. The image was at turns amusing and deeply upsetting, a reminder that, when this all ended, most people would be happy to return to their old lives.

"I shouldn't complain," Will added. "The poor woman puts up with *me*."

"A real trooper."

For several minutes, they remained silent, the only sound the wind rustling the dry brush outside.

"What about George?" Will said. "Unless you're accusing him of spying on you, you rarely bring up his name. He probably talks about *you* all the time. I would if I were him."

"Okay, that's enough," Niki said.

"You don't seem to like him very much," Will observed. "What gives?"

"Well. He has some positive notes. Unlike your spouse, I wouldn't say 'there's absolutely nothing wrong' with him, however."

"Then why?"

"Why *what*?"

"You don't have to stay married, do you?" Will said, and Niki whipped her head in his direction. "You got out of Czechoslovakia. You're a citizen, and you don't have kids. If you wanted to…" He released a small burp. "You could get divorced. Do you even need him anymore?"

Niki stiffened. "Gosh. Divorce is ever the hot topic these days," she said. Will was the last person Niki thought would make assumptions about the reason for her marriage, and anyway, she *did* need George, at least for now. Whether she could or should get a divorce was beside the point. "I'm disappointed, *Demart*," Niki said. "I didn't take you for one of *those*."

"One of what?"

"The people who look at someone like me and see a dirty, scheming foreigner." As Will protested, Niki pushed herself to standing. "No. It's fine. I get it. George came along at a very convenient time, but it did take me *years* to accept his proposal, and I was living in a Nazi-occupied country the whole time. So maybe it's not as straightforward as you think."

"Sorry. It just doesn't seem like you're that enthralled with the guy."

"Good Lord. You're even drunker than you smell. Please help us, dear Eurosia!" Niki said, casting her prayers up to the ceiling. "Patron saint of the demonically possessed, if you're curious."

"All I'm saying," Will continued, at his own peril, "is that if you don't need him, and you don't like him, why are you married?"

"This conversation is over. I don't want you to say anything else you'll regret," Niki steamed. Where did this privileged, white-gloved so-and-so get off interrogating *her* about life decisions? He married his childhood not-even-a-sweetheart and had no idea how the world actually worked. "Come find me when you sober up," she said, and tried to storm off but, because of the dark, only managed to stumble into an adjoining room.

"Nik, I'm sorry," Will shouted, his voice echoing off the bare walls. "I misspoke. For a newspaper guy, I'm miserable with words."

"Don't mention it." Niki meant this in all sincerity—she didn't want him to speak of it again. "This is me, moving on," she said, running her hand along the wall, groping for an exit. "Extinguishing my flame."

"I'm sorry," he said again, his voice cracking. "I didn't mean to give you guff. Obviously, the problem isn't your husband." He belched. "I'm a jealous idiot."

"You got the idiot part right."

"George is not the problem. The problem is, I wish it were me."

Niki froze. Something swelled in her, a feeling awfully close to a thrill. But it wasn't because of Will, she'd later tell herself, or what he said. It was because, at that very moment, the front door opened, and the OSS guard called out their (false) names.

Niki rushed to the foyer, where four wet, muddy men in Wehrmacht uniforms stood holding torches. It was the first team they'd sent out.

"You're back!" Niki said. Somewhere behind her, Will found his way to his feet. "What happened? Did you get the materials out?" She pulled a man's pack off his back, and it thumped onto the ground. The bag was still full.

"We didn't make it," one of the men confessed as Niki's mind swirled. "German patrols were manning the north and south sides of the river and the entire crossing area was under shellfire." They'd been fired on several times before getting anywhere near the line.

Niki kicked at the pack. "Goddamn it all to hell," she said as one of them made the sign of the cross. "What about the others? Have you heard any news?"

The POWs exchanged nervous looks.

"We don't know," someone said. "But I can't imagine they had more success. We were lucky to make it back without being captured. We were lucky to make it back alive."

30

May 1989

Geoffrey Jones clicks through more memorabilia from Operation Sauerkraut, which feels to Niki like a very precise brand of torture.

As the slides flash by, Niki tries to concentrate on her baked Alaska, but the images pull her in, deluging her with old, overwhelming emotions and carrying her back to those heady months in Rome. Her mind replays every memory, every sensation she can recall, from the pride in their work, to the agony of waiting for news, to all the victories and failures, large and small. Niki feels the near misses, and lucky breaks, the pain of each catastrophic decision.

"Cameras were not allowed overseas," Geoffrey says, "but some naughty employee at MO Rome must've snuck one in, because we do have photographic evidence of their exploits."

Ezra. Niki smiles, and the tears catch in her throat. On-screen is a photograph of the printing office, with its mounds of paper, as far as the lens can see. "It seems the folks in Rome weren't the tidiest bunch," Geoffrey says with a wink. The crowd chuckles.

Click. As Niki takes in the next picture, a whimper crawls up from her chest. It's *them*—her and Will. Niki is seated, looking sporty and gamine, like some combination of Audrey Hepburn and a young Judy Garland, which she realizes only in hindsight. Will leans against her desk, all big-chinned and dimpled, eyes crinkled at the corners as he smiles without showing his teeth.

Andrea notices something has shifted. "Mom?" she says, placing a hand on her arm. "What's going on? Is that...?"

Niki scrambles for something to say. *Yes, that's me. Who's the man? Don't worry, he's no one.*

"Did you know those people?" Andrea asks.

Niki feels a thump, as though she's been bumped from behind. She hadn't wanted to answer any tough questions yet is somehow devastated that Andrea doesn't recognize her own mother grinning on-screen. Of course, it is entirely Niki's fault. Andrea has no context for what she's seeing because Niki deliberately kept this part of her life hidden, never willing to disrupt a contented existence to drag her child down into the dark, cobwebby past.

"Hey. Mom. Are you okay?" Andrea says, jiggling her again. "Should we step out?"

"I'm fine, darling," Niki answers, and waves her away. A tear slips down her cheek. "It's the memories. They can be wily devils. Every once in a while, a few pop up out of nowhere." Almost like an emotional attack.

31

NIKI

August 1944

Niki flew into the office, heart flickering like a bird's, hair probably looking like its nest. "Hello, Ezra!" she said, rushing past with a large stack of papers cradled in her arms. "Is Dewart in the office?"

"Sure is. Hey, watch ou—"

Before he could complete the sentence, Niki's feet met with an obstruction, and she was soon hurtling toward a metal cabinet. It was the second live body she'd tripped over this week, but Niki didn't have the excuse of the dark this time.

"Moggy?" she said, circling back and regretting it almost immediately. "Why are you on the ground?" Niki reached down to pet Kunkel's dog, Pierre, who was lying beside her. "This isn't going to turn into a whole thing, is it?" she said. "I really need to meet with Will as soon as possible." By some miracle, Project Sauerkraut was maybe not going down in flames, and Niki wanted to be the first one to tell him.

"It's not a 'thing,' and feel free to carry on with your business," Moggy sniffed. "For your information, I'm conserving energy while I wait for Kunkel to return from his errands." She tried to sneeze, but her position prevented it.

"Where is that stupid man?" Ezra said. "Undertaking errands of mischief, no doubt. You'd think that as much as he leaves the office, he'd walk his own dog every once in a while."

"At least it gives me something to do." Moggy jimmied herself up onto her elbows. "Why am I here?"

Ezra peered over his glasses. "Do you mean, in the world?"

"No!" Moggy snapped. "What is the purpose of my role in Rome? Everyone calls my Jungian studies pointless, but now my entire existence involves feeding a dog, extending the lives of various office products, and occasionally filing a piece of paper."

"Not for nothing, but eking out the supplies *is* very important," Niki said.

"Speaking of," Ezra added, "if a paper clip can't be returned to paper clip shape, probably best to throw it away. Also, I don't need any more pencil nubs."

"I really can't have this conversation right now," Niki said. "I need to discuss some urgent matters with Dewart."

"What's happened?" Ezra said as he walked around to the other side of his desk. "Did something go wrong? You're never this frantic." He scratched his chin. "Hold on a minute. Could it be the opposite? Did MO finally find a modicum of success? Goodness! This is quite the development. We should probably put out a press release."

Niki gave him two middle fingers, nearly dropping her papers in the process. "Yes, we've had success, and I'll fill you in later," she said. After using her knee to reorganize the stack,

Niki pivoted and raced into her office, where Will looked up from his desk, eyes wide as she slammed the door.

"What's wrong?" he said.

"They're *back*," Niki sang, practically dancing up to his desk. "Teams two and three made it through enemy lines!" Because her heart was running at approximately one thousand beats per minute, she couldn't spit out the words as quickly as she wanted to say them. They'd done it. By God, their plan had worked.

"And they're all…"

"Alive! Yes. And unharmed." Niki dumped the paperwork on his desk. "I've spent the past five hours collecting the data. Their observations, mostly. People are reading our newspaper, Will. Some enemy soldiers were quoting from it."

"Wow." Will picked up the first sheet of paper, studying it thoughtfully even though he couldn't read German.

"One prisoner saw an entire eight-man SS patrol huddled around, gawking over the stuff about Hitler being on his deathbed," Niki said. "They even kept the pamphlets. They tucked them into their jackets!" If Niki were the squealing type, she would've done so now. "Honestly, I figured we'd lose a man or two—"

"What? Niki! You can't think like that."

"See? I don't assume everything will work out," she said. "I'm a realist, and our prisoners were interacting with Nazis, who shoot people just for kicks. But they're alive!"

"Wow," Will said again. He grinned, all dimples and chin, and Niki's heart and soul swelled. She couldn't remember any victory ever feeling so sweet. "Congratulations, Niki." His smile expanded. "You did it. You came up with this plan and put it into action."

"Aw, thanks," Niki said, and took a moment to bask in the warmth of his admiration. It was a good feeling, probably a dangerous one, if she stayed in it too long. "But I didn't do it alone. You were instrumental."

The warmth would not dissipate. This accidental affection,

Niki reasoned, was at least two-thirds Paloma's fault. Like an evil scientist, she'd planted the notion of William Dewart as a sexually compelling character into Niki's brain. Then Will exacerbated the situation with his "I wish it were me" comment, even though him being married to an Eastern European refugee was doubtless his family's worst nightmare.

Though neither had brought it up, the conversation was still sitting there, rotting away untouched, hard to ignore but impossible to get rid of. Will was unlikely to raise the point—if he even remembered what he said—and Niki would do the kind thing and pretend it never happened. Men said the most asinine things when they were drunk.

"I'm proud of you," Will said as he walked toward her.

"Of us," Niki clarified. Blushing, she whirled around to plunk down in her chair. "You know what this means, don't you? If the soldiers are reading our propaganda and talking about it to others, it's going to spread like a communicable disease through the ranks. Imagine if this half-assed office made a difference." She reached into a drawer. "Time to report our success. Toot our own horns and prepare for the next mission. I'll bet you regret doubting me now."

"What are you talking about?" Will said. "When have I ever doubted you? Name one time." He sat on the edge of her desk. "Go on. I'll wait. I have all day."

"Well, you didn't say it outright," Niki allowed. "But you were perpetually three seconds from throwing your rifle into the rye. I could tell."

"Here we go with another nonsensical Czech saying." Will tried to roll his eyes, though couldn't complete the gesture to full effect. Instead, he shook his head and laughed. "I was just worried about *patting a snake with my bare feet.*"

"Not the correct context." Niki fed a piece of paper into the typewriter. "Nice try, though." She couldn't remember the last time she was this happy.

TO: Director of OSS

"Hello, comrades," Ezra said, poking his head through the door. He had a camera strung around his neck.

"Don't let Warner see you with that," Niki said. It didn't matter whether someone was stationed on the front lines or in a propaganda office in the Rear Zone. No one in the army was allowed to have a camera.

"I'm sorry, do you follow rules now?" Ezra said with a fiendish smile. "So, what's all the hubbub about?"

"Operation Sauerkraut is an official, unmitigated success!" Niki said.

"Excellent." Ezra brandished his camera. "What do you say, people? A picture for posterity? It's not every day this stupid office accomplishes something. It's usually no days."

He raised the camera to his face, and Niki grinned. The flashbulb popped while somewhere in the office, a door opened and closed.

"All right, there's your souvenir." Niki returned to her typewriter. "Now put that away before you get in trouble, and let me focus on my report. We need to get this out as quickly as possible so we can start on Sauerkraut II," she said, and began to furiously type. "I can't *wait* until they read about our accomplishment in Washington. MO Rome is going to help win this war, and they'll be thanking us with medals. Maybe even a parade."

"Gosh," someone said, and cleared his throat. "A parade? Now that is something."

While Niki's eyes flew up, her adrenaline crashed to the ground. She opened her mouth but would never know whether any words came out.

"Can I help you?" she heard Will say, but it was like an echo, a sound happening in another room, if not another galaxy.

"I don't think so, chap," the voice answered. "The name's George Clingman, and I've come to relieve the loneliness of my beautiful, overly spirited wife."

SECRET

Office Memorandum | **UNITED STATES GOVERNMENT**
TO: Director of OSS
DATE: 3 August 1944
FROM: Pvt. Nikola Novotna (MO, Rome)
THROUGH: Swiss Desk, Bern
SUBJECT: SAUERKRAUT brief

PERSONNEL

Pvt. Nikola Novotna
Cpt. William Dewart
Ezra Feldman
Lt. Jack Daniels
Edward Zinder
Egidio Clemente
12 German Prisoners of War

SITUATION

On 21 July, after we received news of an attempt on Hitler's
life, we convened a meeting to discuss ways to exploit the
situation. Due to a lack of air support and the fact that Swiss
and Italian partisans have proven unreliable, ordinary methods of disseminating propaganda were not available to our
unit. To solve this problem, Captain Dewart and I devised a
novel and daring approach: use a crop of trustworthy German Prisoners of War.

Drawn from the cage at Aversa, the chosen POWs, all of
whom voluntarily surrendered, were thoroughly interviewed
and security-checked. After Captain Dewart and I made the
final selection of men, they were taken to a villa outside
Rome to be trained, equipped, and briefed. Lieutenant Daniels outfitted the men with proper uniforms and equipment,
and Zinder made sure they had adequate credentials. Egidio
Clemente oversaw the printing of three thousand pieces of
material, including pamphlets, leaflets, stickers, as well as

copies of Das Neue Deutschland, the underground peace party newspaper. Within three days, the German POWs were ready to be sent through enemy lines.

EQUIPMENT

The POWs were equipped for their mission with the following.

1. Steel helmets and uniforms.

2. Proper identification papers and passes.

3. Beretta pistols and German rifles.

4. Forty rounds of ammunition each.

5. American compasses.

6. Italian and Swiss watches.

7. 5000 Italian lira each.

8. Stationery.

9. First aid packets.

10. Italian cigarettes for bartering.

11. 3000 pieces of MO material.

DETAILS

Training of the POWs was completed by 25 July. At 1900 on this same date, an OSS officer arrived to drive the men to the infiltration point.

Upon arriving at the infiltration point, the 12 POWs were divided into 3 teams of 4. Group 1 departed at midnight, Groups 2 and 3 at dawn. A different OSS officer led each group across no-man's-land and to a location on the Arno

River. The men crossed the river on their own, after which they were instructed to crawl through the wire and mines to reach the main line of resistance. Safely entering enemy territory was itself a tremendous accomplishment, and we were pleased to learn that both Groups 2 AND 3 made it this far.

Upon entering enemy territory, the men fanned out, depositing propaganda inside officers' quarters, near sleeping soldiers, at aid stations, in ambulances, and in trucks bound for Germany. Materials were dropped in latrines, warehouses, and other high-traffic locations. They were tacked to trees, fences, and buildings, and hidden in toolboxes and gas mask canisters.

Groups 2 and 3 returned at 0500 on 3 August and reported completion of their mission. They had been able to move freely, traveling as deep as three miles into the territory. The POWs reported many instances of enemy troops reading the MO material, including one 8-man SS patrol who discussed the leaflets at length and put them in their pockets.

Group 1 had less success. They returned at 2255 on the 1st, reporting they'd failed to cross.

FINAL CONCLUSION

The new technique of infiltrating POW agents back into enemy lines was a proven success. The agents were thoughtful about dissemination. They didn't "dump" their materials but instead placed the pieces with great forethought and care. Because the agents were German nationals, they attracted little attention and were able to safely linger as soldiers discussed the leaflets.

Throughout the mission, no instance of a double agent was revealed, security was never blown, and only one man was asked for his credentials. The agents reported that the most difficult challenge was avoiding the partisans, who tend to shoot first and ask questions later.

Following these spectacular results, we will immediately put into action SAUERKRAUT II. This will require keeping

8 of the 12 POWs and sourcing 4 new recruits. All twelve POWs used for SAUERKRAUT I were trustworthy, but we now have a better understanding of the type of backgrounds which make for the best agents. We expect only greater success as we fine-tune our approach. Psychological warfare is an important component of the overall battle, and MO Rome will continue to aid the Allies in their march toward victory.

32

NIKI

August 1944

Niki sprang out of the bed and felt on the ground for her trousers and shirt. "I can't believe it happened again," she said, slipping into her pants. She'd been trying to soldier through, fulfill her wifely duties, but was left upset and frustrated, yet again. If they couldn't get the bedroom part of their marriage right, how would anything else work?

"You can't blame me," George called out from the bed. "It's your fault."

"So you keep telling me," Niki said, buttoning her pants.

"Where do you think you're going?" George scooted into an upright position. He snatched a pack of cigarettes from the bedside table. "It's past curfew. Someone could mistake you for a prostitute."

Wouldn't be the worst thing in the world, Niki thought as she tightened her jacket. She was hot with rage, drenched in a furious sweat, but the coat felt like a piece of armor, a layer protecting her from her husband's words.

"I don't know what you're so crabby about," George said.

"Oh, I think you do. Once again, we were unable to—" She waved a hand. "*Consummate.* But I suppose you'll blame me again."

"Who else would I blame?" he said with a mean little chuckle. "Before we married, I had many exploits in the boudoir, and nary an issue until you came along. I say this out of love, but if you worked a little harder, endeavored to make yourself more appealing, you'd likely do a better job." With a deeply smug expression plastered across his face, George cackled again and ran a hand through his black, floppy hair.

Niki leveled her gaze on his. "Speaking of making oneself appealing, what's with the 'do?" she said, incensed, though not really about the hair. "I'd expect men who worked for the *Office of Strategic Services* to be a tad more clean-cut. Especially those reporting directly to Allen Dulles." Niki waited for him to catch on, to break down her words.

After a five-to six-second pause, George shook his head and then laughed exactly like a man who knew he'd always get to call the shots. To think, Niki had once been charmed by his swagger, before she understood that American men were practically baptized in confidence at birth.

"You finally figured out where I work," George said, and lit a cigarette, one of *her* cigarettes, a direct affront. "Sorry for keeping it to myself, but I wasn't authorized to say anything. I dropped several hints but..." He shrugged and inhaled.

"I've known for months," Niki said, with as much nonchalance as she could muster. "Well, Mr. Big Shot, if you're so tight with Dulles, why won't you tell me what's happening with my family? Is my brother fighting? Are my parents alive? You must know more than you've let on."

George frowned, his features collapsing into an expression that could be mistaken for regret. "I don't know more," he said, and Niki almost believed him. "Though not for lack of trying. I keep my ear constantly to the ground and badger Dulles whenever he or someone else mentions the Protectorate, but nothing so far."

"Please. Don't call it that," Niki said. "Isn't there anything you can do, to find out more, if the information isn't coming to you? Can't you dispatch agents into the territory, to see what's going on?"

"Oh. Niki." With that, George's frown spiked back into a smile. A severe smile, honed and sharp like a blade. "You just love to ask for favors, don't you? Special treatment. Planes. Prisoners to do your dirty work. The list goes on and on."

"The prisoners?" Niki said. "Who told you about the POWs?" She'd filed the Sauerkraut memo, but only on her way out the door, *after* George had arrived. How could he have already known?

"The entire point of my office is to stay one step ahead." George shook his head and exhaled. "Niki, you must stop using POWs immediately. It was a cute little scheme, and you got away with it this time, but you're not going to get that lucky again. It will only end badly for you."

"I know what you're doing," Niki said. "You want me to doubt myself. It kills you that Sauerkraut was a success, and that I was at the helm."

"You were at the helm, all right." George took a deep pull on his cigarette, coughing violently as the smoke wound its way down his throat. Niki's stomach curdled. With one inhale, her husband had single-handedly made cigarettes the most abhorrent vice in the world.

"You are full of shit," Niki said. "It was such an ingenious plan, so completely novel, I wouldn't be surprised if it's implemented in other theaters of operation. They'll probably put it in the handbook."

"Yes, indeed, novel it was," George said, and ground his cigarette into the bedside table instead of stretching an inch to reach the ashtray. "So novel it violates the Geneva Convention."

Niki froze. The Geneva Convention? She had only the most basic idea of what this entailed, though thought violations were usually on a grander, more treacherous scale, like using poisonous gases or committing genocide. Niki hadn't killed or maimed anyone, as far as she knew.

"You seem surprised, darling," George said with a snicker. "I thought you were so learned, so knowledgeable about international customs and laws. Well, let me give you a quick education. The Geneva Convention prohibits countries and their representatives from employing prisoners in unhealthy or dangerous work."

"All the POWs returned without a scratch," Niki said, her voice teetering.

"What's more, it also forbids POWs from engaging in any activity directly connected to the operations of war. If what you're doing is so important, so critical to the effort," he said, offering a wink, "then you'd better proceed with great caution, lest you end up accused of a war crime."

"You are full of shit," Niki seethed, her heart booming like thunder. There was no way what she'd done was a war crime. Warner would've stopped her.

"Am I full of shit?" George asked. "Or is this just another story you'll tell yourself to get by? You know, I was skeptical about you being in the OSS, but propaganda really is the best use of your skills."

"I'm going for a walk," Niki said, and swiped her shoes from the floor. "If you're not gone when I get back, I'm going to pay a pack of *ragazzini* to drag you out. I will cause a scene."

"That's fine treatment for your one-and-only. Where do you propose I find a hotel this time of night?"

"There are plenty of empty bedrooms in this villa," Niki said. "Or in one of the others. Fascists have a lot of children, apparently. Figure it out. Goodbye, George."

Niki pivoted on a heel and left, dizzy with loathing as she plodded down the hall. George was bluffing. He had to be. That man was a pro at making Niki question her own interpretation of things.

God, how Niki wished she could cut him out of her life. *Do you even need him anymore?* Will had asked. She didn't need him for citizenship, but he was her sole lifeline to Czechoslovakia, and if she caused too many problems, he could have her dispatched to a different, much worse theater of operation. *C̆urák!* Motherfucker!

Shoes dangling from her fingertips, Niki crept toward the back door. As she passed the courtyard, she saw Ezra sitting in the garden, smoking a cigarette. Where Niki had the roof, Ezra preferred the stone bench as a place to think, and she was not surprised to find him there. Earlier that day, he'd run into friends from architecture school. *Ghosts and shadows,* he'd called them. *Miserable people who don't even realize how bad off they are.* Niki would've joined him, but Ezra wasn't the type who wanted comfort. He'd tell her to mind her own stupid business if she stepped a foot outside.

Instead, without a destination in mind, Niki slipped out of the villa and into the warm night, happy to escape George, but wishing it could be for longer than a few hours.

33

PALOMA

May 1945

I was leaving an assignation—with who, it is none of your business—when I saw a short but determined figure scampering along the road. It was very plainly Nikola, for I have never seen a person walk like her, practically hovering, skimming the ground like a hummingbird.

"Ciao, bella!" I shouted, waggling my arm overhead. *"Vieni qua!"*

Nikola dashed over and, from the look on her face, I thought for a moment that I had done something to upset her. *Ah, che tajo!* Not yet. All in good time.

"I don't have any cigarettes," she told me, though this was not the sole reason I entertained her company. I had come to like the girl, for more than what she could give me. *"Li ha mio marito,"* Nikola added, emphasizing the word *marito*—husband.

"Anvedi! He must've arrived for his much anticipated visit! Here, you share mine." I offered her one of my cigarettes, and she examined it, mouth puckered. *"Me dispiace!"* I said, feeling prickly. "Do you not like this brand?"

"These are perfectly fine," she said, continuing to eye it. "But smoking seems less appealing all of a sudden." She took the smoke regardless.

"It sounds as though you are not having very much fun with the husband," I noted. After a visual sweep of the streets, I backed up and leaned against a building. We were not permitted to be out this time of night, and thus I needed to stay in the shadows. This was one benefit to the lack of electricity—it was easier to work. "What is the problem?" I asked. "What is so bad about the reunion?"

Sucking on her cigarette, Nikola pondered this deeply, revealing without speaking that it was more than one thing. "We work for some of the same people," she said at last. "George and me. Even though he's usually hundreds of miles away, he's a distraction. I can almost feel him peering over my shoulder, which makes it very difficult to do my job, or get any satisfaction from it whatsoever."

"Satisfaction from work?" I pulled a face. *"Non importa, non importa.* Work is for paying the bills. You are not supposed to like it. I've never had an orgasm with my customers, for instance."

Nikola chortled softly. "Well, I don't need *that* level of satisfaction," she said. "I just want to do well, but George wants me to fail." She locked her eyes onto mine. "I can't let it happen, Paloma. I can't let him get to me."

"Because you are the woman of the office."

"Something like that." She took another pull on her cigarette.

"May I ask you, why do you stay married?" I said. "You know I am against divorce, but mostly for good Catholics, and you are not one. War is a nice chance to leave someone, yes? Because there is already some kind of break."

"As lovely as it sounds, divorce is not something I can consider right now," Nikola said. "There are...several factors at play."

"He would refuse?" I guessed. "Or his family would?"

"Yes, that's part of it..." She sighed, and I patted her arm.

I understood her position and am all too familiar with the notion of doing something unsavory for a different but better end. "Where is he now?" I said. "The husband? You should not be out here alone, on these dark and dangerous streets."

"He's back at the villa. We had an argument."

"About what?" I asked.

Nikola ogled me for a great long while. It must've been a very nasty row, I thought, if she struggled to relay the story to a prostitute.

"Nikola?" I pressed.

"Let me ask you a question," she said. "About men, in general. You might be able to solve something for me since you're presumably well-versed in the species."

"Indeed!" I grinned, pleased to be of service in this way. "I've experienced a wide breadth of men, a carnival of every length and shape and fortitude. What is it you need to know? Is something bent slightly to the left, or the right? Is it too small, or too large to comfortably entertain?"

"Jeez, Paloma." Nikola's face flamed, the redness visible even in the deep black night. "Warn a girl before you're going to come out with something like that. The problem is... I don't know how to put this, but... Have you ever slept with a man who is...uh..." She winced. "On the *softer* side?"

"Do you mean...?" I extended my arm straight and then let it fall limp. She confirmed my guess with a nod as her gaze bounced around. *"Ahò!"* I hooted. "No wonder you do not like marriage. Your husband cannot perform." Poor little one. My own husband is much older than hers and has no trouble staying hard. It is one of his greatest qualities as well as his downfall. *"Mia cara,"* I said, trying to assure her. "This happens all the time. *Boh.* Not *all* the time, but I have met many men in the situation. Often they come to me hoping I can fix them."

"And does it work?" she asked. "Are you able to uh…ameliorate the problem?"

"Mostly, no. Sometimes he has a physical issue. Sometimes it is in his head. Many prefer a different type of person. Perhaps this is your husband's ailment?" When Niki gave me a bunched-up sort of look, I amended, "I'm speaking of other men."

"What?" Nikola quacked. "No way. Not George."

"It's more common than you might assume." In my opinion, she should've given this some consideration. With her attire and horribly flat chest, it was quite possible this George preferred the androgynous sort.

"I really can't see it," Nikola said. "According to my father-in-law, George was *quite* the playboy before we met. He had a whole line of girls willing to do whatever he asked."

"That is an interesting comment to make to someone's new wife."

"I think it was his way of telling me I was lucky," she said.

I laughed, all too accustomed to long lines of women. "How is this lucky?" I asked. "Any man can fuck. Except yours, evidently."

"He says it's my fault, and maybe it is," she said. "Maybe I'm doing something wrong. I wasn't, uh…" She glanced away again. "I wasn't *in*experienced when we married, but I also wasn't an expert. I've never seen *that* before, but I don't have many examples to draw from. George swears it never happened to him until I came along."

"Of course this is what he'd swear! Best to blame the woman," I said. "Didn't you tell me something similar, about your work?"

"That's true, but…"

"I'm astounded you've not fully learned this by now," I said. "I thought you were supposed to be smart? Alas, there is something good here. Something you can use."

"The whole problem is, I can't use it," she said.

"No, *sciocchina*," I said. "Two minutes ago, you told me that divorce sounds 'lovely.' Here is the idea. You use this information to get out. Either he lets you leave, or you inform everyone of *il cazzo fradicio*. No man wants this in the public domain."

"Paloma! That is an outrageous suggestion!" Niki said, even as I sensed her squirreling away the information. "No. Absolutely not. I couldn't do that. And it's about more than whether he'd agree to it." She exhaled and used her old cigarette to light a new one. "I've thought enough about George's penis for one day. Let's talk about something else."

And so we did, remaining on the street for another hour, perhaps two. Though we moved on to other topics, my brain was stuck on George's deficiencies. Tell me, do you know what happened with the husband? They aren't together, are they? I am only a whore, but I'd like to think I gave her winning advice, advice I hope she's already used, given what I just revealed. *Boh!* I'd feel terrible if I spilled the secret, if I let the cat out of its very limp bag!

34

NIKI

Now that Niki had seen George off to the train station, accompanied by a dispassionate kiss on the cheek, it was time to put spousal troubles in the rearview mirror. George was not going to intimidate Niki into shutting down Sauerkraut II.

The POWs were at present holed up in the safe house, waiting for their next assignment and growing more restless by the day. Niki hated checking on them now, their salutes and "yes, ma'am"s replaced with catcalls and lewd comments. After one grabbed her by the waist, Niki was left with no choice but to ball up her fist and give him a good old-fashioned knuckle sandwich, to the great amusement of the other prisoners, who whooped and clapped. It was the most entertainment they'd had in months. These men were turning into animals and needed to be put to work, and fast.

"Hello, friends!" Niki called, wafting into the office.

"Hi, Niki," Moggy said, looking up from her daily gossip huddle with Ezra. The combination of his dry, world-weary personality and Moggy's dogged inquisitiveness could be exhausting, but Niki was glad they had each other. If nothing else, the friendship kept Moggy occupied and Ezra from needling them about the POWs. Like George, he thought using former German soldiers was a horrifically bad idea, though his reasons were different. *I wouldn't trust 'em to walk Kunkel's dog.*

"What are we chattering about?" Niki asked, almost afraid to pose the question. With these two, it was never what a person might expect.

"I was asking Ezra what rights he had in Romania as a child," Moggy explained.

"Spoken like a true American," Ezra said. "What are these rights you speak of? We had none! I went to school wearing a numbered nameplate as if I were an automobile—LMB586, for identification and denunciation. The entire educational experience was an inferno of screams, slaps, and heads dunked in toilets. I hardly learned a thing at Lycée Basarab, other than that Jews are social pariahs."

"How awful!" Moggy exclaimed.

"Don't pity me. I was thrilled not to participate in the dreadful so-called 'freedoms' of the upper classes, which were invariably abuses of others," he said. "I'd rather be the underdog."

"Oh," was the only answer Moggy could muster. Niki knew how she felt. Sometimes, with Ezra, it was impossible to know what to say.

"Carry on," Niki said. "I don't want to get in the way of this scintillating conversation."

"I'm glad you find my lack of personal rights scintillating," Ezra carped.

Chuckling, Niki continued on toward her office, shaking her head.

"Finally," Will said when she threw open the door. "Where have you been? You said you'd be here by lunch, and now it's almost dinner. Why are you never on time? You really need to do a better job of estimating how long a task will take."

"It's not my fault. People are always getting in my way, holding everything up." Niki tossed her things on the desk and plopped down in her chair. "I was at the safe house. The boys are itching for their next assignment." She stopped to rub her hand. "I think one guy broke his nose somehow? In any case, we need to get cracking on Sauerkraut II. Internal reports are showing a drop in troop morale in northern Italy, but no one is connecting it to us. For this next go-around, we need comebacks, evidence that our message is getting through."

This was the chief problem with psychological warfare, Niki had learned. It was almost impossible to prove it worked, or that people were reading their materials at all. "The prisoners saw them do it" was worth only so much, and the propaganda skeptics at the top were not inclined to give MO credit for much.

"Comebacks would be great," Will agreed. "But easier said than done. I've spent hours trying to drum up ideas." He shrugged.

"I know, I know." Niki flapped a hand and then paused to ruminate. "What if we—" she began, her germ of a thought broken up by a yell. It was Warner, screaming Will's name.

"Dewart!" he called. "Where the fuck is Dewart?"

Niki glanced at Will. "Gosh. How will he ever find you?"

"My own desk is a tremendous hiding place."

"He's in his office," Niki heard Ezra say. "And please, stop hollering. I have a burst eardrum thanks to playtime with my brother. That's what happens when you don't have toys."

"No toys?" Moggy yelped.

"Well, we got some courtesy of the Hoover relief. Double-decker buses and sailboats. But these were things to revere, not play with."

"Ezra, that is so sad."

"What the fuck is this memo I just read?" Warner said, blustering into their office. "About your goddamned Sauerkraut?" His skin was bright red, his eyes mere dots beneath his heavy brow.

"Are you referring to our highly successful mission?" Niki said, batting her lashes.

"*Successful?*" Warner roared, his spittle flying. "Lady, your brain doesn't work so well if you think routinely using POWs to distribute propaganda is a winning idea."

"Settle down, Warner," Will said, standing, hitching up his pants. "Why are you so worked up about the POWs? You knew about this. You gave Private Novotná the okay."

"I most assuredly did not! Your gal Friday told me the idea was to make Washington give us air support. It was supposed to be a bluff!"

"Noooo," Niki said. As she felt Will's hot gaze on her neck, her nerves began to mount. "It was an either-or situation. Better yet, win-win. Air support or POWs. Alas, no air support, and thus the POW plan was put into action."

"I said you could experiment by having a *few* men distribute a *handful* of propaganda," Warner ranted. "But I was quite clear that you shouldn't view this as an official strategy, and at no point did we discuss writing a goddamned memo spelling it out for all of OSS to see!"

"Huh," Niki said. "I must've misinterpreted the conversation. My apologies." She flashed Will a quick, meek smile. Though Niki might've pushed the boundaries of what they'd agreed to, it was one of those ask-forgiveness-not-permission deals, and she thought Will had understood that. A few POWs for experimentation's sake, or twelve for real, what did it matter? The plan worked, and Warner should take the accolades for being head of the team.

The Geneva Convention, she heard George say. Was it possible he hadn't been full of shit? "What's the problem, Warner?" Niki said, with a hard, dry gulp. "Did someone complain?"

"Well, no..." Warner said, and Niki's heart thumped in relief.

Their clever idea wasn't a war crime. Of course it wasn't. The notion was patently absurd. Niki rattled her head, pitching George's warnings from her brain. "If no one complained, I fail to see the issue," she said as something behind Warner moved, a burst of polka dot. "Anyway, we shouldn't discuss Sauerkraut in the open." The figure moved again. "Not everyone is briefed on the project."

"You're right," Warner said. "You and me, Dewart. In my office. Now." As Niki rose to her feet, the chief waved her away. "Just need the captain for this," he said, then spun around, and immediately bumped up against Moggy. "Jesus Christ! Where the hell did you come from?" he spit.

"I was only..." she began, but Warner shoved her out of the way. Will trailed after the chief, eyes cast to the ground.

"Che cazzo di inferno," Niki muttered, hands on hips. It wasn't that she wanted to be yelled at, but Niki *was* the person who'd come up with the idea, the one who'd authored the memo that'd gotten Warner so hot. Good grief. A woman couldn't even get credit for messing up around here. Not that she had, in this case.

"Do you have a minute?" Moggy squeaked.

"Yes." Niki flopped back into her chair. "In fact, I have all the minutes," she said, and Moggy took a few cautious steps forward, creeping into the room. "Seeing as how those two jokers just cut me out of my own project. Nice outfit, by the way. Someone is trying to revive the bolero."

"Thank you." Moggy dipped her head. "I'm sorry you were excluded. That can feel terrible. But, times like these, I find it's best to let the men be in charge."

"Letting the men be in charge is why we're in a war in the first place." Niki sighed deeply. "Well, Moggy, what do you need? I feel as though I've barely seen you lately. Half the time

I'm convinced you're avoiding me." Niki laughed, and Moggy's face went white. "Wait. *Are* you avoiding me?"

"I'm concerned," Moggy said. "About the conduct in this office, and I've been debating when and how to bring this up. It's about Sauerkraut. The things you and Dewart are doing in this office."

"*George,*" Niki fumed.

Moggy blinked. "My brother has nothing to do with this," she said, then reconsidered. "I mean, a little. But not really. No one can give me a straight answer about what you and Will and Jack Daniels are up to. Even Ezra mutters something about 'supposedly nice Nazis' and clams up when I ask! I recognize that everyone in Rome has their own duties. We're in different divisions, and I should probably mind my own business, but something fishy is afoot. I found this." Moggy reached beneath her bolero and pulled out a postcard. "And others like it."

Niki stretched forward, squinting, at once recognizing it as Sauerkraut material. *Comrades! Hitler will not be able to escape his fate. Even though the latest attempt has failed, he will be executed sooner or later!*

"Where did you find that?" Niki asked.

"The Rumors guy had a stack on his desk," Moggy explained. "He told me the entire point of your division is to create these materials."

"*Zkurvysyn,*" Niki cursed. Rumors guys were the worst, and it seemed they would have to fire yet another one of them. "By the by, there's more to our division than postcards."

"This is not the problem," Moggy said. "From what I can tell, the information on these pieces of paper isn't…exactly based in fact. Niki. Please tell me the truth. Are we making up lies? Creating misinformation? I saw something about Munich being completely destroyed, that there's not a building left standing, but I haven't been able to find anything to confirm that in the English language newspapers."

"I thought you couldn't read German?" Niki said, sweat percolating on the back of her neck. She yanked the postcard from Moggy's hand and used it to fan her face.

"I know *a little*," Moggy said. "There were loads of Germans at the Institute, and Ezra helped me translate the rest."

"How thoughtful! What a reliable friend!" Niki was beginning to think that every male, no matter how great, was obligated to act like a motherfucker a certain number of times per week.

"I found these as well." After reaching back into her dress, Moggy removed several more postcards and slapped each one down on the desk with a thwack, like she was dealing blackjack. Translations were scribbled on every card.

Hitler is on his deathbed.

Several high-ranking German officers have created a new government.

GERMANY HAS NOW BEEN LIBERATED FROM THE BROWN PESTILENCE!

"I also saw the *toilet paper*," Moggy said in a whisper. "It spells out the German equivalent of s-h-i-t!"

"I'm sorry. Are you upset about how Nazis are wiping their rears?"

"Your project," Moggy said. "The reason you keep absconding with Captain Dewart." Her eyes narrowed, zeroing in on Will's empty desk. "You're not really evaluating bomb damage and industrial capacity, are you?"

Niki considered her options. She could come up with an excuse, pile a new lie on top of the others like a bullshit sandwich. But she'd anticipated having to cop to Moggy eventually, and now seemed like as good a time as any, given she was fresh out of explanations. As Niki noodled on this, Moggy read the hesitation in her face.

"So, then I'm right?" she said, her voice quivering. "Your job, the entire purpose of this office, is to *lie*. To create and spread propaganda."

"It's not the entire office," Niki said. "Just MO." She walked around to Moggy's side of the desk. "And it's a stitch more complicated than that. Yes, the truth is stretched here and there, but only to an important end."

"That sounds like rationalization," Moggy said. "Lying is not only morally wrong, Niki, but it feeds into our collective unconsciousness, and we internalize these things, and they become truth."

"Oh, brother." Niki shook her head in disbelief. "Maybe just worry about your own consciousness, eh? For the record, what we're doing will help end the war. Because of *Nazi* propaganda, those saps still believe they're going to win, and they're letting it drag out. Our leaflets and postcards tell them the real story—that Germany is on its heels. We sometimes exaggerate, but the message must be dire to make it sink in."

"You're pretending to be German."

"They wouldn't believe anything from the Allies. Think about it, Moggy!"

Brows furrowed, Moggy weighed the information. Though she seemed to be seriously considering Niki's explanation, like an out-of-season bolero, she wasn't prepared to buy it just yet.

"How bad is lying to the Nazis, really?" Niki continued. "If it spares thousands of lives? Not to mention, Nazis are the most notorious propagandists in the world. We have to fight fire with fire."

In one breath, Moggy's face went from pensive to hard and strained. Whatever Niki had said, it was the wrong thing. "Funny you should bring up Nazi propaganda," Moggy said, spitting each syllable between her teeth. "I hear you're a real fan."

"Come again?"

"Oh, yes, George told me all about it. He gave me *allllll* the details, like how you and Will get your ideas directly from *Mein Kampf.*"

"What?" Niki said. "That's not true at all! I've never once

laid my eyes on that terrible book. Listen, Moggy, I don't know what your brother's angle is, other than to discredit me, but George knows damn well that it was *Bill Donovan* who cribbed his ideas from the Führer."

Propaganda should not be addressed to the intellectuals but always to the masses… Propaganda should be directed to the emotions rather than to the intellect… Propaganda must be popular and its level must be low enough for it to impress itself on the simplest mind… These were the notions on which the Morale Operations manual was based, all of them lifted from Hitler's dastardly text.

"Will and I are just carrying out our work exactly as we were trained," Niki added. "What else did your brother have to say? I assume he had some comments on our distribution methods?" Her mind went to Will, and whatever Warner was saying behind his closed door.

"Distribution methods?" Moggy said, and looked at her askance. "No… I don't recall him mentioning anything about that…"

"Moggy." Niki rubbed her face. "You're a grown woman. A smart, capable woman with a wicked sense of fashion. You were happy at the Institute. Why did you let your family send you all the way to Rome just to spy on me? What's that doing to the collective unconsciousness, do you think?"

Moggy opened her mouth, but no words came out. Her eyes began to water.

"And please, spare me the denials," Niki went on. "It's so obvious. You're forever popping up out of nowhere, badgering me with your relentless queries, and snooping around. Give it to me straight. Did you really find this propaganda on Rumors's desk?"

"Yes, I did…" Moggy's chin trembled. "But that's… That's not." She swallowed. "That's not true at all! What you said about me being a spy for George. How does that even make sense? My family sent me here to work, to do something 'worthwhile.' I swear on my life, no one said anything about looking after you.

If I've bothered you *relentlessly*, it's only because I'm curious, and wanted to be part of something."

In a blink, the conversation flipped, and a new feeling landed on Niki, heavily, like a safe from a second-floor window. Moggy was nothing if not honest and earnest. Niki trusted every word coming out of that lipsticked mouth and now felt like the biggest jerk in the world. "Moggy, I'm so sorry for assuming," she said. "It was the only explanation that made sense." Niki reached for her hand, but Moggy whipped it away and leaped to her feet.

"I can't believe you'd think that about me when I've been nothing but kind. Also, for your information, I love George as a brother but don't especially enjoy him as a person," she said. "He can be quite insufferable!"

"He can and I'm sorry. I read the situation all wrong," Niki said. "Can you forgive me, Mogs? Please?" She put her hands together, as if in prayer.

"I dunno," Moggy mumbled.

"I'll make it up to you. I have an idea," Niki said. She bent down to retrieve her handbag from a drawer. "Why don't we blow out of this office and have a gals' night out, you and me? You've been wanting to do one for so long. Now seems like the perfect time. The question is where…"

It'd be dark soon, and the Allies were the only ones with reliable electricity. The Excelsior Bar was an option, but Niki wasn't in the mood to hang around what amounted to a transient park for the Allied Fifth Army. Niki could probably get them into Fagiano, a dining and dancing club turned officer restaurant, but the place gave her the creeps. An establishment really lost its charm when surrounded by military vehicles and barbed wire to prevent Roman lookie-loos from seeing what'd become of one of their old favorite haunts.

"What about…" Niki began, when an idea popped into her head. "Yes. Perfect. That's the ticket." She scurried over to the door and peered out toward the main office. "Ezra! What was the place you were telling me about? The dance club that's only open on Fridays?"

He'd discovered the club the second week they were in Rome and frequented it often, despite his long-standing fear of Fridays. It was Roman-owned and had power sometimes, though it usually did not, in which case the dancing was done in candlelight.

"Why do you need to know?" Ezra asked, his gaze fixed tightly on the crocodile he was trying to sketch. It was the creature that bedeviled him the most because Ezra could never decide how a croc *wanted* to be seen.

"Moggy and I are going to blow off some steam. Do you think they'd let in a few broads like us?"

Ezra's eyes flew up, practically ripping from the page. "You're thinking of going *with Moggy*?" he said, aghast. "You and Moggy? I'll be damned. Yes, ladies, I think they'd let you in. They are always interested in attracting a *diverse* clientele."

"Gosh, I've never been called *diverse* before," Moggy tittered. She seemed to be returning to a good mood, and thank Ludmila for that.

"What an exciting development. Perhaps I'll meet you there later," Ezra said. "I have a deadline with *The New Yorker*, and also need to finish my croc. If anyone gives you a hard time, tell them you're friends with me."

"Perfect." Niki smiled and flipped around. She threw her handbag over her shoulder, linked arms with Moggy, and off they went.

35

NIKI

August 1944

Ezra had warned Niki that the dance hall was mostly prostitutes and "friends of Dorothy," which were men who enjoyed the company of other men, apparently. In other words, Ezra's favorite kinds of people.

The cartoonist adored bawdy girls not because he was interested in some how's-your-father but because of the very nostalgia he claimed to eschew. Ezra grew up on a street lined with whorehouses—elegant high-end bordellos built alongside run-of-the-mill brothels where the women lived among dogs, hens, roosters, and ducks. On Saturdays, housewives came down from country villages in their aprons and muddy boots to sell not produce but themselves. "Everything happened in the courtyard," Ezra said about that time. "It was part of our daily fabric."

Naturally, Moggy was less accustomed to such types. "I don't think we should be here," she said three seconds after they walked through the door. "This crowd looks...off." She let loose a sneeze.

Niki recognized that bringing Moggy had been a foolish decision. This was a woman who refused to join the others at the Italian cinema because she was terrified of typhus and "certain nuisances" committed in the dark. But now they were here, and Niki figured they should make the best of it.

"Don't worry so much," Niki said, dragging Moggy through the masses. With the thick fog of cigarette smoke and body heat and flickering, intermittent light, the place had a real end-of-the-world mood. Niki tightened her grip on Moggy's sleeve.

"We could get in serious trouble for this," Moggy said. "What if someone saw us? An officer or something?"

"Then he'd be here, too, same as us." Niki let go of Moggy and sauntered up to the bar. They could both use a drink.

"Niki," Moggy whispered. "Niki!" she said again, her hot breath spraying Niki's cheek. "Is this a...you know..." She put her hands on her waist and wagged her rear back and forth.

Niki's eyes bugged. "Come again?"

"A brothel," Moggy hissed. "Are we going to get thrown in an Italian jail?"

Niki laughed and handed Moggy a sweet, watered-down wine. "It's just a dance club," she said. "Anyway, there's nothing illegal about prostitution, if everyone's paying their fees." As though the mere mention of the profession summoned it, Niki turned and found herself face-to-face with her friend from the Spanish Steps. "Paloma!" Niki cried, thrilled to see someone she knew. *"Come te butta?"* She signaled the bartender to pour Paloma a drink, too.

"I am well," Paloma said, and indeed she looked spectacular with her low-cut blue dress and that explosion of bright red hair. "A drink for Generosa, also, yes?" she said.

Niki nodded and laid down a few more coins as Paloma's friend waved from the other side of the room. She'd met Generosa a time or two, and with her dull hair, missing incisors, and four-feet-nothing of height, she paled next to Paloma. It was a miracle that she got regular work, though they probably had vastly different price points.

"Who do we have here?" Paloma said, eyeing Moggy up and down. "I like your little jacket."

"Bolero," Moggy corrected her.

"This is my sister-in-law, Mary Margaret Clingman," Niki said, widening her eyes in what she hoped was a meaningful look. "Sister to my husband, *George*." It suddenly struck Niki this encounter could go sideways fast. She considered Paloma a friend, but in truth they hardly knew each other at all.

"*Anvendi!* I'm very inclined to meet you," Paloma said awkwardly, before offering a curtsy. It was the wrong greeting, the sort of artless gesture Moggy might've made, which rendered it some kind of charming. "*Mi chiamo Paloma.*" She extended a hand.

"Hello, Paloma. Wow!" Moggy said, goggling her bulky, glittering rings. It was nothing more than costume jewelry, but Moggy's tastes weren't strictly high-end. She fancied anything that grabbed the eye. "I love your jewelry!" she exclaimed.

"*Grazie,*" Paloma answered. "I do work ever so hard for it."

"Oh, Lord," Niki said, deciding it was time to break up the party. Her sister-in-law would like prostitution even less than she did propaganda, and though Niki didn't think Moggy was spying on her anymore, she couldn't have this getting back to George. "Come on, Mogs," she said, pulling the cocktail from her hand. "Let's cut a rug."

At the suggestion, Moggy was as horrified as she'd been all night. "You want me to dance?"

"It's time to let down that hairpiece and live," Niki said, and hooked her arm around Moggy's shoulders. "I think we could *both* use some fun."

And Moggy *would* let her hairpiece down, by and by, at times nearly losing the blond-streaked pageboy altogether. By the end of the night, she'd completely relaxed her stiff-as-a-board smile and stopped assaulting passersby with "useful Italian words and phrases" from *A Soldier's Guide to Rome. Il menu, per favore. Che cosa ci consiglia? Sono allerga a...*

Even Niki managed to cut loose, realizing it was the most carefree she'd felt in some two or three years. When the band struck up a Latin number, she drafted a younger fellow for the St. Louis Swing. From the edge of the dance floor, Moggy snapped her fingers and swayed her hips, holding on to the back of her head to keep her clip-on in place.

The night passed in a blur, and soon the two women were stumbling home, arm in arm, through the very neighborhoods the guidebooks warned them about. "Gosh, that was fun," Moggy said as they tripped through the villa gates. "Should we go back tomorrow night?"

"It's only open on Fridays, and let's not get ahead of ourselves," Niki said. They rounded a corner. "We still have work to do. And I have a feeling that neither of us will feel very productive tomorrow."

"Well, well, well, what do we have here?" said a voice.

Will emerged from the shadows, and the two women jumped.

"Jesus Christ!" Niki said, and gave him a little shove. "You scared us half to death. You can't go creeping around like that when the electricity is out. For your information, we were *dancing*. Reveling. Taking a load off. You should try it." She brushed her hair back with both hands. "How was your meeting with Warner? In hindsight, I'm glad to have avoided all that. Moggy and I had much more fun."

Despite the dark, she could see a pain pass over Will's face, like a cloud across the sun. "The meeting is why I'm here," he said. "We need to talk. There are some, er, complications."

"Oh, great," Niki said. "Now you drag me into it. No thanks! You were the one called into the office. What do you need me for? I'm sure you have everything under control."

"I need to warn you about something. Something big. You're not going to like it, and should hear it from me, first."

Office Memorandum | **UNITED STATES GOVERNMENT**
TO: MO MEDTO
DATE: 4 August 1944
CC: OSS Director
FROM: MO Chief, Rome
SUBJECT: Promotion

I am recommending for promotion Captain Will Dewart from Captain (OF-2) to Major (OF-3). Please process the paperwork, and ensure he receives the appropriate increase in pay.

36

NIKI

August 1944

Only a man could walk into his boss's office a captain and walk out as a major. *Zkurvysyn.* Son of a bitch.

Warner was steamed about the POWs, but once William Dewart had his ear, he changed his tune. For one, the men had been vetted far better than the partisans the OSS used. Those ad hoc secret agents weren't subjected to hours of interrogation, Will pointed out, or made to sign oaths of allegiance. All they had to say was "down with Hitler," and the OSS welcomed them into the fold. Once Warner learned the full details of what went down at Aversa, and the extreme care they took, he allowed that the scheme *did* make wise use of untapped resources. It was maybe even revolutionary.

"I never meant for it to happen like this," Will said, as if it were some consolation. "I was trying to take the heat, but the conversation turned. By the end of it, he completely misunderstood my role in the operation."

"I'll say! What was that thing you told me, about shit flowing uphill?"

To think, Niki momentarily felt bad that Will had to take the heat on his own.

In the days that followed, Niki could barely stand to look at the man, not that he'd bothered to notice. The POWs were still at the safe house, awaiting their next mission, so they'd have to speak eventually, but for now she did her best to avoid him while sketching out plans for Sauerkraut II.

With Will presently out of the office—doing important major things, no doubt—Niki was racking her brain for comebacks when her focus was interrupted by a loud footfall and the telltale clearing of the throat. It was Moggy, her new dancing friend.

"Hello, Miss Clingman," Niki said. She looked up, then pulled back sharply, shielding her eyes. "Good Lord," she blurted. "What are you wearing?"

"This?" Moggy stroked the nest of white straw and sweet peas perched atop her head. "It's called a half half-hat," she said. "The smallest hat ever made. Isn't it darling? I just received it from Mother."

"A half of a half?" Niki said with a crooked look. "Wouldn't that be a quarter hat?"

"You're so funny!" Moggy helped herself to a seat directly opposite Niki, and clasped her hands together atop the desk. "I was thinking... Now that we've come to an understanding— daresay, I believe we're friends—I have a proposal. Something that will benefit us both."

"Uh-oh..."

"I *thought* Kunkel left for Tuscany three days ago," Moggy said. "Ostensibly to assess the political attitudes of the region now that it's freshly liberated, but no one's heard from him since."

"I'm sure he'll be back soon," Niki said. "Kunkel does this. Give him time. Do you mind if we talk later? Maybe we can go to lunch. I'm kind of in the middle of something."

Niki glanced back at her scrap paper. "Safe conduct pass" was her only comeback idea so far, and it wasn't great. If a German used one to safely surrender, it did offer proof he'd read the propaganda, but most Nazis weren't going to arbitrarily give themselves up. She'd have to think of something else that would cause a person to show up at a specified place, with what amounted to a receipt in hand.

"Ezra thinks he's gone full AWOL," Moggy said.

Niki jiggled her head. "Who's that?"

"Kunkel...?"

"Oh, right." Niki put down her pencil nub. "I doubt that's the case. But either way, what do you want me to do about it?"

"Here's my proposal," Moggy said. "If he doesn't return, I'll join your team."

"Ha!" Niki barked. "Ha! Yes. Let's sign you up." When she realized Moggy was serious, Niki shook her head again and tried to back up. "Hold on. You want to join Morale Operations?" she said. "I thought you were against propaganda?"

"I didn't say I was against it. I said I had some *concerns*," Moggy emphasized. "Maybe if I understood how it's used, my view might change. You said it could help win the war, and that is something I'd like to participate in. If I just sit around waiting for Kunkel to return, what is my purpose? What am I doing for the betterment of society?"

"Um. Okay. Well. That is...something to consider." Was it? They could always use another pair of hands, but would Moggy help, or hold them back?

"You mentioned a manual?" Moggy said. "Mind if I take a look?"

Niki eyed her for a minute. Never before had her sister-in-law acted so decisively, which meant she'd been ruminating about this for days. *Oh, what the hell?* Niki thought, sliding a hand into her drawer. Reading a manual never hurt anyone. She didn't think.

"If you're up for it, here it is," Niki said, and flopped a book onto the desk.

MORALE OPERATIONS FIELD MANUAL

"All the rules and philosophies are right here, laid out in black and white. Give it a whirl. Let me know what you think."

As Moggy thumbed through the booklet, a vein pulsed in her neck. *The objectives of a subversive morale operation are to incite and spread dissension, confusion, and disorder...*

Like Rome when the sun went down, Niki could practically see Moggy being turned off. Luckily for the both of them, between the unsavory aspects of black propaganda and Kunkel's inevitable return, Niki didn't see any danger of Moggy actually joining their team.

"Thank you for lending me the book," Moggy said, scanning the next page. "I'll get reading right away, though I do need to walk Pierre first. I'm quite peeved about it all." She glanced up and adjusted her half half-hat. "Kunkel didn't even ask me to look after him this time. When I arrived at the office this morning, the mutt was just chained to my desk. No note. Not a single please or thank you. Can you imagine?"

"Oh, God." Niki's heart stopped. "Pierre was chained to your desk?" When Moggy nodded, Niki threw back her head and wailed. "This is not good, not good at all."

"I didn't know you were such an animal welfare nut," Moggy said. "I don't mind helping out, here and there, but it was so presumptuous. Ezra also found three of Kunkel's hats stuffed into his drawer. What's that about, do you think?"

"He didn't."

"He did. That's why he thinks Kunkel is AWOL, though I don't know what headwear has to do with it?"

"Do prdele!" Niki shouted, using one of the many Czech equivalents of "fuck." In this case, the direct translation was "go to ass."

"Unfortunately, Ezra is right," Niki said. She laughed, and it hurt on the way up. "When a person departs a post, it's tradition to leave one's most cherished belongings for the colleagues staying behind. It seems Kunkel is gone for good, and you are now the proud owner of one black Labrador."

"Niki!" Moggy sprang to her feet. "I can't look after a dog. I don't even agree with the concept of animals as companions."

"I don't know what to tell you, Mogs," Niki said as she heard the open and slam of the office door. "Pierre isn't really going to care about whether or not you believe in pets. He seems like a good pup." More stamping and slamming continued as Niki spoke. "Good Lord. What *is* all that commotion out front?" She poked her head around Moggy just as Warner materialized, a sheepish-looking Will lingering behind him.

"How exciting!" Niki trilled. "Look who it is. The boss and Captain America. Oh, sorry, *Major* America."

"We have a situation," Warner said.

"A situation? Neat. Dewart, sounds like you might be in line for another promotion."

"Niki..." Will warned.

"I'm demanding you stop all work on Sauerkraut II," Warner said. As Niki went to protest, he put up a hand. "Save whatever retort you have lined up, whatever sassy remarks. There is a problem with your *assets*."

"Our assets?" Niki said, trying to divine what he meant. This office had no assets to speak of, which had been the problem all along.

"We've received a dispatch from the cook at the sub-base

where..." Warner's eyes skipped toward Moggy, and back again "...where said assets are kept."

"I don't understand," Niki said, though she could already feel the color drain from her face.

"Your assets have been breached," Warner said. "Private Novotná, I order you and Major Dewart to proceed to the sub-base immediately." He released a long, phlegmy sigh. "No surprise that Kunkel left this godforsaken office. If I had any sense, I'd be the next one out."

37

PALOMA

May 1945

I was at the villa, in bed with one of the prisoners, when that blessed squawk crashed through the house. Right away I recognized the voice as Nikola's.

The man and I exchanged glances but chose to linger. It wasn't that we were in a state of postcoital rapture. *Ahò!* The thought of it! This boy Max had no more than three hairs on the full of his chest. He was barely a man! None of this matters, though, for while he got the proper screw, what he really needed was to be held. Everybody just wants to be loved when you get down to it.

Regardless. With each passing second, the shrieking intensified, and we soon heard the pit-a-pat of angry feet. When the door flew open, Max ducked under the sheets. I scooted onto my elbows, flicked a piece of hair from my face, and grinned.

"Nikola!" I sang. "Lovely to see you."

The woman was furious. Her face was red, and she had demons for hair. After casting about for a minute or two, she placed her hands on her hips and bellowed, *"Che cazzo!"*

This made me giggle, all the way down to my derriere. One thing I appreciate about Nikola is her ability to curse in Italian, and with such colorful language. She might've said, *what is happening?* Or, *what are you doing?* Or, *what the hell?* Instead, Nikola was direct and to the point. *What the dick?*

"You are very funny," I told her, "for an American. *Come te butta?"*

"How's it *going?"* Nikola growled, stalking deeper into the room. *"Voi siete pazzi?"*

The query was rhetorical—*are you crazy?*—but the answer was the same for most of us. "Yes," I said. "A little bit."

As I reached for one of Max's cigarettes, I noticed William Dewart standing behind her. As I have mentioned, Americans do not appeal to me, but I nonetheless toyed with him, letting the blanket slip and expose the tops of my full, pale breasts. When his eyes flared, I loosened the blanket further to reveal one perfectly round pink nipple. The man looked away with such force he might've injured his neck.

"What are you doing here?" Nikola asked me. "Did...did someone hire you?"

"I told you five thousand lira was too much pocket money," William said, his eyes attached to the floor.

"Relax," I said. "No one paid me! This was an impromptu gathering. Just a bit of fun, no? One of his friends—" I swept a hand toward Max "—snuck a note to one of mine, saying men were lonely in a villa, looking for...what is it called in America? *R & R.* We thought to give it to them. Or they could give it to us." I thrust my hips in case she missed the point.

"Paloma!" Nikola moaned and threw her hands over her face. "You've really put me up a tree." She dropped her hands and flipped around, instructing William to escort Max from the room. Holding a pillow over his *cazzo*, Max scurried away, and Nikola's tall, bent-nosed colleague closed the door.

She crossed her arms. "What are you doing here?" she asked again.

"It is a funny question," I said. "What am I doing here? When, really, I'd like to know this about *them*. Are you keeping prisoners in this villa, Nikola?" I struck a match. "This is what they told us. You didn't do anything stupid, did you?"

Here is the point at which I did not know whether anything was wrong, exactly, but I understood something was amiss. Was this official? Approved by your government? Or was she using Germans for her own personal projects? Mostly I wondered what they were doing with the Italians they'd captured, and were any nearby?

"It's really none of your business." Nikola sniffed, though the quake in her voice told me she was not as indignant, or assured, as she pretended to be. "Classified information."

"*Va tutto bene, tesoro,*" I said. "We came for some fun. Nothing more. In case you're worried, no secrets were spilled. We Italians are on your side." I took a drag on my cigarette.

Nikola plunked onto the bed and raked all ten fingers through her hair.

"Americans are so puritanical," I said. "The Czechs must be, too. Maybe you should try one of the men out, given the situation with your husband."

Nikola glared. "I don't care about the sex," she said. "They're not supposed to be around *anyone*. That's for everybody's safety, including yours. Now I'm going to have to..." She wouldn't finish the sentence.

"Replace them with new ones?" I guessed. Max told me they were doing very important, secretive work. He didn't spell out what kind.

Nikola rubbed her face. "Something like that," she said.

"Very smart, very smart. Replacing them should solve everything." I cackled and ground out my cigarette. "I'm sure these boys, they are anomalies. Ah, Nikola." I clucked. "Tell me, what will you do the next time?"

"The next time *what?*" she said, and looked at me sideways.

"The next time your men get horny?" I said. "You can take them away, Nikola. You can lock them up or swap these men for others and swap them again. But you will never get to the end of it because, eventually, everyone needs a good fuck."

38

NIKI

August 1944

"It's pretty funny when you think about it," Will said as they drove through the countryside, past smashed pink-and-blue villas and piazze littered with decapitated statues. In each town, people picked through piles of burnt rubble while others wandered aimlessly beneath gnarled olive trees. Everyone was desperate for food, or anything of value, but they also had endless hours to waste. There were no jobs, and Nazi-planted land mines prevented farmers from returning to their crops.

"I don't find it funny at all," Niki said, steering the truck with one knee as she lit a cigarette. Up ahead, their path was decimated, like a giant had taken several great chomps from the road. "Never mind potential security breaches. We put in all that time, and now we have to find a whole new group of

POWs. As you may recall, anti-Nazis are not easy to come by. We're talking about German prisoners!"

Niki was frustrated, but it was about more than logistics and starting from scratch. The old group, who'd done a fine job until they brought girls into the equation, were at that moment being driven in the opposite direction, to an entirely different POW cage where they'd begin a new incarceration, with new paperwork and new names. Something about this unsettled her.

They were the enemy. Niki understood, yet she felt a pang of regret about their identities being wiped away so easily. She kept picturing Paloma's friend Max, the one with the hairless chest and toothy smile, the one who so resembled Niki's little brother.

"I don't like treating them as though they're...expendable," Niki said, mostly to herself.

"Having to replace the POWs is not the most ideal situation," Will agreed, "but we've learned our lesson, right? Next time we'll be more explicit. No girlfriends."

"I'm sure that'll do it," Niki muttered, doggedly smoking her cigarette as Paloma's words rang through her head. *Eventually, everyone needs a good fuck.* The woman wasn't incorrect.

They rumbled along in silence, the only sound the rocks and gravel clinking against the bottom of the truck. Wanting to get this damned drive over with, Niki gunned it, thumping over potholes and narrowly avoiding houses-turned-piles-of-rubble. Through it all, Niki kept the cigarette pinned between her teeth.

"Are you upset about something?" Will asked, and Niki shot him a look. "I don't just mean right now, but before. Did I do something wrong?"

"I'm not speaking to you."

Will laughed for a second before realizing this was no joke.

"Tell me," Niki said, and stopped to suck angrily on her cigarette. "How much of a pay bump did you receive with your promotion? Ten percent? Twenty?"

"I'm not sure..."

"Ah, so it's that inconsequential. Lovely. I couldn't afford the rent for a decent flat on what they give me." She flipped her cigarette out the window. "You know what the new Rumors guy told me? When they promoted him to captain, he made *double* what he did as a professor of theology at Yale."

"I don't think theology professors are known for their incomes."

"That's not the point," Niki said, making sure to hit all the biggest bumps. Up ahead a branch hung low, near the passenger side. *Perfect*, she thought, steering toward it.

"Jesus! Niki!" Will said, ducking just in time. "I was nearly impaled!"

"Can't believe I missed," she groused.

"You can't seriously be mad," Will said. "It's not as though I asked for the promotion. I was covering for you, and it just happened. I thought you might, I dunno, be happy for me. It benefits the both of us."

Niki's eyebrows popped up. "*Happy* for you? So typical. A man achieves something on the back of another and expects a damn parade."

"Who said anything about a parade? Why do you even *want* a promotion? It just means more stress, more responsibility."

"I can see you are greatly suffering. Poor darling," she cooed. "Warner drags you into his office and throws money at you. Terrible."

"First of all, he's still pretty hot about the POWs, and he's threatened me with a 'firing squad' if anyone else finds out the extent to which we're using them," Will said. "Second, he's not exactly going to pat me on the back for the mess with the prostitutes."

"They have names, William."

"This incident will be reported," Will reminded her. "I'll probably get remanded to a lower post."

"Didn't that already happen?" Niki asked. "Is there anything lower than Rome?"

"Once it goes through Washington *and* Bern," Will continued, "my goose will be cooked."

All at once, Niki's fire went out, but alarm bells rang on. "Warner's reporting it to Bern?" she said, jerking her head toward Will. "Are you sure?" Even though she couldn't fathom the men who'd participated complaining, Niki imagined George would view this incident as an abuse of the prisoners, too.

"Niki!" Will shouted. "EYES ON THE ROAD!"

It was too late, and now they were halfway up a small hill. Niki cranked the wheel hard left, and the truck skidded along on only the left-side wheels before thudding back onto the dirt ten yards in front of a flock of chickens.

"Huh. This truck is nimbler than I thought."

"Hand to heart, your driving is the scariest thing I've endured in this war," Will said. "I don't even fear getting shot anymore."

"You probably should worry," Niki said, and jammed the truck into Park. "About getting shot." She pushed away a curl stuck to her forehead and hopped onto the ground. "I'd love to finally put the firearms training to use."

"Very funny," Will said, peering out the window. "What happened? Did we get a flat or something?"

"The truck is fine, Dewart," she said, and broke into a jog. "I'm going to grab a few chickens, bring them back with us."

"Another pet?" he said. "Do you think that's smart? Moggy just inherited Pierre."

"These aren't pets. In case you haven't noticed, people are hungry in Rome. I'm bringing back food."

Niki launched herself into the flock, sweeping up whichever ones she could grab. Within minutes, she emerged from a cloud of feathers and dust, covered in scratches but with three chickens under her arms.

"Success!" Niki said as she marched toward the truck. She

shoved the chickens through the window and onto Will's lap. Then Niki jumped into the driver's seat and tore off.

"Stealing chickens," Will said as one of the birds gave him a face full of chicken ass. "Ridiculous, even for you." He turned and spat out some feathers. "First the silent treatment and now this."

"Ah, you noticed. I wasn't sure."

"I was trying to give you room to cool off," Will said. "But you seem really intent on punishing me."

"Believe it or not, starving Romans have nothing to do with you."

"I'm sorry you're upset," Will said. "Sauerkraut was a great success, and you *should* be heralded for your work. In the event that I survive this, uh, situation with the women, I'm going to insist that you get a promotion. It will happen, Niki. Just be patient."

"No thanks for the help," Niki snapped. "I'm not a damned charity case." *SQUAAAAWK!* "Even with your golden word, no one's going to magically promote me. That only happens to people like you."

"People like me?" Will said, crinkling his forehead. The smallest bird leaped up onto the dash. "I assume you mean a loyal employee with a good head on his shoulders."

"Ha!" Niki scoffed as they thumped over something large but that had a little give. An animal carcass, if she were to speculate. "You could've done nothing more than stand around and look pretty and still you would've been promoted. You're a man, with the 'right' education and pedigree. They don't call it the Oh-So-Social for nothing. It's an old boys' club. Also, you're a rich bastard, which always helps move things along."

As Niki swerved around the bend, she saw they were closing in on Aversa. They'd shaved some serious time off this trip, despite stopping for the chickens. She hoped the commandant had a decent batch of POWs lined up. It'd help her get past the sting of losing the first group.

"Your daddy probably knows Donovan personally," Niki added as Will stayed silent, stroking the back of a hen. "Maybe even Roosevelt. No doubt Papa Dewart called one or both and said, 'Give a hand to my boy, eh?'"

"Unlikely, as my father is dead."

"Oh, shit," Niki said. She turned toward Will but could not catch his eye through the fan of tail feathers. "Oh, God. Will. My gigantic mouth strikes again. I'm sorry. Really, I am. Why haven't you ever told me?"

Will shrugged. "We weren't close," he said.

"I'm so sorry, Will. I shouldn't have assumed."

"Lots of people have family members who die. It's just the way of things."

"It is," Niki said, swallowing hard as they reached the end of the road. Up ahead, a man stepped out of the gatehouse. "I'm sorry. Again. I can be a bit of a hothead sometimes."

"Really? This is new information."

Niki could *feel* his smirk as she leaned out the window to greet the guard. "Hi there," she said. "The commandant is expecting us. Private Flingman and Captain Demart." She looked back at Will. "Did Demart get a promotion, too?"

"Hilarious," Will said as the guard waved them through. "By the way. The thing you said about my 'proper education and pedigree'? I should probably tell you…well…" He squeezed his eyes shut. "This is embarrassing to say out loud, especially to you, but I never graduated college."

Niki threw him a glance, nearly giving herself whiplash in the process. "You didn't? What's with all the secrets?" She felt a little stung, though recognized she had no right to. "The father thing I understand, but we've discussed university and degrees."

"I was embarrassed," he mumbled. "Because you have three degrees. Because of your—" he swept a hand "—accomplishments."

Niki said nothing as she cast about for a response. A small voice warned her not to tease or make a production out of it. "What's the big deal?" she said. "Lots of brilliant people never finish university." Niki lightened her foot on the gas to give them more time before they reached the barracks. "What happened? I thought attending college was a birthright for someone like you?"

"In a way, I suppose," Will said. "My father and grandfather both graduated from Harvard. I went for one miserable year, but it never felt right. I hated my professors and struggled to make friends. I just didn't fit in with the hard-drinking, old-money types."

Idiots, Niki thought, overcome by the urge to give him a hug. Though she razzed him endlessly, and he did not deserve that promotion, Will was one of the best fellas she'd known. Admittedly, the bar was none too high, but Niki could only imagine the caliber of men who didn't let him "fit in." A dozen variations of George, she presumed.

"It was a given that I'd eventually take over the newspaper," Will continued. "Degree or not. One day I looked around and realized I wasn't doing anything to prepare for the rest of my life. So, right after my twentieth birthday, I left college for good."

"Bold move," Niki said, and really tried to mean it. All things considered, a rich boy abdicating Harvard wasn't *that* big of a risk. Did it even matter whether he had a degree? William Dewart Jr. wouldn't end up in the cheese line or on the dole. On the other hand, Niki understood the gut-wrenching agony of disappointing one's family, and what he'd done was a quiet kind of bravery. "Is that what you meant?" she asked. "When you mentioned being a screwup?"

Will craned over his chicken. "Huh?"

"The thing you said, about why you married your wife." Niki's heart raced as she recalled their conversation. "You figured you'd finally do what was expected of you. Or something along those lines. Maybe you don't remember the discussion. You were pretty drunk."

"Oh. Right." He scowled. "Sure. I guess."

"What'd you do in lieu of college, then? Go straight to work?"

"I spent one year at the Empire State School of Printing," he said, "then tried out a bunch of different jobs to get a sense of the industry. I started on a delivery truck. After that, I apprenticed in the stereotyping department of a small journal. I won't bore you with the rest. It bored *me* enough, though it gave me what I wanted, which was experience."

Niki brought the truck to a slow, rolling stop. "I'm impressed, Major," she said, barely sarcastic when mentioning his rank. "You have more grit than I thought." She kicked open the door.

"I'm sorry you didn't get a promotion, too," Will said as he gently, almost lovingly, placed the chickens on the floor of the truck. "You deserve one, and I don't blame you for being mad at Warner, or Dulles, or, hell, even Donovan. But we're in this together, and if you really want to make it work, you're going to have to forgive me."

"Even college dropouts can make a good point every once in a while," Niki said, jumping onto the ground.

"So, you're not still mad?"

"Nah," Niki said, and flung a hand. "What's there to be mad about? You're only a man. And you're right. We do have to work together, and we've got enough obstacles around here without making our own."

"I apologize for not acknowledging the silent treatment," Will said as he lurched out the car. "In my defense, your brooding never lasts long, and it's usually replaced by a quick, hasty action of one kind or another. Not to sound Jungian, but I've concluded that you stay busy to avoid being upset."

"Oh, you've *concluded*, have you?"

"Yes. Picking up these guys, for example," he said, gesturing to the chickens. "That's half the reason you're so damned productive."

Niki laughed. "Unrelated," she said, though she briefly wondered whether he might be right. "The chickens are because people need to eat. Jeez. I didn't realize that in less than a year of knowing each other, I've been upset so often you've detected a *pattern*."

"It's more than just when I've done something stupid." Will paused, gnawing on his bottom lip. "There's a lot to worry about. It must be stressful, with your family in Czechoslovakia, and not knowing what's happening at any given time. It makes sense you'd give yourself distractions with work. Or chickens."

Niki stiffened, glad at that moment her back was turned. "The situation in Czechoslovakia isn't my favorite thing," she said evenly. "But if you want to know the truth, I hardly think of them at all."

The New York Times

6 Factories Razed in Reich Air Blow
—
Crushing U.S. Attack by 3,000 Bombers and Fighters Also Destroys 50 Nazi Planes

By Wireless to The New York Times

The crushing weight of American airpower descended on the Luftwaffe again today after a period in which oil and industrial targets had received their periodic mauling.

Today 3,000 bombers and fighters in the United States Strategic Air Forces destroyed at least fifty Nazi machines, and wrecked six factories and an unspecified number of ground bases serving the German Air Force at home...

Nearly 1,000 aircraft, all told, took off from Italian fields to attack targets in Czechoslovakia.

Vital Targets Attacked

The places attacked today were a bomber assembly plant at Wismar, a components plant at Luebeck, an assembly factory in Rostock, a research center at Rechlin, and air force stations at Anklam, Schwerin, and Neu Brandenburg near Stettin.

The Mediterranean-based bombers went to the Brnö-Líšeň factory in the Moravia area and the Brnö-Kuřim engineering works.

Tales of enemy opposition varied. Some pilots said the Germans most definitely "did not put out the welcome mat," and others found it hard to believe that the Reich had any defenses. Flak was pretty hot over Peenemuende, from all accounts.

39

NIKI

August 1944

Niki's hands shook as she read the article. *The Brnö-Lís'en' factory in the Moravia area. The Brnö-Kur'im engineering works.* Right in the belly of things, near her family's factory.

"Are you okay?" Will called out from his desk, stretching around stacks of freshly printed copies of *Das Neue Deutschland*. This edition was their thickest yet because of a spate of real-life news, beginning with the liberation of Paris. The city was finally free, and at that very moment, thousands were cheering, *"Vivent les Américains!"* along the banks of the Seine.

"I'm fine," Niki said. "There's just a lot to take in. I need to focus. We have so much work to do."

She returned to reviewing Ezra's sketches of Wehrmacht soldiers. The Nazis had modified their uniforms yet again, and Niki

needed to get these drawings to Jack Daniels so he could procure and reproduce the right patches and insignia as quickly as
possible. The new POWs were trained and ready, and Niki now
appreciated the danger of leaving them unattended for too long.

"We have the liberation, but what other Nazi setbacks can we
capitalize on?" Niki said as the words from the bombing article
hung in her mind like clouds that wouldn't burn off.

If Niki's parents manufactured underwear and uniforms for
the Wehrmacht, they were likely now dead, with nothing to
show for their collaboration other than a blown-up factory and
a daughter whose memories would be forever soiled. But what
if they hadn't played nice? Every once in a while, Niki could
convince herself they'd abandoned the factory and were holed
up somewhere, hatching plans. This never gave her comfort for
long. Her parents weren't resister types, and neither was Pasha,
and the underground was no place to hide. Resistance was a
dangerous lifestyle, especially with rumored plans of a partisan
revolt. Many hundreds if not thousands of Czechs would soon
die for the cause.

"We almost don't need anything beyond the liberation," Will
said. "If the Nazis can't hang on to their favorite playground,
what will they keep? Everything hinges on this. Paris is a bell-
wether for a full retreat."

"Fair point. Maybe we should threaten that they're in danger
of ending up French themselves. That'd really plummet their
morale," Niki said. Shaking her head to toss away her thoughts,
she crumpled up the article and pitched it into the trash. "Did
you read the latest intelligence briefing, about the entertainment rules?" she asked. Germans were now permitted to enjoy
only radio, and violation of the new sixty-hour workweek was
punishable by death.

"I did," Will said. "So nice of them to give us fodder for our
campaigns. We won't even have to bend the truth."

As *DND* would soon report, the Nazi regime was in chaos

at home and abroad, desperately attempting to stave off disaster while they prepared for a last-ditch stand. Meanwhile, their Axis compatriots were dropping like flies, leaving everyone to wonder which domino would next fall. What did it mean that Hungary had dissolved all political parties? What was Nazi-aligned Finland going to do? Would Bulgaria follow Romania out of the war?

Not even Hitler could keep up the pretense of strength. He'd recently issued a decree calling for "total mobilization of the Reich." In *DND* they'd pondered, mobilizing *who*? Weren't all able bodies already either in service or dead? If Hitler was asking for every last person in the Reich to join up, it was a bleak situation indeed.

"All they've got left are the grandmas," Ezra said, and whipped up a cartoon to demonstrate exactly this point. He'd drawn two heavyset old ladies on roller skates wielding umbrellas and brooms, with the words *Schwere Panzer* written beneath. These old battle-axes were the only "heavy tanks" the Nazis had left, and Niki chuckled every time she pictured it.

The Nazis' ongoing response to last month's failed assassination was also a Morale Operations gold mine. Hitler hung eight of his generals in retribution, and newly imprisoned officers were retaliating by spilling military secrets to the Allies whenever they had the chance. For a regime that fancied itself the very image of discipline, order, and patriotism, they were now operating like a disorganized jumble of underworld gangsters. *Morale is so low*, Niki wrote in an op-ed, *that officers are resorting to telling troops that Himmler has been killed or Göring is gravely wounded, just to cheer them up.*

"Something's bothering you," Will said as Niki stared at the wall, tapping her pencil on the desk. "What's wrong? *DND* is twice as meaty as it's ever been. You should be thrilled."

"That's all great," Niki said. "But after the incident with the girls…"

Will nodded. They were hanging by the thinnest of wires, even with Warner's promise to keep the prostitution business under wraps. "You're in enough trouble as it is," he'd said. According to him, the top brass deemed their efforts "lamentable" and were questioning the efficacy of psychological warfare full stop. Who was to say their propaganda was getting into the right hands, or producing results at all? It was a big investment to make when their bodies could be used somewhere else. Sauerkraut II had to prove their worth, or the whole thing would be shut down.

"We need better comebacks," Niki said, even as she debated whether tangible proof of their efforts would be enough. The *New York Times* had reported on *DND—SECRET REICH PAPER HITS NAZIS!*—believing it was a legitimate rag. Warner told them it'd been chalked up to coincidence.

"Hello!" squeaked a voice. It was Moggy, standing in the doorway with a book in her arms and Pierre at her heels. "Mind if I join you?" she asked, and Niki fought back a sigh. Before she could respond, Moggy was seated, and Pierre had army-crawled beneath her chair. "I'd like to discuss Morale Operations," she announced. "I've extensively perused the manual you lent me."

"Beg pardon?" Will said. "Our manual?"

"I've decided to offer my services to your unit," Moggy said, and Will sounded as though he was having a choking fit. "I'm a little skeptical about the propaganda, mind you, but we're saving the world from Nazism, so how bad can it be?" She sneezed into her elbow.

"Gosh, Miss Clingman," Will said, and passed Niki a glare. "I didn't realize you had become involved! It's the first I'm hearing of it."

"Nobody's involved," Niki said. "No promises have been made. Moggy, if we can bring you on board, I will need to run it by Will first." Niki gave Will a feeble smile, and he further narrowed his eyes. "And Warner, I guess."

"I recognize that I'm not an expert," Moggy prattled on, "and I haven't even been trained, but maybe a fresh point of view could be beneficial?"

"Moggy—"

"Please? I'm so bored. And lonely. I just want to be a part of something."

Niki grumbled softly. How could she possibly say no now that Moggy'd so thoroughly plucked at her heartstrings? Niki had a real soft spot for outsiders, probably because she was one, too. "You know what?" she said. "Fine."

"Fine?" Will took three brisk strides across the room. "*Fine? We're* not authorized to bring new people into MO!"

"I'm sure Warner will be fine with it. He's barely paying attention." Niki grabbed a piece of scrap paper and scribbled something down. "First, I want you to send a telegram to your brother," she said. "Tell him that Warner—not me—is asking for details on yesterday's Allied bombing campaign. What other targets were hit? How badly?" Niki fished the article from the trash and flattened it on her desk. "Reference this newspaper clipping."

"Aw, Nik," Will said, reading over her shoulder. "Why didn't you say anything?"

Niki gently pushed him out of the way and unlocked the bottom drawer of her desk. "Second, here are some interviews we did with prisoners early last week," she said. "Assuming you can interpret my chicken scratch, it'd be helpful if you typed up my notes."

Moggy swapped her harlequins for the pair of real glasses tucked into the front of her dress. "I'm happy to type the notes," she said, scanning the sheets. "But my German is still fairly weak."

"That's all right. Just transcribe what you see." About this arrangement, Niki was feeling better by the second. Bringing Moggy on board might save them loads of time and, more critically, give Niki another avenue with George. Maybe he'd be less withholding with his sister, or if he thought OSS Rome was asking, instead of merely his wife. This was what they called "killing two flies with one hit" back in Czechoslovakia.

"Why did we interview German prisoners again?" Moggy asked, brows pushed together as she tried to decipher Niki's handwriting. "It seems a little...wrong. Why do we care what they think?"

"Moggy, you're either going to help us or you're not." Niki rubbed her forehead, feeling as though she were sprinting at a very high altitude. "This is not the time to overthink it."

"Why are we interviewing prisoners? Miss Clingman, I'm astounded you'd ask," Will said. Niki glanced up and he winked knowingly. "Since you've read the manual, you must know that the first general principle of psychological warfare is to carefully tailor each program to a specified group."

"Hmm," Moggy said, twisting her mouth. "If I recall correctly, that is the *second* principle. The first is to focus on special groups versus painting everyone with a broad brush."

"Touché!" Will smiled, gritting his teeth, and Niki detected the smallest quiver in his knifelike jaw. It wasn't always easy being the nicest guy in the room, and he was working damned hard at it. "Focusing on special groups is the very reason we've interviewed the prisoners," he said. "We need to understand what makes a German soldier tick. What makes him happy, what gets him down. This is what you're holding in your hands."

Will slid his gaze toward Niki, and she gave him a thumbs-up. She was impressed by his version of propaganda, and how swiftly he'd come to her aid.

"Fascinating," Moggy said, and ticked through a few more pages. "It makes me wish I spoke the language better. Ezra's been tutoring me, but I'm far from fluent."

"I'd wager you'll find your German is stronger than you think," Will said. "If anything strikes you about the prisoners' states of mind, feel free to make a note of it. This is where your Jungian training should come in very handy."

"Wow, Major Dewart," Niki said, marveling.

"What am I looking for, exactly?" Moggy asked.

"We want to home in on their fears, their doubts. It's much more compelling to play on personal insecurities than to constantly remind them they're losing. That can only take you so far."

"Makes sense." Moggy stood, clutching the interviews against her significant bosom. "I'll get on this right away," she said, and her attention skittered toward the stack of communist newspapers piled on Will's desk. "I'm curious. How do you get the propaganda into enemy hands?"

"A very good question," Niki said, and she searched Will's face, hoping he had more trickery up his sleeve.

Moggy beamed. "Thank you. It's just... I don't think that printing machine ever stops running, and I've heard you and Will complain about having no air support. You're not personally taking it across enemy lines, are you?"

"Me?" Niki gave a shrill, high-pitched laugh. "No, absolutely not." She again looked at Will, who gave a quick lift of his shoulders. "Generally, we use partisans or other OSS agents. We have a network of resources. A real mixed bag." That much was true.

"Oh, okay." As she went to turn around, Moggy noticed the drawings scattered across Niki's desk. "Wehrmacht uniforms?" she said, and Niki nodded.

"Ezra draws them to help Lieutenant Daniels source uniforms for our, uh, partisans."

Moggy leaned further forward, pursing her lips. After studying the pictures for some time, she declared, "Those are incorrect. Ezra must not have seen the latest intelligence briefing."

"What? No!" Niki said. "Ezra never gets it wrong."

"It just came this morning?" Moggy said. "Maybe it hasn't crossed his desk yet. This division right here." She tapped the drawing with a bright pink manicured finger. "They changed the shoulder patch. Let me show you." Moggy scrabbled around Niki's cluttered desk for a pencil nub and a blank scrap of paper. "It's no longer just the small diamond," she said as she sketched, still hugging the stack of interviews against her breast. "It's now one small red diamond, plus a larger one."

She dropped the pencil and turned the paper to face Niki and Will. "These proportions might be off," Moggy said. "I'm certainly not an artist! But you get the idea. Might want to have Ezra check the latest brief."

"Moggy, that's amazing," Niki said, more bewildered than she'd been by the half half-hat. "You must have some kind of eagle eye." There was at least one benefit to Moggy's tendency to think a topic to death. The girl never missed anything.

"It's a by-product of all that filing and doing-of-nothing. All right, then, I'll get to work on these," Moggy said, using Niki's desk to straighten the stack of interviews. "I'll let you know what I find!"

After she scuttled off, Niki turned toward Will. "That was... unexpected."

"It was more than that," Will said with a wry smile. "Private Novotná, your sister-in-law just saved at least a dozen lives."

40

NIKI

August 1944

"Remind me again why we're voluntarily dining alongside the British press corps?" Ezra said as they tromped up the stairs toward the Hotel de la Ville, which sat at the top of the Spanish Steps. "They are such an unhumorous bunch."

"I need a break from the American joints," Niki said, pulling open the door. She paused to let Ezra, Will, and Moggy walk through. "The barbed wire, the chow-and-cafeteria style. I'm craving a real meal. Look! They even have candlelight. We can pretend we're on holiday."

"But Americans are so much better company," Ezra grouched.

"Are they, though?" Niki said.

"You really are a better American than the rest of us put together." Will laughed as they selected a table in the furthest recesses of the dim, oaky bar.

"None of you appreciate our country," Ezra said, and plopped down into the booth. "It is a miracle. The most fascinating cultural kaleidoscope of the Western world."

"He actually believes this," Niki said to the others in a fake stage whisper.

"Mind-boggling," Will agreed. He turned toward Ezra. "Surely you find some aspects of this 'miracle' less than ideal? What about your difficulties getting in? The bribes paid to Dominican dictators and a forty-three-year wait?"

Ezra slapped the air. "Quotas don't bother me," he said. "They're a necessary evil. And America's beautiful, glorious contradictions are part of its enchantment. Burlesque and tragedy, modernism and old-fashioned ideals, everything side by side. It's why the best ideas originate in the States."

"Our beloved country did come up with the devilishly *ingenious* way to avoid banning Jews outright," Niki said. "Much easier to go around that unsavory notion and instead prevent an influx of immigrants from the countries Jews are fleeing. To wit…" Niki twirled a hand. "The forty-three-year wait."

"I don't want to hear it," Ezra said. "Compared to what's happening in Europe, America's brand of anti-Semitism is a joke."

"What about Mickey Mouse?" Moggy said. "You hate Mickey Mouse."

"I didn't say America was perfect," Ezra said as his features pinched together. "You know how I feel about that cursed mouse. He has far too much influence on the street. I find him positively abhorrent and am still trying to figure out why."

The study of Mickey Mouse was Ezra's version of Jungian analysis, and he was certain that decoding the creature was key to decoding the American spirit. The slightly feminine characteristics superimposed on a macho culture needled him greatly, and there was also something racist about his visage Ezra couldn't quite put his finger on. Mickey was half-black, and demonstrated *some* human characteristics yet was still very much "other."

"We'll solve the Mickey conundrum eventually. I'm sure of

it," Moggy said, craning, trying to get a gander at their surroundings. "Gosh. This is an interesting restaurant."

Niki noticed that her sister-in-law looked as unsure and out of place as she had at the dance club. Maybe it was her outfit—a loud, banana-print frock—which was fine for sweltering August afternoons but jarring amid all this testosterone and cigarette smoke. "It is interesting," Niki said. "I think you and I are the only females in the joint."

"Only females for now," Ezra said, and Niki silently groaned. She'd forgotten prostitutes liked this place, due to its steady stream of customers and proximity to the Spanish Steps. All Niki wanted was a nice, relaxing meal and now she was anxious to leave.

"We're not here to ogle the clientele," Niki said. "We're here to eat and discuss Sauerkraut II. Everyone was instructed to brainstorm ideas for comebacks. As a reminder..." She glanced at Moggy. "A good comeback would be anything that could prove Sauerkraut materials are getting through."

"I've been thinking. Are comebacks really that crucial?" Will said as a waiter delivered their drinks. "Given the amount of energy we're expending trying to think of them, I can't help but wonder whether this is a good use of our time."

"Not a good use of our time?" Niki said. "What are you talking about, Dewart?"

"This conversation is boring," Ezra said with a yawn.

"My point is, we do know the messages are being received, because our own agents watch as the opposition reads them."

"Yes, *we* know this," Niki said. "But the brass does not."

"Here comes the cavalry," Ezra sang. He slipped an anchovy into his mouth. "By cavalry I mean prostitutes," he added, speaking directly to Moggy. She swiveled around.

"Moggy, focus on our discussion, please! Not the other patrons!"

Zkurvysyn. Son of a bitch. The Spanish Steps were Paloma's territory, and she could walk in at any second. It wouldn't take Moggy long to realize Niki's friend wasn't a housewife, and the problems would only spiral from there. Paloma might sidle up and reference her occupation, and Ludmila help them all if she mentioned sleeping with the POWs, and that Niki caught her bare-bottomed.

"What is a soldier's biggest dilemma?" Niki said, hoping to refocus the table's attention. "What gets to him the most?"

"Love," Moggy said. The rest of the table whipped in her direction. "Love is the answer to every problem, big or small."

"Love?" Niki's face went slack, as if slapped by surprise. Moggy never struck her as a romantic type. She'd never had a serious beau, as far as anyone in her family knew. "Where are you getting this?" Niki asked.

"I noticed it in the interviews you gave me to transcribe," Moggy said. "In all of them, love was the common theme."

Ezra guffawed. "I don't recall translating anything like that!"

"Not directly," Moggy said, and ever-so-subtly rolled her eyes. "When you asked what news from home bothered prisoners the most, the answer was never air raids or lack of food. They were most tortured by the thought of their wives messing around. I don't think this is the result of jealousy, per se, but a deep longing, a desire for companionship."

"Companionship is important," Niki said, thinking of the POWs as she sipped her beer. "You might be onto something, Mogs. Love, sex, companionship. At the end of the day, isn't that what we all want?" She took another sip and pushed the beer aside, unsatisfied. Would she ever in her life have another Czech lager?

"Love, sex, and companionship are three different things," Will said, and Niki lifted one very skeptical brow. "Besides, Ezra has already produced several cartoons addressing the idea of the top Nazis taking all the best women and food."

"The cartoons are fantastic," Niki agreed.

"Of course they are," Ezra said. "I am incapable of mediocrity."

"But what if we could go further, and attach a comeback?" Lips pressed together, Niki tried to pull some ideas into her brain. Love. Companionship. Something exploitable, but what, and *how*? As she pondered this, Moggy repeatedly peered back toward the restaurant as the number of women grew.

"Moggy, pay attention!" Niki snipped.

"Are those really prostitutes?" she asked, frowning. "I'd expect more from the British. It must be so distracting! I'm glad the American GIs don't engage in this sort of behavior."

Ezra snorted. "Our choirboys? Never," he said. "There are very strict rules against it."

"Good. I'm glad to hear it," Moggy said, her eyes tracing a stunning black-haired woman as she moved through the room. "Where do they find each other, anyway? Like, how do the men know where the women are going to be, and vice versa? Is there some kind of pass code, or ticket, or something?"

As Moggy spoke, a seed planted in Niki's mind.

"A ticket?" Ezra looked up. "Heavens, who needs a ticket? They're all just right out there in the piazza."

"Anyway!" Niki said, slamming her palms onto the table. "Back to the topic of love, and companionship. Wouldn't it be fantastic if we could replicate this scene?" She waved a hand. "But instead of Brits, it'd be German soldiers."

"You want to *lure* a bunch of Nazis into one room?" Will said. "Using prostitutes?"

"I'm not talking about prostitutes, necessarily," Niki said. The root of her idea took hold, and a stem began to sprout. "What if we could get men to show up somewhere, at a specified time? An accidental defection?"

"We could promise them girls, and when they came to collect, arrest them." When Niki's eyes widened, Moggy frantically flapped her hands. "No! Never mind!" she said. "Forget it. What a stupid idea. Where would we even get so many women?"

"No, Moggy. That's not stupid. It's *brilliant*."

"I don't like where you're going with this," Will said.

Ezra sniggered. "I don't mind it too much," he said.

"We could offer companionship," Niki said. As the pieces came hurtling together, she felt winded, practically knocked over. "We tell the men to show up at a certain time, in a certain place, if they wish to meet women who are as lonely as they are."

"Where are we going to get these women?" Will said. "AFHQ is not going to let us use prostitutes."

"That's what makes the plan so brilliant. We don't *need* real women on the other side," Niki said. "The promise is enough. It's better if there aren't any, in terms of rock-bottom morale. Can you fathom how hopeful they'll be at the idea of a date, then devastated when they discover they've been stood up? Even if we can't get enough officers to arrest the men, damage will be done."

"It reminds me of the events Mother sends me to," Moggy griped. "Forcing me to light out to some bar or restaurant to meet potential love matches, and it never ends well. If we choose this route, the men should wear a pin or a rose, some signal as to why they're there, like a real lonely hearts club. This is a magnificent plan." Her glower deepened. "Quite humiliating. An absolute decimation of morale."

"It was a fun experience, is what you're saying?" Ezra joked.

"Mary Margaret Clingman." Niki lifted onto her feet. Seizing Moggy by the shoulders, she gave her a hardy but loving shake. "You, my friend, just created a goddamned comeback."

"Brava," Ezra said with a clap.

"I'm not sure about this…" said Will.

"It's perfect." Niki returned to her seat. "Either they're arrested, or these poor saps are ruined when they're expecting a date and find only other sad, forsaken men. We could use a heart, or some other symbol, instead of a flower. We'll include it in circulars and in *DND*, with instructions to cut it out and pin it to their chests."

"Where will we tell them to show up?"

"Intelligence can dig up a list of the places they're allowed to go for their measly half days of R & R," Niki said. "We'll focus on the restaurants and bars in these towns."

"I do not like this," Will said. "In case anyone's keeping track."

Niki loved that he was always so concerned with propriety and being a stand-up guy, but now was not the time. "It's a great plan," she insisted.

"Well, looks like we're off the clock, Dewart," Ezra said. "MO doesn't need men anymore. The Lipstick Bureau is getting it done."

"Cute name!" Moggy squeaked.

"You realize this will never work," Will said.

"And why not?" Niki said. "Everybody's lonely, particularly men at war. Hence, a booming women-for-hire business wherever there is a large accumulation of soldiers." She gestured toward the room.

"Well, if you go through with this cockamamie plan," Will said, "you'd better tell whoever's delivering the circulars that the invitation isn't real. You know how 'girl crazy' our *couriers* can get." He puckered his lips. "The only comebacks we'll probably get will be from our own side."

Will was right—this *was* a potential problem, as Paloma and her friends proved, but Niki had a solution in mind. *Three cheers for the Lipstick Bureau*, Niki thought. As Will passed her an inquisitive look, Niki gathered her composure and tried to quash the grin taking over her face.

41

PALOMA

May 1945

Nikola was very direct in asking for assistance. "Paloma," she said. *"Potresti farmi un favore?"* You see? It was right there in the question. A favor.

I was happy about this turn of events. It meant she'd cooled off about the incident with the men, and there would likely be an exchange of some kind. Cigarettes. Chicken. Money. *Chissà,* who knows. When she invited me to dine at the villa, I understood it might be more than one thing.

Though Nikola said she was no cook, she performed admirably, tossing freshly made pasta with powdered eggs and bacon from American military rations. This was a fresh surprise in itself. Usually when I was with an American, he brought a crate of food and expected *me* to cook.

"I hope it's palatable," Nikola said as we sat down. "It's the best I could do, given my skill level, and under the circumstances."

"Looks like a feast to me," I answered, for the last thing I'd eaten was a cup of boiled dandelions. "Any time you have extra food around, I'll take it off your hands. Valuable as a sack of gold." *In realtà*, it was better, for if I'd had gold, there'd be nothing to buy.

Nikola's cheeks pinked. "This is a bigger meal than I usually have," she claimed. "The army sends us extra rations to encourage us to invite sources—I mean, *locals*—over for dinner. So, really, this is supposed to be for people like you." She shook her head. "I'm sorry. I should've had you over sooner. The food situation in Rome is hideous."

"It's more akin to a *lack* of food situation," I pointed out.

"Yes, absolutely terrible!" Niki said, and had a quick gulp of wine. "That you've been able to endure it all these years says something about the Roman character, I think."

"Perhaps. But for most of the war, we ate well," I said, and my comment left Nikola perplexed.

Until Mussolini's regime fell, our restaurants were open, and almost every type of food was available. Then the Germans took over, transportation ceased, and the cafés closed. As bad as it was, in some ways, the food was more plentiful *before* our so-called liberation, because the Germans controlled the entire country. With the Nazis controlling northern Italy, and the Allies the south, half the country's food supply was not available to us, or the Vatican soup kitchen.

"We were thrilled to be rid of the Germans," I said when explaining this to Nikola, "but it came at a cost. Maybe one of these days, the Americans will get around to fixing it."

"I hate that it's all so difficult, but it shouldn't be too much longer until you'll notice an improvement," Niki said, and I tried not to scoff audibly. "I recognize that things have been..." She swallowed. "Slow to progress. Sometimes large organizations don't move as quickly as we'd like."

"That is one way to put it," I said with a cackle. "I do hope someone is warning the Parisians about potential delays. All that celebrating and cheering and *'Vivent les Américains!'* I expect they'll find liberation is not all it's cracked up to be."

Nikola blinked. "But they're free?" she said.

"It's better than the Nazis, of course." I took a sip of the wine—Brunello di Montalcino. She'd brought out the big guns, as you might say. "But most of the time," I continued, "your liberation feels like another form of occupation. It amuses us that your government is so surprised that we are drawn to communist ideals. Peace and everyone enjoying an equal share? This is much better than what we've seen of your democracy so far."

"I understand what you're saying," Nikola said, with an evenness that was strained, almost painful to hear. "But it's not that simple, to fix everything."

"No matter." I flicked my wrist. I didn't want to complain *too* much and end up depriving myself of a meal. "Let's eat!"

Though I sensed a wariness on her part, we dug in, chatting amiably and pouring ever more wine as the night wore on. Finally, after a great long while, Nikola got around to the point of the meal. *Per me va bene,* in light of the food and the wine.

"Paloma," she said. *"Potresti farmi un favore?"*

"Ahò!" I said, and helped myself to another healthy glass. *"Buon cibo e ottimo vino!* You will ask me something very big, I assume. Are you seducing me? I expected you'd be sleeping with your tall colleague by now." I pretended to look around. "Where has he gone, anyway? The one with the dimples?"

Nikola offered a shaky, unconvincing giggle. "You are so funny about him. I am not sleeping with Major Dewart," she swore. "His villa is next door, though I believe he's spending the night at another location, looking after some of our…" She cleared her throat. "Some of our assets."

"And your sister-in-law, the one from the dance club?"

"Doing her calisthenics, and then early to bed." Nikola splashed a very moderate amount of wine into her glass. "Don't worry, Paloma, we are all alone. To that end, I wanted to discuss a special project. You made an interesting comment when we last spoke."

I took another sip. As the warm, calming salve made its way down my throat, I was thrown into the past, back to days of family and friends and abundant meals. *Sì, certamente,* life was not perfect. With that angry, horny husband of mine, there was very much fighting, but I had my son in the home, a few lira under the mattress, and plenty of bread on the shelf. Vast riches, in other words. Even now my eyes smart with the knowledge I'll never return to that place.

"Paloma?" Nikola said, leaning forward. A look passed over her face. A hesitation.

"I am fine," I said, waving her away. "What was this comment? I don't remember much speaking. Mostly, there seemed to be a great deal of shrieking by you."

"I don't know about *shrieking,* but the gist of it was…" Nikola quirked her mouth and ran a finger along the rim of her glass. "That everyone needs a good screw, eventually," she said.

"*Dai!* This is plain fact!"

"That's why I found it so memorable." Nikola had a glug of wine. "There's a new crop of men at the villa. That's where Will is tonight."

"Now this is getting exciting." I gathered my hair and pulled it over my left shoulder. "What are you up to, naughty girl?" I asked, leaning forward onto both elbows. "Americans treat their prisoners very well! How do you get them to stay away from you? Your figure is not very interesting, but you have a nice face."

"Don't worry about me. I have my ways of keeping the men in line. But in that regard, I could use your help." After sizing me up for a moment, Nikola let her body relax, a softening I recognized as a decision to trust. I can see what you're thinking. If this woman was so smart, why'd she put her faith in a common whore? What I'd ask you in return is, why *not* a whore? Who would I tell?

You know what happened next. You want me to say it out loud? All right. She offered to pay me and my friends to "entertain" the POWs. In the bedroom. You must deem this salacious, but Nikola was merely taking care of these men's primal needs. If they were getting food and water, why not this? Also, their work was very important to the Allies, and this was one way to keep them loyal.

Did I have qualms? Only a few. But they were deserters and whoring is a good job, if you can get it. Plus, I still had hope. Maybe, one day, a prisoner might give me an answer when I asked, "Have you met an Italian POW named Paolo?"

PART FOUR

LEAGUE OF LONELY WAR WOMEN

DEAR FRONTLINE SOLDIER!

When will you have leave again? When will you be able to forget your arduous soldier's duties for a while, for a few days of joy, happiness, and love?

We at home know of your heroic struggle. We understand that even the bravest get tired sometime and need a soft pillow, tenderness, and healthy enjoyment.

We are waiting for you: for you who must spend your leave in a foreign town; for you whom the war has deprived of a home; for you who is alone in the world without a wife, a fiancée, or a flirt.

We are waiting for you: cut our symbol from this letter. In every coffee shop, in every bar near a railway station, place it on your lapel so that it can be clearly seen.

The dreams you had at the front, and the longings of your lonely nights, will be fulfilled... We want you, not your money.

Therefore, you should always show our membership card to anyone who may approach you.

There are members everywhere, because we women understand our duties to the homeland and to its defenders. We are, of course, selfish too—we have been separated from our men for many years.

With all those foreigners around us, we would like once more to press a real German youth to our bosom.

No inhibitions now: your wife, sister, or lover is one of us as well. We think of you and Germany's future.

League of Lonely War Women

42

NIKI

September 1944

Niki was on her fourth—no, her fifth—letter of the day. As the hours flew, she found herself getting caught up in her own tales.

Take this heart and display it visibly, Niki wrote. *Soon a member of our League will take charge of you and your dreams and longings.*

She drafted each one carefully, using the appropriate wording and slang. As with all materials she produced, Niki wrote the missives in German first. Nothing was ever translated from English.

There are members everywhere, since we German women understand our duties toward the defenders of our country.

Varying the letters was key. The League of Lonely War Women needed to present as a muddled collection of Frauen sprinkled throughout Germany, all with a common mission. To get screwed.

Don't be shy. Your wife, mother, sister, or sweetheart is one of us. We think of you and we think of the future of Germany.

Grinning, Niki set this draft aside, atop the others. She stood and stretched, the sweat gumming her shirt to her back. It was almost one hundred Fahrenheit outside. Her office had no windows, and therefore no breeze, and someone had helped himself to their fan. That was the way of Rome. Anything of value left unattended was purloined.

"Almost there," Niki said to Will, who was sulking in the corner.

Tomorrow, their newly trained POWs would depart for Prato, twenty kilometers northwest of Florence. After breaking into three teams of seven, they'd cross the line in two waves, the first group along the road from Prato to Pistoia, and the second and third one hour later, on the road to Bologna. Their mission was the same as before: disseminate the materials, observe reactions, and report back. Upon their safe return, they'd enjoy a few days of rest before heading back north, to the cafés and bars where lonely hearts were instructed to meet.

"Why do I feel like this is going to bite us in the ass?" Will said as Niki fanned herself with a pamphlet.

"You always think that," Niki said. Overhead, the light bulb faltered.

"You know we can't arrest enemy soldiers for walking into a bar, unless they're wearing a uniform, and openly bearing arms."

"A minor detail," Niki said with a blithe little shrug. "Our job isn't to detain people. It's to lower morale, which this does in spades."

Will crossed his arms. "Fine, then. What happens when not a single man finds the woman he's after? If our POWs are hanging around watching, and attempting to collect comebacks, we're putting their covers in jeopardy. Not to mention, if the Nazi soldiers realize it's a hoax, it could completely discredit *DND*. All these risks for what benefit?"

"The promise and then denial of companionship is infinitely

more demoralizing than reading some communist rag," Niki pointed out. "Plus, we'll have comebacks when all those men march into the very bars we dictate, with paper hearts on their breasts. *That's* why we're doing it."

With Will's misgivings about the lonely hearts club, Niki would hold on to the information about her deal with Paloma until a better, later time. After the League of Lonely War Women was successful, Niki could more easily persuade him that the arrangement was necessary to keep the men obedient, and loyal. Anyway, *Will* was the one who brought up the likelihood the prisoners would want to join the club themselves.

"I'm here to retrieve the last batch," Moggy said, stamping into the room.

With Warner having approved her official transfer from R&A, she was now a full-time MO employee. "Just go ahead and take her," he'd said. "We're all swimming out here with no raft. Grab whatever you can to float."

Niki teased that *they* weren't meant to be the ones with the flagging morale, and he'd better be careful or he might end up in a love affair with a German. As always, Warner couldn't find the joke.

"Behold, my latest works of art," Niki said, extending a stack of newly typed letters toward Moggy. "Take them to Clemente and have him do his thing. Not for nothing, but these are damned good. I should write love letters for a living." She chuckled. "I guess I already do. It's really so much fun."

Penning these fictions also made for a terrific distraction from the news coming out of the Czech Lands. The Slovak partisans were now in full revolt, working alongside Czechoslovak underground forces to wrest control from the Germans. They'd seized most of Slovakia, and similar uprisings were expected to flare up in the Protectorate. The partisans in both areas had asked for Allied support, and liberation seemed only a matter of time, but countless questions remained. Who'd save them?

The Americans or, more likely, the Russians? And how much blood would be shed?

"Niki?" Moggy said. Niki startled, having mentally left the room for a minute. "I'm, uh, I'm sorry to ask this question, and I appreciate that we're running full steam ahead." She inhaled. "But do you ever have doubts?"

"Doubts about what?" Niki said, narrowing her eyes. Good God, had Moggy caught a case of Will's hems and haws?

"It's hard to explain," Moggy said. "This sounds silly, but part of me feels sorry for them." She waved one of the letters. "Getting duped in this way. I recognize that I helped spark the idea, not that I'm giving myself undue credit!"

"You *were* critical to the entire plot, you brilliant thing," Niki said, pinching Moggy playfully in the side. "And is it really 'duped' to agree to sleep with someone else's wife?"

"I suppose that's true—" Moggy began.

With a final crackle, the light bulb went dead. Niki stared up at it, frowning, wondering whether the situation would get better or worse now that the governing of Rome was being transferred back to the Italians, a change that should please Paloma to no end. She loved to complain that the Americans couldn't properly run things and in general made democracy seem both tedious and unfair.

"No one's forcing them to be adulterers," Moggy allowed, her teeth shining in the near dark. "It's just...if it works, it'll show how desperately lonely people are that they'll risk everything for an hour or two of companionship."

"Oh, God, Moggy. Please stop. We'll never get anywhere if you go around trying to humanize the bastards," Niki said. "The fact that loneliness is so universal is what makes your idea so genius! Now, take those letters to Clemente."

"All right," Moggy said. She turned and stumped off.

"Hey, Mogs," Niki called out. "Did you get a chance to send that latest memo to your brother, asking about Czechoslovakia?"

Moggy bobbed her head. "I did, but we haven't heard any-thing back. That is the third one we've sent…"

"Please try again," Niki said. "Inform him that it's impor-tant this office is kept apprised of the latest intelligence about the revolt." Niki didn't imagine she'd get a proper answer. He hadn't given her even a morsel about what was happening in-side Czech borders or hope that he ever would. It was this last part that terrified Niki the most. If she didn't have hope, then what was left? As that Czech proverb said, *naděˇje umírá poslední.* It was hope that always died last.

The New York Times

Nazi Chief Warns Prague

—

Governor Says Revolt Will Be Drowned in Blood

STOCKHOLM, Sweden, Sept. 11—The Nazi governor of Prague, in an article in the press today, warned the population of the so-called protectorate not to revolt. The governor said the protectorate was part of the Reich and not an occupied area.

It would not pay, the governor said, if Czech patriots tried to organize or start a revolt, as the Nazis would not give up Bohemia, and any attempt to relieve the country of the Nazi yoke would be drowned in blood.

SECRET

Office Memorandum | **UNITED STATES GOVERNMENT**
TO: Private Clingman, MO, ROME
DATE: 12 Sep 1944
FROM: OSS, Bern
SUBJECT: Operation Dawes

Czech Intelligence Services in London has learned that several British and American fliers who were recently liberated from German POW camps in Slovakia are at Banská Bystrica, 115 miles north of Budapest, where Czech partisans are currently defending a liberated area against enemy troops. OSS will be sending a team of agents into Slovakia to evacuate the downed airmen, provide supplies to the partisans, and gather intelligence. It is worth noting that this "Operation Dawes" will represent the first OSS units to operate in central Europe. We will keep you apprised of any developments.

43

NIKI

September 1944

Dear George, Niki began, writing from the desk in her bedroom, the candlelight flickering against the dingy white walls. *Thank you for the memo. Though it gives me no pleasure to read about more bloodshed, I appreciate the information. That this is OSS's initial foray into the area came as a surprise.*

Niki never would've envisioned that writing to her own husband might be so taxing, but George's memo felt like a gift. He'd given her faith another length of rope and deserved *some* positive attention in return.

There seems to be movement in the region, Niki added, choosing each word with the censors in mind. The Swiss were notoriously heavy-handed, so aggressively neutral that taking a staunch position about the war could land a person in jail. Their smugness about neutrality was maddening. In Niki's view, impartiality was its own kind of side, closer to enemy than ally.

The news out of Romania was unexpected, she wrote.

Last week, Romania's dictator was toppled in a palace coup, and Ezra's home country switched its allegiance to the Allies. This development didn't right any wrongs, and it couldn't bring back the dead, but at least Ezra's home and family were now in the hands of the "good guys."

"Good guys? Who are they?" Ezra had said, incredulous. "Don't believe the propaganda. It's the same people doing the same things!"

Niki didn't know whether he meant his parents, or the people in charge. When she pressed, Ezra claimed, "it doesn't matter," and proceeded to joke that he was glad all his possessions were stolen on the boat to America because he had nothing left to remind him of "terrible Romania." It was a classic Ezra deflection, and Niki understood he felt more than he let on. She hoped a free Romania was a sign of positive things for Ezra's family as well as more liberations to come.

As for our work in Rome, she continued, *I read the latest report from Bern—30 recently captured prisoners mentioned DND. You can imagine how pleased we are that our efforts are producing a notable effect! Alas, there is more work to do. Men are returning from SKII, and enjoying some much-needed "R & R" before the next phase begins.*

Though it appears that this mission is also destined for success, we'll have full results in 2 to 4 weeks, when the comebacks fully infiltrate the public. I'd take credit for this operation—not too shabby for an immigrant, eh?—but accolades must also go to your sister, believe it or not. Speaking of, did you know Moggy has a dog now? His name is Pierre.

Pausing with a pen pressed to her lips, Niki evaluated where to go next. "I miss you"? There was no reason to lie to the man. "I've been thinking about you"? A true statement but only on occasion and not in the right way. Fifteen minutes later, Niki was still staring at the page. That she found it easier to write love letters to Nazis than her own husband did not portend great things.

I hope all is well in Bern, she went on, exerting maximum effort with each word. *Here in Rome, we chug along with minimal assistance. Our government has forgotten us, so we've had to pull out all the tricks to get by. Alas, we do what we must!*

Niki set down her pen and rubbed her forehead, trying to recall the state of their marriage as they'd left it back in the States. She remembered being on relatively decent terms, but their disastrous meeting in Rome lingered, leaving a bad aftertaste, like her mother's tripe soup. Thinking back on all the fights they'd had in their brief marriage, Niki was unable to remember what was her fault, and what had been his. That was the problem with time. It changed stories, somehow.

When they'd met, George had been handsome and cocksure with his slick, dark hair and well-cut suit, his shiny shoes and equally polished personality, which turned out to be a mirage. Men in Czechoslovakia didn't have that kind of overflowing self-confidence, and Niki hadn't realized this was a somewhat ordinary American personality trait, that bluster and flourish did not make him anything special.

But no matter how hard Niki worked, how ardently she hearkened back, even the pleasant things she could recollect were overshadowed by the bad. If she'd married George for citizenship, allegedly, why the hell had he married her? He didn't even seem to like her that much, inside the bedroom or out.

Hope you are well, Niki scribbled hastily, then signed it with "all her best." She folded up the letter, crammed it into an envelope, blew out her candle, and prepared for bed.

It was early, not quite ten o'clock, but Niki was tired, so exhausted she didn't bother getting into proper pajamas. Yawning, she extinguished her bedside lamp, slipped on a mask, and crawled into bed.

"Sleep!" she admonished herself as her eyes refused to close,

her lashes snagging on the silk each time she blinked. *"Go to sleep, damn it!"*

As she flipped onto her side, she heard a faint knock.

"Niki?" said a voice—Moggy's—from the other side of the door.

Normally Moggy's timing would've set Niki on edge, but since she wasn't sleeping anyway, she sat up, pushed the mask on top of her head, and told Moggy to come in.

"Sorry to bother you," Moggy said as the hinges creaked. Wearing a navy-and-white-striped piqué dressing gown and holding a candle to her face, Moggy looked like the resident ghost at a seaside resort. Niki swallowed a laugh. "Will's outside," Moggy said. "Parking the jeep. The last of the men have returned. All twenty-one, no covers blown."

"All of them?" Niki said, the now familiar thwack of her heart propelling her out of bed. "Where are they now?" After glancing around for something to throw on over her shirt, Niki swiped an old coat from the floor.

"Being deloused," Moggy said. "Niki? Twenty-one is a lot of men."

"It is," Niki agreed, putting one arm and then the other into her jacket. She froze, remembering that Moggy didn't know about the POWs. Will knew about the POWs but not the arrangement with Paloma. At some point, Niki was going to have to find a way to keep this all straight. "Twenty-one strapping partisans," she added, cringing at the lie.

"The number surprised me, but that's good news?" Moggy said, her words at odds with her furrowed brow. "You're always complaining that we're so shorthanded."

"That's true, but it's just like with the office supplies," Niki said, and ran a hand through her wild hair. "Sometimes you think you're shorthanded, and then you have a stroke of luck and are able to make it work."

"So that's all we're relying on? Luck? That seems...unwise."

"Oh, Mogs." Niki chortled. "Sometimes luck is all we have."

SECRET

Office Memorandum | **UNITED STATES GOVERNMENT**
TO: MO Chief, Rome
DATE: 12 Sep 1944
CC: MO Branch, OSS Washington; MO MEDTO
FROM: AFHQ
SUBJECT: German contingent

Based on intelligence received through Bern from SI contacts in the field, we have concerns about the degree to which your outpost is making use of enemy POWs. The facts as we know them are as follows.

1. POWs (numbering in the dozens) are being used by MO Rome and are a key component of Operations Sauerkraut, I and II.

2. When MO Rome elects to use POWs in an operation, they are taken from the cages at Aversa, stripped of their identities, and sent to a sub-base for training.

3. Once trained, the POWs are given cover stories, then asked to deliver "black" propaganda behind enemy lines, thereby placing these men in dangerous if not deadly situations, and for extended periods of time.

4. After the operation has thoroughly wrung out all usefulness of the POWs, the men are returned to a different cage, where they are given new records, as if they have recently surrendered.

5. Though it is our understanding they are properly housed and fed, the POWs do not receive compensation, and one can argue that they are being used in a manner strictly forbidden in Article 31 of the Geneva Convention. Violation of this and Article 32 (forbidding the em-

ploy of prisoners in unhealthy or dangerous work) would be deemed a war crime.

6. While we can recognize that you've been understaffed, this is not an excuse. Further, see the enclosed details about a mission the 15th Air Force will be completing at the end of the month. You may include your materials if you can find a way to incorporate them into the drop.

During a war, it is all too easy to dismiss actions as justifiable that would otherwise be considered obscene. Just look at what Germany has done. While treatment of detainees does not compare to the atrocities being committed in German prisons and labor camps, our standards must be higher than "not as bad as the Nazis," and this could very well rise to the level of "international incident" if you do not get the situation under control.

Beyond the problem with the POWs, we once again ask that you reevaluate the purpose and effectiveness of your work. Kesselring recently denounced the DND newspaper, saying it did not come from inside German borders. Propaganda is no longer "black" if the enemy knows who produced it. The printing office is a valuable asset, and it's a shame that it's being wasted on your middling efforts.

You are requested to attend a meeting at Caserta on 13 September at 1100 to discuss these matters and the future direction of your base.

The New York Times

28 Czechs Executed

—

Accused of Sheltering Patriots Hiding from Gestapo

LONDON, Sept. 13 (AP)—Czechoslovak patriot forces were harassing Germans today in preparation for the expected Russian entry.

The Germans, in a new terroristic attempt to put down this stroke in the rear, have executed twenty-eight more Czechs, including six women, Czechoslovak authorities in London announced. The victims were accused of sheltering the patriots from the Gestapo and of other activities.

44

NIKI

September 1944

Niki squatted beside the jeep. Damn it all to hell, they'd busted a tire. "Get the spare," she ordered Will. Then she stood and brushed her hands on her pants.

"We don't have a spare," Will called back. "Or a pump."

"This is perfect. Just perfect," Niki groused as she walked around to the back of the jeep. "Of all the goddamned luck," she said, and cursed the empty spot where a spare and pump should be. "Do you think the universe is trying to tell us something?"

"Yes. That you drive too erratically."

"You're such a card!" Niki huffed, kicking one of the good tires. "I didn't even want to attend this meeting in the first place. We don't have time for these pointless journeys. We actually have things to take care of back in the office."

At the end of September, they'd get air support, a full month later than promised, but better than never, Niki supposed. Now they had only two weeks to finish printing miniature versions of *Das Neue Deutschland*, two weeks to roll up the copies and stuff them into long, thin canisters, which would then be shipped off to Foggia and packed into bombs. The bombs were designed to explode fifty feet aboveground, at which time *DND* would flutter down, providing the latest underground information to anyone who cared to read it.

Though General Kesselring had denounced *DND*, Niki and Will saw this as good news. It confirmed the paper's popularity, and whether soldiers thought it was produced in Germany or somewhere else didn't matter. They were consuming it with enough frequency that one of their leaders felt compelled to deny its legitimacy, and they had to keep putting it out. This new plan was no League of Lonely War Women—in fact, it was "Pig Iron"—but it was good enough, especially because they were forbidden to use POWs. Their last batch of prisoners distributed the fake love letters, and the Nazis would show up to claim their women, but there'd be no one to gather proof that it'd worked.

"We're only losing a day," Will reminded Niki. "We can get back to Pig Iron tomorrow."

Grunting, Niki swept a piece of hair off her forehead. "A day's not nothing," she said. "Clemente is printing a *million* copies. I hope we have time to pack them all. And what is Warner doing that's so important he can't bother to attend a meeting *he* was invited to?"

"In fairness, the meeting *is* about Sauerkraut," Will said. "And Warner hasn't been involved in the planning or execution at all. He wouldn't even know how to answer questions about it."

"You have a point there. I wonder what they're so peeved about?" Niki stomped out to the road and squinted down its long, crooked emptiness. "He could've at least shown us the memo instead of saying the brass is mad, and good luck, suckers. Instead he's sending us into the lion's den. *Hladit hada bosou nohou.* Asking us to pat a snake with bare feet. *That's* the proper use of the expression." Niki walked a few more steps down the lane. "Wait…is that…?" she said, and shielded her eyes.

In the distance, Niki spotted two figures cycling in their direction. Young boys, she deduced. As they got closer, Niki let loose a sharp whistle. *"Ragazzi, venite qui!"* she hollered. *"Venite qui!"*

"Ciao, bella," one of the boys said as they pedaled up. He and his friend hopped off their bikes and heaved them into a fennel patch. From the looks of it, they were about nine or ten years old.

"Come state oggi, gente?" Niki said.

"Mi chiamo Matteo," said one of the boys. He had a smattering of freckles across his nose, and his hair was the color of a shiny new penny. *"Lui è Gio,"* he said, indicating his friend. *"Una gomma a terra?"*

"Yes, and we don't have a spare," Niki answered in Italian. "Any idea how often army types drive along this road?"

"Usually by the late afternoon, a convoy is coming through," Matteo said.

"Mortacci!" Niki said, and put her hands on her hips. It was ten o'clock in the morning, and already their day had been shot. Even with her efficient driving, there was no way to make the meeting, and Niki wasn't going to stand around for hours baking on a hot dusty road. "I don't suppose your village offers much in the way of cafés or rest stops?" she asked, and they shook their heads. "Yeah, I didn't think so." In this part of Italy, towns rarely had more than one or two buildings left. "Do you gentlemen have any suggestions for how a couple of Yanks might while away the day?"

"There's a good place for swimming," Matteo said. "The sea's about five kilometers that way." He tilted his head. "It's a very nice spot. No land mines."

"A dip sounds heavenly," Niki said, wiping the sweat from her forehead. "It's hot as Hades out here." She closed her eyes, conjuring the blue of the ocean, the taste of salt water on her lips. The sea had always been a salve, and her family used to spend summers on the island of Krk, in Croatia, where Niki and Pasha would lie on their backs for hours, drifting aimlessly, buoyed by the salty Adriatic. When Niki opened her eyes again, they were stinging with tears. "William." She pivoted to face him. "I want to take a dip."

"We're meant to be in Caserta."

"*We're* not," Niki said. "Warner is. Anyhow, someone could drive by right now and we still wouldn't make it."

"But we don't even have bathing costumes," he said.

"*Potrete nuotare senza costume de bagno,*" said Gio, and Freckles smacked him on the chest.

"What he means is that you would be safe," Matteo said. "If you wanted to swim." He blushed all the way to the tips of his ears. "No one is around to see anything."

"We never use them," Gio said, and Matteo looked at him with murder in his eyes. Meanwhile, Will smiled tightly, pretending to grasp the rapid-fire Italian whizzing back and forth.

"*Sembra allettante,*" Niki said. "Five kilometers is a haul, but we do have the rest of the day."

"Five KILOMETERS?" This, Will understood. "I am not walking five kilometers in this heat."

"I have an idea," Niki said, her eyes skipping toward the discarded bikes. "What if we borrowed those? We'd compensate you, of course. We have food. Cigarettes. Lire and United States dollars."

"Did you just say *lire*?" Will balked.

"What do you think, boys?" Niki asked. "Could we pay you to stay here, look after the jeep, while we borrow your bikes?"

"*Sì!*"

"*Sì, assolutamente!*"

The boys were thrilled, lit from within, and no surprise, at this point in the war. Niki imagined a stretch of endless days in this battle-weary countryside, and the pair trying to pass the time while avoiding thoughts of fathers and uncles and brothers off fighting or dead. Watching an American's jeep could likely pass for an adventure.

"Oh my God, Niki, what did they just agree to?" Will said.

"I'll pay you a little bit now," Niki said, reaching into her pocket, "and more when we return. Here. To get you started. The package is almost full."

"We don't smoke," Matteo said.

Niki made a face. Until now, she hadn't met an Italian over age eight who didn't.

"YOU'RE GIVING CIGARETTES TO CHILDREN?"

"Why don't you take them anyway?" Niki said. "I'm sure you could sell them or give them to your mothers or grandmothers. We have a few cans of rations in the back you can eat while we're gone. And later, lire or dollars, whatever you want."

The boys exchanged glances, consulting each other without a word. Niki could practically see them weighing what they wanted for themselves, or what their mothers might be pleased to have.

"Can we play in the jeep?" one of the boys asked. "Just mess around, not turn anything on?"

"Of course!" Niki said. "Do whatever you want. Just keep everything intact. If all looks good when we return, you'll be justly rewarded."

As the boys scrabbled toward the jeep, Niki turned to Will and grinned. "I believe this day is going to turn out all right," she said.

"We can't just leave a military vehicle unattended. Especially one with a push-button start."

"We're not." She crooked a thumb. "They're looking after it. Plus, it'd be awfully hard for someone to steal a jeep with a flat tire."

"You always have an answer for everything, but Niki—"

She grabbed his arm. "William. We haven't had a break since we landed in Algiers almost a year ago. Not a day of R & R. It's just an afternoon. We need this," she said. "*I* need this, and I'm biking down to the sea, with or without you."

Although Will was now shaking his head, Niki saw this as a yes.

"Gio! Matteo!" she said, and the boys popped up over the jeep's canvas top. "We'll meet back here at sixteen hundred hours. If an army vehicle comes past, flag it down and see if they'll exchange our tire for one of their spares. I'll leave a note, just in case."

Niki marched to the rear of the jeep. Into her satchel she tossed a bottle of wine, some food, and an old blanket. Through it all, Will was saying *something,* but Niki was accustomed to his protests and had trained herself to tune them out. After scribbling a note—*GONE SWIMMING*—Niki stuck it to the windshield and slung the bag diagonally across her body. The boys were already pretending to drive, ducking for cover against the crash of phantom bombs.

"Let's get to it," Niki said, selecting the less rusty bike. "If we're going to spend our war in Italy, we might as well have some fun."

◇◇◇◇◇◇

Niki stood at the top of the hill, gazing down at the Tyrrhenian Sea as it spilled out in turquoise infinity. No matter how many times she saw it, the sight always left her breathless. "Pretty, isn't it?" she said.

Will's expression was equally astonished. "It's more than beautiful," he said. "It's otherworldly. All the times we've driven on that damned road. Back and forth, to the prison camps. This was on the other side of the hill. I knew that, of course, but never took a moment to think about it. Not a single time."

"You're welcome," Niki said. She grabbed his shirt and pulled him down the embankment, through the deserted fishing village, and toward the black sand beach. Matteo and Gio had been right. The place was a ghost town. Homes were boarded up, and shops were empty, waiting for their owners to return, if they would return at all. But Niki didn't want to think about that now, nor the possibility that the area wasn't fully cleared of mines, despite the boys' promises.

At the entrance to an abandoned German pillbox, Niki stopped. Between them and the sea were more bunkers and a trench running the length of the beach. Funny how a person could forget the sea driving to and from a POW camp, but there was no forgetting the war.

"I brought some snacks," Niki said, and laid her bag against a cement wall. "Let's swim first." Inhaling, Niki flung off her shirt.

"Niki!" Will said, slapping a hand over his eyes. "Warn a fella if you're going to do that."

"Oh, for Pete's sake, it's nothing you haven't seen before," Niki said, and kicked aside her pants. She was pretending to be confident, unperturbed, all the while praying he didn't detect the tremble in her voice. Standing in broad daylight in only her knickers and bra was terrifying. It was exhilarating. It was everything at the same time.

"See ya there," Niki said, jogging down the hill, feeling Will's eyes on her the whole way. She was never the va-va-voom type—her body was closer to the village boys' than a pinup model—but she knew there must be something appealing about it. She'd always received plenty of attention from men.

At the shoreline, Niki paused, letting the water lap at her feet as her eyes began to smart. Son of a gun, the beautiful world was still right there waiting for them. It was almost too much to take in.

"Get yourself together," Niki muttered. She looked back toward the beach. "Hurry up, slowpoke!" she called out to

Will, who was now cautiously making his way down the hill. "You're—"

She froze, and her insides dropped. Miracle of miracles, the fella had stripped all the way to his skivvies. There was a little whimsy in him yet.

Niki waded a few inches into the water, adjusting her pointed bra and high-waisted knickers. The decent move was to leave these two pieces intact, but she would have to get back into the jeep at some point and didn't relish the thought of chafing against damp undergarments for multiple hours over bumpy roads.

Oh, what the hell. She unhooked her bra and carefully stepped out of her underpants, lobbing both onto the beach.

"Jesus!" Will said. "Are we doing birthday suits, then?"

"Whatever you want," Niki said, laughing, trying her best at joie de vivre even though she was wobbly from the inside out. As she hustled into the sea, even her lamentably shapeless derriere jiggled.

"This is going to be very embarrassing if we're caught!" Will shouted.

Niki laughed again, held her breath, and ducked beneath the water. She resurfaced and slicked back her hair. In long, confident strokes, she moved further out. As her muscles tightened, she swam harder, spurred on by the challenge of the open water.

Niki stopped and pinched her nose. She sank down, stretching with one pointed foot toward the bottom, but couldn't reach it after a dozen tries. Stirring her legs, she watched Will lumber into the water, moving with all the grace of an intoxicated gorilla.

"I think you missed your calling as a—" Her smart remark died in her throat when she saw that Will had jettisoned his underclothes, too. *Holy hell.* The man had no business being insecure with *that* dangling between his legs.

To calm her flaming cheeks, Niki went back under, sputtering when she resurfaced. Will was now rushing toward her in a rapid, assured stride, resembling a proper soldier, almost. "Hold on! I'm almost there!" he called. "Keep your head above water!"

"No, no, I'm fine," Niki said, stifling a giggle.

"Damn it, Niki." Will swiftly shed the hero act. "You scared me half to death, and now you're cracking up?" he growled. "I thought you were drowning or choking or something! How am I supposed to know whether you can swim?"

"I can, and quite well, in fact," Niki said, studying the flashes of red in his sandy-blond hair. It was strange how his features could change, depending on the light. "Anyway, *you're* the one who startled *me*. Honestly, I didn't expect you to remove your undershirt, much less..."

His face grew serious. "I'm sorry, is this inappropriate?"

"No! I like it." Niki's face reddened again. "I mean, it's good. It's a good thing."

"Okay..." Will smiled, awkwardly, using only half his mouth, and Niki's heart filled to the brim. They'd come a long way since defective bombs on golf courses, a long way since patio lunches at the Red Cross club in Algiers. Will was now an inextricable part of her days, like a tire on a jeep as well as the spare—critical, deeply missed if he wasn't there.

"What?" Will said, eyeing her suspiciously. "What is that face?"

"This is nice," Niki said. "Being out here, together. You seem much freer, less constricted than usual."

"Nudity will do that to a person. This is..." Will began, squinting toward the horizon. "Knowing life can be this beautiful one day, when the war ends, is what keeps me going half the time. I don't know how something can feel so near yet far away at the same time."

"I understand completely."

"It's hard to imagine what will happen next," he said. "Where will we go? Who will we be? Will our families even still recognize us?" Will glanced back at Niki just as she swatted at the tears that were once again building. "What is it? Are you okay?" He reached for her arm, but she jerked it away.

Niki's breaths were contracting, becoming hiccupy, and every last nerve ending felt exposed. "It's the salt water," she said. "Bothers my eyes." Niki held the bridge of her nose, like Moggy did to prevent a sneeze. "Carry on!" she sang. "What were you saying? It was quite poetic!"

"Niki." Will inched closer. "Tell me."

"It's nothing."

"Liar."

"Fine. It's everything. The news. The war. I don't know!" Niki tried to laugh through the two years of emotions amassing in her chest. "I don't want to go into it. You know I prefer to work with my blinders on and not think about all the horrible things I can't control. One track, dead ahead."

"But you have to get off the track eventually," Will said. "And the blinders must come off."

"What do you want me to say? It's too much. The fighting. The atrocities. All the roadblocks at work. I'm even mad at Ezra!"

After the royal coup, Ezra learned that an American plane was being sent to Bucharest to recover several prisoners of war. They'd offered him a seat to visit his family, but he declined, recommitting to his vow to never go back.

"Why didn't he accept the flight home?" Niki said. "To make sure his family is okay, if nothing else? No matter how he feels about the place."

"He's never changed his position on this," Will reminded her. "Can you blame him? We can't possibly know what it was like to be treated as he was, to experience such aggravation and outright fear."

"You're right, of course," Niki said, Ezra's words playing in her head. *I never want to lay eyes on the people who betrayed my fam-*

ily. I never want to see my family, who refuses to view them as cowards.
"I recognize that I'm not being entirely rational," she added.

"What's 'rational' when it comes to war? But, and I say this with kindness and your best interests in mind, you're *not* mad at Ezra," Will said. "Or the fighting. Or all the minor, ticky-tacky irritations in the office. It's whatever's happening in that part of the world." He gestured, more or less, toward Czechoslovakia.

"Why can't we get in there?" Niki cried. "Why can't we liberate it like we did Paris and Rome?" The question was rhetorical, for Niki already knew the answer. Not every battle of a war was won, and sometimes tough choices had to be made. Czechoslovakia existed for a scant twenty years before it was broken up and sold for parts, which rendered it inconsequential, something to sacrifice to achieve broader goals. Italy and France were important.

"Forgive me if I don't know what the hell I'm talking about," Will said, "but it seems the partisans are taking control of the situation? There's an undeniable whiff of change in the air."

"Yes, but how much more destruction will happen first?" Niki shook her head.

"I'm sorry, Nik," Will said. "I can't comprehend the worry you must be living with on a daily basis, but the Russians, I think, are moving in to free the area? Liberation *is* on the horizon."

"The Soviets." Niki snorted. "Perfect. I'm sure it will go swimmingly. Perhaps you recall a little something called the Russian Revolution? They might be our allies, but Nazis aren't the only monsters."

"Yeah, they don't really give me warm feelings, either." Will sighed. "I don't know. Maybe, to get by, you can imagine a conclusion that isn't terrible? I realize that sounds incredibly naïve," he said, his voice trailing off.

"What is there *but* terrible?" Niki said. "You've seen the news. Czech factories have been bombed, burned to the ground.

Brnö was once the center of a huge textile industry, but now only four plants remain. My parents own a wool factory, so…" She finished the sentence, though only in her head. Either they were helping manufacture Nazi underwear and uniforms, or they were dead. "Sometimes I think I could've worked a little harder," she said.

"At what?" Will asked. "Convincing them to leave?"

"Yes, but more than that," Niki said. "I picture the people in our neighborhood, my professors from law school, and wonder if I could've helped more."

"Aw, hell, you can't go there. A million people could say the same thing."

"Yeah. That's the problem. My story is only one of millions."

Niki exhaled and closed her eyes, grappling for anything else to think about. Pig Iron. Sauerkraut II. The League of Lonely War Women. Were the Nazis really drinking beer out of sacred Catholic chalices, as they'd written in *DND*? Or was it just a rumor they'd passed along as the truth?

"Niki?"

"Let's change topics," she whispered. "Please?"

"Whatever you want," Will said. He was quiet for a moment, the only sound his body swishing through the water. Niki snuck a glimpse of his face in time to witness a sly grin stretch across it.

"Oh, no…" she said. "What is that look?"

"No look. I'm just happy. Pleased to discover you are capable of harboring fears and regrets like the rest of us mortals," he said.

"You can be such a pill!" Niki slapped the water's surface, dosing him with a large splash. He turned away, shielding his face. "Please forgive me, Major," she said. "I apologize for mentioning anything, and ruining our perfect day."

Will turned back toward her. He lifted both eyebrows cutely, sweetly, and Niki's heart melted. "Perfect?" he said. "Really?" As he spoke, Will seemed to be swimming backward, *away* from her.

"Well, mostly perfect," Niki said, feeling at once cold. Only a few yards separated them, but it might as well have been miles, yet another reminder that Niki was inexorably alone. As her jaw began to tremble, Niki wasn't sure how much longer she could keep the tears dammed up.

"You can't cry and tread water at the same time," Will said, and opened his arms. "Come over here. Hang on to me."

"I'm not crying," Niki said through the knot in her throat. "And what are you trying to do, anyway? Drown us both?"

"This might come as a surprise, but you and I are not the same height. I can touch. Come here," he said again, and Niki's pulse quickened. Maybe she *wasn't* alone. Maybe, if only for a moment, Will could be her solid ground.

Without letting herself stop to reconsider, Niki allowed her body to swim toward him. She wrapped her legs around his waist, crossing her ankles at his lower back. Well aware of their nakedness, Niki pressed herself against him, and he pressed back. She buried her face in his warm, salty neck.

45

May 1989

Geoffrey Jones lingers on the photograph as Niki's heart flails around her chest. *Move on*, she thinks, not sure whether her brain is addressing Geoffrey and his slideshow or her own thoughts. *Make it go away.* Niki squeezes her eyes shut and clasps her hands, almost like a prayer.

"Wow. That guy's pretty hot," her daughter says, and Niki looks up. "You didn't know him, did you?" As Andrea continues to study the screen, her smile fades. "That woman..." She leans forward, eyes squinched. "Hang on. Mom? Is that you?"

Niki bites the inside of her cheek, and the tears begin in earnest. She nods, or maybe she doesn't, at least not enough to confirm Andrea's guess.

Geoffrey Jones advances the slide. The last one contains only numbers and words, a summary of Morale Operations accomplishments, from leaflets to newspapers to the radio programs conducted in other theaters.

"Though not everyone in the OSS bought into the idea of psychological warfare," Geoffrey says, attempting to summarize what couldn't be described in a thousand slides, "the various MO outposts were important contributors to the overall war effort. These fearless agents—including some of you—destroyed enemy morale. Without pulling a trigger or deploying one bomb, they destroyed enemy lives."

Geoffrey smiles. He means this as a compliment, but the words push Niki to the brink. Even though he's moving on to R&A, Niki can't stay a second longer.

"Excuse me," she says, springing to her feet. "Excuse me."

"Mom?"

Niki throws her napkin onto her chair and scurries out of the room.

46

NIKI

September 1944

After a meal of Triscuits, deviled ham, and a bottle of cheap Frascati, they lay on their backs on the hot black sand, Niki's left foot touching Will's right, their fingers intertwined as Will snored gently and Niki replayed what'd just happened.

In this dreamy haze of sunshine, it almost didn't seem real, but there was no mistaking how Niki felt, like a person turned inside out. After she'd clung to Will in the ocean for an incalculable length of time—it might've been seconds, it could've been hours—they'd stumbled out of the water, pawing each other as they made their way onto the beach. Niki fell onto her back and pulled Will on top of her. She expected him to do what men do, and go straight for the sex, but he trailed his lips down her body, stopping with his head between her legs.

Will's stubble was at first rough against Niki's thighs, but all discomfort soon vanished. With the first flicks of his tongue, she gasped in astonishment. He'd struck fire, and each movement was a shock. Rolling her hips and crying out, Niki felt herself thrum against Will's mouth until suddenly, he drew back.

"What?" Niki wheezed. "Why?"

He kissed her again, on the mouth, sending Niki into a writhing agony as she feared the flame going out. Somehow, despite their difference in height, she managed to flip him over and position herself on top. Will held her firmly against him, and when at last he slid inside, Niki took in a sharp breath. The brief shot of pain was followed only by slow, rhythmic sweetness.

"Oh," Niki breathed. He kissed her along the collarbone, his lips unbearably gentle. "This is the best thing ever." He laughed, and she felt it vibrate in her own body.

So this was how it was supposed to be. The kind of sex she'd read about no longer seemed like a myth, and she definitely wasn't worried about Pig Iron anymore.

"Hi there," Will said now, turning toward Niki. "How are you?" His voice was thick and gravelly.

"Hello!" Niki chirped. "Feeling fine. Did you have a nice nap?"

At the sound of his voice, already the joy was slipping away, replaced by a cold blanket of regret. Will was *married*. Niki was, too, but she didn't love her husband, and George seemed to feel the same, even if he'd make her act like they both did for the rest of their miserable lives.

No, this nauseating shame had absolutely nothing to do with George. It was all about Will. He was a good man. He prided himself on this, but if Niki knew one thing about the male psyche, it was that sex could really scramble it up. She adored Will, deeply, for the person he was, and didn't want to be the reason he hated himself.

"That was the best nap of my life," Will said. "Listen..." He squeezed her hand more tightly, but Niki scooted away. She rotated onto her side, and hopped to her feet.

"We should go," she said, wiping the sand from her backside. "It's getting late." She bent down and checked the watch in her pocket. *Shit.* They promised the boys they'd be back ten minutes ago. "Get up!" Niki said, softly nudging Will's leg with her foot. "It's after four. We've wasted the entire day!"

"I wouldn't call it a *waste*," Will said as she winged his pants at his face.

"We have to get back. Hurry!" After hastily throwing on her clothes, Niki chugged up the hill toward the bikes, pumping as hard as her legs would allow. She rounded one bend, and then another. Panting and dizzy from the wine and heat, the whole day, probably, Niki looked back, but Will was nowhere to be seen. After disentangling her bike from a bush, Niki hesitated for a second before deciding he'd catch up soon enough. She pressed her feet onto the pedals and took off.

On the ride back, to avoid thinking about her miraculous and degenerate afternoon with Will, Niki tallied up all she had to offer the boys, from cigarettes to rations to hard cash. They'd given her something like a holiday, and Niki would never have enough to repay them.

"Matteo?" she called out as she approached the jeep. "Gio?" Niki set the bike against a tree and stalked through the brush. The car appeared to be in fine shape, replete with a fresh tire.

"*Buongiorno!*" Matteo said, peeping his head out the left side.

"*Santo Cielo!*" Niki yelped. "You scared the shit out of me!" The boys cackled. "I see the car's been fixed," she said. "I take it some of our army friends were in the area?"

Matteo said they'd driven past about an hour before, and traded the busted tire for a spare. Niki smirked to imagine the soldiers' expressions when they stumbled upon two Italian adolescent boys instead of their colleagues.

"Did you have a nice swim?" Gio asked.

"It was splendid," Niki said, blushing and looking away. "Thanks for the tip. It was the perfect way to spend an afternoon."

"What happened to your friend?" asked Matteo.

"Oh." Her eyes shifted toward the road. "He should be along shortly. The man tends to get lost sometimes. Thank you, again, for watching our truck. Here's a little something for your efforts." Niki reached into her pocket and pulled out all the money she had, plus a crumpled-up quarter-full package of cigarettes. "I know you boys don't smoke, but someone in your life will want these. Or you can sell them to a neighbor."

"Not many neighbors left to sell them to," Gio said, though took the package nonetheless. "Almost our whole village is destroyed."

Just like that, Niki was back to war. "I have some crackers, too," she said flimsily, rifling through her knapsack for the last remaining Triscuits. "This is tough goin', isn't it? The desolation of war? I'm from Czechoslovakia, and by the end of this, I'm afraid my home will be mostly gone, too."

"Huh," Matteo said, crunching into a cracker.

Niki smiled. She'd forgotten this about young boys. They had a hard time feeling sorry for someone else.

"When do you think your friend will be back?" Gio asked, wiping the crumbs from his mouth. "We need to get home, and my grandmother will beat me if I do not have my bike." He shivered. "She is terrifying."

"There he is!" Matteo said. "Your friend!"

Niki's eyes followed the point of his finger to where, up ahead, Will teetered and weaved like he'd never ridden a bike in his life. "What in the world?" Niki said.

"What's that on his lap?" Matteo asked.

"Did he run into a bush?" Gio wanted to know.

Niki squinted into the fading but still brilliant sun, trying to decipher the scene. "Oh, God," she said, wanting to sink into the ground. *William Dewart, what are you doing?*

"Greetings, gents," Will said as he pedaled up, the gravel crunching beneath his tires. "Thank you kindly. *Grazie.* For watching everything and lending us your bikes. I'm sorry, you probably don't understand a word I'm saying. *Grazie, grazie, grazie.*"

The boys tittered.

"Mamma si arrabbierà," one of them said.

"Andiamo!" said his friend.

"Ciao!" they sang in unison, and rode away.

Niki waited until she heard their tracks retreat before opening her eyes again. "What took you so damned long?" she said, her gaze landing on the wildflowers clutched in Will's hand—a bounty of purple stock and bellflowers and bright pink gladiolas, along with hollyhocks and flat-petaled periwinkle. "We're late, and you decided to stop and pick flowers?" Niki scowled, hard, as if this might scare away what was right then coursing through her veins, a feeling dangerously close to complete delight.

"They're just kids," Will said, extending the flowers. "I figured they could wait. These are for you."

"Honestly," Niki mumbled. She crossed her arms and looked away for a minute before giving up. "Aw, hell." She snatched the bouquet from Will's hands. "Thank you. This is actually very charming."

Will grinned as the sweet smell of stock filled Niki's nose. "I'm glad you think so," he said. "That was the whole idea."

47

NIKI

September 1944

"A busted tire?" Moggy said. She was waiting in the kitchen because whenever Niki did something not at a prescribed time, or in a prescribed place, there was Moggy, tapping her foot and asking questions. "Did you change the tire yourself?" she pressed. "Is that why your hair looks so terrible?"

"It's been a long day," Niki said, trying to squeeze past, only to find herself out of nowhere seized by the head. "Ouch!"

Moggy jammed her nose into Niki's scalp and sniffed. "You smell like the beach," she said, and pulled back, releasing her hold. "Also, your neck is bright red. This one over here—" Moggy gestured toward Will, who seemed stuck in the doorway, as though he couldn't decide whether to come in or go out. "Major Dewart is so sunburned he might as well have spent a week with the devil. This looks like a capsize situation, not a flat tire. What's your explanation? No propaganda. Remember, I'm part of the team now!"

"I don't know what to tell you. We had a flat tire," Niki said, wiggling her shoulders. "As for the hair, the jeep doesn't have windows or doors, and that briny sea air really wreaks havoc on my crazy old locks. They've been out of control lately. I could use a trim."

Moggy exhaled in vast relief. "Yes! Thank you!" she said. "I've been *dying* to mention it." Moggy grabbed Niki once again, this time by the arm, and threw her into the room's only usable chair. "Lucky for you, I happen to have an innate talent for hairdressing. We can fix you right now."

"You're not touching my hair," Niki said. She tried to stand but Moggy pushed her back down. "Aren't you always telling me to grow it out?"

"I thought that at one time, but you might be a special case." Moggy whipped her attention toward Will. "What are you doing still standing around? Can we help you with something? Why aren't you at your villa?"

"I'd like to see how this plays out," he said.

"Suit yourself." Moggy turned back to Niki. "Don't worry," she said. "I cut everyone's hair at the Institute. I'm kind of a professional. I don't have my regular tools, but I can use the scissors from my sewing kit. Don't move. I'll be back in two shakes!"

Before Niki could protest again, Moggy darted from the room, brusquely shoving Will aside, though the doorway was wide enough for at least two or three people to walk through simultaneously.

"You're really going to let her do it?" Will said, and arched a brow.

"It doesn't seem like I have much choice," Niki said, her eyes skimming the marks Moggy left on her arm. "Sweet Ludmila, that woman has a helluva hold. I'm surprised she doesn't break bones every time she shakes someone's hand. You should probably leave." She glanced up with a watery smile. "I'd hate for this lovely day to end in a nightmare."

It *was* a great day, a perfect day, made all the better because Will hadn't immediately tried to dissect what happened. They'd simply enjoyed the drive back to Rome in cheerful, companionable silence. If and when he did bring it up, Niki had already decided what she'd say. Their tryst was a one-time event, a glorious memory, a beautiful keepsake from the past. She had no desire to ruin his life.

"I *could* leave," Will said, "but I also feel as though supervision might be required."

"I'm back!" Moggy warbled, returning within her promised two shakes. She had a comb and pair of scissors in hand, a mirror tucked under each arm, and Pierre nipping at her heels.

"*Two* mirrors?" Niki said.

"So you can see the finished product! I really should've insisted on doing this before," Moggy said, almost singing the words. "First things first. Where do you part your hair? I've never been able to tell. Most of the time, it seems to be going every which way, like you've been recently electrocuted."

"I guess I just let it fall where it wants."

"Ha! Yes, well, that is quite evident," Moggy said, dragging the comb over Niki's scalp. "Most people don't appreciate the importance of the right part. It can alter a woman's appearance as effectively as plastic surgery."

"Are you saying I need plastic surgery?"

"We could all use a little help," she said. "Now, for your edification, center parts are best for heart-shaped faces, and deep side parts for rounded ones. Blunt-cut bangs are all the rage but should only be used on people with angular cheekbones, so don't get any ideas. You, my dear, are a heart-shaped gal." Moggy began to comb with more gusto, hacking through her locks.

"Jeez, Moggy," Niki said with a staccato laugh. "Were you this rough with the folks at the Institute?"

"I didn't have to be. I've never seen so many knots," Moggy said. She tugged and snipped, and Niki bit down on her tongue to keep from crying out. "By the by, you two are going to be in hot water at the office tomorrow. Warner was *furious* when he received word you never showed. Now that I'm officially on your team, he went straight to me for answers. Made me feel foolish, to be so thoroughly in the dark. On the plus side, the rest of us made a lot of progress on the Pig Iron project!"

"Oh. Right." Niki had nearly forgotten about it. "Thanks, Mogs. It's much appreciated."

"In any case..." Moggy blew out a puff of air. "AFHQ was none too pleased about the no-show. I hope you don't receive a formal reprimand."

"I appreciate your concern," Niki said as she wondered when justifying herself to Moggy had become part of her job. "But the blown tire was random bad luck, and this was Warner's meeting to attend. If anyone gets reprimanded, it'd be him. We were doing him a favor when fate intervened."

"Not according to George—"

Niki whirled around, nearly getting impaled by Moggy's scissors. "You spoke to George?"

"Careful!" Moggy yelled. "You could've lost an eye!"

"What did he say? Why did he call?" George never rang. Did he have news about her family? The idea choked Niki with hope and terror in equal measure.

"Warner had me ring *him* when you didn't arrive at the meeting," Moggy explained. "He thought George might know where you were. I knew he wouldn't, but..."

"Oh, okay," Niki muttered. She was suddenly exhausted, physically depleted, as though she'd narrowly survived a crash. It was a strange state of being—so hungry for the same information she desperately feared.

"I'm curious," Moggy said. "About the flat tire. Why didn't you just throw on the spare?"

"We didn't have one," Niki said, and glanced down. There seemed to be an awful lot of hair on the ground. "Another convoy came by eventually and gave us theirs, but it was too late to make the meeting by then."

"What did you do to kill the time?"

"Uh, Moggy..." Will said. "Do you think...?"

"What?" she said. "Why are you still here?"

It was a good question and Niki hoped he wasn't waiting to dissect what happened on the beach.

"I think there's a bald—" Will began. "You know what, never mind. I'll leave you two alone. Good night, Moggy, Niki. I'll see you tomorrow."

"Bye, Will!" Niki called out, and waved over her shoulder.

"Jeez, that guy can't take a hint," Moggy said as more dark chunks of hair fluttered to the ground. *Snip, snip, snip.*

"You about done?" Niki asked. "It feels like it shouldn't take this long, given my hair was already fairly short."

"Almost," Moggy said. "Actually, sure. Why not? This is as good as I can get it."

"Uh. Moggy. You're not inspiring a lot of confidence."

"Well, it's not perfect," she said. "But it's decent considering what I was working with, and the fact I didn't have the right tools. Also, the lighting in this kitchen is wretched! When are the Italians going to get it together with the electricity?"

"Do prdele," Niki groaned, dread crawling through her. She'd never been overly concerned about her appearance but wasn't looking to scare any schoolchildren, or herself, whenever she passed by a window. "Moggy. Please hand me a mirror."

"Now, before you fly off the handle," Moggy said, "promise you'll take a day or two to get used to the new length. I *do* think it's an improvement. And the good thing about hair—it always grows back out!"

"THE MIRROR!"

"Please don't get mad," Moggy said, shrinking, handing over one of the mirrors. She held the second to Niki's face.

"Holy shit!" Niki barked as she waved the mirror around her head, able to make out three distinct bald patches. "*Che cazzo! Moggy!* This is horrific! Worse than I expected!" Niki leaped up, and the mirror clattered to the ground. "It's almost like you did it on purpose."

"Please, don't be mad," Moggy begged again.

"Mad doesn't even begin to cover it!"

When Moggy went to reach for the mirror, Niki pushed her away. "I'll get it," she said. "The way things are going, you'll break it and bring me more bad luck. People are going to think my hairdresser has a vendetta." As she crouched down, Moggy released a long, strangled scream. "What?" Niki peered over her shoulder. "What is it now?"

"Niki!" Moggy said, choking, spluttering, clapping both hands over her mouth.

"Are you telling me I didn't even see the worst of it?"

"It's not your hair. You're not wearing…" she wheezed. "Niki! What happened to your underwear?"

48

PALOMA

May 1945

It was the middle of September. Days were still hot, but the nights were getting that early fall bite. My friend Generosa and I were strolling along with linked arms, the soles of our worn-out shoes flopping on the cobblestone streets.

As we walked, I had the sense of being followed. Without telling Generosa, I picked up our pace. Soon I felt a dog's hot breath on my ankles. I spun around and was confronted by the visage of Nikola's sister-in-law. What was her name? Mary Margaret? Yes, that's right. I recognized her right away, on account of her clothes.

"Ciao!" I said. My greeting spooked her, and for some reason she tumbled into the road. "Careful!" I said in English. "Do you know how dangerous our streets are?"

She could've died or, worse, gotten hurt. Our hospitals were already at capacity on account of how often Romans were run over by American military vehicles. With a shortage of beds and a total absence of medicines, when it came to serious injury, it was preferable to expire on the spot as opposed to dragging things out.

"I'm sorry," Mary Margaret said. She staggered back to safety as her dog watched, intrigued. "Paloma, right? We met a while back, at the dance club? My sister-in-law is Niki?"

I nodded. "I like your brooch."

"Oh. Thank you," she said, fingering the riot of diamonds and pearls. They looked real to me, but I am admittedly no expert. "I didn't expect to run into someone I know." She blushed. "Well, not *know*. How are you? This is my dog, Pierre."

I looked at her sideways. "Is something wrong?" I asked. "You seem distressed."

"Oh, golly," she said, and fluffed her fringe. "Yes. I'm a tad out of sorts. Niki and I just had a row. She was disappointed with the way I trimmed her hair, even though I did my best." Mary Margaret spoke hurriedly, as if racing against the clock. "Then I, uh, noticed something strange, and Niki got a bit churlish, and told me to leave her alone and—" The woman stopped short. When she glanced up, her eyes were damp and wide. "You're not in the middle of something, are you? Or on your way home?"

"Home is not where we are going," I said, with a small snicker.

"Excellent." She exhaled with great force. "I could really use someone to talk to. Would you mind terribly?" As she spoke, I exchanged curious looks with Generosa. "You know. *Parlare.*" Mary Margaret flapped her hand like a puppet's.

"Yes. I know talk. *Prego.*" I sat on the curb and patted the ground. Lighting a cigarette, Generosa backed up against a wrought iron gate.

Top lip curled, Mary Margaret inspected the sooty cement for several moments before putting a scarf beneath her rear and sitting down. "I'm so overwhelmed," she said, "and I don't know where to turn. Niki is my sister-in-law. But there are secrets, not to mention a wall, and I can't seem to get over or around it. She's supposed to be my family, my colleague, my friend."

"That is a lot to ask of one person," I noted, but Mary Margaret carried on.

"I'm supposed to be part of the group, part of her life, but Niki keeps me perpetually on the outside," she said. "She excludes me from most things, then gets angry when I want to be involved. Sometimes, I have the sense that she's lying, and I'm *positive* she's hiding things."

"Everyone hides things," I said.

"Not healthy people, but I recognize the point." Mary Margaret gently tossed her eyes. "This is different, though. It's almost impossible to trust anything she says. Her entire job is to bend the truth, to tell people a curated set of so-called facts." She froze, and something passed over her face. "I mean that figuratively," she said.

"Of course." I didn't understand the hesitation, as this all sounded very American to me.

"I've told myself a thousand times that I'm overthinking it," she continued, "as I'm prone to do, but my brother—her husband!—today called her a 'slippery character.'" Mary Margaret curled her fingers into quotes. "Claims she tricked him into marrying her. What am I supposed to make of that?"

"*Ehi, aspettate un attimo.* Your brother told you this about his wife?" I said. "*Che palle!* What balls! A man should not discuss with his sister the troubles in his marriage. He sounds plenty slippery himself."

"Oh, it wasn't like that," Mary Margaret swore. "We spoke because Niki was missing for the afternoon, and I was beside myself with worry. George was merely assuaging my fears. He insisted that Niki always turns up fine, and with some grand excuse at the ready. Sure enough, she and Major Dewart came tromping in, with a fish tale about a flat tire."

"*Ahò!* Missing with Major Dewart," I whooped. "Congratulations to Nikola! That sounds like very much fun! What were they doing together, do you think, for the hours they went missing? Did you check the boudoir?"

"Oh!" Mary Margaret peeped. Her face turned crimson. "No! I don't think it's anything like that. Niki's not the type to cheat. Although, when she got back, she wasn't wearing any—" She made a sound like a hissing balloon.

"Any what, *mia cara?*"

"No. No way." Mary Margaret's eyes jumped toward Generosa, who was still pleasantly smoking her cigarette.

"She's not listening," I said. "Her English is very poor."

"I'm sorry. No." Mary Margaret shook her head. "I shouldn't be doing this. I'm not one to pass untoward rumors. I need to go. I've taken up too much of your time."

As she stood, two GIs walked past. They let their eyes stick to me, and I gave them a look, a plea to move on. From their view, I hardly had a say in the matter, but they chose politeness, maybe because I was with an American.

"Good grief," Mary Margaret groused. "Why are there so many damned soldiers around *all* the time? Shouldn't they be winning a war or something? They're a scourge."

"I rather agree," I said. "Your prisoners seem to do more work than your soldiers. Maybe you should swap them."

"Our prisoners?" Mary Margaret wrinkled her nose. "Are you referring to the POWs?"

"We know the POWs!" Generosa said, nearly startling me out of my shoes. She must've been spending more time with GIs than I thought, because her English was never so good. "We know them very well," she added. "Because of Nikola!" Generosa grinned, showing all the teeth she still had.

"*Niki?* The POWs?" Mary Margaret swung her gaze back in

my direction. I reached into my dress for a match and a second to think.

"*Alfred! Franz! Rolf!*" Generosa writhed, grasping her bosom with both hands, and disappearing her eyes into her head. "*Oh, Heinrich!*"

I reached back to give her a playful slap on the shin. "You need to practice more," I said. "If this is how you fake *la petite mort.*"

"*Il mio preferito era Otto,*" Generosa said. "Otto Berger. *Era piuttosto bravo a letto. Molto, molto sexy.*"

Mary Margaret blinked heavily, her false lashes sticking together. "I'm so confused."

"Don't listen to my friend." I paused to tell Generosa—in Italian—to clam up if she wanted to continue fucking Otto Berger. "Generosa is the one who is confused. She thinks you and Nikola and Major Dewart work with the German prisoners. There is some mistake. She is not the brightest."

"Well, we interview them from time to time, but…"

"A miscommunication," I said. "Different languages, you know."

"That must be it," Mary Margaret said, though I understood she was merely attempting to end the conversation. "Thank you, Paloma. It's lovely to have someone to talk to." She touched her brooch with one gloved finger and then, in a single move, unlatched the pin. "I want you to have this," she said, extending the glittering jewel in my direction.

I wish I could tell you I demurred, or refused, but in truth I allowed Mary Margaret to pin the treasure right onto my blouse. The exchange filled me with gratitude but no second thoughts.

You may think it strange that in a starving, desperate city, I held on to a piece of valuable jewelry, but I hated the thought of selling it for a pittance and had the arrangement with Nikola to keep my belly full. We'd serviced the men a week before, and I expected there'd be a new group soon. Life was so difficult by then, and I longed for something different, something I couldn't get from every GI who passed me on the street. I wanted to feel pretty, special for once.

"*Grazie*," I said to Mary Margaret. "*È molto dolce.* Very sweet."

"Thank you for being so kind," she replied, "and for not shooing me away at the first opportunity."

"Never!" I said, running my fingers over the diamonds and pearls, fantasizing about the other treasures she might one day bring. "You are my friend now, *cara mia*. You come and see me whenever you want."

49

NIKI

September 1944

Will was standing in the doorway, slack-jawed and glassy-eyed. Though his hair resembled a haystack, Niki's was ten times worse, even a week and a half after the mauling. Niki still couldn't decide whether Moggy was really that terrible or had done it on purpose, to get back at her for something.

"You look like shit," Niki said, brushing past him and straight into his villa.

He answered with a long, gaping yawn.

"This should wake you up." Niki threw herself across a half-broken chaise, one of the few pieces of furniture no one had bothered to loot. "We have a comeback," she announced.

Thirty minutes before, as Niki was preparing to leave the office, Lieutenant Jack Daniels had stormed in, hooting and hollering and hoisting a large envelope overhead. "You won't believe what we found in a cache of captured documents! Where's Major Dewart?" he'd asked, glancing around.

"Gone for the day," Niki said, and snagged the envelope from his hands. She peered inside and saw it right away: six safety pins stuck through hearts. Their League of Lonely War Women tags. Niki pulled out one of the circulars. *The dreams you had at the front, and the longings of your lonely nights, will be fulfilled...*

"German women will sleep with anyone," Daniels said. "What a bunch of whores." Though he'd pulled together uniforms for the very men who'd ferried the messages across, Daniels did not recognize the hearts as MO's handiwork. It gave Niki great satisfaction to tell him.

"Can you believe it?" Niki said to Will now. "It's only been a couple of weeks since the men returned. I thought we'd have to wait a month. Then again, perhaps I underestimated how briskly men will accept free sex." Niki chuckled to herself.

Sitting on the low, rickety table across from her, Will rested both elbows on his knees and clasped his hands. "Well. Good job," he said flatly.

Niki walloped his leg. "Good job? You could be a little more enthused," she said. "It's exactly what we've been hoping for! All right, we need to repeat another round of the League, and go bigger this time." Pondering this for a minute, Niki performed some basic math. "I'm thinking we recruit ten more prisoners on top of the ones we already have. Clemente has the printing capacity now that we've shipped out Pig Iron."

"Niki."

She flicked a hand. "I recognize that everything is 'on hold,' but the men are at the safe house, twiddling their thumbs. I don't see any benefit to waiting. We might as well put them to use."

"No. Absolutely not."

"William. We can't wait around for AFHQ to, quote-unquote, 'find another solution,'" Niki insisted. "When it comes to busting morale, there's no room for delay. We must capitalize on every ding in the armor, and each day this war drags on, more atrocities are committed, and more people die. We have to *do* something."

Will shook his head. "Our work has some purpose, I'll grant you," he said. "But we're not exactly saving lives. It's not *that* urgent."

"If we're doing even the slightest thing to help end this war, then yes, it is," Niki said. "I'm not going to let our resources, or our momentum, go to waste."

"No," Will repeated, and Niki could feel her blood pressure spike. All their work, all their progress and success, and he was going to let his nerves, his do-goodism overtake common sense. Here was one downside to Will's principled heart.

"Sheesh," Niki said. "Who put the shit in your shoes? Maybe we should discuss this rationally before you completely shut me down."

"Swear to God, Niki!" Will said, and exploded onto his feet.

Niki pulled back as if slapped, though she was also the tiniest bit stirred by his burst of passion. "Goodness, Major Dewart!" she said. "While I enjoy the unexpected peacocking now and again, this probably isn't the time. Listen, I recognize and appreciate your tendency toward caution, but strongly believe we should go ahead and use the assets we have. It's the only option that makes sense."

Will let out a strangled yell and dug his fingers into his hair. "You really just do whatever the fuck you want, don't you? Without a care to anyone you might trample along the way."

"When did you and Warner become such bosom pals?" Niki asked, though understood he was not talking about work. She had many jobs right now, not the least of which was to keep herself and Will and their relationship away from any uncleared land mines. Unfortunately, Will knew her too well to be led.

"I don't give two shits about Warner," Will said, narrowing

his eyes, declaring with one look that they were about to have the conversation she'd been dodging for two weeks.

Niki guessed this was coming. Though she'd felt him circling, getting closer, like an impending cold, Pig Iron preparations had allowed her to put him off, as did the fact that Will spent several days avoiding *her* while acclimating to the haircut. Each time he saw it anew, he involuntarily cringed, and then degenerated into a fit of embarrassment over having shown a reaction. *I'm sorry! I can't help it! It's not really that bad!* His response was almost cute. Because they'd gotten this far, part of her believed he would let it go altogether. But Will wasn't like her, and she should've known better.

"You want to talk about the beach? Fine." Niki stood and threw up her hands. "Let's do it. One discussion. *One.* And then we'll leave the incident in the past, where it belongs."

"That's all it was to you, an 'incident'? A way to lower my morale?" He thumped a palm against his chest. "That hurts."

"Your morale should be sky-high," Niki said with a heavy wink. "You're quite good at it, and very well-endowed." This kind of talk could usually soften a man up, but Will was not having it. She saw only fury in his eyes. "Don't get me wrong," Niki said. "I'm not upset it happened. It might've been my favorite day of the war so far. For one afternoon, we could pretend we were different people, living in a different time. You were...it was..." She cleared her throat and jerked her head away. "Remarkable."

"Why, then? Why do we have to pretend?" Will said. "And imagine it's other people? Why can't it be us, all the time?"

"Will." Niki reached for his hand, but he snatched it away. "The day was pure magic. Better than the very best dream, but we live in the real world."

"Meaning..."

"We're both married, for one."

"Motherfucking George Clingman," Will grumbled, getting

to his feet. "I do not understand that guy or your marriage at all. One minute you act as though you can't bear the sight of him. The next you're losing your head because you missed his call."

Niki blinked. "Huh? His call?" She had no idea what he was referring to.

"When we were at the damned beach!" Will shouted. "Moggy told you about it when she was cutting your hair!"

"Oh, that?" Niki laughed. "The only reason I was 'losing my head' is that he *never* calls, and I thought he might have information from home. As soon as Moggy said it was *she* who called *him*, I lost all interest. You know how I feel about him. I don't love George, but I have to keep the line of communication open."

"Here you go with the propaganda again," Will steamed. "You say he's your lifeline to home, but what has the man given you, aside from one crumb about Operation Dawes, which you would've learned anyway in an intelligence report? You're using him as a shield, to avoid having to admit how you feel about me."

"How I feel about you is not in question," Niki said.

"If that's the case, why can't we try to make it work? What's stopping us?"

"Gosh, I can't think of a thing!" Niki said as a surge of anger rushed through her. How very like a man to lob an idea into the air, and expect everything to fall into place. "Tell me, Major Dewart, what's the game plan? You want me to commit to an affair for as long as we're in Rome, and then we all go home, and pretend it never happened?"

"What? No!" Will looked genuinely taken aback. "That's not what I meant at all. I was thinking more...long-term."

"Long-term?"

"Why is that so outrageous? You're not planning to stay married to that creep, are you?"

Niki coughed out a laugh. "Brilliant. Okay. Say I did divorce 'that creep.' What then? Will *you* get divorced, too? That's the only way this pans out, you know."

Will opened his mouth to speak, and Niki put up a hand. "Don't worry. I'm not really asking you to answer," she said. "I get it, Will. You have a business and family and obligations and can't give it all up for some foreigner."

Will sat back down. He had nothing to say. As Niki took this in, the wind fell out of her, a punch to the gut. She realized she'd wanted him to respond, to make a promise he'd never be able to keep. This was the one benefit to a war, was it not? It put into perspective petty concerns and encouraged people to live their most fulfilling lives.

Life is short, Will would say, in her wildest dreams. *We might as well be happy. Let's find a way to be together.* Niki was disappointed in herself for clinging to these impossible hopes, but the reality was, she'd come to love William Dewart.

"I appreciate your position," Niki said, with as much grace as she could muster. "You have a name and a career. Children. More people to answer to. I care about you, Will, and you mean too much to me to be your piece on the side. I'm sorry, but I can't—"

As she spoke, Will stared into space, rubbing his jaw. Niki flipped around so he couldn't read her face. "No hard feelings," she said, and got up to leave. "Absolutely none at all. This is reality, and a person would be foolish to think it could be any other way."

50

NIKI

September 1944

Ezra stood at the baseline, ad side, bouncing a tennis ball, a ciga-rette clenched between his teeth. On the other side of the court, Will seesawed between his feet and prepared to return serve. The men were in a second set tiebreaker in a best-of-three sin-gles match, and Will had to win it to force a third.

"Four-three!" Ezra announced. He bounced the ball one last time, hurled it into the sky, and came down upon it in a thrash-ing squall. Unlike Will, who had textbook-smooth strokes, Ez-ra's lack of formal training was obvious. Every time he hit the ball, he moved with the clacking grace of a puppet missing its strings.

Will split step as the ball spun into the service box, and used his pretty backhand to return it deep. The cigarette now between his fingers, Ezra slapped at the ball, flinging it back. *Thwonk*, another artful forehand from Will. *Clunk*, this time, against Ezra's frame. The ball hit the top of the net, and after briefly contemplating life, it dribbled onto Will's side. He dove for it but had no chance.

"Bravo!" Moggy said, clapping wildly. "What a point!" From beneath her seat, Pierre barked.

"Nicely done, all." Niki smiled, keeping both hands tucked beneath her rear. Throughout the match, Will glared whenever she cheered for him and grunted when her favor swung to Ezra. There was no winning for Niki today, and she'd resorted to wearing a pair of Moggy's oversize sunglasses to avoid any misconstrued expressions.

"YES!" Ezra trumpeted, flinging both arms overheard. Behind him, a white marble statue of a boy soldier-sportsman loomed. The figure was tautly muscled, dressed in a pair of gym trunks, but he toted a rifle and gas mask instead of a tennis racket. "You only have two chances left, Dewart," Ezra shouted.

"We'll see about that," Will yelled back.

They were at Foro D'Italia, formerly known as "Foro Mussolini," a sprawling sports facility built by Il Duce for the Olympics that never took place. The complex sat on the west bank of the Tiber, forty-five minutes north of the Vatican—thirty-five if Niki drove—and in addition to the courts, it boasted several state-of-the-art gymnasiums and a mosaic-lined swimming pool. Though its dramatic stadium was recently rededicated as a Fifth Army rest center, no one had bothered to lop off the fascist statuary that encircled the place. Between the statues, a thousand "Duces" inscribed in the tiles, and a monument honoring Mussolini near the entrance, a person visiting the Foro could be convinced that Rome's liberation never happened.

"Five-three!" Ezra called out. He served. Using his forehand, Will ripped it short. Ezra slung his racket at the ball, knowing he'd never reach it with his feet. "Stupid shot," he said, and Will lived another day.

As the men switched sides, Niki felt herself wishing she could play, too, not that she was any good. Unfortunately, the fascists who'd once owned Ezra's villa only left behind two rackets. Niki pictured the villas' other residents rushing to pack, throwing in their tennis gear, just in case.

"This is so much fun to watch!" Moggy said. "Go team!"

It'd been two days since Niki's argument with Will, and she had to consider the possibility that the rest of their time in Rome would be spent like this, with chaperones. Regardless of what did or didn't happen between them, they needed to move forward, especially with twenty men at the safe house waiting for orders. Niki still believed they should proceed with a second League of Lonely War Women mission but couldn't get Will alone for more than a second or two to discuss their next steps.

Even Moggy seemed to be in on it, forever planting herself between them, asking inane questions, like what kind of perfume did Will's beautiful wife wear, and what was his favorite thing about her? It was as though she was playing the buffer, even if half the time it seemed Moggy wanted a buffer, too. Earlier that afternoon, Niki had asked Moggy if she wanted to skip out of work and go to the pool. Next thing she knew, swimming plans were ditched, and half the office was trooping to the Foro, tennis gear in hand.

"Four-five," Will said, and hit his first serve into the net.

Niki leaned forward, elbows on knees, playing the serious spectator when really, she was weighing her next steps. Each day of inaction was like sinking deeper into quicksand, and soon they wouldn't be able to move. Will was champing at the bit to take back the POWs, and Niki was trying to delay this as long as she could. They'd already had to return two men who'd become squirrelly and bored, and Niki didn't want to squander any more of their hard work.

"ONE MORE!" Ezra sang when Will double-faulted. He won the next point, too, taking the victory for the day. As Niki untied Pierre, Will exited the court, dragging his feet through the ruddy clay.

The foursome made their way toward the entrance, treading atop a kaleidoscope of mosaics that heralded great moments in fascist history, such as the founding of Mussolini's newspaper, and the conquering of Ethiopia, Libya, and Abyssinia, interspersed with authoritarian slogans.

"Who's the victor now?" Ezra murmured, as his eyes swept over one of the plaques. *Molti nemici, molto onore.* Many enemies, much honor. Ezra smiled quietly, as though his victory had become even more satisfying. When Niki tried to catch his eyes, he refused to look.

"What a fun afternoon," Niki said. "Next time, Moggy and I get to play. Doubles, maybe? We'll take on you and Will."

"Personally, I'd rather watch," Moggy said. She gave Ezra a soft punch to the arm. "I'm so proud of you! The underdog came through! And you did it while wearing your uniform."

"And leather Italian loafers," Niki added. She glanced back at Ezra and he seemed a million miles away.

"Meanwhile, Dewart was no doubt handed a racket at birth," Moggy went on. "He probably grew up with his very own tennis court!"

"That's a fine insult," Will said. "When one might make the same assumptions about you and your...*brother.*" He spit out this last word in disgust.

"We had two courts, actually," Moggy said as they walked past the towering obelisk with *Mussolini Dux* inscribed on the side. "One clay, one grass. That's how I can so easily recognize the type of people who have them."

When they reached the car, Niki hopped up into the driver's seat. Ezra howled and scrambled into the back. "Lord help us all! Dewart! Please? Can you drive?" he begged. "The ride here was death-defying, and I would hate to have survived the Nazis and fascist prisons only to expire because they let women operate cars."

"Sorry, friend," Will said, slumping his way to the front. "She doesn't listen to me."

"I'll join you," Moggy said, and she and Pierre climbed in behind Ezra. "When Niki is driving, I, too, feel safer back here."

"You all are a bunch of babies," Niki said, and started the engine. "I am the best and most efficient driver you'll ever meet. By the by, speaking of efficiencies, I'm planning to stop at the office to check on Warner." She threw the car into Drive. "Since we didn't tell him where we were going, those of us who look like we've just played tennis should probably stay in the jeep."

"Will is the only one who qualifies," Moggy said. "Ezra didn't even change his shoes."

On their journey back to the city, Ezra relived the match, growing more animated with each point, while Will remained quiet, his eyes resting and his head cocked back. Through it all, Niki kept her eyes trained on the road, wondering why she felt so trapped, and helpless, and even a tiny bit bereft. *I should skip the office*, she thought, but by then, they were a block away.

As they veered onto Via Baccina, a tickly sensation flitted across Niki's arms. The narrow alley behind their office was busier than usual, blocked on both ends by several long, shiny cars. "What in the world?" Niki said, craning forward to inspect the dozen or so people milling about.

They were men, all of the same stripe, like a group of clones from a science fiction film or a very boring sports team. It was the army uniforms, Niki realized. She begun to feel itchy, almost desperate to get out of her own skin.

"Busy evening," Ezra noted as their jeep slowed to a stop.

Will opened his eyes as the last stiff, starched visitor exited his car. "Oh, shit," he said. "Is that who I think it is?"

A rosy-cheeked, silver-haired man strode forward, swinging his leather briefcase, looking every bit the former war hero turned Wall Street lawyer. A gaggle of colleagues scurried frantically behind him, trying to keep pace. One aide—his hair was darker, a little longer than the others'—followed like a shadow.

"It's him," Niki rasped, as Moggy appeared over her shoulder and squinted through the filthy windshield.

"I'll be damned," Ezra said. "It *is* him. Wild Bill Donovan. The only man in the world Roosevelt fears. The President can't stand that there's someone more popular."

"No," Niki said. "I mean, yes. It's Donovan. But also—"

"Oh my gosh!" Moggy said, clambering forward, pushing on Niki's seat. "Help! How do I get out of this thing?"

"What's happening?" Ezra said. "Moggy! Don't forget your dog!"

"He's here!" Moggy said, sweat flying off her brow. She hurled herself out of the car. "It's him! My brother, George!"

51

NIKI

September 1944

Niki stood with her arms crossed, a lit cigarette dangling from her fingertips. If George was hoping for a cheerful reunion, he was in for a surprise, especially after ignoring his wife for weeks and then turning up at her workplace accompanied by a band of G-men.

"This is quite the fanfare," Niki observed. "You must like giving people heart attacks."

"Is there a reason our appearance would make you so nervous?" he said.

Shifting positions, Niki examined George. His hair was longer than she'd seen it, and he'd been dyeing it black. The more Niki stared, the more he seemed like a portrait of someone she'd known once but had mostly forgotten. "I wouldn't use the word *nervous*," she said at long last. "But a little warning would've been nice. At least one person was unflinchingly thrilled to see you."

George laughed without moving his mouth. "I do believe that's the first time Moggy has ever voluntarily embraced me," he said, and Niki was curious whether he'd noticed she hadn't done the same.

"So, what brings you to our fledging Rear Zone operation?" Niki asked. "It can't be anything good."

"Donovan and Dulles were already coming, and I decided to tag along," George said. His eyes were droopy and tired, his voice that of someone reading a long and dry list. He looked annoyed to be there, as though she'd demanded he come. Finally, he exhaled and shook his head. "I warned you, Niki. The thing with the POWs is a problem. Dulles and Donovan are here to conduct a special study to determine just how bad it is."

"Oh, for fuck's sake," Niki said. "How long are they planning to stay?"

"I'm not sure," George said. "A week or two?"

"Jesus!" Niki groaned. "Just what we need, a bunch of uptight wolves prowling around. Well, good thing Moggy did this." She gestured toward her hair. "I won't have to worry about slapping anyone for getting too fresh."

George managed a smile. "I was wondering about that—"

"I know, I know. I look like a young lad who's gotten his head stuck in a wheat combine."

Tweaking his mouth to prevent a laugh, George straightened his spine. "It is a rather unfortunate result," he said. "Though I'm concerned you might have bigger problems than whether Donovan will make a pass."

"Let me guess. The Geneva Convention?" Niki inhaled deeply on her cigarette, letting the warm tendrils fill her body. All this smoking was probably not very healthful, but she couldn't fathom giving it up. On some days, it was the only comfort she had. "The point of the articles is to prevent the mistreatment of political prisoners," she said. "But nobody is being mistreated.

We only use men who enjoy the work, who *want* to participate. We even returned two whose hearts were no longer in it." These prisoners had tried to escape, but Niki didn't reckon George would benefit from hearing this detail. They weren't harmed in any way, just bored. "It's really the ideal arrangement. We have a vast repository of able bodies who speak perfect German, and know the ins and outs of Nazi life. Why shouldn't we use them to infiltrate enemy territory?"

"I understand, but—"

"Plus, what is war but a series of small and large violations of one sort or another?" Niki ranted. "There's not a damned general who hasn't broken a few laws, and with all that's happening in Europe, I hardly think this could be considered a war crime. Why would anyone punish a lowly private doing her best when they need to go after the Hitlers and Himmlers of the world?"

"While I appreciate your point," George said, "and agree about the spirit of the Convention, you are playing with fire. I know your modus operandi is excuses and justifications and skirting convention, but eventually you're going to find yourself ensnared on a hook that you can't easily slide off."

Niki flicked her cigarette into the street. "Why are you so concerned with what I'm doing, anyway?" she asked, studying her husband again.

Her husband. A legal fact, yet incomprehensible all the same. There'd long been a gulf between them, and it'd grown ten times over the past year, starting well before the business with Will. Somewhere along the way, George had become a less familiar and less welcome presence than his sister.

"I'm worried," he answered. "Simple as that."

"Yes, but you're not worried about *me*," Niki said. Although George seemed like a stranger, some facts of her husband remained crystal clear. "You're worried about how I'll make you look."

"You're my wife," he said, glowering, emphasizing the *my*, the possessive. "Whatever dirt you get on your name is also on mine."

"I'm not even using Clingman!" Niki said. "The only reason people know we're related is that you keep bringing it up. That's probably the whole reason you're here. To remind everyone I belong to you."

"No, Niki, that's not it..."

"Ha!" Niki scoffed. "I don't believe you came all this way to tell me to be careful—again—which you could've easily done in a letter or on the phone."

"You're right," George said, and closed his eyes for a beat. "I *do* think you need to be careful, but that's not the main reason I'm here. I came to Rome because there's something I must tell you in person."

"Really?" Niki said with a flash of hope. Did he want a divorce? Was he harboring a chippie in Bern? Dulles and Donovan were notorious for their roving eyes, and perhaps George had fallen in love with a charming Swiss Miss. *Oh, please, sweet Zdislava Berka, let it be true.* "Is it about...?" In one breath, Niki's hope crashed to the floor. If George had a chippie, he'd keep her a secret so he could have both a wife and a gal on the side, which meant there was another reason for the visit. "Do you have news about Czechoslovakia?" she said. "About Brnö?" Niki braced herself, waiting for impact.

"In a manner of speaking." George sighed, and for a moment looked sad. "Dawes remains the only source of information coming out of the Protectorate, and I don't know what's happening in Brnö. That said, I do have news. It's about your brother." As he spoke, Niki's body went cold. "Pasha is alive, and I know where he is."

SECRET

OFFICE OF STRATEGIC SERVICES

9 October 1944

Summary Report on Observations in Rome for the period 27 Sep 1944 to 8 Oct 1944

I have been at MO Rome for almost two weeks and although my study is far from complete, I wanted to put together a few preliminary thoughts.

Recruiting POWs

To the credit of this outpost, great thought and consideration was put into the vetting of candidates for their missions. According to interviews conducted with Major Dewart and Private Novotna, when selecting the POWs, they focused on maturity, intellect, and a history of anti-Nazi behavior, with preference given to anyone punished for their beliefs. Further, they interviewed only those prisoners who voluntarily surrendered.

Upon narrowing down the group, the men were put through hours of interrogation, using many of the same questions as were asked during OSS training school. After they were trained and given the proper documentation and credentials (produced by R&A), the men were sent across enemy lines.

Problems & Concerns

While MO Rome reports no problems with the process, several issues have been noted by other groups (for example, SI), including but not limited to the following:
1) the risk of recruiting double agents
2) violation of international protocols

3) ineffectiveness (e.g., each prisoner can only carry so much propaganda)

SI agents have encountered the MO recruits in the field on multiple occasions, and feel the men get in the way of their efforts. As no specifics have been provided, one can assume that some of these SI agents mistook the men for bona fide Wehrmacht soldiers.

MO Rome Response

First, it must be established that Morale Operations is naturally at a disadvantage due to its late start relative to other OSS divisions (founding: January 1943). This has greatly hampered MO's ability to secure first-class equipment, and first-class personnel.

There's a real "flair" to how things operate, and a modicum of success can be claimed. Some of their propaganda offered tangible comebacks and is so "black" not even The New York Times sniffed it out (see the attached, published in the paper this week).

MO Chief Warner recognizes the "Wild West" nature of the operation but chalks it up to "work-arounds" due to the aforementioned lack of equipment and personnel, combined with minimal communication/advice/guidance from Washington and AFHQ. These "work-arounds" include use of the POWs.

While the use of POWs has been an interesting experiment in distribution, it's not without significant downsides. In addition to the issues already raised, I'm concerned about the possibility the practice violates articles 31 and 32 of the Geneva Convention. Furthermore, one of our agents has uncovered an alarming association between the prisoners and local women, possibly prostitutes. We've interviewed two men who were part of the operation, and they recalled only the first names of these ladies: Rosa, Paloma, Antonella, Generosa, and Sally. It's likely these are aliases. The men have asserted that the women are being paid by MO Rome employees. I've asked the Office of Inspector General (MTOUSA) to look into these and other matters.

Chief Warner claims that they've stopped using POWs until our investigation is complete, though it's impossible to verify the accuracy of the statement, given the lack of adequate record-keeping. I will continue to keep all interested parties apprised of the developing situation.

William J. Donovan
Director

The New York Times

LEAGUE CIRCULATES VALENTINE TO SOLDIERS ON LEAVE

By Cable to The New York Times

ROME, Oct. 9—A rather incredible prospectus of the "League of Lonely German Women" was distributed here this morning as having originally been published in Hamburg and discovered on the Eighth Army front.

The circular bears a valentine-like emblem of overlapping hearts, and the theme line is:

"We are waiting for you."

What it comes down to is that any German soldiers in a strange town on leave are invited to display the emblem, and it will attract a local member of the "Lonely Women's League."

"Don't be shy," reminds the document.

52

PALOMA

May 1945

Mary Margaret stomped into the club *in modo aggressivo*. Though Rome had grown wild by then, she drew many looks with a dog leash wrapped around her elbow. People speculated that it was for something salacious and not a pup named Pierre.

"Paloma!" Mary Margaret screamed through the pulsing and the heat. She wore a pale blue jacket lined with crushed raspberry over a pine-green suit—quite lovely but far too much fashion for the place.

"Ciao, bella." I plucked the pink artificial flower from her hair and placed it behind my ear. "How are you, my new friend? Where has your sister-in-law been? I have missed seeing her." Nikola gave me the impression that the business with the prisoners would be a regular occurrence, but already a month had

passed. Until she went silent on me, I hadn't realized how much I'd come to rely on her dollars and chickens. What was at first a lark, a money-making gambit, was now a necessity. Winter was coming, and for the first time since the war began, I worried about my ability to get by.

"Huh?" Mary Margaret touched her ear, then cupped her hands around her mouth and leaned forward. "I need to talk to you," she said, and I felt her hot, damp breath on my face. "It's important."

"Andiamo!" I grabbed her arm and dragged her through the club and out into the alley. Because I'd forgotten about the dog, I had to reopen the door to let him out, too. "You are sweating. Do you maybe want to…" I mimed removing a jacket.

"I've wanted to all day," she answered, lightly panting. "When I got dressed this morning, I didn't think about the fact my suit is green. People are funny about anything that even vaguely resembles a Nazi uniform, and now I'm paranoid about taking it off."

"At least lose the ascot," I said, and she complied. "Why have you come to find me? I presume it's not to dance."

"It's not." She shook her head. "I'll get right to the point. Our office is being investigated about the use of POWs. It's a very serious situation, and my sister-in-law is at the heart of it." Mary Margaret paused to laugh, though with a complete absence of cheer. "George was right. Niki always has some grand scheme underway, and now she's lured poor Major Dewart into her gambits." The woman's brow darkened. "In addition to whatever she lured him into before."

An investigation? What did this mean? I trusted Niki and, all this time, assumed money was a day or, at most, a week away, never once considering that I might've seen the last of it. "Okay…" I began evenly. "Why have you come to me with this news?"

"I saw your name in a report," she said.

"Dai!" My heart galloped. "That can't be correct!"

"It's true. I'm acting as the top guy's secretary while he's in town for the investigation. His name is *Wild Bill*," she said. "In fairness, the report lists only first names—"

"First names of *what?*" I pressed.

"Er, it doesn't matter." Mary Margaret looked away. "Maybe it's a coincidence, but Generosa said that thing about the POWs, and then I saw your name, and everything clicked. I thought I should warn you."

Warn me about what? I longed to ask. Mary Margaret was no doubt worried about potential reprimand, but angering some American military figure was not an ingredient in my pot of concerns. What I truly wanted to know was the context of my name being used, and whether there would be more POWs, which is to say, more money.

"Will your office stop using the prisoners?" I asked.

Mary Margaret shrugged. "I don't know," she said. "According to Niki, it's a technicality, and soon it will be back to business as usual." With these words, my entire body released. "But I don't know what to think. The thing with Niki is—"

"No," I said, and put up a hand. "No more." I wasn't prepared to digest further bad news. For now, I needed to believe in Nikola, and that she would come through for me.

"I'm sorry. I hope you don't think I'm a terrible gossip," Mary Margaret said, misreading my gesture entirely. "But this all seems very bad. My friend Ezra says regularly consorting with German prisoners was bound to go south, and maybe he's right. There was even a whisper of *prostitution...*" She passed me a weighted look.

I cackled. "*Santo Cielo!* Prostitution! How scandalous!" I said, playing along. This Mary Margaret was truly precious. She'd learned what I was up to and had come to caution a prostitute about the men she was sleeping with. Ordinarily it was the other way around, and it was nice to be on this end of things, to be enough of a person that someone else was concerned. It nearly brought me to tears.

"But it's not just the report," Mary Margaret added. As tears welled in her own deep brown eyes, she wrapped the leash around her hand and pulled the dog closer to her side. "I'm surrounded by people who tell lies, and people make decisions based on these lies, and getting to the truth of any one thing feels impossible. It's like I'm swimming and swimming but can never find the surface."

"Lying is bad," I agreed. "But we must take responsibility too, no? Sometimes the lies are obvious, and we choose to believe them regardless."

Mary Margaret startled. Her eyes grew very round. "Wow. That's…that's quite Jungian. I'm a follower, an admirer of his work."

"Nikola told me about your scholarship," I said. "What a fun story." Mostly, it highlighted the chief difference between someone like her and someone like me. I would never find myself in a position to follow an analyst around the world merely because I liked what he espoused.

"It *was* fun," Mary Margaret said sadly. "Until it was over. Oh, Paloma." She squeezed her eyes shut. "I wish I could leave. I *would* leave, if not for Pierre, and the possibility of being court-martialed for desertion. What we're doing, here in this office, I don't like it."

"I find it is very rare to agree with a government," I said. "Yours in particular. This is why so many of us want to become communists. Try not to worry so much. You can't take it personally. This is a war, and people do what they must to get by."

"Too many excuses," Mary Margaret said, her gaze now leveled on the darkened street. "I don't know how you and Generosa got mixed up with these men, and I don't need to know." She spun back toward me. "But you've been so kind, and I'd hate for *you* to land in trouble. I should probably mention Niki is being accused of sending *prostitutes* to entertain the men, and that's how your name is involved. I'm sure it's a misunderstanding. Can you imagine anything so depraved?"

"The very worst!" I said, laughing again. When Mary Margaret blanched, my laughter stopped short.

"Hold on a minute," she said, and rattled her head. "*You* knew about this? *How?*"

"*Pensarci, bambina,*" I said. "Think about it. You are a very smart girl."

Though her face maintained a certain blankness, I could sense the wheels turning in her head. "You're not…" She let out a gasp. "I thought you were a housewife!"

"I am. Or I was, at one time." Even as I smiled, my spirits began to flag. She hadn't come to warn *me* about the investigation. She'd come to warn a different girl, one she'd concocted in her mind. I decided to let her off the hook, as you Americans might say. "I understand that you're not permitted by your army to speak to women like me," I said. "Since your office is in enough trouble, you and the dog should probably return home. I can pretend we did not have this conversation."

But Mary Margaret did not move. "Wait. Is this…" The wheels turned and turned. "So, the report is correct? You *do* have an arrangement of some kind? Is Niki or someone else paying you, to—" she cleared her throat "—entertain the men?"

"I certainly can't be giving it away for free!"

"How many have there been?" she asked, calmly, confounding me with her composure. Based on what Nikola said, I would've expected her to expire from shock. "The prisoners?"

I thought about this. "A few dozen, spread between me and four friends. I have a ledger if you'd like to see the details." As with any business, it's important to keep thorough records, for financial purposes and to remember who made the best customers. It was also a map, I hoped, of the many paths that might lead to Paolo.

"A *ledger*?" At last the curtain of horror fell across Mary Margaret's face. "Oh my God, Paloma! I wish you hadn't told me."

"It is okay, *cara mia*," I said. "I am not ashamed, and I am in possession of all the proper paperwork and stamps." From my dress, I pulled out the yellow card of the *mignotta indipendente*, the independent whore. "I am very diligent," I told her. "I never miss a weekly inspection. It is a very lucky job, and unlike in your country, I cannot get into trouble for working."

"I'm so sorry," Mary Margaret said. "I didn't mean to insult you. Whatever your job, whatever your…" She flung a hand. "I hate that Niki got you mixed up in this. She has a real knack for taking advantage of other people's desperation. Is William Dewart in on this, too? He can't be." She appeared to mull this over. "He's too nice."

"I cannot say. It was only Nikola who made the arrangement, but they work together, and it's impossible to know the ins and outs of their pillow talk."

"Pillow talk." Mary Margaret's face soured, and she turned to face me again. "Are we friends, Paloma?"

"Yes, we are friends!" I said, and pulled back my hair to reveal my left shoulder. "You see, I'm wearing the brooch you gave me!"

Mary Margaret touched her heart. "I'm so glad you're finding a use for it," she said. "Part of me worried you might sell it." She gave an abashed smile. "Not that there's… You absolutely should if you need to!"

"Sell a gift from a friend? *No, mai!* I will cherish it," I said, praying that I'd always be able to scrape together enough money to make this true. "Tell me. Is there something you need to ask your friend?"

"Oh, jeez. I don't know how to put this, exactly." Her eyes darted away. "It's about Niki and Will. I sometimes get the feeling that they *are* sleeping together. Is that terrible?"

"*Avoja!*" I let out a hoot, and Mary Margaret drew back. "Not terrible because I believe the same thing. I knew it all along. I said to myself, *e finiranno a scopare*. Eventually, they're going to fu—"

"Paloma!" Mary Margaret chirped. "She's married to my brother!"

"Yes, but he does not fulfill her needs, if you catch my drift," I said, winking, though she did not in fact catch it, from what I could tell. "To me, Nikola denies she and William are fucking, but I've divined the truth. *Dice un sacco di cazzate*. She's full of shit. How did you find out?"

"I didn't find out anything," Mary Margaret said. "You made that comment the last time we spoke, about checking for them 'in the boudoir,' and the idea's been plaguing me ever since. It was after the flat tire incident that the mood really changed, and they began acting incredibly uptight, like something unspeakable happened."

"I do not understand what a flat tire has to do with this?"

Mary Margaret bit down on her lip, thinking this through. "Well. I didn't tell you this before, but when they came back from their little misadventure, Niki wasn't wearing her underwear!"

I whooped again. "Now this is getting exciting!"

"When I asked her about it, Niki said she ditched the underwear because she fell off the roof!"

"The roof?" I looked at her cross-eyed. "What roof?"

"Not an actual roof. She was having, you know, a *personal problem*? Flying her colors?" Mary Margaret waved her hands around her head as if this might summon my understanding. "I'm talking about her monthlies, Paloma."

"Oh, *certo*!" I chuckled. "In Italy it is different. We have guests, or the red week, or a flood." A thought occurred to me then. "How long ago was this 'outing' you described?"

"Three weeks ago? A month, maybe?"

I nodded, my suspicions confirmed. "This would make sense," I said. "During this time, I have also noticed a change between them." From my perch on the Spanish Steps, I could see something had shifted over the past few weeks. It was a longing on his face, a nervousness in hers, and always a grand space between them, a very wide berth. "It seems to me you are correct in your assumptions," I said. "They've touched fire, and are afraid of it happening again. This may explain why your sister-in-law has been so 'uptight.'"

"Maybe... Though, in fairness, Niki has had a rough go of it lately. She got some news about a family member, and..." Mary Margaret stopped. "Hold on. I thought you two hadn't seen each other in a while?"

"We haven't *spoken*," I clarified. "But I have seen her and William Dewart together, many times, though usually they are accompanied by you or the cartoonist."

Mary Margaret exhaled. "For the sake of my faith in humanity, I hope our suspicions are off base," she said. "I should go." She tugged on the dog's leash, and I could see she was sweating again. With a mumbled apology and a hasty thanks, she staggered away. I watched until she disappeared, admiring the swish of her blue raspberry-lined coat.

When did we have this conversation? Sometime in mid-to-late October. Yes, I'm sure. It's easy to remember because that's the last time I ever saw her.

53

NIKI

November 1944

Because of the torrential rains, Niki hadn't come up to the roof in weeks. No one had been much of anywhere as most of the roads leading to and from Rome were impassable and people had died trying to cross the gushing rivers. The poor weather also meant a stop to fighting in northern Italy, giving the Germans time to recover and regroup. It was another delay, on top of waiting for Donovan's investigation to conclude. Niki felt as though she'd lost control but couldn't do anything about it.

Lighting a cigarette, Niki gazed out across the rooftops. She loved this time of day, when Rome was bathed in a golden, late-afternoon light. It was damned beautiful, if she didn't look too closely at the thinly clad housewives haggling at the food stalls below, fighting over a few pieces of cauliflower. Around the piazza's sad, cloaked statue, the *ragazzini* gathered to barter with the GIs, or beg from them, or offer them women they had no right to sell.

Niki took a pull on her cigarette. It was a shame. She might've loved Rome, if not for the war. The idea of staying in the city much longer was almost intolerable, yet Niki was also scared by how quickly they were hurtling toward the finish line. Weather delays aside, progress *was* being made on a wider scale, such as the recent naval victory in the Philippines and the crumbling of the Holland defensive line. In Paris, shops had reopened, and bridges were being built. Even Goebbels was yammering about peace. In three months or in six, this war would end, and Niki hardly knew what she'd do. Her dreams of Czechoslovakia were smashed, blown away in a Red haze. Returning to life with George was the only option, but Niki couldn't bear the thought.

Nor could she bear to consider her brother's fate, and after a month, Niki still struggled to digest the information from George. Though her parents' whereabouts remained a mystery, Niki now knew that Pasha was in the Monte Rosa area of northern Italy, fighting on behalf of the fascists. They were in the same *country*, and somehow both closer and farther apart than Niki could've imagined.

Pasha was part of the First Battalion Vládní Vojsko, once the military force of the Protectorate tasked with keeping peace at home, until recently, when they were deployed to Italy to support German military operations. Hitler called for all hands on deck, and while MO Rome had been mocking his desperation from the safety of their office, hee-hawing at the idea of old ladies on roller skates, it turned out that Hitler's backup players included the Vládní Vojsko and Niki's little brother.

Now Niki had this answer but understood little. She didn't know whether Pasha joined up or was conscripted, or if he was happy about the work or trying to escape. Niki remembered with grim clarity what she'd said when Moggy had second thoughts about the League of Lonely War Women. *We'll never get anywhere if you go around trying to humanize the bastards.* The memory made her sick.

"There's a decent chance he's not fighting," George said, in an unprecedented attempt at calming his wife's fears. "Reportedly, the First Battalion has limited responsibilities on the front, mostly construction of fortifications and field positions."

For this small mercy, Niki was grateful. George hadn't needed to travel all the way to Rome to deliver the information, nor did he have to be so kind when he relayed it.

More news had come in the weeks since. Recently, there'd been another series of air raids in Brnö—nearly three thousand bombs dropped in one day. It used to be that folks in her hometown only saw Allied planes when they were flying on their way to somewhere else. Now they had to worry about bombings from all sides, more so with the Czech partisans acting up, and the Germans desperate to shut them down.

"Niki?" said a muffled voice, followed by three raps. "Are you up there?"

Niki crawled over and flung open the hatch to find Moggy peering up from the ladder. "Is it terribly high up?" she asked. "I'm wearing slick shoes."

"It's safe," Niki said, extending a hand. "Come on." After hoisting her up, Niki stepped back and placed both hands on her hips. "Slick shoes." She clucked. *"In realtà, sono pantofole."* Moggy wore silk slippers along with some kind of cherry-red tunic ensemble that had cheerful bands of turquoise and lime at the sleeves.

"Dinner pajamas," she said before Niki could ask.

"Very nice. Welcome to my office," Niki said, stretching her arms.

Since Donovan and Co. swooped into town, Moggy had been fretting herself sleepless about the POW investigation, and Niki found herself having to assure Moggy daily. "Those military types are obligated to sniff around wherever someone's breaking the tiniest rule," she'd said a dozen times. "But they have real criminals to worry about." The longer they went without news or follow-up, the firmer Niki's conviction, and the more she was able to believe her own words.

Though Niki cut a persuasive argument—in her opinion—Moggy had been unusually quiet and distant, not to mention busy being Wild Bill's gal Friday. Son of a gun, Niki missed the woman's spirit, from the amateur analysis to her wide-eyed surprise at everything, even the mundane.

"It's nice to have you up here," Niki said as Moggy lurched her way toward an overturned crate.

"Good Lord, this is higher than I thought," she said, taking a seat. "What are you doing up here?"

"Oh, just ruminating." Niki chucked her cigarette off the roof and ferreted around in her pocket for another. "It's a good place to mull things over. Or let your mind go blank, take your pick."

"What are you mulling over? I thought you were grounded from your little..." She waggled her fingers. "Scheme."

"For now," Niki said. "But no news is good news, and they'll have to let us act soon. Especially now that the rains have stopped."

They were back to those early days in Rome—producing endless reams of propaganda and watching it pile up. Meanwhile, the Reich was spiraling into greater chaos, revealing more tender places to poke.

"To date, we've focused on the morale of soldiers," Niki mused, "but I think civilians are our next frontier. The recent infrastructure problems should be good for that." German administrative services were in such disarray that citizens had been ordered to use "any means necessary" to deliver the mail. If somebody stumbled upon a letter addressed to a person the next town over, the onus was now on him to get it there. As usual, noncompliance was punishable by death.

"Feel free to pitch in with another idea," Niki added. "I was thinking, if we can find a way to get *our* materials into *their* postal system, we can serve up propaganda to everyone, every day, like cornflakes for breakfast. Hey!" She pointed at Moggy with a cigarette. "Project Cornflakes. That's not a bad code name. Don't let me forget."

"Niki, I need to ask you something."

"If they give us air support, we can drop the propaganda onto their postal trucks and wagons," Niki went on. "Bombed-out trains. The open road! Do you have any dastardly thoughts about what materials we can include? Maybe some kind of reverse Lonely Hearts Club, though not that exactly."

"Niki—" Moggy tried again. When Niki put up a hand, she batted it away. "Are you and Major Dewart having an affair?"

Niki's neck snapped in her direction. "What?" she said as heat spilled across her cheeks. "Of course we're not having an affair." This much was true. The tension was thicker than ever and they only spoke when required. There was exactly no sex or even eye contact going on. "Where'd you get that idea?" she asked.

"I have my reasons," Moggy said. "Niki, I can't do this anymore. I can't keep working here. I need to put in for a transfer, or something."

"A transfer? What in the name of Ludmila are you talking about?"

"The situation is untenable," Moggy said, and covered her eyes. "This office feels like a massive propaganda machine, and I'm not only talking about *DND* and the leaflets. Nothing is what it seems, and it's screwing with my brain."

"Is this about the POWs?" Niki asked. "I've told you a thousand times, you should be *glad* I didn't let you in on it. And besides, all the men we used have been returned to camps. A huge waste, if you ask me, but what could they possibly get mad at now? We are not actively using POWs."

"That's part of it, but the problem is so much bigger." Moggy dropped her hands. "Yesterday, I walked into the printing office and stumbled upon Clemente taking pictures of Lieutenant Daniels wearing a Swiss uniform."

"Oh that?" Niki gave a dismissive flick of the wrist. "In the next issue of *DND*, we're going to put Hitler's head on Daniels's body to make it appear as though the Führer was photographed surrendering to the Swiss."

"That's exactly what I mean!" Moggy wailed. "Everything is a plan, or a trick, or an outright lie. I don't trust anyone anymore. Not even myself!"

"Here's an easy clue," Niki said. "If it's written in German, don't believe it. That goes for whatever *we're* producing and what their government puts out."

Moggy crossed her arms. "And what about the *other* POW arrangement?" She hardened her face, gritting her teeth with such intensity that Niki experienced it physically, like an electric shock. "The one with your friend Paloma? The prostitute."

Niki forced a laugh. "What would Monsieur Jung have to say about such judgment? Yes, Moggy, she's a prostitute, but in case you haven't noticed, there's a war going on, and these are desperate times. Anyway, it's allowed by the Italian government. Half the brothels in this town are state-run."

"I don't care about Italian brothels!" Moggy yelled. "I care that you're paying someone to have sex with the POWs."

"That is not what's happening," Niki said, the lie snapping like a rubber band out of her mouth. For a second, she contemplated recanting but immediately decided against it. Not even Will knew about Paloma, and Niki was doing them both a favor by keeping this secret. If it came up in the context of this or another investigation, she wanted everyone to be able to truthfully plead innocence.

As she rolled this over in her head, Niki's breath stopped short. Did Paloma's name come up in the investigation? Was that how Moggy had gotten wind of it?

"You're telling me this isn't true," Moggy said, jawline quivering. "Paloma is not sleeping with the POWs? Because she told me that she is."

Niki almost passed out from the swiftness of her relief. Better for Moggy to have heard it from Paloma than a government file. "Listen, what Paloma does on her own time isn't my business," she said. "A girl has to make a living. You're getting too mired in the trivialities, Mogs. The ins and outs. I know you're worried about how all this…" She waved a hand. "How psychological warfare plays into the collective unconscious. But I'll have you know that your precious Jung might be working for us soon."

"That can't be true," Moggy said as the blood drained from her face. "You're feeding me more propaganda."

"Au contraire," Niki said, smiling in triumph. "In the next few weeks, MO Washington is sending a guy called Mellon to Switzerland for the sole purpose of interviewing Dr. Jung for a role. Wouldn't that be wild, if he worked for MO, too?"

Moggy's face went whiter still.

"I'll show you the memo that outlines everything," Niki said. "Jung has been advising Donovan since '42. Never mind all that." She threw an arm around Moggy and pulled her close. "It's funny. When I married your brother, I never imagined *we'd* become friends. But somehow you managed to wiggle your way into my heart." Niki's words were meant to placate but had the added benefit of being true. She didn't want Moggy to leave at all, much less while feeling this unsure about things. "You're not transferring. You're not going anywhere. We need you here."

Moggy looked at her. "You do?"

"I do, in any case," Niki said, and Moggy's shoulders loosened, her body relaxing against Niki's hold. "You're a brilliant woman, Moggy. Don't spend too much time overthinking things or listening to others. You can always trust your gut, and you can always trust me. I have only your best interests at heart."

The New York Times

CZECHS JOIN ALLIES' FORCES

LONDON, Nov. 13—The Czech Government in exile reported today that approximately 400 members of the Czech puppet army had deserted while fighting partisans in northern Italy and escaped across the Alps to join a Czech brigade fighting with the Allies at Dunkerque. The men were part of the German police corps in Prague and were sent to Italy when they were suspected of subversive activity. They fought their way into the Allies' lines in France without equipment or food.

54

NIKI

November 1944

"George thinks we're in the clear," Niki said as she and Will walked toward the office, along Via dei Serpenti. It was one of the only times they'd been alone in months. They'd returned to a state of almost normal, or normal enough to continue their work.

"Really?" Will tossed her a look. "He said that?" He seemed unbothered that Niki had spoken to George recently enough to know this.

"His logic is that it's been almost two months since Donovan was in Rome," Niki said. "And we haven't heard a peep. The holidays are coming up, and they would've done something by now." *George isn't quite as useless as you implied*, Niki thought but did not say. She was never overly worried about the Geneva Convention bluster, but George's highly informed opinion did help Niki sleep a little better at night. The brass had bigger fish to fry, but as they said back home, *malé ryby taky ryby.* Even small fish were fish.

"Interesting," Will said, considering George's assurances as their shoes clopped like horse hooves on the frozen streets. "I wouldn't say we're home free, but it *does* put my mind at ease. I appreciate his point about this possible infraction being small potatoes in the grand scheme of things."

"Precisely what I've been saying all along," Niki said, bristling, though she couldn't let her irritation show. Whatever it took, she needed to stay on Will's good side to mentally prepare him for another trip to Aversa. Using POWs was practically the only thing that'd worked, and she wasn't giving up yet.

"Did George mention anything else?" Will asked. They swung around a corner, nearly tripping over two hunched, shivering forms.

As Niki staggered, she tried not to glance back. "Um, no. Nothing of significance," she said, and stole a look at the two homeless men. They hadn't put their palms out, or said a word at all. Niki's heart cracked. Moggy was worried about propaganda, but the city's beggars were now too weak and malnourished to panhandle. This was the real stain on their collective unconsciousness. How much more could the world take?

"All this waiting," Niki said. "It's pointless. We have a small window between the rains and the snow, and the weather is only going to get worse. We need to act while we can."

As with Rome's indigents, by all reports, German soldiers were also starved beyond recognition, including those on the Italian lines. Niki wasn't concerned about the nutritional intake of Nazis on the whole, but she worried about Pasha, and her mind refused to lump him in with the others. He remained forever her curly-haired little brother, waving, chasing her down the road.

"Warner put in for air support," Will said as they dodged

the *ragazzini* offering to shine their shoes. "I'll follow up with him today."

"Thanks," Niki mumbled. Hundreds of fake mailbags sat in the printing room, ready to go, but she had little faith that Project Cornflakes would ever get off the ground. It was another potentially meaningful operation stopped in its tracks. "I was thinking," she said, pulling a lock of hair over one of her partially bald spots. Moggy's crime against beauty was growing out and not a moment too soon, with winter on the approach. "Did you read about the hundreds of soldiers who deserted this week in northern Italy?" Niki felt Will hesitate in his step.

"You mean the Czech soldiers?" he said, and she nodded, unable to look up.

Will understood what the phrase "Czech soldiers" might mean to Niki, but he didn't know the half of it. Niki told the others that her brother was confirmed alive but left the details hazy. No one knew about the First Battalion, or that Pasha was fighting for fascism.

"I was wondering what made them desert en masse like that," Niki said. "Maybe it's something we can replicate in other areas."

"My guess is that the weather and lack of food caused the surrender campaign to have a multiplier effect," Will said. "A soldier contemplating desertion needs either a decent reason to give up or belief that surrendering won't be worse than his present situation. White propaganda gave him both."

Niki suspected Will was right. For years, troops were kept sufficiently terrorized by warnings of what would happen in the event of an "unconditional surrender" to the Allies—the breakup of Germany, exile, sterilization, eternal slavery. For most, dying while fighting for one's country was more palatable than castration at a Siberian labor camp.

But now the Allies could point to Italy, Romania, Bulgaria, and other newly liberated areas to demonstrate Allied prisoners had it better than most, and "unconditional surrender" meant not only saving German homes, industry, and soil, but returning sons, sweethearts, and husbands to their beloved. MO planned to bolster white propaganda's efforts by providing information about the luxury of Allied prison camps, as described to *DND* by people supposedly on the inside, but these and other efforts were gathering dust beside the printing machine.

"Redefining the notion of surrender is definitely helping," Niki agreed. "But it doesn't account for the waves of surrenders. Four hundred at a time."

"Maybe the situation is really that dire? According to intelligence reports, the Czechs and Slovaks are doing all the dirty work along the front," Will said, which aligned with George's comments about the First Battalion building fortifications. "Temperatures are dipping below freezing. It can't be that compelling to stick around if they don't truly believe in the cause."

"I'm sure that's it," Niki said, her jaw lightly clenched. Will spoke as though defecting was a careful decision, the outcome of weighing several viable choices, each with pluses and minuses, instead of what was for many likely the only option left. "I suppose it'll mean more defections as it gets colder," she added.

"That's what I'd expect." Will reached for the office door and held it open for Niki to walk through. "Could your brother be fighting in Monte Rose?" he asked. "Are you thinking he might be one of the defectors?"

"Never crossed my mind," Niki snipped as the door thwacked closed behind them.

"Come on. I know you better than that," Will said, touching her arm. "You *are* worried, and who could blame you? Can't your husband—"

Niki pushed past him. "George doesn't know jack shit," she said. "Even if he did, how does that help? There's no good answer, not a solitary comforting thought. Hello!" Niki called out. "We're here."

As she stepped from the entryway into the main office, the

entire room froze. "What is it?" Niki said, feeling the weight of a dozen eyes upon them. She locked gazes first with the Rumors guy, and then with Ezra. "Is there news? From AFHQ?"

"Um…" Ezra said, without a comment for maybe the first time in his life.

"What?" Niki said as her alarm ratcheted up. *"What?"*

"You might want to check your office," Lieutenant Jack Daniels offered.

Niki surged forward, dizzy and off-kilter. "What is it?" she asked again, and was answered by a single clear bark. Pulse racing, Niki flipped on the light. Perched on her chair was a half half-hat. Pierre was tied to her desk. "Oh my God," she gasped as Will slid up behind her.

"What happened?" he said.

"Moggy deserted!"

55

May 1989

In the wide, empty hallway outside the ballroom, Niki stops to catch her breath.

"Mom?" Andrea says as she approaches, her ice-blue gown swishing on the ground. "Are you okay?" She hands her mom a tissue. "What's going on? I think that's the first time in my life you've ever made a scene."

"It's the nostalgia," Niki says—the easy excuse—and dabs her eyes.

"Nostalgia, I understand. Still, it's an awfully big reaction from my very even-keeled mom," Andrea says, and Niki gives her a wobbly, sideways smile. "That was you, wasn't it? In the photograph? The cigarette was a shock. Completely new information. But you were so pretty!"

"Thanks, Andi. That's very sweet." Niki sniffles. They are quiet for a minute, the only sound a burst of muffled applause on the other side of the ballroom doors.

"It's strange," Andrea says, breaking the silence. "You never talk about those years." She pauses for a moment before continuing on. "Though I suppose that's a generational thing. Growing up in Washington, DC, in the fifties, it seemed like all my friends had parents who were born somewhere else, who left Europe in the wake of some tragedy. It almost didn't matter the situation, or what country they'd come from. The vibe was the same."

Niki smirks. "Move on and never speak of it again," she says.

"Exactly!" Andrea laughs through her nose. "In your situation, I get it. The way you lost your family..." Niki has told her daughter the basics. Her parents stayed behind—at their own peril—and Niki fled. She married a man named George Clingman, long since deceased, and this helped her survive. Not everyone in her family was so fortunate. "Honestly, Mom," Andrea says, "I understand not wanting to rehash all that trauma, but you could've told me you were in the CIA!"

"Not the CIA. The OSS."

"Same thing!" Andrea says, flinging her hands overhead. "I knew you worked in Italy during the war, but whenever it's come up, you've made yourself out to be some cog in a back office helping with translations. I never questioned it since you spent a career translating at the UN. Now all this! It's almost too hard to process."

"It's difficult for me to process sometimes, too. Rome was..." Niki ponders this, chewing on her bottom lip. "It was a very short period of time. Less than a year. Barely a blip. But it was complicated. Wonderful and awful and everything else."

"I'd love to hear more," Andrea says, drifting closer while Niki fights the urge to step back.

"This is going to sound terrible, but I loved those months. Not *everything* about them..." Niki chuckles sadly. "There were some real dark spots, and we were at war. But..." Because there's nothing more she can say, Niki lets her voice fall away.

Andrea smiles. "If a person can find a bright spot during a war, that's a good thing," she says. "You have to take the silver linings where you can get them."

"Perhaps," Niki says, exhaling. "But the repercussions of what I did—it's hard to shake sometimes, despite my best efforts." These "efforts" being that Niki spent the last half century trying to forget, laser-focused on her sweet family and the road up ahead.

"What you *did*? Do you mean the propaganda?" Andrea says.

"That's part of it," Niki admits, recalling how unsettled she felt the first day of training, when the instructor told them to address their propaganda to the lowest common denominator. Where would she be now if she'd listened to her gut and bowed out?

"Mom...?" Andrea presses.

"The propaganda was necessary," Niki says. "But that doesn't mean I feel one hundred percent proud of my contributions. I had this friend. She..." At the thought of Moggy, tears spring to Niki's eyes. "My friend Moggy, she thought disseminating propaganda was messing with our collective unconscious. She actually *deserted* over it."

"Dang! A New Ager before her time."

"A self-styled Jungian," Niki says. "Good old Mogs." She sighs again. "Oh, Andrea, I've made such a mess of things. If I tried to unravel it all, I wouldn't know where to begin."

First, there was leaving her family to marry George, and then going through with the wedding, despite her misgivings. Ultimately, George drank himself to death. It happened a few years after the war, and they were no longer married, but Niki had to wonder whether meeting her was what sent his perfect, neat existence savagely off course. She made many mistakes during the war and, afterward, spent years pretending her parents were gone. Then there was all that happened with Will...

Andrea places a hand on her mother's arm. "You're being hard on yourself," she says. "Which isn't like you but completely understandable. You must be physically and mentally spent with what's going on with Dad."

Niki nods. She *is* exhausted, because of Manfred, but also, she realizes, from holding on to so many secrets for such a long time.

"Do you want to leave?" Andrea asks. "We can get out of here, like right now."

"Andi, there's more I need to tell you," Niki says, and peers around her daughter. "We should sit down." She gestures toward a white leather bench. "It's important that I get everything out, and it will take a while to explain."

56

NIKI

December 1944

Niki didn't know how or why she ended up at St. Peter's on this cold, blustery night, other than she found herself caught up in the throngs of jeeps and command cars and people journeying across the Tiber toward Vatican City for Christmas mass.

Though Niki didn't believe in God, she was overcome with emotion upon reaching the basilica, where the scene was electric, both metaphorically and in fact. After all these months in darkness, the entire square was ablaze, with enormous spotlights fixed on the cathedral's stately columns. Some fifteen thousand soldiers from the Fifth Army were given passes, and Niki suspected it was the first time some had seen lighted buildings in years.

However Niki felt about religion—the questions it couldn't answer, the problems it caused—this felt like a refuge, and it beat staring at Moggy's empty desk, or walking the gloomy streets of Rome, Pierre moping alongside. Niki hadn't known it was possible, but after the food riots earlier in the month, the city had even less of everything. Less light, less transportation, less work, less food, and less hope. No wonder so many Italians were leaning toward communism. The United States had occupied Rome for half a year, and Niki didn't blame its citizens for deciding democracy didn't seem so great.

Around her, the crowd waited in buzzing anticipation, as though everything might change on one magical night, as it had those thousands of years ago. It was the promise of religion, though everyone was probably also happy to get out of the cold.

At thirty minutes to midnight, the silver trumpets sounded, and the Swiss Guards processed, their red plumes wafting as they moved. Soon, the Pope came through, riding on his throne as the crowd cheered and waved their hats. Pasha was *(is?)* a devoted Catholic. He would've loved every word, every ounce of pomp.

"Evviva il Papa!" the people shouted as the Pope blessed congregants along the way. Upon arriving at his altar, His Holiness positioned himself beneath a magnificent bronze canopy, then donned his white-and-gold vestments and began the mass.

Niki couldn't hear much, though she didn't try particularly hard. After the service, the Pope distributed communion to the several hundred people near the altar, mostly Allied officers, and members of the diplomatic corps. In other words, those who needed blessings the least. When everyone filed out, Niki remained seated, unable to move. Maybe it was the choir, she reasoned. They were very good. Or perhaps she was simply waiting for the crowd to thin out, so she wouldn't get trampled on Christmas.

Niki stayed for the second mass, too, and it started and ended, same as the last. At the end of it, Niki sat alone once again, frozen for reasons she couldn't explain. She really needed to get back to the villa—it had to be almost three o'clock in the morning by now. As Niki debated how and when to move her limbs, someone tapped her on the shoulder. She whirled around.

"*Buon Natale*, Niki," Will said. He was smiling, his hat scrunched up in his hand.

"William!" she said, turning to face him all the way. "You've learned a drop of Italian! Bravo! What are you doing here? Did you follow me?"

"Sure did. You left the villa after nine o'clock. By yourself." He clicked his tongue. "People are desperate in this city, and it's not safe for a young, beautiful woman to be out alone."

"I can look after myself," Niki said, though she was flattered by his concern. Will must've been sitting there for hours, and it was the longest they'd been near each other in months. She'd worked hard to joke with him, to be excessively kind, and bring him back out of his protective shell. Tonight, it seemed as though her efforts might've paid off. "You're very sweet to worry about me, but the curfew's been lifted for Christmas," she reminded him.

"That doesn't change the time. Whaddya say?" He tilted his head toward the door. "Should we get back? It's practically dawn, and Pierre doesn't like to be left alone this long."

"You sound like Moggy," she said. "You're obsessed with that damned mutt!"

"Apparently I am," Will said.

As Niki took his outstretched hand, a thrill ran through her body, followed by the warm comfort of having his skin pressed against hers. Maybe this night could make miracles, after all.

Hands still entwined, they walked through the nave in silence, past the pillars with their etched-in saints. Listening to their shoes echo on the hallowed floors, even Niki had to admit to the holiness of the place.

"Did you enjoy the service?" Will asked as they stepped outside.

"Sure." Niki affected a shrug. "It was wonderful to be part of history. The first public mass ever given by the Pope!"

Will puckered his lips to suppress an encroaching smile. "Ah. Yes. The history of the thing was its only redemption. Which is why you stayed for two masses."

"So did you." Niki pulled her hand out of his and gave him a playful swat on the shoulder. "I was only trying to take it all in," she said. "And stay warm!"

"Sure, sure." He winked. "You keep telling yourself that."

As they crossed St. Peter's Square, Niki tightened her coat and picked up her pace. Only when she reached the other side did she speak again. "Where do you think she is?" Niki said.

Will didn't need to ask which "she" Niki meant. "Impossible to know," he answered, his breath making puffs of smoke in the air. "Her parents have money, which means she could be anywhere in the world."

"They claim they don't know either," Niki said. "According to…" She stopped her train of thought, not wanting to bring George's name into this beautiful night. "They're in a state about it, apparently. Afraid she's dead or in a ditch somewhere. It's kind of faithless, if you ask me. Moggy's perfectly capable of taking care of herself." Some part of Niki wished she wasn't, and that she'd come crawling back. Damn it, she missed the girl. She missed her with her whole heart.

"I agree," Will said. "Wherever she is, Moggy will be fine."

They walked a few more paces. The night was quiet, too quiet, almost, and Niki could feel Will straining against an avalanche of words. She wondered if he'd say it again. *Why can't we try to make it work?* Out here, in the desolate night, beneath a three-quarter moon and a dreamy, star-speckled sky, Niki might've said yes.

"What are you thinking about?" Will asked, nudging her shoulder.

Niki shook her head. There was no use going down that dead-end path. "Oh. You know." She blew out a mouthful of air. "How FDR said this would be our last wartime Christmas. Do you think that's true?"

Will snickered grimly. "Who the hell knows?" he said. "Might be our government's version of propaganda. Keep fighting, soldiers, the end is in sight! Just like the Germans do it."

Niki smiled without looking up. "You're probably right," she said.

"I don't know, though," Will said, dragging his feet along the icy ground. "I have a feeling that maybe 1945 will be our year. I guess we'll just have to see."

"Or we don't have to *just see*." Niki swung around to face him. "I don't think we should wait anymore," she said. That was all this past month had been—waiting. Waiting for air support, or an alternate means to distribute Cornflakes. Waiting for a bolt of lightning, some genius plan to inspire more defections from Monte Rosa. It was almost a new year, and tonight she and Will had reached a new, better place. They couldn't fritter away another minute. "I've been very patient," Niki added. "But I won't do it anymore. I'm tired of rushing to check the pouches every day for some report or memo from AFHQ about whether using POWs is approved. Reports, by the way, we were supposed to receive weeks ago."

"Oh, God, Niki, not this again—"

"You heard what George said. They're probably just going to let the POW matter drop, and hope we forget about it," Niki said. "They don't want to tell us 'okay,' but if they say it's a violation, they open up way too many cans of worms."

"They're playing out the clock," Will said, and Niki felt him waver, bend almost imperceptibly in her direction. "You're telling me you want to move forward on Cornflakes, even though they're planning to bomb the train lines in January, which means air support?"

"That's what they *say*. And Cornflakes will only be part of it," Niki said. She paused, and threw on a grin. "I have another idea. It's going to require more POWs."

Will groaned. "You and your big plans. I gave Warner my word that we'd remain on our best behavior." Though Will was technically saying no, his conviction was weak. Niki could see the cracks, the light peeking through.

"They had their chance to respond about the POWs," she said. "But I'm not going to sit around and hope for the best. Haven't we done enough of that? Wars are not won by 'playing out the clock,' to use your term."

"You'd like to take matters into your own hands," Will said, his face pained. "In true Niki style."

"Yes, sir." Niki's grin widened. "I'll give you a little break for the holidays, but beginning January first, we proceed with Operation Cornflakes, and another project I've begun to cook up. This war is almost over, and we have to finish strong."

PART FIVE

OPERATION MONTE ROSA

SECRET

Office Memorandum | **UNITED STATES GOVERNMENT**
TO: Director of OSS
DATE: 1 Jan 1945
CC: Swiss Desk, Bern
FROM: MO, Rome
SUBJECT: OPERATION MONTE ROSA

PERSONNEL

Maj. William Dewart
Pvt. Nikola Novotna
Lt. Jack Daniels
Ezra Feldman
Egidio Clemente
~~Mary Margaret Clingman~~

SITUATION

One of the last German strongholds is the fascist Monte Rosa region, in the mountains of northern Italy, near Lake Como. The Nazis have deployed thousands of Czech and Slovak nationals to fortify the front. Already there have been hundreds of desertions in the area, and the opportunity to flip more enemy soldiers is great, especially if we move quickly.

OBJECTIVE

Disseminate propaganda to the Czech and Slovak nationals that will cause them to question why they are continuing to fight on behalf of their occupiers. Drop "safe conduct" passes written in Czech and Slovakian throughout the region, encouraging submission in the face of a hopeless situation. Ultimately, cause hundreds of desertions.

REQUIREMENTS

1. Paper stock.

2. Czech and Slovak typewriters.

3. MO printed materials, including DND as well as "Hitler skull" and "Hitler death head" stamps.

DISSEMINATION

By any means possible (e.g., POWs, as used successfully before, or support of a Special Leaflet Squadron). We must ride the wave of desertions now, before it's too late.

NOTE

All requirements outlined herein are <u>in addition to</u> what has been previously requested for Operation Cornflakes, the German mailbag infiltration, in the memo dated 30 December 1944.

FROM THE DESK OF NIKOLA N. CLINGMAN

8 January 1945

Dear George,

Happy New Year! Or is it? Impossible to know.

Do you recognize the stationery? It was a wedding gift from your parents. I thought paper was for the first anniversary, but I don't keep track of these things. Did you spend the holidays in Bern? Surely you were given leave. I haven't seen any updates regarding your prior visit to Rome. Seems as though it was a lot of fuss for nothing. I do appreciate you "checking" on me and providing the information on Pasha. As I presume there's nothing more to know, I am in the process of teasing out some of his compatriots. No doubt the memo has come across your desk.

Speaking of checking on things, I've asked you about Moggy thrice, but have yet to receive a reply. If you do know where she is, please tell her that I only want the best for her, and also that Pierre is being well tended to, and I ~~forgive~~ miss her. She warned me she was leaving, but I didn't listen.

I don't mean to be one of those demanding wives, but it'd be swell if you could answer me, every once in a while.

All my best,
Niki

57

NIKI

January 1945

She'd done it. Niki had worn down the MO chief, at last convincing him that if anyone really cared about using POWs, they would've officially stopped them by now.

"Fine. Do whatever you want!" Warner had cried. "Just leave me out of it."

Because enough time passed, not even Will could demur. Now they had two operations to manage: Cornflakes and Monte Rosa.

For Cornflakes, Niki and Will culled thousands of names from German phone books and sent them to Siena, where OSS typists worked around the clock addressing envelopes before returning them to Rome to be stuffed with propaganda. Several freshly recruited POWs had been postal workers in their prior lives and were on hand to evaluate how everything was labeled and sealed. The tens of thousands of completed letters were then crammed into sacks, which the Fifteenth Air Force would drop on the rail lines in Austria and Germany they planned to bomb next week.

My Dear Comrades, Niki wrote. *The Führer is in danger. The reactionaries have learned of his weakened health and know he is unable to carry the burden of his office. They wish to do away with our Führer and subject the Reich to a military dictatorship.*

As with the League of Lonely War Women letters, Niki had a ball with these fictions, in pretending to be Franz or Heinrich, Klara or Elke. Housewives and military officers and factory workers, Niki impersonated them all. She'd even sent a few letters to the Führer himself, commenting on his raging case of gonorrhea and notoriously small penis. She also mentioned his lackluster art and pointed out three grammatical mistakes from his latest speech. As she wrote, Will sat nearby, inspecting cancellations on completed envelopes. Pierre lay beneath him, his head resting on Will's feet.

When Niki finished her last letter—from a concerned East Prussian gauleiter, a Nazi Regional Party Leader—she returned to Monte Rosa, the operation she cared most about. If this didn't get her closer to her Pasha, she didn't know what would.

"I think these are ready to go," Niki said, eyeing the safe conduct passes with a sickening quake in her gut. She'd typed the messages—*good for one return trip to Czechoslovakia via Allied lines!*—in Czech and Slovakian, using special typewriters at the Vatican. "God, I hope they work."

"I'm not worried," Will said, smiling. Since their moment at St. Peter's, the relationship had turned a corner. He was no longer so perpetually grumpy, and Niki was thrilled to have her old friend back. "You always manage to get it right," he added.

"I don't know about that," Niki said. "Though I do try."

Will walked over and dropped a stack of envelopes he was reviewing onto her desk. From the other side of the room, Pierre groaned and flipped onto his side. "Mind taking a look?" he asked. "See if everything is correct?"

"Sure, sure," Niki said. "Whatever we need to do to get these letters out." The quicker they finished the envelopes, checking the spellings of *München*, *Köln*, *Länderbank Wien Aktiengesellschaft*, and *Wiener Giro-und Cassenverein*, the sooner Niki could focus on Monte Rosa. "They look good to me," she said, and slung them aside.

"Should we run them past the POWs?"

"Nah. I'm sure they're fine." Niki returned her attention to the safe conduct passes. Placing the final pass atop its stack, she conjured the image of Pasha picking it up a week from now, somewhere in the snowcapped mountains above Lake Como.

"Good luck to you, little one," Niki said to the paper. "I'll see you on the other side." She closed her eyes and prayed to Good King Wenceslas, he of heroic virtue, that Pasha would read the letter, and know exactly what to do.

SOLDIERS OF THE 1 BATTALION OF VLÁDNÍ VOJSKO!

You have been thrown into the line to be sacrificed. You are replacing a unit that has been almost wiped out. You are expected to hold an already broken section.

Whoever remains in this line will not survive the murderous barrage that's coming!

COME OVER TO US!

Many of your comrades have surrendered. They are already out of the battle zone on the way to an American POW transit camp. *They* are in safety!

You were told a lot of silly lies about American captivity. The truth is that we treat every one of our prisoners decently, regardless of nationality.

When coming across, wave this leaflet or some other white object, or show us in some other way that you want to quit!

Act at once!

Shed this German yoke of shame, cross over to the partisans!

SECRET

Office Memorandum | **UNITED STATES GOVERNMENT**
TO: MO Branch, OSS Washington
DATE: 23 Jan 1945
CC: OSS Detachment, OSS Bern
FROM: AFHQ
SUBJECT: Use of POWs

Per the orders of Maj. Gen. Bill Donovan, Gen. Dwight D. Eisenhower, and President Roosevelt, and in light of the rules established under the Hague and Geneva Conventions, all use of POWs must stop, effective immediately. As of the date of this letter, any recruitment of POWs will result in a Court Martial. This applies to all branches, in all theaters of operations. Any questions should be directed to Allen Dulles, at OSS Bern.

58

NIKI

January 1945

"As of the date of this letter," Niki repeated. Will was lying prone on the floor, Pierre's head in his lap. "This doesn't seem like the largest problem in the world."

"Did you not read the part about the court-martial?" Will said.

"Yes, but the memo is entirely silent on anyone recruited prior to January twenty-third," Niki said. "Pointedly silent, in fact." She put both hands on her hips. "It's almost as though they're sending a message."

"It's not a message. It's an order!"

"What if we went ahead with the POWs we already have? The brass would never find out."

"Jesus, Niki. They're not idiots."

"Eh..." Niki waggled her hand back and forth.

Will pushed himself up onto his elbows, careful not to jostle Pierre's snoozing head. "They'll surely figure it out," he said, "when hundreds of men turn up with safe conduct passes. I'm sorry, Niki. We can't go forward with Monte Rosa. I have a horrible feeling about how this will turn out."

"You always have a horrible feeling! That's why you've lost seven kilos in the past two months," Niki said. She wiped the sweat from her brow. "Will. This doesn't change anything. We recruited the Monte Rosa men *before* January twenty-third."

"We can claim ignorance about anything we did prior to reading the letter," Will said, gesturing. "But I can't, in good faith, pretend I haven't seen it. I hate to pull rank on you—"

"You really do not. You love it."

"I'm forbidding you from sending them across." Will put a hand on her shin, and she jumped. "Sorry," he said, and let go. "You know damned well they're not giving us an allowance for any previously recruited prisoners. Why are you so upset? We still have Cornflakes."

"Cornflakes is nice, but we *have* to finish Monte Rosa," Niki said, lip trembling. She bit down, debating whether she should admit the truth. But no, it wouldn't change anything, other than to make Will feel sorry for her. "The men are trained," Niki said instead. "They have uniforms and are ready and waiting to go. We can't abandon another mission. Too much has been invested."

"You really don't listen to anyone, do you?" Will said. "Part of me wishes Moggy were here. I think she might be able to talk some sense into you. Or give you food for thought, if nothing else."

"Moggy?" Niki's jaw dropped to the floor. His invoking of Moggy felt like direct fire. *Get a hold of yourself. Moggy is your sister-in-law. Not even a blood relative.* "The question isn't whether she'd get all morally twisted up," Niki said. "We both know she would. The question is why I'd concern myself with what a deserter thinks."

"Aw, Niki." Will tilted his head and frowned. "The only person you really think she deserted is you."

Niki hopped to her feet and swiped an empty sack from the floor. She couldn't abide another second of that smug, handsome face. "You should come with a warning," she said, cramming safe conduct passes into the bag. *"Seems like a nice guy but is really an ass."*

"What are you doing?" Will asked as Niki finished filling one sack and started a second. "I'm forbidding you from taking anything to the POWs. Don't make me report you."

"I can't make you do anything," Niki said as she attempted to storm off, an action closer to a lumber on account of the bags. She'd nearly escaped when her coat pocket caught on the door handle, flinging her back into the room.

"Speaking of messages," Will said.

Niki's cheeks flamed as she heaved the bags over her shoulder, resembling some kind of down-and-out St. Nick. *"Jdi do hajzlu!"* she said, and then plodded through the main office, dragging the bags.

"Didn't you tell me *hajzlu* means toilet?" Will called out.

"Niki, do you need help with something?" Ezra asked.

"No thanks! I'm fine!" She knew Ezra would be on Will's side when it came to the POWs.

After slamming the door behind her, Niki stopped to regain her bearings, and figure out what the hell to do next. She was going forward with Monte Rosa, that much was certain, but she had to act quickly, before news of the POW ban traveled through the rest of the OSS channels and all her coordination points on the road to northern Italy. But Dewart would be watching her every move, and Niki couldn't complete the operation on her own. She'd need to enlist someone else, and there was only one person Niki trusted to make it happen.

59

May 1945

Yes, it's true. She wanted me to take the bags to the men. This, after we hadn't spoken in months, aside from the occasional *"Ciao!"* as we passed on the street.

"You wish me to deliver letters?" I'd said, not understanding what this was about.

"Technically, I want the men to deliver the letters," she clarified. "But you will take them to the men."

I considered this, scrutinizing her face. On the one hand, I needed the money. On the other, she had some nerve, soliciting more favors after having gone dark on me for so long.

By then I was awfully sick of Americans. Niki might've been born in Czechoslovakia, but I didn't see much daylight between her and the others. You promised us the troops would leave once

Rome was back under Italian control, which it had been for months, yet you still occupied our city, same as before.

You promised us transportation, but no new buses came, and you used the few the Gestapo didn't take to haul soldiers to and from leave. Food riots happened daily, and even the strongest anti-fascists were saying how much better life was when Mussolini was in charge. Back then, at least we had food, and the trams ran on time. This was my state of mind when Nikola came to me.

"Why are you asking me?" I said. "Is it because you don't want to take the risk yourself? My life is more expendable?"

"No! Of course not! I'm being watched," Nikola claimed, "and need an intermediary."

"Mmm-hmm," I said, crossing my arms. Mary Margaret told me Nikola was one to fudge the truth, and I was done letting her do it to me. It is strange, in hindsight, that I find myself firmly on the side of that strange, well-dressed woman. "You abandoned me," I added.

"Abandoned?" Niki blinked. "What?" She could not have looked more astounded if I'd whipped off my top and swung around *mie tette*.

"Our arrangement," I said as she cast about. "With the men?"

"Oh! Right. I didn't realize you were waiting for me," she said, and now I was the one amazed. "You should've told me you were upset. I didn't mean to abandon you. We weren't able to use them for a while, and there was no one to bring you to see. But that's about to change…"

"I know about the investigation," I said. "Your sister came to warn me. It was very kind of her to do."

"My sister?" Nikola said, forehead lifting. "Do you mean Moggy?" She took me by the arm. "Is she okay? When did you see her? What did she say?"

"It was months ago," I said, wiggling out of her clutches.

Nikola's face fell. "I hadn't known you and Moggy were so

chummy," she said. "Are you aware she's left town? Just blew out of here." Nikola whistled and fluttered her hand like a bird. "No warning and without her dog. She left everyone in the lurch, including me."

"I'm fairly certain *you're* the reason she went," I said. "Mary Margaret was tired of your lies and false promises. Your propaganda." Nikola flinched at the words, but I pressed on. "I understand your work, I think. You abuse information that is maybe only a little true." I pinched my thumb and index finger together to demonstrate. "As I always say, we do what we need to get by, but you should be careful about who you are lying to, especially because liars usually get caught."

"I did not lie to Moggy," Nikola insisted. "There were certain things I had to keep from her. In her best interests!"

"In her best interests." I tossed my eyes. "Is a relationship with Major Dewart also in her best interests? Spare me your protests, your ear-piercing squawks. I think all this lying to Germans has left you confused, and now you are lying to everyone, including yourself."

"Now that is plainly ridiculous," she huffed.

"You don't know who you are, or what you want."

Nikola gaped. "Gosh, Paloma," she said. "You *have* been hanging around Moggy. You sound like a Jungian, by and by. Don't worry about me. I may not have a country, but I know exactly who I am."

"Then tell me, what are you going to do when the war is over?" I said, and Nikola squinted as though this wasn't the most obvious question in the world. "Are you going back to that husband of yours, the one who cannot get hard? The man doesn't appear to have a single redeeming quality. Even his sister would agree. I get the sense she loves him, because he is her brother, but doesn't like him all that much."

"Oh, that's just Moggy," Nikola answered, though I could see confusion like scribbles on her face. What I said affected her. She was spinning these words around in her head. "You know what?" She gave a curt, cold laugh. "Forget I asked. I didn't come to you for amateur analysis. I wanted to offer you a job. If you're not interested, I'll find somebody else. Good luck, Paloma. I wish you all the best." Shaking her head, Nikola began to walk away.

"I'll take the bags," I shouted.

Nikola paused, waiting several long beats. "Really?" she said without turning around. "After all that, you want to help me?"

"Yes, really," I told her, though what I really wanted to say was, *fuck you, Nikola, fuck you and your dead bastard ancestors.* Alas, a girl must eat, and Nikola understood she had this on me. "I'm not helping *you*, though," I said. "Unlike you, I know who I am, and that's someone who will do almost anything to keep herself fed. Someone who has very little left to lose."

And just like that, we were united for one last operation.

60

NIKI

February 1945

"Private Novotná," Warner said as he stuck his head through the open door. "I'm stepping out but will return in five minutes, at which time I'd like to address a most urgent matter. Don't leave your desk."

Niki flashed a glance at Will, then looked back to Warner. "Pertaining to what?" she said, her voice cracking. "Project Cornflakes?" She closed her eyes and prayed to all the saints.

"Not Cornflakes," he said. "Well done on that, by the way. There are several signs the mail is making its way through German households, and the air force has already agreed to another drop with the next rail bombings. In any case, that's not what I'd like to discuss. I won't spoil anything, but think Italy. Think *mountaintops*." He tapped an envelope on the door frame, and

Niki's stomach collapsed. "See you shortly." With that, he spun around and strode away.

Niki began to perspire. *Do prdele!* When a bunch of Czechs and Slovaks surrendered with safe conduct passes, Niki understood there'd be inquiries, interrogations, even, but relied on the chance the top brass wouldn't connect it to Rome. She'd written the Monte Rosa memo but, as far as most knew, the operation never got off the ground. How could it? They didn't even have the proper typewriters for the languages.

She'd already played it out in her head. The Czechs (including Pasha) would give themselves up in droves. Afterward, a bunch of OSS men in suits would stand around, befuddled, wondering what happened before eventually shrugging it off. Why quibble with how the safe conduct passes got into the hands of soldiers, when it resulted in defections by the hundreds? Like money, success covered so many ills, which didn't mean Niki hadn't been silently tormenting herself for weeks with alternate, much worse scenarios.

"Are you okay?" Will asked.

"Uh. Fine." Niki had never perspired so much in her life. "I'm just, uh, curious about this so-called urgent matter."

Will stood. With both hands in his pockets, he walked over to Niki's desk. "I've never seen you like this," he said. "Sometimes you're frustrated, or irritated by something I've done, but you're not one to worry until you know there's something to worry about. And sometimes not even then."

"Ha!" Niki warbled. She had to tell him. For five weeks, Niki had been on edge about the Monte Rosa scheme, wondering how it'd turn out. Would she get into trouble, and did she even care, if it meant finding Pasha? There were many things to fret over, but the worst by far was having duped Will.

"Warner *just* complimented Cornflakes!" Will said. "And you saw the latest report from Bern. For the first time, they're giving us credit for lowering morale."

"True…" Niki dabbed her forehead with her sleeve. She had this win, at least. Field orders found on recently captured soldiers revealed a growing problem amongst the Nazi ranks. Men were purposefully injuring themselves so that they might be sent home, and a general in their targeted area had ordered death sentences for any self-mutilation attempt. This threat seemed rather beside the point, but it did serve as a grim kind of comeback, and Wild Bill Donovan applauded MO Rome for the bleak morale these acts of self-injury had proven.

"Why am *I* the one talking *you* up?" Will said, and moved closer to Niki's desk. "Usually, it's the other way around. We can't trade roles this late in the game."

"I have to confess something," Niki blurted, and Will took in a sharp breath. "It's about Monte Rosa. You thought it was strange that I was so dead set on the mission."

"I did. But I'm accustomed to your stubborn determination by now."

"I didn't tell you the whole story," Niki said, speaking quickly to spit out the truth before she changed her mind. "Among the Czechs and Slovaks holding the line is Pasha." It was the first time Niki said it out loud, and it landed with a jab to her chest. "My baby brother."

"Niki!" Will gasped. "Why didn't you tell me? You must be so worried. Shit. It wasn't my decision, but now I feel like an ass for shutting you down."

Niki squeezed her eyes closed. "Please. Will. Don't feel bad. You didn't shut down anything. I, uh, went forward with the operation," she said, choking out the words. When he asked what she meant, Niki clarified. "The safe conduct passes were dropped in Monte Rosa."

Though Niki's lids were still clamped tightly shut, she imagined Will's face, picturing him as a cartoon figure, with a muddled cloud of characters and symbols overhead. "I'm confused," he said. "You told me you burned the passes. How'd they get into enemy territory?"

Niki dropped her head into her hands. The pain of telling Will, of knowing it'd change the way he saw her, was unbearable. "A friend took the bags to the POWs," she said, voice muffled against her palms. "And they took them across."

"YOU USED THE PRISONERS AGAIN?" Will shouted, and Niki could feel the power of his heat, like a fire's back draft. "For the love of Christ, tell me you're joking!"

Ever so slowly, Niki shook her head. "I only used six men. One team." Niki looked up and straight into Will's furious, green-rimmed eyes. "They all returned safely?" she added, though this wasn't going to make anyone feel better.

"How did you get new men? When did you go to Aversa?" Will paused to work something out. "Hold on. Is this the reason you were dragging your feet on taking them back?"

Niki nodded and let out the smallest of whimpers.

"That means that when we *did* take them back, they'd already gone to Monte Rosa." As Will stitched the details together, Niki began to grasp the extent to which her deception had metastasized. To protect the one lie, she'd told a hundred more, and each one had continued to grow unchecked.

"Who helped you?" Will demanded. "Who else was in on this?"

"The OSS guard from the safe house. The contacts at the infiltration point. Others along the route." Niki closed her lips and swallowed Paloma's name. "I'm so sorry, Will," she said. "I hate myself for lying to you, but I couldn't *not* do it, if I had a chance of reaching my brother."

At that moment, someone rapped on the door. Niki jumped. "Greetings, I'm back," Warner announced, tramping into the office with either the best or the worst timing in the world. "Are you ready to talk?"

"Yes, sir," Niki said as Will slunk over to his desk. Whatever Warner had to say, Niki was ready for it. Nothing could be as tormenting as the expression on Will's face, aside from the knowledge that she'd caused it. "Give it to me straight, Warner," she said. "What'd I do this time?"

"A most excellent job," he said, and Niki's eyes flew up. "On Operation Monte Rosa."

"You've got to be fucking kidding me," Will said.

"We have defections." Warner placed something on Niki's desk. Three pieces of paper, with many columns of names. "Seven hundred so far. A truly remarkable achievement."

Niki stretched forward, scanning the list, her heart caught in her throat. *Prazak. Wacha. Plsek. Apel. Dvorak.* In no particular order.

"Donovan was quite curious as to how the passes were distributed," Warner said. "I told him through partisans. If that's not the case, please keep it to yourself." He offered Niki a look and gave Will one, too.

"The partisans. Of course." She flipped to the second page. Names, ages, and hometowns. The words were dizzying, but Niki couldn't find her brother's name. *Petr Novak* was as close as she got.

"Whatever the situation," Warner continued, "Washington is very pleased. Not sure we can run Monte Rosa again, especially with whatever *clandestine* methods you used to get the passes across, but, as I mentioned, we are bombing more trains in Austria in a few weeks, which means air support for Cornflakes. That's something, isn't it?"

"Terrific," Niki answered flatly, still digesting all that was or wasn't on the list of defections.

"There's more," Warner said. "Washington is so happy that they've decided to promote you to corporal."

"A promotion?" Niki said, and rattled her head. "What?"

"That doesn't sound right," observed Will.

Warner tittered through his red and bulbous nose. "What's

with that face? I expected you to be more jubilant," he said. "Given how furious you were when Dewart was named major. You should feel very proud. You have some clever little ideas. Aren't you going to say anything? Should I tell them you don't want it?"

"Yes, I want it. Thank you for the honor," Niki managed to croak. She glanced back at the list.

Warner laughed again. "You're a tough broad to figure out," he said. "Well, *Corporal* Novotná, I'll let you get back to your Cornflakes. Congratulations. This time, you got away with it. Carry on!"

The second Warner left the office, Will sprang up and shut the door.

"Please," Niki said, afraid she might vomit. Nearby, Pierre circled and paced. "I know you're angry, but can we save the argument for another time?" She returned to the list, searching for possible misspellings, or phonetic errors, but couldn't scare up even the smallest coincidence to latch on to. As she set the papers down, Niki felt the loss of her brother all over again, this time as a burning, physical pain.

"Not on there?" Will guessed. He stepped closer, and closer still.

"How is it possible?" Niki said. "I was certain... If he hasn't defected, he's either a full-blown Nazi, or..." She swept a hand, and they both knew she meant dead.

"I'm sorry, Niki," Will whispered.

"What am I supposed to do?" Niki said. "When we're done here? I imagined going to Brnö, to check on things. Now, what's the point?"

Will put his hands in his pockets and dipped his head. "It probably sounds ridiculous," he said. "And my situation is far more mundane, but I don't want to go home, either."

"Not ridiculous," Niki murmured. "The whole world has changed, including in leafy American suburbs."

"It's not the suburbs that I dread," Will said. "I want the fighting to end, of course, but I don't want to leave. I'm not ready to move on. I'm not ready to accept a world where I don't get to see you every day."

"Will," Niki said. "Stop." The tears were falling now.

"I've felt this way for a long time," he said, "but I haven't appreciated the extent until right now. I should be absolutely disgusted with you for lying—"

"*Disgusted* might be a bridge too far."

"But all I want to do is hold you and tell you it will be all right." Will sighed. "Niki. Hear me out. If everything's going to change, then why not make sure it changes in the way we want? The very purpose of war is to upend things, blow them up."

"Golf courses are also good for blowing things up, or so I hear." It was a joke, a distraction, a lame attempt to steer Will away from the pitfalls ahead. If Niki let herself lean in to what he was saying, she might crack all the way open.

But Will recognized her pivot for what it was, and he wouldn't let her get away with it. "You asked if I would ever get a divorce," he said. "The answer is yes." Niki glanced up to find Will grinning. "Wow," he said. "My stomach doesn't even hurt. I think this might be what relief feels like?"

"Will! You can't just declare you're getting divorced."

"I'd wager most divorces begin with someone declaring it."

"Your family will be furious!" Niki said. She felt panicked, and it was the first objection that popped into her head. "They'd probably disown you!"

"Don't care," he said. "I'm getting a divorce, and my little brother can take over the paper. He *wants* to be in charge. I'll need to stay close to New York for the kids, and find a new job. Publishing will certainly be out." He thought about this, seemingly for the first time. "I do love photography."

"You're not going to make any money as a photographer!"

Will laughed. "A pilot, maybe? I'll figure it out," he said.

"Something only a man could say."

"Maybe, but I want you to figure it out with me. No more bullshit. I love you, Niki. I do. And with everything about to end, I can't pretend anymore."

"Oh, Will," Niki said, lining up all the protests in her mind. *Our day at the beach didn't mean anything. You're in love with a time and a place. Everyone feels romantic after swimming naked in the Tyrrhenian Sea.* Or, the most truthful of all: *I have a dreadful track record as a wife.*

Then Niki thought of Paloma's accusation, the one she couldn't get out of her head. *Non sai chi sei. Non sai cosa vuoi.* You don't know who you are. You don't know what you want.

"I think I'm... I think I'm getting a divorce, too," Niki said, tucking a piece of hair behind her ear. George hadn't responded to any of her questions about Moggy, or her last half dozen letters at all, and neither George nor his parents had acknowledged Niki's recent birthday. It was starkly clear that the family was keeping Niki on the outside, preparing for her inevitable excise. There was no other explanation for the silence.

"You're leaving George?" Will's grin spread, flattening the cleft in his chin.

"I think so..." Damn it, Niki loved the man. She well and truly did. After this war was over, there'd be enough people Niki would never see again, and she didn't want Will to be one of them. *Non sai chi sei. Non sai cosa vuoi.* In fact, she did. She'd just been too scared to admit it. "Not sure who will get around to 'declaring' it first, me or him," Niki said, then narrowed her eyes and lifted a finger. "Don't get a big head about it. It was going to happen regardless."

"Typical *Corporal* Novotná qualification," Will said, and they both broke into a laugh. "Get over here." Will opened his arms.

Niki rose to her feet and walked into Will's waiting embrace. It was the feeling of stepping into sunshine, a whole new world.

"I love you," he said.

"*Snesl bych ti modré z nebe,*" Niki replied.

"Uh-oh, when you start speaking Czech, it usually means trouble."

"Not at all," she said. "Just an old saying I've always liked." *Snesl bych ti modré z nebe.* I would take the blue from the sky for you. Something more than mere love.

FROM THE DESK OF NIKOLA N. CLINGMAN

1 Mar 1945

Dear George,

This will be the last time I ask: Where is Moggy?

I've been thinking a lot about this war, and that it seems to be ending. Tell me the truth. Can you really envision returning to Philadelphia, to "normal life"? We both know there's no such thing.

When it's over, I imagine everyone will scatter. The people in this office. You. Me. Everyone else. War changes people. Or maybe it helps us figure out who we are.

I can't go back to Philadelphia. You must know this. Otherwise, you would've worked a little harder at maintaining the bond between us. Lucky you—I'm gently guiding you off the hook! Where will I go? Czechoslovakia, maybe, though this is looking like less of a possibility.

I'd like to find Moggy, unless someone in your family can tell me where she is. Then it'll be straight to Reno, for a divorce. Don't worry, I won't ask for a dime. As for your sterling reputation, just tell your family I'm a wanton hussy from Eastern Europe who only wanted citizenship. In other words, exactly who you thought I was all along.

All my best (truly),
Niki

61

NIKI

March 1945

They sat in front of the crackling fire in the men's villa, Niki leaning against Will, Pierre resting between her legs. Although they were still at war and taking very minor steps to keep their relationship under wraps, Niki could almost imagine living this life. It'd been less than two weeks since they'd decided to be together, but they already felt like some version of a family.

"You could be an interpreter," Will said as they brainstormed future jobs. "You know a hundred languages."

"Or, seven. Eight if you count Brünnerisch, which you probably shouldn't. So far, all the ideas you've offered have been for me. Is this the plan?" Niki teased. "I'll support us while you live out your photographer dreams? Gosh, sounds like a lot to take on." She gave him a playful nudge.

"You wait," he said. "I'll be successful, by and by."

"So you keep telling me." Niki snuggled more tightly against him, and he wrapped an arm around her chest. "First, though, I need to go to Brnö. I know I've wavered, and I'm not going to like what I find, but I can't leave Europe without checking, one last time." She still regretted how quickly she left the first time. The circumstances were different, but Niki didn't want to spend the rest of her life haunted by her tendency toward haste.

"We'll both go to Brnö," Will said, and kissed Niki's hair, which looked almost normal now.

"But the question is when," Niki said, thinking of the latest front-page news from *Stars and Stripes*. Victory was all but guaranteed, but the army's newspaper was eager to remind everyone of several important facts. Following VE-Day, relatively few people would be discharged. There might be *some* furloughs, but most folks would be part of a swift transfer from Europe to the approaches of Japan. In short, the work was not over yet.

"You have to stop obsessing about that article," Will said, and Niki wondered for how long he'd been able to read her mind. "They're referring to soldiers. GIs. The fighting types. They already have MO in that region, and Japanese is one of the only languages you don't speak. Let's worry about furloughs and discharges later." He gave her a squeeze. "Back to daydreaming. Okay. Let's think this through. After we go to Brnö, and you find Moggy, we'll get our respective divorces, and then move to New York. What about children?"

"You have children," Niki said.

"Yes, but what if I wanted more?"

"Now you're trying to spring kids on me?" Niki said. "I think I'll just admire yours from afar. Children seem like a hassle, and I hate the idea of bringing innocents into this terrible world." Niki was putting on a good show even as she thought, *maybe, just maybe…*

Suddenly, a great commotion broke out near the front of the

house. Niki sat up, and Pierre did, too, his ears perked to attention as he released a quick, nonthreatening bark.

"You can't just storm in here," someone said, and Niki recognized the voice of the latest Rumors guy. They were on their eighth so far, and Niki still didn't know what happened to them when they left. Were they reassigned or dispatched to some rumormongers' graveyard?

"Er, they're in a private conference," Rumors said. "I'm under strict instructions not to open that door. They're discussing very top secret things!"

"I need to speak to Nikola," the intruder said. "And someone in her villa told me she was in yours."

"Paloma?" Niki whispered as thoughts raced like horses through her mind. Paloma had been furious at Niki for all those months of no work, but she *was* recently compensated, after Monte Rosa. Then again, Romans were growing increasingly desperate, and desperate people did unpredictable things. Why, oh, why had Niki shown her where they all lived?

"Is that a woman's voice?" Will said.

"Yes, I think it's—" Niki stopped, realizing with a great thud that she'd never told Will about their arrangement, and she now hated herself anew. How could a decent person hide so many things from the man she loved that she *forgot* some of them? The answer was straightforward, plain as toast. Niki was not decent.

"I'll only be a minute," Paloma said. *"Ho un affare molto importante."*

Niki leaped up, hoping to intercept Paloma before she entered the room, but it was too late. Paloma had already thrust open the door, and there she stood, in her redheaded, big-busted glory.

"What in the world?" Will said from his spot on the floor.

"Abbiamo un piccolo problema," Paloma began.

"Let's step outside." Niki took Paloma's arm and pulled, but the woman was immovable. *"Puoi parlare in italiano per favore."*

"No," Will said. Even from across the room, Niki could sense him tighten. "Please speak in English."

Paloma considered this, whipping back and forth between them as trouble scurried across her face. She exhaled. "One of the men escaped his new camp," she said, deciding on English. "He came to find Rosa. One of my girls. Says she gave him…" Paloma's gaze hopped toward Will and back again. *"Una malattia venerea,"* she said, switching to Italian.

"Malattia venerea?" Will said, and Niki's heart at once plunged. It was about to be over, the best almost-two-weeks of her life. "I know you're talking about VD," he said, and Niki hated the army for being so obsessed with gonorrhea that they'd practically turned it into a national advertising campaign. *Be sly, VD is high. Though Russians rush us, and Yankees crush us, she'll give the VD to you…and you…and you!*

"Ah, you're very smart," Paloma said as something in the periphery snagged her attention. It was Pierre, sitting on his hindquarters, staring with those big brown eyes. *"Ma che bel cane che ha!* Such a good boy." She squatted to scratch his chin. "The problem, you see, is that one of your prisoners got the VD from one of my friends, and he came to confront her, rough her up a bit."

"He what? Oh my God, is she okay?" Niki imagined Ezra shaking his head, saying, *I told you not to trust Germans.*

"She is fine now," Paloma said, and stood. "But she requires medicines, and who knows when she will next work, so compensation is also in order."

"Um, forgive me for saying so," Will interjected. "What happened is terrible, but this feels like a shakedown. It sounds as though your 'friend' wants money, and you've come to the closest American. I fail to see how it's any problem of ours."

Niki moaned softly. She loved that Will had said "ours," adopting himself into her troubles. It was a sweet gesture already beginning to rot. There was nothing to do now, and Niki braced herself for Paloma to say the next words.

"It is your problem because Nikola is the one who arranged it!" Paloma said.

"What you're telling us doesn't make sense," Will said.

"*Certo che sì!* Do you need me to be clearer? It is very simple! The two never would've met if Nikola hadn't paid me and my girls to sleep with your POWs."

The words landed with a crash. Niki glanced at Will, pleadingly, but his entire body had turned to stone. That was it. He'd forgiven her for many things, but Will would never look past this, and Niki's dreams of this happy life were officially over. It was all her fault, every last bit, but good Lord, it had been magnificent while it lasted.

62

May 1945

Oh, yes, William Dewart was fighting mad! He'd always seemed a teeny bit *noiosa*—boring—so it was nice to see the fire in him. He stormed out of the villa, *inveire come un pazzo*. Cursing like a madman. I suppose Nikola isn't the sort for pillow talk after all.

That was the last group of prisoners I entertained. Do I regret it? You would like me to answer "yes," but the true response is "not at all," even though I know what your posters said, that we were Axis agents, ready to take down the Allies with our sexing and disease. No matter. I've stayed fed all this time, and I've stayed alive, and I never had to fight one of my neighbors for cabbage. I won't say much more on the matter. I did what I did, and Nikola did what she did, and I think you know the rest.

63

NIKI

March 1945

There was nothing left to say, and Niki had tried everything. She was sorry. She was protecting Will. Seventy-five percent of GIs reported visiting prostitutes, and German men were no different. If they were going to patronize *una casa di toleranza* anyhow, why not keep them happy and loyal to the Allies' cause, while providing the women a means for food and warm clothes? Niki said these things over and over, but Will remained unswayed, and she didn't blame him. It all sounded like propaganda, even to her own ears.

The wait for "the end" of this war was draining. Every exchange with Will sapped what energy Niki had left, and so she spent most days with Clemente, addressing envelopes for the next Cornflakes drop. Despite the heat and intermittent electricity, the printing office was preferable to her own, where Will's presence left Niki so perpetually faint with longing she feared evaporating on the spot.

"Printing them out as quickly as I can. I live to make you happy," Clemente said, ever gallant, as he dropped a new stack of envelopes onto the table. Though he asked no questions, Clemente understood. There had been something between Niki and Will, and now it was gone.

"Thank you," Niki said, ticking through the envelopes. Without POWs to inspect postmarks, her own set of eyes would have to do. "How many more do you think—" she began, only to be interrupted by the sound of metal squeaking.

The large door lifted an inch, and a slice of daylight shot through the gap. Niki and Clemente froze, watching as one sparkling black shoe nudged the door up half a foot, and another half. In a single move, it rolled the rest of the way up to reveal George Clingman standing with both hands on his hips.

"George?" Niki said, shielding her face from the light blasting through. "What are you doing here?"

As he marched in her direction, Niki noticed his hair was even longer and darker than before. It'd taken on an almost bluish hue, leaking out of his head like someone had knocked over a bottle of ink. From Niki's perspective, he was far more dashing with a proper cut and a little gray mixed in, but George probably wasn't in town to solicit coiffure opinions from his future ex-wife.

"What is the meaning of this letter?" George bellowed, waving a piece of paper in her face.

Niki's head was swimming. She'd committed so many mistakes of late, she couldn't fathom what she'd done this time. "You'll have to be more specific."

"It's the letter in which you call yourself a wanton Eastern European hussy. Overall, the missive is outrageous, but on this point I quite agree."

"Oh. That one." Niki stifled a laugh. Her failed marriage was hardly comical, but it felt like she'd written it a lifetime ago. Will had still been speaking to her then. "Sorry, I'd forgotten. There's been a lot…going on."

"For Christ's sake. How many men are you writing to, asking for a divorce?"

Clemente chortled, and George looked at him with the stab of a thousand daggers. "I'll let you two catch up," Clemente said before escaping to the office through the side door.

"You're unbelievable," George said. "You try to divorce me by *post* and then act like you don't know what I'm talking about? That's insolent, even for you."

"I wasn't pretending. I'm sorry. It was a lapse. It's just…" Niki counted backward. "I wrote that letter, what, three weeks ago? You really take a long time to work yourself up, don't you?"

"I just received it! Do you know how much of my mail is confiscated? Both ways? The damn Swiss are the worst when it comes to censorship. Neutral, my ass," he said.

"They shouldn't even be calling themselves impartial," Niki agreed, trying for a moment to get on the same page.

"Why?" George said. "Why are you leaving me? Am I really that terrible? Our marriage isn't perfect, but it's better than most. Whatever's wrong, we can fix it."

"You want to *fix* it?" Niki gaped. Was George really upset, or was this his own stab at propaganda? Did he simply want to bring someone back under his control now that the war was about to end? "If we were to try, I wouldn't even know where to start."

"This is unacceptable. You can't divorce me," George said. "I'll have you sent back to Czechoslovakia."

"I'm a citizen, George. And Czechoslovakia doesn't exist anymore." Niki could almost see the heat crawling up his neck. Why was George clinging so tightly to what was, even at its best, never that great?

"All I've ever wanted to do was help you!" he screamed. "I won't let you walk away that easily!"

"I'm sorry, but it's over," Niki said, speaking softly, trying to get him to turn down the heat. "Surely you understand this by now." Her calm tone must've worked because, like the drop of a curtain, a new expression fell over George's face.

"We know about Monte Rosa," he said, with an unmistakable sneer.

"Monte Rosa?" Niki repeated, wrinkling her brow. "Where is that? Somewhere in Italy?"

"Oh, save it," George hissed. "You know exactly what you did and this time you didn't merely bend the rules, you intentionally broke them. Was it worth it, Niki? All that effort and risk with no sign of your brother. One of your biggest downfalls is that you're the most reckless when it involves the people you love."

"I had to do it," Niki said, and she willed her eyes not to water. "It may not have turned up Pasha, but the operation worked. Nearly a thousand defected."

"Once again, you got lucky," George said. "For now. But I sincerely hope this grave violation of the customs of war doesn't land you in court, or worse. Alas, nothing's a crime until someone finds out about it, until someone writes up a report."

In one breath, all air seemed to leave Niki's body. Her head was whirling, and she could no longer see straight. "You wouldn't," she said. "You wouldn't file a report on your own wife."

"Ex-wife, apparently," George said, and removed a toothpick from his pocket. "I'm only interested in doing what is right. Patriotic. Unfortunately for you, I have the ear of the highest levels of government." He stopped to pick his teeth, flicking small bits of his lunch into Niki's face. "We know about the arrangement with that prostitute and her friends."

"Really, George. You're resorting to threats?" Niki straightened her shoulders and lifted her chin. "Why are you so adamant about keeping me as your wife, when you claim that our bedroom problems are my fault?" Niki laughed dryly. Now that she thought about it, *that prostitute* might've been the cleverest one of them all. "It's funny," she said. "I believed you there for a minute. I really gave you the benefit of the doubt, but I'm glad I decided to find out for myself."

"What the fuck is that supposed to mean?" George roared, leaning toward her, his stale coffee breath wafting over her face.

"You know exactly what it means," Niki said. "Now, regarding my alleged violations of international law…" Her heart was beating so fast she could barely hear her own words. "Do what you need to, but remember this is war, and you're not the only person carrying ammunition."

64

Hans Haseneier was weary after a long day of sorting the post. A long week, now that they were mandated to work sixty hours, under the penalty of death. He'd been an officer once, high up in the Wehrmacht, and now they were hiding him in this bureaucratic position. Germany's loss was only a matter of time and the Allies would want to hold people accountable. Hans would likely be on the list, but was toiling away here truly better than facing a trial?

He would've been proud to work for the Reichspost if the postal system wasn't in such shambles. Mail was vital, to the men fighting and the women and children at home, but now there was no guarantee that any letter would make it to its recipient, and entire train cars carrying letters were routinely blown up. In light of these challenges, Goebbels called postal workers "brave soldiers" for trying to march onward, and it was easier for Hans to endure each day if he could think of himself as a hero again.

Hans heaved a sack onto the counter, one of two found after a raid on a train near Sankt Pölten. With a deep inhale, he plunged a hand into the bag and extracted a fistful of envelopes. He took to sorting them into their appropriate piles. *Flick, flick, flick.*

Twenty percent, perhaps a quarter way into the bag, something caught Hans's eye. In his weariness, it took his brain a second to catch up. Bringing the envelope to his face, Hans appraised the return address. Everything clicked into place.

Wiener Giro-und Cassenverein.

Hans dropped the envelope as if it were on fire. "Cassenverein" should've read "Kassenverein," and no German could've made this mistake. The letter *C* never preceded a vowel and was only used in combination with other consonants. Hands still quivering from the shock, Hans retrieved the piece from the ground. Though even a former officer could be shot for doing so, he ripped the envelope open to find an unflattering rendition of Hitler looking like literal death. Hans opened another letter from the mailbag, and another after that, and the realization struck him like a bat to the head. It's true what Goebbels had said. The Americans were dastardly. They were sending propaganda through his beloved Reichspost.

Tucking the offending mail into his jacket, Hans rushed to find his supervisor. Through all his shock was a small speck of glee. He didn't think this discovery would change the tide of the war, but if he could make a small difference, maybe he *could* be a hero, and this demotion would've been worth it in the end.

PART SIX

DEMOBILIZATION

OFFICE OF STRATEGIC SERVICES

WASHINGTON 25, D.C.
15 April 1945

Dear Eugene,

With the final push in Italy under way, and the recent discovery by the Germans of MO Rome's black propaganda operations, we are closing your branch within the next forty-eight hours. Employees will be given immediate discharge.

We will continue to investigate the Kassenverein incident, as well as reports of the use of German nationals and the allegations regarding the local prostitutes. Rest assured, we have determined that you had no knowledge of any potentially rogue behavior, and you are not being personally investigated. We will keep you apprised of our findings, and whether anyone associated with MO Rome will be subject to court-martial.

Good luck in these last days, and I'll pray for everyone's safe return to the States.

Sincerely yours,
William J. Donovan

65

NIKI

April 1945

Niki's flight bag was packed and propped against the wall, just as it had been over a year ago, when she left her Washington boardinghouse for Algiers. It almost hurt to think about how different she was then, certain she was so hardened and wise, incapable of having her heart broken. Niki wished she could warn that girl.

"Vienna, then?" Ezra said, scrutinizing her paperwork. They were the only two people left in the office. The rest, including Will, had moved on. "That's where they've agreed to take you?"

She nodded. "The Army has secured me a flight to Vienna and a hotel in the American zone," she said. "After that, it will be up to me." It was one hundred thirty kilometers of land mines and bombed rail lines between Vienna and Brnö. For now, the

Krauts kept a tight hold on the Czech Lands, their last piece of empire, but once they finally gave up, Niki would leave Vienna to traverse the wasteland alone.

"I wasn't sure that you would choose to go back," Ezra mused. "Given your brother's allegiance, and the fact that your hometown must be chockablock with Russians and fascists. If you weren't so foolish…" He gave a wink. "You'd come with me to the States, where I will be enjoying life and milking that huge American cow."

From Rome, Ezra would proceed directly to Manhattan, and a job at *The New Yorker*, no regrets or rearview mirrors for him. In the eight months since Romania was liberated, Ezra hadn't changed his view once, though his sour feelings were more deeply rooted than hers. Niki only had a few years to develop a bitterness toward her home, whereas Ezra had a lifetime. Plus, there were likely large swaths of the population who didn't want him back at all.

"In the end, my decision was easy," Niki admitted, checking the top of her bag, to make sure all was in order. "I have to find out what happened to them, good or bad. It'll be difficult, but it's for the best." She just wished she wasn't going alone.

"What about Major Dewart?" Ezra asked, as if reading her mind. Or maybe he only had to read her face. "Any idea where he's gone?"

Niki shook her head. The week before, Will was summoned to AFHQ in Caserta, ordered to report the same day, and with all his belongings. He'd left the office hastily, offering a blanket goodbye, with nothing special reserved for Niki. No one had heard from him since.

"They probably sent him to Japan," Niki guessed. "Or somewhere else to continue his OSS work."

"The only one of us worth a damn," Ezra said as a car honked outside. "That must be for you." He wrapped Niki in a hug, startling her with the strength of his embrace. "It's been a wild time," he said, with an extra squeeze. "I loathe sentimentality, so I'll make this quick. I'm glad to have spent my war with you."

Niki stepped back, smiling as the tears bubbled. "Me, too," she said. "More than you'll ever know. I'd love to stay in touch, but you don't seem like the type."

"Letter writing is a stupid waste of time. Alas, should you ever need me, you know where to look." Ezra grinned. "You can find me in the pages of *The New Yorker*."

"I wish I knew where you'd find me," Niki said as the horn blared again. "I guess you'll just have to keep your eyes open. I could turn up anywhere."

The New York Times

TWO CAPITALS STILL OCCUPIED

LONDON, May 4 (AP)—The capitulation of German forces in the Netherlands and Denmark leaves the Germans only two satellite capitals from their once imposing empire—Oslo, Norway, and Prague, Czechoslovakia.

TWO ARMIES GIVE UP

—

Germans Now Fighting Only U.S. Third Army in Czechoslovakia

—

By Wireless to The New York Times

PARIS, May 5—The final defeat of Germany is a matter of hours. The whole left, or southern, flank of the German Army facing the western Allies collapsed today when Army Group G, a shattered, demoralized force of between 200,000 and 400,000 men, surrendered to Gen. Jacob L. Devers and his Sixth Army Group, composed of the United States Seventh and French First Armies.

Czechoslovak Pocket Stormed

The Czechoslovak bastion, last of the three great redoubts left to the Germans, is under heavy assault by the United States Third Army from the west and two Russian Armies striking from the east and, according to reports from the United States Third Army front, Gen. George S. Patton's divisions drove deeper into western Czechoslovakia today.
Continued on Page 3, Column 1

66

NIKI

May 1945
Vienna

Hitler was dead, but the Germans were clawing onto the last bit of land. More than once, Niki decided, *to hell with it*, and packed her bags, determined to travel forth into Czechoslovakia, Nazis be damned.

Luckily, her better sense had intervened so far, usually when she had one foot out the door. The OSS had given Niki the name of someone who could drive her from Vienna to Brnö when she was ready, but the region remained under heavy assault. It was one thing to get herself killed, but Niki didn't want anyone else's blood on her hands.

Instead, day after day, Niki sat in her hotel room, in the American occupation zone, biding her time as she pondered whether Brnö would be more or less of a disaster than the city she saw through the window. In Vienna, a quarter of homes were destroyed, and more than three thousand bomb craters marred the urban area alone. Bridges into and out of the city were crumbled beyond repair, and there was a gas, water, or sewer pipe exposed and spewing something every other block.

Having divided Vienna into quarters, the Allied victors governed from an "interallied zone" in the middle, with one representative from each country. Anytime, day or night, the four men could be seen tooling around in their jeep: the American always at the wheel, with the Brit in the passenger seat, and the Soviet and Frenchman in the back. "The four in the jeep" was recognized as a legitimate form of government, which said much about the overall state of affairs.

After struggling through each day, Niki spent her evenings nursing a long list of regrets, like that she never told Paloma goodbye. Unable to find her in those final hours, Niki asked Generosa to deliver a note, along with an invitation to take whatever she wanted from the villas. Most of Moggy's trunks remained stacked in her old room.

During these endless, sleepless nights, Niki also wrote letter after letter to Will. Angry letters, heartbroken letters, and chirpy ones that belonged to a world where nothing had happened between them, good or bad. It made her feel better, though Niki had no place to send the missives and, in the end, burned them for heat and light. Later, she'd lie in bed and pray to her saints that, tomorrow, she'd wake up in Vienna for the very last time.

The New York Times

PRAGUE SAYS FOES ACCEPT SURRENDER

—

Czechoslovak Radio Reports All Fighting in Bohemia Will Be Ended Today

—

LONDON, Wednesday, May 9—The Czechoslovak-controlled Prague radio announced today that the Germans in Prague and throughout Bohemia, a last major holdout pocket of German resistance, had accepted unconditional surrender.

The announcement came as the United States Third Army was reported to have advanced to the outskirts of the Czechoslovak capital, and three Russian armies hammered toward the same goal from the east and the north.

"The German military plenipotentiary is negotiating with the Czechoslovak National Council on the modalities of unconditional surrender," said the **broadcast Continued on Page 11, Column 2**

67

PALOMA

May 1945

I must say, these are very fine quarters for a government building. The former Savoy Royal Palace! I suspect you're not required to pay rent. No, Americans like to requisition things. You prefer to own them.

Well, you have the list of names, of every POW my friends and I entertained. What are you planning to do with them? Though you're not likely to listen to my counsel, I don't think you should give those boys too much trouble. Humans need sexual gratification, and are going to seek it, one way or another.

You have promised me a visa, a path to America, as a trade for this list, but I would rather have information about my son. I presume your records aren't as thorough as the Germans', but surely you have *something*, unless he's merely a number to you, another head.

Va bene. If you can't or won't give me information about Paolo, then I will take the visa, along with the cash—five hundred American, you said?—and the ticket on the *MS Vulcania.* Generosa will let me know whether Paolo returns. If I'm already in America, it should be easier for him to come, too.

How can you question my leaving? It is simple. I don't know whether I'll ever see Paolo again, and he is an adult. It would drive me mad to languish in the ruins of my old city, searching in the faces of the haggard, limbless soldiers for my son. As for my husband, one of his girlfriends can look after him. He's not my problem anymore. No, I will not be getting divorced! What kind of Catholic do you think I am?

It's getting late, and I would like to go home, so I can prepare to leave Rome. We're waiting for someone? Who? I don't love surprises but will play along. Is that a knock? Has our guest finally arrived? I'll stand. I know you Americans appreciate ceremony.

Santo Cielo! What do we have here? *Ciao, mio caro!* It is so very nice to see you, Major Dewart. As I told Nikola, you're very much not my type, but I always knew you'd come see me, eventually!

68

NIKI

May 1945
Brnö

As Niki crossed from Austria into Brnö, Germans filled every north-and westbound road out, hoping to be captured by the Americans as opposed to the notoriously savage Soviets.

Upon entering the city center, Niki wept at the sea of flags billowing from every window—resurrected Czechoslovak flags, homemade American ones with sloppily stitched-on stars, the Soviets' hammer and sickle. But neither the windows nor the buildings were as plentiful as they'd once been. Niki's homeland was in ruins.

She'd come to learn that the war leveled fifty percent of residences and the majority of churches, businesses, and schools. Downtown Brnö had more piles of rubble than buildings, and endless blocks of teetering frames and exposed pipes. The Red

Army and their tanks were everywhere, and the Soviets strutted around like conquerors, failing to grasp that Czechs were already on their side. Niki couldn't believe a country founded on democracy was now in Russian hands.

The brutes made their presence known at every opportunity, forever staggering down streets with bottles of vodka, occasionally stopping to pick fights or assault a woman or girl. Still suffering the lingering consequences of Moggy's haircut, and with her perpetually skinny frame, Niki could pass for a malnourished teen boy, which allowed her to move about the city without too much fear for her life. Moggy almost deserved thanks for what she'd done.

After checking into one of the only hotels left standing, Niki set down her bags and waited two hours for a taxi to ferry her out to the suburbs, where she discovered that, like so much else, her childhood home was mostly flattened, save one and a half rooms toward the back.

Niki stood in the drizzling rain, watching the house, conjuring what might've happened to its residents, unable to simply move on. Ten or maybe fifteen minutes later, an elderly woman appeared out of the wreckage. She was all gray, from her hair to her skin, and moved with great effort as she picked through the mess. This war had turned everyone into looters and thieves, even grandmotherly types.

"Excuse me, but this is private property," Niki called out, though was this even true? What were the rules, once a place had been taken over, and taken again? Did the original owners get everything back, or did their lives now belong to some new tyrant? Niki thought of Vienna, sliced into fourths. *"Dobrý den!"*

The woman didn't hear, and Niki moved closer. *"Promiňte!* This is my—" She stopped and took in a breath. No. Yes. Could it be? *"Maminka!"* she cried. The woman looked up and her mouth formed into an O of surprise. Between this and her coloring, Niki could see only a ghost. *"Maminka!"* she said again, and sprinted straight into her arms. Niki wrapped herself around the figure and they tumbled to the ground.

"I can't believe you're here, in the flesh," Niki said. She helped her mother to her feet, though she could not fully stand up. The woman seemed to be permanently hunched, curled forward as if protecting something at her core, and looking decades older than her forty-eight years. "What are you doing?" Niki asked. "Why are you here?"

"What am I doing?" her mother repeated, nostrils flared. "This is my home. What are you doing here? Where is your husband?"

"Oh, George is in Switz—"

"Do you want to come inside?" her mother said, getting down to business. She didn't care about George any more now than when Niki first left. Back then, they had Pasha to help in the factory and were just glad Niki found someone to marry, even if it took her away from home. At least she would no longer be putting a target on their backs with all her shenanigans and protests. "Your *táta* is here."

"He is? Yes, I'd love to come inside." Niki's heart swelled. Her parents. Both had made it! What were the odds? But as soon as hope surged through her body, everything sank again. The odds of survival were low, and Niki did not believe in miracles.

As she followed her mother through the wreckage, Niki recognized several things from her former life—a chair, a painting, blue-and-purple shards of her mom's favorite pottery. All this evidence of an existence, much of it literally turned to dust. The disorientation left Niki breathless.

"Here he is," her mother said when they reached the kitchen. "Your *táta*. Karel, look! It's Nikola."

Niki smiled. For the longest time, the words were stuck in her throat. *"Ahoj,"* she wheezed at last, removing her rain cap only to feel several fat drops land on her scalp. Overhead, where a roof was supposed to be, Niki saw gray sky. This was her childhood home, but it wasn't a place to live. What would her parents do when the temperatures dropped and the entire country began to freeze?

"*Táta,*" Niki said, kneeling as tears mixed with rain on her cheeks. "I can't believe it's you." She wrapped her arms around her father, who was ashen, fifty pounds lighter, and wearing tattered clothes that hung on his body like shirts on a line. Taking his hands in hers, Niki swallowed, and conjured the nerve to ask the big, painful question. *What happened?*

For an hour, he described how they survived the war. Just as Niki feared, they made uniforms for the Germans, but the Russians bombed their factory last month, and now it was gone. Was this a tragedy, Niki wondered, or exactly what they deserved?

"You sold your soul," Niki whispered. "You sold your soul and got nothing in return."

"We didn't have a choice, Nikola," her father said. "It was that or the camps."

"But it *was* a choice," Niki said. "Not a very good one, but a choice all the same. You understood the alternative and elected to play nice." She saw no indication that they'd doubted their decision or felt the slightest contrition at all.

They must've read about the atrocities at Buchenwald. It'd been in the papers constantly, the specifics more wretched than the outer reaches of anyone's worst nightmare. Nazi party officials were committing suicide by the dozens, starting with the Führer, and Goebbels the very next day, which meant the horrors likely went beyond all the terrible things they already knew.

"We didn't understand what they were doing to the Jews," her father insisted, imperiously, though his voice was every bit as weakened as his body. "How would we know this? We were just citizens. Dedicated workers." Niki remained unconvinced. There were camps nearby.

As for Pasha, poor Pasha, he'd left his battalion in January, deserting not thanks to a safe conduct pass but because the weather in the mountains was too much to endure. Under an assumed name, he'd taken a job at a gun factory in Prague and was killed during one of the Russian bombing raids, days before the Germans surrendered. While Niki had been preparing to leave Rome, her little brother was still alive. How did they all let the war go on for so long?

"You see? Our decision was correct, for your mother and I both survived. There was no other choice we could've possibly made," her father concluded, and Niki was so furious she couldn't speak.

Two weeks later, Niki was still in Brnö, helping her mother track down her sisters. Each day, Niki slogged back and forth between her hotel, the records office, and the library at Masaryk University, where she'd gotten her law degree. The stately white building was in decent shape, though the facade for the Faculty of Law, which had served as Gestapo Headquarters, was crumbling like a piece of old cake. Niki could make herself sick contemplating how many of her beloved professors were hauled off and killed. Yet classes were already resuming. People were getting on with life.

Regarding her aunts, Niki wasn't having much luck. She searched court records and death records and prisoner and passenger lists, but the information was sparse. Another day, week, or month would change little, and Niki began to realize she had to leave soon if she truly intended to go. She didn't want to give her parents false hope, and needed to get to Reno and start her divorce.

But Niki was stalling. She dreaded what awaited her on the other side of the world, and her fears were both vague—*where would she go? what would she do?*—as well as clear-cut. While at Masaryk one day, Niki finally confronted her fears and researched the Third Geneva Convention "relative to the Treatment of Prisoners of War," adopted in 1929, to which the newly formed Czechoslovakia was a party. George was right. In a strictly legal sense, a case *could* be made against her. The only debate was whether the violation was grave enough to be considered a crime. As anxious as Niki was to leave Brnö, she couldn't help but imagine walking off a plane and directly into the arms of MPs.

They have bigger fish to fry, Niki assured herself time and again. *They have real war criminals to worry about.* If they didn't all kill themselves first.

These were the fears swirling in Niki's mind as she pushed through the hotel doors after yet another long day of fruitless research. Evening was draping across the city, and the Brnˇáci—the citizens of Brnö—were gathering in great numbers. There remained few places left to congregate, and each evening her hotel lobby filled with cigarette smoke and people swigging beer, but everyone was too beleaguered for the scene to connote any sense of cheer. Alas, they were trying, God love them. They were trying to be normal.

On that night, Niki wound her way through the crowd, politely excusing herself or shoving where necessary, and inhaling deeply, relishing the smell of cigarette smoke. She'd run out of cigarettes weeks ago and hadn't found a way to get more. Practicality had robbed her of this old habit, it seemed.

"Promin'te," Niki said to a person who blocked her path. She tucked her notebook more snugly beneath her arm. *"Promin'te,"* she repeated to someone else, careful to avoid eye contact.

"Pro-e-men-e-tay?" the person repeated. "Come on, Nik, you know I don't speak any other languages."

Tripping on her own two feet, Niki staggered. Upon bracing herself against a pillar, she looked up and directly into the face of Major William Dewart. "Will!" she cried. Niki stumbled forward again, hurling herself into his arms, praying that he still cared enough to catch her.

69

NIKI

May 1945

Around them the room swirled, the voices and people smearing into one long blur. "How did you find me?" Niki said. She was drained, utterly depleted, and ached to lean into Will's body for rest.

"If you thought you were hiding, you picked a pretty bad place." Will flashed a grin, and in his wobbly lips, Niki saw he was nervous, too. "As soon as I heard an order was issued for all German units to abandon Brnö, I knew exactly where you'd be."

Niki nodded, eyes watering with one glimpse of his smile and that crooked, off-center nose.

"Once I got to Brnö," Will continued, "it didn't take long. There are only so many places around here a person might be." He glanced back. "Is there somewhere we can speak more privately? Upstairs, perhaps?"

"William! I can't take a fella up to my room!" She gestured toward the man at the front desk. "He'd kick me out of this hotel in five minutes flat, and then I'd have to stay in a pile of rubble formerly known as my childhood home."

"Aw, hell, Nik." Will frowned. "I'm sorry. This must all be so hard."

"It is, but I'm more fortunate than most," Niki said. "I have a roof over my head." Of course, when it came to her parents, their lack of roof was by choice. They were too prideful, too stubborn to move on from what they so staunchly believed was theirs.

Will took her hand. "Let's step out of the thoroughfare."

As he pulled her to the side, a sharp, cold dread snaked up Niki's spine. It was the sudden thought that he'd not come all this way just to say hello.

"Why are you here?" Niki asked, her tone all over the place, not unlike her emotions. "I thought they were shipping you off to Japan? You weren't discharged, were you?" The questions rose in time with her panic. "Have you come to arrest me, inform me of an imminent court-martial?" she said. That would be just like George, to send Will to deliver the news.

"A court-martial?" Will said, dropping her arm. "That's a helluva question. What have you heard, because I've been—"

"I researched the Geneva Convention," Niki said, "and while I think it'd be an egregious overreach, an argument could be made..." She swallowed. "You probably think I'm being paranoid, but George made some threats, and he could create real trouble for me if he wanted to."

Will put up a hand. "Niki." He laughed. "Slow down. I'm aware of Mr. Clingman's threats, but there is no way I'm letting you be tried for a war crime. I hope you're still divorcing him, by the way. The man's a real bastard."

Niki snorted. "Well, he has his good points. But yes. On both counts."

"I've spoken to AFHQ," Will said, and reached into his jacket.

"And I believe we have the solution to save you from future retaliation by George, or anyone else. Think of this as an insurance policy."

Niki took the paper from his outstretched hand, scanning what appeared to be a list of names. When she reached Maximillian Borgwardt, Niki understood what she was looking at. The POWs were to have been stricken from the record, but here they were enumerated, one by one, with a hometown and signature beside each name.

"It's every POW we ever used," Will said. "With signatures attesting they agreed to the work and were well-fed and well treated. I've spent the past few weeks hunting them all down. It's why it took me so long to get here."

"But..." They locked eyes. "How did you have all their names?" Niki asked. "Were you keeping a list?"

"It wasn't me. I didn't think that far ahead. Fortunately, some prostitutes maintain meticulous books."

"Paloma." Niki gasped, and a smile snuck out. "I can't believe she did this. I can't believe *you* did. Listen, about Paloma, about not telling you. I don't have an excuse. Well, I do. I have a million of them," she said, and Will pretended to roll his eyes. "I'm beyond sorry for lying to you. Sorry is not enough. If I could take back only one thing from the past year, the past *three* years, it would be that."

Will shook his head. "I'm not mad," he said. "Not anymore. If I'm going to learn to live with you, I'll need to accept that you're always hiding that last ten percent."

"Learn to live with me?" Niki repeated as her heart climbed all the way up into her throat.

"I'll have to work off the assumption that there's always a reason behind whatever you're holding back," Will said. "Maybe, over time, I can whittle the ten percent down to nine, maybe eight."

"Will." Niki clamped her lips together, afraid she might burst.

"Do you think this will work? The list?" She didn't want him thinking the "this" in question was the two of them.

"Should we need to use it, I am fully confident that we will," he said.

"*Fully* confident? There's a first time for everything, I guess," Niki teased.

"Oh, you're very funny." Will rolled his eyes, for real this time. "The purpose of the Convention is to protect the abuse of prisoners, but no one can accuse us of mistreatment if each one signed an affidavit stating the opposite. I think, in hindsight, after enough time has passed, people will realize how brilliant it was to attack the enemy with their own kind. They'll appreciate that the men's contributions were critical." His mouth twisted into a sly smile. "One could argue that stopping the use of German nationals *led* to the Kassenverein mistake."

"Oh, God," Niki groaned, and smacked a hand over her face. "Don't ever say that word again. The letter *C* followed by a vowel! It's like I never spoke German at all."

"Don't be so hard on yourself," Will said. "We sent out millions of pieces of propaganda. One mistake, during a very harried time, is an excellent record. Personally, I was thrilled to learn you were human."

Niki felt herself flush. "Just remind everyone of that before they send me to prison."

"You're not going to prison," Will said. "Whatever happens, if you land in hot water, then I'll be right next to you, boiling away." He held out his hand. "We're in this together. You and me." Niki went to open her mouth, but instead of responding with a smart remark, she smiled and accepted Will's hand. "Aw, Nik." Will pulled her into his chest and Niki exhaled, his heart fluttering against her cheek.

"Will?" Niki said, her voice muffled. "Where's Pierre?"

He chuckled. "I gave him to Clemente. The man needs a friend now that he won't have the printing machine to keep him company," he explained, Niki softening into him as he spoke. "In addition to the names, Paloma gave me one more piece of information. She knows where Moggy is."

Niki pulled back. "She does?"

"Apparently she sent Paloma a letter, and a jeweled bandeau? I'm not even sure what that is. In any case, Moggy mailed it to a dance club, and somehow Paloma got it."

"Can you...can you tell me where she is? Do I even want to know?"

"Yes, I can tell you," he said. "Better yet, I can take you to see her."

OFFICE OF STRATEGIC SERVICES

WASHINGTON 25, D.C.
May 30, 1945

Dear Eugene,

You should have received word by now that you and Major William Dewart will be decommissioned next week. This is not meant to be a punishment but a reward for your service.

Before the curtain comes down on your work, I wish to send you a word of appreciation. You have put your brains, your imagination, and your doggedness into every pursuit, and your results have been (mostly) exceptional. Your operation showed its mettle beginning with the Hitler putsch one year ago and ending with the defection of over 1,000 Czechs and Slovaks thanks to your "Monte Rosa" safe conduct passes.

Even now, your efforts continue to show. During the past two months, between 30 and 50% of POWs who've surrendered to Allied forces quoted from copies of DND. Here is a sampling of overall impressions when prisoners were asked for their opinions.

"Good."

"Very good."

"It was believable."

"We didn't believe the Nazi papers and radio anymore."

"The newspaper gave us hope that we would be able to live as free Germans again when the Hitler system collapsed."

All that to say, your work has certainly helped hasten the end of the war.

While there has been much consternation about the use of POWs, based on interviews with key players, and the evaluation of relevant documents, we have concluded that the idea of using German nationals in day-to-day work was to the benefit of the Army, and no charges will be brought.

In summary, your office should be commended for its splendid teamwork and high morale despite many hardships, including but not limited to inadequate equipment, an insufficient number of trained personnel, security restrictions, and a rapidly changing tactical situation. You have reason to be proud of what you accomplished. I wish you the best on all future endeavors.

Sincerely yours,
William J. Donovan

70

NIKI

June 1945
Davos

As Niki waited in the bright, almost blinding solarium, she felt like she might come out of her skin. It'd been over six months since she'd seen Moggy, and Niki didn't know what she'd find, but when Moggy at last walked into the room, all misgivings fell away.

Niki leaped to her feet, thrilled to see her friend, who looked like the same old Moggy she'd come to adore. She was perhaps a little thinner, a tad less clenched, but with her bright cherry dress and gold snakeskin belt, her fashion was still high, a sign that everything was as it should be. It took Niki a second to get a hold of herself.

"I'm so relieved to see you," Niki said, snuffling into Moggy's shoulder. "I've been so worried!"

Moggy stepped back. "You've been worried about me?" she said. "You were still at war!" She reached out and pulled on one of Niki's loose curls. "Your hair is growing out. It looks pretty!"

"It's taken some time," Niki said. "After you left, it *was* nice to be able to say your name every once in a while. Granted, it only happened whenever I passed a mirror, and it was usually accompanied by an expletive. Gosh, Mogs." Niki glanced around. "This place is awfully nice, and you can't beat the views. The Alps are glorious. But a sanatorium? At least you're allowed to dress like yourself. You stand out."

"Mother had to file for a special dispensation for the outfits," Moggy said, running a hand over her skirt. "This place might seem bleak to you, but these past few months have been as near to heaven as a person can get on this earth. My family is coming to get me in two weeks, and I'm not altogether looking forward to it. I'll miss the people, the fresh air, the mornings spent on the porch, sipping coffee on a fur-covered rattan chaise."

"That does sound heavenly," Niki agreed. Davos was famous for its restorative effects, and it was easy to understand why. "But I'm still concerned about how you ended up here."

"It's hard to describe," she said. "I just got so mixed up, so lost, I couldn't keep anything straight and had to step out of the world for a spell. We must be made of different stuff, because the propaganda was too much for my brain."

"Maybe you're the only one who's acknowledged it," Niki said. "I'm sorry, by the way. Not just for the things I kept from you, but the fact that after you left, I called you a filthy deserter to anyone who would listen. You didn't defect, though. You only needed a break."

"'Filthy' might be a stitch harsh, but the plan *was* to stay here until the end of the war," Moggy said. "And I'm certainly not alone."

She snickered, and it was good to hear. According to Moggy, there were a dozen sanatoriums on this hillside, and whenever "patients" convened in town, Davos's streets teemed with an unholy mix of Jewish refugees, Nazi officers, Russian princesses, and hundreds of American pilots who'd crash-landed in Switzerland. Niki laughed, wide-eyed, trying to picture it.

"I've met so many interesting people," Moggy added. "One in particular." Her eyes drifted toward the dining hall. "Maybe, when she's finished breakfast, you can meet my very dear friend. She's American, too!"

"I would love to. Listen, Mogs." Niki reached out to take her hands. "I'm sorry about how things ended. I appreciate why you were frustrated with the nature of our work, and the secrets and obfuscations."

"The lies, you mean."

"Sure," Niki said, and glanced away. "It's strange. When it comes to MO, sometimes I'm proud of what we accomplished, and other times I feel like a terrible person. Maybe I'd better check into this place. Whaddya think?"

"You don't need it because you know what you're doing, and you very much know who you are," Moggy said. "It wasn't the lying that made you good at your job. It was your ability to see the good in others, and the enemy's humanity."

"You have the same skill." Niki smiled, thinking of their League of Lonely War Women, though she didn't bring this up. Moggy was happy, and at peace, and Niki would not ruin that.

Moggy cleared her throat. "George came to visit recently," she said. "Is it true? Are you going to divorce my brother?"

Niki felt herself wince. "I'm sorry, but yes," she said. "It's truly the best choice for us both. Are you terribly mad?"

"Not mad. Sad we won't be in the same family, though." She sighed. "William Dewart?" Her voice was timid, as if stepping back. When Niki nodded, Moggy bobbed her head in return. "I understand," she said. "You have a special relationship. Any fool could see."

"Aw, Mogs, thanks. I'd like to think so, too. And there's

no reason we can't keep in touch," Niki said. "You're the best damned thing to come out of that family."

"I don't know about that," Moggy said. She frowned and released a long stream of air. "Whatever you do, Niki, follow your heart, and those incredible instincts. That's one of the things I've learned since being here. As Jung himself said…" She stopped to throw on a smile. *"The privilege of a lifetime is to become who you truly are."*

◇◇◇◇◇◇

Will waited outside, leaning against an idling car. With packed bags in the trunk, their next stop was the airport, and after that, America, though Niki anticipated a few detours. They were still traveling courtesy of the United States Army, after all.

"How was it?" Will asked, opening the driver's-side door.

"Better than I expected," Niki said. "Moggy looks fantastic. Happy. She didn't sneeze once!" Niki peered over her shoulder. "You're letting me drive? Boy, you're really trying to play the dashing beau."

"Nope." Will shook his head. "We're in a bit of a time crunch. Before we board our plane, we need to stop in Rome, and I don't want to be late."

"Rome? Oh, God!" Niki threw back her head as Will gently closed her door. "I don't know if I can go back."

"You can, and *we* will." He poked his head through the open window and planted a kiss on her mouth. "We have a very important engagement. Before you ask, I've been sworn to secrecy, so you're going to have to be patient. Not your strong suit, but trust me when I say it'll be worth it."

71

May 1989

They are seated on a white tufted bench outside the ballroom. Niki faces slightly away from her daughter—a quarter turn—contemplating her black beaded clutch. Inside the purse is something that will explain what Niki is feeling, and reveal to her daughter that her big emotions are more than nostalgia.

"I want to hear everything," Andrea says. "Whatever it is, I can handle it. I'm not a child. I'm over forty years old!" She rubs her mother's hand. "Talk when you're ready. I can hang around for hours. Remember. I have teenagers. I'm used to waiting up all night."

Niki glances at her purse again. *Something* compelled her to come tonight, and something compelled her to bring Andrea, at Manfred's encouragement. Maybe, when she opened her mailbox to find that ivory cardstock, Niki saw it as more than an invitation to a banquet. Maybe it was a summons to confront the past.

"The entire time we were working in Rome," Niki begins, an easy place to start, "the top brass didn't think we were pulling our weight. Psychological warfare was new to the US, and many of those buzzed-hair types thought fake newspapers and Hitler toilet paper seemed like a waste of time and resources."

"Personally, I found the toilet paper hilarious," Andrea says.

"My friend drew the Hitler," Niki says, smiling at the memory. "Do you remember Ezra Feldman, the cartoonist?" She's not surprised that Ezra is famous now, so renowned that MoMA, the Smithsonian, the National Gallery of Art, *and* the Pompidou in Paris have asked for his work when he dies. In true Ezra fashion, he deems the request "stupid," as well as profoundly insulting. *I intend to live forever!* Niki thinks he just might.

"You met Ezra a few times?" Niki says to her daughter. "When you were younger?"

Andrea shrugs and rolls her head around, as in, *sounds vaguely familiar.*

"He came to the house wearing a Braves jersey?" Niki adds. In his endless quest to better understand the American essence, Ezra spent years following the Braves, having decided that baseball was the perfect allegory about the country he loved. It had everything—courage and fear, good luck and mistakes, and constantly changing self-esteem in the form of a batting average. To him, baseball and America represented the triumph of the "incredible individual spirit combined in a loosely collective manner."

"I don't know. Maybe?" Andrea says, and Niki feels a surge of disappointment.

"Anyway, in Rome, we were constantly trying to prove our worth," she goes on, "when we weren't digging out of whatever trouble we'd gotten ourselves into. In our line of work, we had to bend a few rules."

"You? Bending rules?" Andrea puts a hand to her chest, feigning shock. "I can't fathom it!"

"It was all for the cause, but I did spend several months *after* the war worrying that I was about to be court-martialed. At one point, I found myself having to stand up in front of a large contingency of the top brass."

"Mom!" Andrea yelps, her awe genuine this time. "That doesn't sound like you! What'd you do?"

"Nothing, as it turns out," Niki says. "Rather, nothing I was punished for. One could argue I violated a statute or two, but when it came to my time at MO, the big guns had something different in mind."

72

Niki

June 1945
Rome

Niki stood on the parade grounds, surrounded by a sea of ca-
dets in dress blues and flanked by a detachment of representatives from Rome—Ezra, Lieutenant Jack Daniels, Warner, the
final Rumors guy, and Major William Dewart.

The Bronze Star was awarded to members of the United
States Armed Forces for heroic or meritorious achievement in
a combat zone, and Niki still couldn't fathom how she'd qualified. The official reason was Operation Monte Rosa, because it
resulted in the defection of over one thousand enemy soldiers,
but Donovan said Niki should think of it as encompassing everything she accomplished in Rome. Funny how briskly the
tides of favor changed.

Now Niki waited, wearing her starched uniform and "a little

bit of lipstick," as instructed. A stiff wind tore across the hills of Rome, and Niki's heart whipped just as wildly as the American flags overhead. For what felt like ten minutes, a spit-and-polish officer recited a long list of formalities until, at long last, the band struck up "The Stars and Stripes Forever," and the man called out her name.

Niki stepped forward, feeling the cheers and the power of her OSS compatriots at her back. As Donovan pinned the ribbon and star onto her chest, she glanced over her shoulder and caught Will's face in the crowd. She grinned. As great as this moment was, Niki couldn't wait to see what would come next.

73

May 1989

"You were awarded the Bronze Star?" Andrea says. "Mom! That's incredible!"

"It was pretty incredible," Niki agrees. "It never seemed real. It still doesn't. Of course, winning a medal was not why I came up with the plan."

Andrea frowns. She'd known Niki's brother died at the end of the war, but this is the first she's heard of Operation Monte Rosa. "I'm sorry Pasha wasn't one of the defectors," Andrea says, when Niki lays it all out. "But it did help bring the war to a speedier end. That's not nothing."

Niki smiles feebly. "I suppose," she says.

"Do you still have it?" Andrea asks. "The medal?"

Niki nods. "Somewhere," she says. "In the jewelry box in my closet, I think?"

"Oh my God!" Andrea thwacks her forehead with her palm.

"That is so you! Just over here keeping Bronze Stars next to old pantyhose. Shouldn't it be in a safety-deposit box or something?"

"I don't think so?" Niki says, and wrinkles her brow. With an inhale, she flicks open the latch on her purse, then rotates toward her daughter to face her square on. "There's more," she says. "And this part isn't going to be quite as...decorative."

"You have a very strange look on your face."

From the clutch, Niki pulls out an old xeroxed copy of a newspaper article. Why she removed it from the recesses of her lingerie drawer before leaving, Niki can't begin to speculate. On the other hand, maybe she can. "Read this first," she tells her daughter. "And then I'll explain the rest."

PLANE CRASH KILLS
PUBLISHER OF SUN

Special to The New York Times

RENO, Nev., Jan. 3—William Thompson Dewart Jr., publisher of The New York Sun, was fatally injured on a ranch about eight miles south of Reno this afternoon when a private plane which he was piloting as a student flyer struck the top of a tree and crashed.

Suffering from a crushed skull, he died here an hour later at the Washoe General Hospital, where surgeons had found that his condition made it impossible to operate.

Joseph M. Williams, an instructor for the Silver State Flying School, was with Mr. Dewart in the plane but his injuries were not critical. Officials of the school said that Mr. Dewart was to have received a private pilot's license tomorrow.

John S. Belford, attorney for Mr. Dewart, said he was awaiting instructions from the family, but an inquest will probably be held tomorrow, and the body sent to New York.

Mr. Dewart came here four weeks ago and was said to have planned establishing residence to file suit for a divorce.

© *The New York Times*, 1946.

74

May 1989

Andrea ogles the article, though unlike Niki's, her eyes are dry. It doesn't take long to piece the information together. William Dewart died in January 1946. Andrea was born several months later.

"Wait. This man who died in the crash?" Andrea says. "*He's* my father? Is that what you're telling me?"

"Correct," Niki says, struggling to catch her breath. Each time she reads the article, the feelings make a rushing return, and she's thrown back to that unbearably dark time.

How ironic, Niki thinks now, that the first person to come to her rescue was the last person she expected to see again. But Ezra was indeed the one who got her through, who invited her to stay in his apartment in the West Village. It was Niki's own version of recovery, like when Moggy went to Davos, though with less fresh air and more crying involved.

Even now it seems like a miracle that Ezra had the time and

inclination to help, given how busy he was with his own life. When he wasn't drawing cartoons for *The New Yorker*, or entertaining hours of Niki's keening, Ezra worked on getting his family out of Romania now that the communists were in charge. So many people helped him reach America, it was the right thing to do, just as it was the right thing to help Niki. But with the Iron Curtain falling across the region, Ezra had to act quickly.

Though his parents wouldn't be subject to any quotas, the United States was out of the question, for Ezra's own sanity. He lobbied for Palestine, where they'd be surrounded by friends, family, and some hundred thousand other Romanian Jews, but his mother wouldn't hear of it. Her goal wasn't to live near family or old neighbors she despised, but to experience luxury after years of wartime deprivation and be the envy of her sisters. In the end, his parents went to Paris, and Niki moved back to Washington. By then, she didn't feel like dying anymore, which was progress.

"But… But…" Andrea stutters, shaking her head. "I'm so confused." Until now, about Niki's background, she's known two things. Her mother was married for several years during the war and Andrea's father died in a plane crash before she was born. Niki told her daughter these facts when she was four or five years old, and little Andi conflated the facts, assuming they were about the same man, and Niki let her believe this.

"My father *wasn't* George Clingman?" Andrea says, staring at the paper again.

"No. He wasn't. I suppose I felt that divorce *and* a lover were too much for your preschooler's brain to process," Niki says. "Will was dead, either way, and explaining everything in exact detail seemed beside the point. Your father supported the decision. Manfred, I mean. This all happened around the time he legally adopted you."

As the years ticked on, there was never a perfect entrée into the impossible discussion, never the right time to open old wounds. When they were happy, it was easier not to rock the boat. When there was a problem, she didn't want to pile on. Niki told herself she'd get around to it eventually, though this might have been a resurgence of her old propaganda techniques. After all, the longer a person keeps a secret, the more deeply it's ingrained, until it becomes something like the truth. Even Manfred seems to have let it go. He hasn't pressured her to come clean in well over a decade.

Manfred. Niki takes in a quick breath. She can't believe she's about to lose him, too. A fresh crop of tears springs to her eyes.

"I'm sorry," Niki says, taking her daughter's hands in hers. "I never meant to lie. I just…" She just *what*? "I guess too much time had passed. Or the truth was too painful. Or something."

"Or it was easier to keep it under wraps." Andrea is visibly shell-shocked, struggling to digest what she's just discovered. "You've never been the most open person in the first place," she points out.

Niki nods, feeling deeply embarrassed, remembering what she once overheard Andrea's high school boyfriend say. *Your mom definitely seems like she's from a communist country.* Czechoslovakia had been democratic when Niki lived there, and the boy was a turd, but Niki understood what he was implying.

"This is so sad," Andrea says, lightly touching the article. Niki's heart could burst. How generous her daughter is, when outrage would be justified. Andrea doesn't even seem mad, and shows no hint of feeling betrayed. Granted, she's forty-three, and has never been one for tantrums, but her kind reaction reminds Niki of Manfred. It reminds her of Will, too. Maybe there is something to tonight's table, the lucky number eighteen.

"What did you do?" Andrea asks. "After the crash? Since your family was gone, I figured you had your in-laws, the Clingmans, to lean on. But…" Her voice trails off.

"They were definitely not willing to help me at that point," Niki tries to joke.

"You mentioned being close to his sister? Weren't you in touch over the years? I swear you've mentioned her before."

Niki smiles. She and Moggy have indeed kept in loose contact, but it's been a while since either wrote. Last she knew, Moggy was living in Cherry Hill, New Jersey, with her partner, a woman she met at the Davos sanatorium. She's also a well-respected psychologist with a thriving Jungian analysis practice. "I haven't heard from Moggy Clingman in many years," Niki says. "Listen. There's something else I need to explain." She takes a deep inhale. "When I told you my parents were gone, that wasn't entirely true."

"I have grandparents?" Andrea says, and she seems more disturbed by this than the part about Will.

"Had," Niki emphasizes. "They died when you were young, but by then I hadn't spoken to them in years. As you know, my brother, Pasha, was killed in the final months of the war, but they lived until the late 1950s."

Niki describes traveling to Brnö that final time, after she left Rome. She'd wanted to make peace, or sense, or *something* of the mess, but came up short. It was sad to realize she'd arrived in a place where no U-turns could be found, but Niki had been consoled by the idea of eventually starting a new family with Will.

"Why didn't you speak to them again?" Andrea asks. "Your parents. Was it because you were pregnant, and they didn't approve?"

"Nothing like that. I'm not sure they even knew about you." Niki swallows, struggling with the next words. "They stayed in Czechoslovakia during the occupation. They turned away from the violence and suffering, continuing to prosper as they made uniforms for the Nazis. Collaborators, in other words." When Andrea gasps, Niki squeezes her eyes closed. "I know. It's horrific. I'm so ashamed, which is why I haven't been able to bring myself to talk about it."

"What? That's ridiculous! It wasn't your fault."

"No, but it doesn't make me feel any better about things." Niki sighs. "You came from such a good man, and were raised by a good man, too. You're an incredible person and I couldn't risk letting your lineage affect your sense of self."

"What your parents did has nothing to do with me, with either one of us," Andrea says, quite reasonably, and Niki falls in love with her all over again. "What happened after Will died? I assume pregnant single women in 1946 didn't have a lot of options."

Niki chuckles flatly. "No. We did not, though once again I was lucky. I stayed with Ezra for several months," she explains. "He was lovely company, but eventually, it was time for both of us to get on with things. Ezra was traveling a lot back then." Niki smirks, recalling how he would accept any engagement, no matter how inconsequential, just to see a new part of the country. He once judged a children's art contest in Pittsburgh, awarding first place to a seven-year-old for his watercolor of a woman being decapitated.

"When I left Ezra's," Niki continues, "I was going into my third trimester and had to find a job before you became impossible to hide. I managed to stay pretty small for a good, long while." She pats her flat stomach. "Anyhow, I returned to Washington and used an OSS connection, a man called Warner, to get my translator job. I met your father at work. You know the rest." Three years later, Niki married Manfred Brzozowski, and in 1986, she retired from the UN after a four-decade career.

"This is… I'm just…" Andrea says. "Did William Dewart know you were pregnant?"

Niki bows her head. "He did," she says, remembering how happy she'd been those few months before it all fell apart. "He was so excited. We both were." Niki bites her lip. "He had older children, with his first wife. His *only* wife. I'm not sure what happened to them, but I can give you their names, if you'd like."

"Okay. Um. Maybe. It's going to take a while for everything to sink in. I'm sure I'll have a lot more questions."

"And I promise to answer them, the best that I can."

Andrea glances up, tears now glistening in her own eyes. "I'm sorry, Mom."

"Why are you apologizing to me?" Niki says. "I'm the one who kept this from you."

"It's all so tragic."

"What happened *was* awful," Niki says, and stops to smile. "But it's been a really good life."

Niki has said this many times over the years, and it's never felt truer than it does now. Manfred is Andrea's father, without question, but their daughter still carries a piece of Will. Niki sees it in Andrea's yellow-rimmed hazel eyes, the dimple in only one cheek. Sometimes Niki believed she'd gone years without thinking about William Dewart, but maybe because of Andrea, he's been in her mind and heart the whole time.

"I know you've been happy," Andrea says with a frown. "It's just...well... I'm sorry for what you went through. I'm sorry you missed out on the love of your life."

"The love of my life?" Niki hesitates, finding herself for a moment perplexed. "What are you talking about?" She studies her daughter, and the realization hits her with a thump. "Oh, Andrea. Will died, and it was terrible, but the true love of my life has always been you."

★ ★ ★ ★ ★

AUTHOR'S NOTE

The character of Niki Novotná was inspired by Barbara Lauwers. Niki is meant to be fictional, so while the women have many similarities and share several biographical details, there are a few ways in which their stories diverge.

Both women were Czech natives with multiple degrees. Both women married Americans and immigrated to the United States in 1941. They both joined the OSS and ultimately went to work for Morale Operations in Rome. Both women divorced their first husbands shortly after the war, though George Clingman is an entirely fictional character.

Barbara and Niki participated in many of the same operations, from Sauerkraut to Cornflakes to Monte Rosa, though the Rome office undertook many more projects than are included in this novel. Like Niki, the real Lauwers also received the Bronze Star for her work on Monte Rosa, albeit a few months earlier than Niki does in the book. Whereas Niki finds the ceremony emotionally stirring, her real-life counterpart had a different recollection.

"I was unable to listen and absorb," Lauwers told a reporter once, "because suddenly I felt the excruciating need to pee so terribly that I thought I'd faint. It occurred to me that if I should let go, it would run down my legs into my shoes, onto the pale gray concrete of the slight incline where I was facing the Brass. The puddle would proceed, grow, and spill toward the detachment of soldiers behind me.

"I started to pray to all my saints, not knowing which one could handle such a situation. I prayed that the ceremony would end before I burst. I obviously reached the right saint, and I was spared that final ignominy."

Both women also worked closely with Major William Dewart, who was indeed the scion of a publishing family and died in the manner described in this book (the article is taken verbatim). Though I read nothing that suggested an affair between Lauwers and the real Dewart, Barbara did have a daughter three months following his death, and the father was never named. I'd like to think this was one piece of William Dewart that got to live on.

On a personal note, later that same year, a different pregnant young woman also lost her beloved in a plane crash. The woman was my grandmother, and the child she had was my mom. This is how I know that despite the heartache of losing Will, Niki still could've gone on to marry a great man and live a happy life.

Although the real MO unit in Rome was comprised of twenty-two people, I kept the core group small, with the occasional reference to others, to better serve the narrative. Ezra, Warner, Jack Daniels, Clemente, and the other employees of MO Rome, aside from Moggy, are all based on real people. Ezra's background was modeled after the famed *The New Yorker* cartoonist Saul Steinberg. If his name isn't familiar, most readers should recognize his work, as it graced everything from magazines to Neiman Marcus catalogs to Jell-O commercials. For many decades, his name was considered synonymous with *The New Yorker*. "I am the writer who draws," he famously said.

The real Ezra wed his formerly married mistress during the war, but I made my Ezra single. As Niki does with Ezra in the novel, Barbara lived with Saul for several months in the West Village while she was pregnant and figuring out what to do next.

For plotting purposes, I slid around and combined dates, and did the same with official memos and orders. I also tried to streamline and detangle the OSS structure to the best of my ability. As Niki mentions, the organization changed frequently, as did its hierarchies, and I didn't want to bog down the story with the minutiae of government reporting structures.

My goal was to bring attention to the work of Barbara Lauwers and capture the spirit of a time and a place—specifically, Rome, at the end of the war. (Interesting note: the Foro D'Italia, where the crew plays tennis, remains in the same state as Niki, Will, Ezra, and Moggy would've found it, replete with fascist slogans and statuary.) Overall, I aimed to tell a good story while staying true to the historical timeline as well as the people and type of work done in Rome. As with all my books, my greatest wish is that this story sticks with you, and inspires you to learn more about a person, or a moment in history, or both.

SELECTED LIST OF SOURCES

Government Publications:

FM 35-20 United States Women's Army Corps (WAC) Physical Training 1943.

Morale Operations Field Manual—Strategic Services.

A Soldier's Guide to Rome.

Other:

Aline, Countess of Romanones. *The Spy Wore Red.*

Alper, Benedict Solomon. *Love and Politics in Wartime: Letters to My Wife, 1943-45.*

Anderson, Carolyn. *Accidental Tourists: Yanks in Rome, 1944-1945*, Journal of Tourism History.

Bair, Deirdre. *Saul Steinberg: A Biography.*

Bancroft, Mary. *Autobiography of a Spy.*

Brown, Anthony Cave. *The Secret War Report of the OSS.*

Dunlop, Richard. *Donovan: America's Master Spy.*

Failmezger, Victor. *Rome—City in Terror: The Nazi Occupation 1943-44.*

Griebling, Erik K. *Intelligence Professionalism: A Study of Developing Intelligence Professionalism in the Office of Strategic Services in Italy and th- ͡   ιι ̣. Mediterranean, 1941-1945.*

Hayes, Alfred. *The Girl on the Via Flaminia.*

Heideking, Jürgen and Mauch, Christof. *American Intelligence and the German Resistance to Hitler.*

Jason, Sonya N. *Maria Gulovich, OSS Heroine of World War II: The Schoolteacher Who Saved American Lives in Slovakia.*

Kloman, Erasmus. *Assignment Algiers: With the OSS in the Mediterranean Theater.*

Lisle, Debbie. *Holidays in the Danger Zone.*

Hoehling, A.A. *Women Who Spied.*

MacDonald, Elizabeth P. *Undercover Girl.*

McIntosh, Elizabeth. *Sisterhood of Spies.*

O'Donnell, Patrick K. *Operatives, Spies, and Saboteurs: The Unknown Story of the Men and Women of World War II's OSS.*

Petersen, Nancy H. *From Hitler's Doorstep: The Wartime Intelligence Reports of Allen Dulles, 1942-1945.*

Pym, Barbara. *A Very Private Eye.*

Sevareid, Eric. *Not So Wild a Dream.*

Smith, Richard Harris. *OSS: The Secret History of America's First Central Intelligence Agency.*

Stursberg, Peter. *The Sound of War: Memoirs of a CBC Correspondent.*

Todd, Ann. *OSS Operation Black Mail: One Woman's Covert War Against the Imperial Japanese Army.*

Tompkins, Peter. *A Spy in Rome.*

Wilson, Edmund. *Europe without Baedeker: Sketches Among the Ruins of Italy, Greece and England.*

ACKNOWLEDGMENTS

I must start by thanking the team at Graydon House for assembling this gorgeous book: art director Kathleen Oudit and designer Laura Klynstra, who created the stunning cover, copy editor Jennifer Stimson, sensitivity reader Dill Werner, publicist Justine Sha, and marketing managers Pamela Osti and Diane Lavoie. It's amazing how many talented people are involved in the finished product. The utmost gratitude goes to my editor Melanie Fried for a hundred things, like suggesting the 1989 timeline, which solved oh-so-many problems. As always, huge heaps of appreciation for Barbara Poelle, my agent of nearly fifteen years. You never make me feel like I'm being too demanding or histrionic, even when I am!

Everybody needs colleagues, and I've loved my time around the watercooler with Liz Fenton, Lisa Steinke, Kristin Rockaway, Allison Winn Scotch, Kate Quinn, and Kristina McMorris. Thanks especially to Susan Meissner, Shilpi Somaway Gowda, and Tatjana Soli for our monthly chats over tea. And thank you to all the writers who came before me, the women who bravely served overseas and kept the diaries and wrote the memoirs that helped me imagine this tale.

To Lisa Kanetake—can you believe we made it to 2022? Thank you for sharing this incredible journey, and I know there are many more great moments to come. I'm also sending love to the rest of the Kanetake-Bergan family—Audrey, Emily, and Charles—for being a second family to us.

While writing this book, my quietly heroic husband, Dennis, once again picked up his undue share of slack and played along with/suffered my variant moods. He even agreed to a second dog when I expressed an intense need for another comfort pet. As my oldest daughter said, "We're about to leave home and Mom's trying to fill the hole in her heart with Jindos." She's not wrong. Speaking of daughters, I can't express how grateful I am for mine. Paige and Georgia, you've stayed strong and flourished in a difficult time. You're so fun and independent and easy to parent, and I admire you both so much.

And to all the readers—every email, every kind tweet or Instagram post—you are often the reason authors find the mettle to write on any given day. Thank you, thank you, thank you! This is all for you.

THE
LIPSTICK
BUREAU

MICHELLE GABLE

Reader's Guide

GRAYDON
HOUSE

1. Discuss themes of truth and source in the novel. How do these subjects still resonate in the world today?

2. Discuss how Niki's gender impacts the way the OSS and some colleagues treat her. Does the way they underestimate her also influence her own actions in the novel? How so?

3. Who was your favorite character among the employees of MO Rome (Niki, Ezra, Will, Warner, Jack Daniels, Clemente), and why?

4. Which was your favorite MO Rome campaign?

5. Did you think Niki was wrong to lie to Will about her agreement with Paloma? Why or why not?

6. Did you understand Moggy's reaction to the propaganda and MO Rome's activities?

7. Why do you think Niki hid her OSS work from her daughter, Andrea? Would you have done the same in her place? On the flip side, how would you react if you found

out a close relative or friend withheld such a secret from you all your life?

8. The novel is loosely based on real-life OSS operative Barbara Lauwers, who was awarded a Bronze Star. Had you heard of her previously? How does her story reflect the larger historical trend of women's stories being ignored?